shy girls
can't date
celebrities

shy girls can't date celebrities

MILLY ROSE

One

I carry my books along the hallway on Monday afternoon, thankful for the last bell. It's not that I dislike school. I dislike how many people they cram into one building. My favorite part of the school day is when I can hide in the library and escape into the latest short story I'm writing. In the times I'm forced to walk alongside the masses, I wall-hug. I'll admit, I've gotten pretty dang good at becoming invisible.

"Hey, how was your last class?" my best friend Kylie asks when we meet at our lockers.

"Piece of cake," I reply. "I'm already ahead in my reading."

Kylie smirks. "AKA, you've already written your history assignment?"

I shrug, pulling my backpack from my locker. "If a subject involves reading and writing, it comes easily to me. Math and science, that's where things come undone."

I already have so many check marks against my English, history, and social studies classes. It makes breathing a little easier.

"And that's why we're such a good team," Kylie says, hooking an arm behind my neck. "We have such nice skills to trade off."

"Hey, ready to go?" Parker, Kylie's boyfriend, calls out to her.

Kylie nods ahead. "Want me to ask Parker to drive you home?"

"No, I'm cool. I'll take the bus."

"It's no problem," she insists.

I give her a hug and hoist my backpack over my shoulder. "No, it's fine. You've been buzzing about your date since first period. I won't cramp your style."

Kylie clicks her tongue. "You never do that."

I give her a bright smile. "Go. Have fun."

She waves me off and moves across the hall to Parker.

I dawdle behind some seniors as I make my way out of the school building. Two cliques pace on either side of me, babbling about the latest gossip. As the crowd funnels toward the front doors, my pulse runs high as oxygen is squeezed out of the packed space. I close my eyes tight, hug my waist, and force my feet forward. When sunlight hits my face, I open my eyes and gasp for air.

The girl to my left gives me a strange look, but I shake it off and keep moving toward the bus stop. As I wait for my bus, I spy Kylie and Parker moving into the student parking lot. Parker is talking to two of his friends. Their movements are casual and effortless. I seriously don't understand how anyone can get through those hallways without some kind of mini panic attack.

But maybe I'm the weirdo.

I'm glad Kylie has found some confidence since being with Parker. She's happier and livelier now, hanging out with him and his friends. Now, when I'm hiding out and creating a new story, I also have free time to fantasize about being with the guy that got away.

The bus arrives, and I find a seat near the front. I do my best to avoid the middle and the back. The middle is where any object can become a projectile, and the back is gossip town. The number of mornings I've spent on the bus, listening to the newest hookup or breakup news, irks me to my core. Since my middle school sweetheart became headline news for gossip websites, I have zero tolerance for rumors.

I get off the bus and into my house about ten minutes before my mother drops the twins home. Casey and Callum are ten-year-old handfuls. Well, Callum is sweet as pie, but can be easily led by Casey, who is the reason they got banned from the school bus. Casey is on a conspiracy theory kick at the moment, and she likened everyone on board the bus to sheep being driven to a meat factory. Needless to say, she freaked everyone out, and our parents agreed to an indefinite pause on the twins taking the bus.

Now, it's my job to ensure they do their homework and wash up before Mom comes back from work. If my parents hadn't had me, Mom would have had to switch to part-time hours. She already panics about the thirty minutes she needs to make up for pickup. If only I had learned to drive, I could help out a little more. But I'm already an anxiety-riddled mess walking side by side with other students. I couldn't imagine getting behind the wheel of a car and being part of crowded traffic.

Nuh-uh.

No, thank you.

Dad already works such long hours, he's usually home well after dinner. Money always causes such deep wrinkles on my parents' faces. Anything I can do to relieve their stress, I'll do. Even if it means playing third parent to my younger brother and sister.

By the time Mom gets home, I've prepared dinner. The relief and gratitude on her face raise my spirits, and I leave it up to her to pry the twins away from their video game.

With a moment to myself, and all my homework up to date, I give in to the nagging voice inside my head. I unlock my phone and check what they're saying online. My stomach knots just thinking about it.

Wyatt Hayes.

Suspected brain injury.

That's literally the biggest news going around social media right now.

Oh please, please, please.

Be false.

Be a big nasty rumor without a shred of truth.

But the truth is, no one has seen him in public for a few months.

Production of his new movie shut down.

Something massive happened, and it was covered up for weeks, until someone leaked that he had been in a serious accident.

"Josie!" Casey calls out to me.

I drop my phone and move into the living room. "What?"

Casey stands in the living room, her arms crossed. "Mom said you cooked eggplant lasagna."

"That's right."

"I thought it was *real* lasagna."

I huff and roll my eyes. "It is *real* food."

Callum's lip upturns. "What the heck is eggplant? Did you put an egg in a pot plant?"

I snigger at his comment. "No, it's the purple vegetable."

They both screw up their faces. "*Eww.*"

I huff again, turning to leave the room. "Hush, you two. You'll enjoy it."

We get through dinner, and it's finally past the twins' bedtime. Sometimes, getting them to shower, brush their teeth, and tucked in feels like a full-time job. I leave Mom downstairs to chill in the living room, and Dad should be home any minute. The twins still love hearing a bedtime story, and I always read them something I've written. But something about tonight's story has really riled them up. As I leave for my bedroom, my sanctuary, I hear their mischievous little voices calling out to me again.

I trudge to their doorway, about to snap. "Oh my gosh, will you two just go to bed?"

It's like their only mission in life is to give me a mammoth crater of a headache.

They giggle and blow raspberries at me from their twin beds.

"Ugh. You guys are the worst."

I move back to my bedroom, unlocking my phone. Between opening Word docs and refreshing my newsfeed, my phone is getting a massive workout. I lie flat on my back, diagonally across my double bed, with my curls cascading away from my face. As the queasy sickness vortexes in my stomach, I keep an eye on the posters lining my walls to keep a semblance of grip on reality.

Since something happened on the set of Wyatt Hayes's latest movie, the tabloids and social media have been speculating about his current condition. Piecing together the scraps of information, the reports say he's in a private hospital called The Clearview Clinic, and worse, there are rumors he has amnesia.

I don't even want to fathom it being true. Kylie keeps telling me that if so many online commentators are saying it's true, it can't be one-hundred percent false. But my heart just won't let me believe it's true.

I try my best not to look at what people are saying online. Sometimes, I go days without checking social media, and that's the way I prefer it. Instead of letting the speculation fester its way into my brain, I open the notes app on my phone and jot down lines of poetry. Unlike my short stories, which I share with friends and family, the poetry is just for me. I've never told a soul I write it, and I'm fairly positive I'll never share it.

I reread a stanza I wrote earlier.

To love you then,

And love you now,

Another chance is when,

I have you somehow.

I mull over the words, feeling something off about the timing and phrasing.

My fingers itch by the phone's keypad, and it dawns on me how to fix it.

To love you then,

And love you now,

Another chance when,

You're here somehow.

I drop the phone with a sigh, wondering how Wyatt could possibly be back here one day. I sit up and pan around my array of posters, paparazzi candid snaps, and professional event photos that I have plastered on my walls. I reach over and trace around the line of polaroids we took three years ago. The one where he's kissing my cheek still makes me blush.

When I started sixth grade, it was one of the best times of my life. Wyatt joined my class because he had been held back and needed to repeat sixth grade. He was nervous, shy, and a bit of a loner. I gravitated toward him right away and was thrilled when our teacher asked me to help tutor him. I've always loved reading and writing, and he was one of the first people I ever shared my short stories with. The more eager he got to hear me read something I wrote, the more enamored with him I became.

My gut cramps, and I slouch forward. Deep down, I know the idea of amnesia hurts so badly because I've spent the last two years fearing he's already forgotten me. I don't hold it against him that he stopped replying to my texts. It was a whirlwind when I got messages and photos after he won his season of Talent Quest. When recording studios and movie sets became the norm for him, I can see why he got too busy for his former life.

I pick my phone back up, feeling another stanza simmering inside me.

In my heart near,

Body too far,

An ache it sear,

Longing for the star.

It's okay that he stopped catching up with me because I've never stopped following him and his career. I move off the bed and place my phone on my desk as I wake my laptop. It's not healthy, but I can't help refreshing the news site still loaded on my browser. With much of the same in the headlines, I change tabs to my favorite streaming site that has Wyatt's movies.

I hover the cursor between 'No Chance, Goodbye' and 'Without You,' struggling to decide which to watch. In 'No Chance, Goodbye' he plays a popular, jock-type who's forced into a volunteering role with a bookish, goody-goody type. They start out as enemies, and of course, end up in love.

In 'Without You' he's a sensitive and sweet guy who gets dumped by his ultra pretty girlfriend and tries a list of grand gestures to get her back. That is, until he realizes his best friend was the girl he wanted all along. In 'Without You' he's more the type of guy I remember him being. But 'No Chance, Goodbye' is an absolute crack-up. And right now, I think I need a good laugh.

Just as I'm about to hit play, I'm startled into a jolt.

Buzz, buzz, buzz.

The harsh vibration from my phone grinds against the wood grain of my desk. I frown at the private number and hit decline.

"Not today, telemarketer."

I settle back in my desk chair, and I'm interrupted by another call. The private number calls another two times, and on the third ring, I give in.

"Hello?" I answer.

"Hi, is this Josie Bartlett?" asks a female voice.

"Umm, yes. Who's asking?"

"My name is Erika Hartley from Circle 8 Management, the team that represents Wyatt Hayes."

The air is snuffed out of me. I choke and bang a fist onto my chest.

Wyatt?

"Josie? Are you there?"

I cough roughly and clear my throat. "Yes. Yes, I'm here."

"Are you aware of Wyatt's current condition?"

"Umm. Only what online gossip is saying."

Erika sighs into the receiver. "Wyatt suffered a blow to the head. He took some time to regain consciousness, but we're grateful to say he's doing much better in his recovery."

My heart pounds with adrenaline. "Oh, thank goodness. I'm so relieved." I sink into my seat. "But, why are you telling me this?"

"There's been some setbacks," Erika says hesitantly. "Wyatt is suffering short-term memory loss. He doesn't remember me or my team. In his mind, he never left Victoria Falls or starred in his season of Talent Quest."

My mouth falls open. "You're kidding."

"Josie, he wants to see you."

I stammer a few sounds as my heart leaps into my throat. I swallow hard and exhale swiftly. "He does?"

"We can arrange a flight for you, first thing in the morning," Erika says. "Can you get to the airport by eight a.m.? We'll have the Circle 8 Learjet ready and waiting for you."

I choke on the words, "Like, a private plane?"

"Yes, Josie. It's important that you come here. We want him released from the clinic, but the medical team is hesitant. We're hoping a blast from the past can help kick-start his memory."

"I'd do anything to help him, but..."

"But, what? Tell me anything you need, and I'll make it happen to get you here."

"Well, I have school, and my parents can't just pack up and leave."

"You'll come without them."

I puff out air nervously. "They won't like that."

"Where are they?" Erika asks in a rush. "I'll speak to them now and get them to sign-off."

Sign-off? Why does that word make this sound like a business proposal?

"Umm, okay," I say with a tremble in my voice. "I'll go downstairs and find them."

"Very well."

I lower the phone and slink out of my bedroom. An unsettling surge of adrenaline bolts through me, and my head wobbles from side to side as I descend the stairs.

"Mom?" I call out, the tremble in my tone worsening. "Mom?"

Mom backs out of the living room. "What's wrong?"

I lift the phone in my clammy hand. "Umm, there's a woman on the phone..."

Mom makes her way over, unnerved by my demeanor. "Yes?"

"Umm. She works with Wyatt."

"Wyatt?" Mom's brow furrows. "Wyatt as in Hayes?"

I gulp, slowly nodding.

"Hello? Hello?" Erika's voice calls through the phone.

I hit speaker on the phone. "Hi, Erika. I'm with my mom."

"Hello, Mrs. Bartlett," Erika says. "I'm Erika Hartley, management for Wyatt Hayes. I called your daughter because Wyatt has requested to see her."

"What? When?" Mom asks in alarm.

"We will have the Learjet at Victoria Falls airport tomorrow morning for an eight a.m. departure," Erika replies matter-of-factly.

Mom gasps in shock. "What? She has school, and her father and I work. Not to mention her siblings. She can't just leave."

"She can," Erika replies. "My assistant, Randall, will be there to escort Josie on the plane, to the hotel, and to the clinic to visit Wyatt. Your accompaniment is not required."

Mom laughs with nervous shock. "You want us to send our daughter off with a stranger?"

At that, Dad walks into the house, arriving home from work. His expression becomes serious when he takes in the bewilderment on my and Mom's faces.

"What's going on?" he asks, loosening his tie.

Mom gestures at my phone. "There's this woman who..."

"Mr. Bartlett?" Erika butts in. "My name is Erika Hartley, management for Wyatt Hayes."

Dad's chin drops as surprise colors his face. "Wyatt Hayes?"

"Yes, the same Wyatt who Josie grew up with," Erika replies. "He's requested Josie come to Cherry Beach to see him."

"*Tomorrow,*" Mom blurts, astounded.

"Tomorrow?" Dad asks, flinching. "All the way to Cherry Beach? There's no way we can make that happen. We both work, plus the kids..."

"As I was already saying," Erika cuts in, "you and your wife can stay home with your other children, and we'll arrange everything for Josie to have a safe flight and trip here."

Before my parents can repeat their lines again, I pivot between them and say, "He has amnesia. The rumors are true."

"No..." they breathe out in unison. "Can't be."

"It's true," Erika says. "He's forgotten the past three years. The medical team hopes a familiar face will help with his recovery."

Mom blinks at me. "And that's Josie?"

"Mom," I murmur, shivering with adrenaline. "He's forgotten his fame, but he hasn't forgotten me."

A tear buds in the corner of her eye, knowing how I've kept tight hold of my former relationship with Wyatt.

"How do we know this is legit?" Dad asks, crossing his arms. "You could be some nut who's trying to lure our daughter away for nefarious reasons."

Erika sighs into the phone. "Believe me, Mr. Bartlett, I'm far too busy to play games with a sixteen-year-old. But, to put your minds at ease, I'll call you back on video."

The call abruptly ends, leaving my parents and me staring at each other.

"This is unreal," Mom mumbles.

Nervous energy bubbles inside me. "Mom, it's Wyatt."

Dad grunts. "I've called her bluff. It's a total scam."

I groan. "*Dad.* What would she get out of that? Do you really need to put your skepticism cap on right now?"

Mom hugs an arm around me. "Josie, we can't have you leave with strangers."

Before I can reply, my phone buzzes in my hand.

Incoming video call: Private number.

With a shrug, I hit answer. When Erika Hartley fills the screen, I aim the phone higher, getting me, Mom, and Dad in frame.

Erika's phone is being held by someone else as she shows her ID near her face. "This is me, Erika Hartley," she says, and then the camera zooms out and pans around the opulent space behind her. "And this is the presidential suite at the Gran Palacio Hotel we have reserved for Josie while she visits Wyatt."

I almost drop the phone as Mom and I gasp at the same time. "Pr-pr-presidential suite?"

"Does it look legit yet, Mr. Bartlett?" Erika asks with a smirk.

Dad shifts his weight, keeping his arms folded. "Certainly doesn't look like a dime was wasted."

I let myself grin. "Sorry, Erika. My dad is skeptical about everything."

"Perfectly reasonable," Erika replies. "We should never accept things at face-value."

At that, my dad loosens up.

"Will you be here, Josie?" Erika asks, looking right down the camera lens.

I slouch, eyeing my parents. "I don't want to risk ruining his recovery. Please, can I go?"

Dad pulls me into a hug. "We know how closely you've followed Wyatt all these years. I'm just afraid of what you're getting yourself into. He's not the same boy you used to know."

I chew my lip, thinking about the implications of his memory loss. "But he doesn't remember the boy he became."

Mom smiles, tracing a finger under my chin. "I remember that boy," she says tenderly. "He was sweet, kind, and joyful. Ever since hearing about his accident, I haven't stopped thinking about him." She sighs, looking at Dad. "Daniel, if Josie can help, she should go."

Dad nods. "I know, but I don't want her getting into trouble over this."

"What trouble would I get into?" I ask in the midst of our group hug.

Dad smiles kindly, brushing the side of my face. "I don't want you to get hurt or lost in the shuffle."

"I'm just visiting Wyatt," I reply. "Please, let me do it."

"I guarantee her safety," Erika says through my lowered phone. "We have the best security in the business."

Dad narrows his gaze at Erika. "When do you expect to turn the jet around and get her back here?"

"It'd be great if she could stay for a few days."

Mom and Dad share a look and reply together, "Three days max."

I squeal, almost dropping the phone. "Really? I can go?"

Erika's tone becomes upbeat. "We can arrange for a car to pick up Josie at your house."

"No," Mom blurts. "I'll drive her to the airport. I need to meet this Randall before I let Josie go anywhere."

"Very well," Erika says, gesturing at the phone. "Randall, do you want to turn the camera around to you so they'll see a familiar face tomorrow?"

The camera changes, showing a man in his early twenties in a fancy suit. "Good evening, everyone."

As soon as we utter our hellos, the camera flips back to Erika.

"Thank you for your cooperation," Erika says, like we're making a business deal. "We'll have your accommodation and meals covered while you're here. Josie, all you need to bring is yourself."

"Okay, thank you," I say, breathless. "Nothing will stop me from seeing him."

"See you tomorrow, Josie."

"Yes, bye."

Erika ends the calls, and I'm left stunned.

I breathe out, trying to reconcile the amount of adrenaline pumping through my body. "Wow. One hour with Wyatt would be more than enough time for me. I can't wait to soak every second."

Dad smiles. "I'm glad you're so happy, darling. Just remember to keep your wits about you."

I huff. "Yes, Dad. Can you now stop being Mr. Doom-and-gloom?"

"I have to admit," Dad says, "I've been glued to my phone, waiting for updates about Wyatt."

"What the heck is happening?" a small voice calls from the top of the stairs.

We turn to see Casey and Callum in their matching striped pajamas.

Dad turns to them. "Josie's going on a trip. She'll be gone by the time you get to school in the morning."

"What?" they blurt at once, hurrying down the stairs.

"*Daniel*," Mom grouches. "Did you have to fire them up?"

"They have to know," he reasons.

"Where are you going?" Casey asks as she and Callum invade my personal space.

"Umm," I falter. "Cherry Beach?"

Callum's face screws up. "Where's that?"

"A four-hour flight away," Dad answers.

"You're going on a plane?" Casey asks. "Why can't we go?"

Mom gets between the twins, clutching both their shoulders. "Because Josie has a very important meeting. Your father and I aren't going either."

"I want to go," Callum whines. "This isn't fair."

"I'll have to call the Marshalls to pick the twins up earlier for the carpool," Mom says to Dad.

"What?" Callum whines. "We have to leave the house earlier tomorrow morning?"

Casey crosses her arms, pouting. "This sucks."

I bend my knees and look the twins in the eyes. "Guys, I'm going to visit Wyatt Hayes."

"The guy on your wall?" Callum asks.

I nod with enthusiasm.

Casey blows a raspberry. "Why the heck would he want to see you? Sounds like a scam."

When I stand and roll my eyes, Dad can't help laughing at the comment.

"The mini-skeptic, here." I sigh. "Guys, I told you. Wyatt and I were friends. He even played with you guys in the treehouse."

"The boy in your polaroids looks nothing like the guy in the movies," Casey says, arms still locked across her torso.

Mom chuckles with exhaustion. "It's the same boy. Now, you two, move it back upstairs. I'll get you tucked back into bed."

"We need another story," Callum says, staring me down.

"I need to pack," I protest.

Casey glares at me. "You're leaving us. We're owed another story."

Mission accomplished. Crater-sized headache.

"Mom, I'll take them upstairs. I have a quick story I can read."

"No, a long one," the twins whine in unison.

"Oh my gosh," I say in exhaustion. "Would you two just get your butts upstairs?"

The twins hightail it upstairs, and Mom and Dad move into the living room, discussing the enormity of our recent phone call.

As I move upstairs, the adrenaline resurfaces mixed with a heavy dose of ick. I'm beyond excited to see Wyatt, but my excitement feels obscene, considering how he's struggling. My knees weaken with every step up, and my stomach cramps.

Is he excited to see me? Is he scared? Does he remember everything from the past, or is his memory patchy?

My heart works overtime, and I force myself to level out my breathing. Getting worked up won't help Wyatt. I need to settle these nerves so I don't freak him out. They want me there to help with his recovery.

A smile tingles on my lips.

Oh my gosh.

I actually get to see Wyatt tomorrow.

I don't think this will ever sink in.

Hurriedly, I text Kylie. *"Wyatt's manager just called and said Wyatt wants to see me. They're arranging a flight."*

"Josie!" the twins yell from their bedroom.

"Coming!" I yell back, opening the Docs app on my phone.

It is super cute; the twins love hearing the short stories I write. Callum is always delighted by anything he hears, but Casey is a harsh critic. She definitely helps me tweak and perfect my story plots. But when I need an ego boost, I bring Callum over to my laptop in secret.

I have a new story that's only a page and a half long. I can already hear Casey telling me to beef it out, but right now, I just need to get to the end so I can pack my bag. The story has some spooky elements, which has Callum pulling his bed covers up to his chin. Casey sits on edge, listening to every word.

When I drop the cliffhanger ending, they both lie stiff as a board and speechless.

Ahhhh.

Peace at last.

"Guys, I'll be home soon, I promise," I whisper, moving to the doorway. "Love you."

"Love you too," they reply in unison.

My heart swells as I leave for my bedroom. Okay, sometimes they're not complete devils.

Before I get to my bedroom door, the front doorbell rings. Jitters course through my body, picturing Erika or her assistant at our front door. Could they possibly be here to pick me up already?

Oh crap. Was Dad right? Was it some kind of elaborate scam?

I slowly descend the stairs as Mom moves toward the front door.

"Who the heck is coming here this late?" Mom asks. She opens the door, and her demeanor softens. "Oh, Kylie, Parker, hi."

I hurry to the first-floor landing as my best friend and her boyfriend enter our home.

"Oh my gosh." I gasp, pulling Kylie into a hug. "What are you doing here?"

"This is huge," Kylie blurts into my ear. "How did you expect us not to come right over?"

I pull out of the hug. "But weren't you two on a date?"

"Are you kidding?" Parker says excitedly. "We have too many questions to wait for text message replies."

"I don't know if I have many answers," I say, leading them upstairs and toward my bedroom. "This has all come out of the blue."

"Whoa," Parker puffs, jolting back as he takes in my bedroom. "Someone's obsessed."

Kylie laughs and elbows his ribs. "What did you expect? I told you, she's a superfan."

"Not stalker vibes at all," Parker mutters.

I click my tongue, folding my clothes. "I'm not a stalker."

"Well, something's off," Parker says, walking into my bedroom and gesturing at the pictures on the wall. "You've pasted your face over the girl in his arms."

My jaw rocks as I look at the body of the popstar Portia, with my face covering hers.

"There's nothing wrong with fantasy," Kylie defends.

"Don't you think it'd freak him out if he saw all of this?" Parker asks.

I cringe. "He'd never see this."

Parker wriggles his eyebrows. "What if you hit it off, and he wants to visit your home?"

Kylie gasps. "Oh my gosh, what if Wyatt Hayes comes back to Victoria Falls?"

I shiver. "Why are you guys trying to freak me out?"

Kylie wraps an arm around me. "Sorry, Josie. This is just so surreal. You're leaving on a private plane to visit a celebrity. Our minds are running wild."

"I just don't need speculation right now," I say with a sigh. "I need to focus on Wyatt and what his condition actually means. He's forgotten his life, but he remembers me. I need to take this one step at a time."

Kylie grins. "You know, we're gonna need pictures."

I giggle, thinking about being close to Wyatt again. "I'm not going to immediately ask for a selfie."

"Yeah, but you're walking into glitz and glamor," she replies. "We need to see it all."

"He's still in the hospital, or clinic, whatever it's called," I reason. "It's not like I'm going to a red carpet event."

Parker smirks. "Didn't you text Kylie something about a presidential suite? Sounds pretty swanky to me."

I cup a hand over my mouth as a flood of giggles spills out. "I can't believe this is happening."

"You never lost faith in seeing him again," Kylie whispers with wonder in her eyes. "Now you're getting your wish."

My heart sinks as I frown at her. "But I never wanted it like this. I'd do anything to reverse his pain."

Parker grins. "Maybe seeing you is just what the doctor ordered."

There's a knock on my open bedroom door. I view Dad as he looks at Parker. "We have a no boys in the bedroom rule."

Parker lifts his hands in surrender.

"Dad, he's Kylie's boyfriend, not mine."

"We should get going anyway," Kylie says and pulls me into another hug. "Best of luck with everything tomorrow."

I squeeze her, needing all the good luck I can get. "Thank you."

"And, remember, photos, please?" Parker says, backing out of my bedroom.

I giggle, blushing, as Kylie follows Parker out. "I'll try."

Kylie sighs, looking me up and down in my Wyatt-clad bedroom. "I really hope it goes well. Give him our best. I can't imagine how he's feeling; forgetting a huge chunk of his life."

"Thanks," I reply. "I really have no idea what I'll be walking into."

"Wyatt remembers you," Dad says gently. "You just keep your guard up around this management team."

I click my tongue and clutch my elbows. "Yes, Mr. Skeptical."

Two

Did anyone expect me to sleep a wink? It was hard enough getting a few hours of sleep a night when there were only scraps of information about Wyatt's accident online. But now, knowing I'll see him today, my nerves kept me staring at the ceiling.

After we got the twins ready for their carpool, and Dad gave me a mixture of best wishes and lectures before leaving for his hour-long commute to work, I'm finally able to focus on myself. With a good dose of product in my curls, a natural face of makeup, and wearing my best outfit, I take my carry-on bag downstairs.

Mom and I forced breakfast on everyone else, but we're both too nauseous to keep anything down. Knowing we should eat something, we both scarf a protein bar on the drive to the municipal airport.

Mom grunts as she takes a bite. "I hate these bars. I wish you'd let me buy the ones we used to get."

"*Mom,*" I complain. "You know I'm trying to go vegan. You said you'd support me with this."

"I am, darling. It's just, I preferred the taste of the other brand."

"I guess you can get the other brand for yourself?"

"I'm not buying two different boxes. And are you really going vegan for yourself? Or is it just because you saw an interview where Wyatt said he was vegan?"

"I believe in it too, Mom. I'm just having trouble adjusting."

Mom mutters under her breath, "Maybe because you need all the food groups to survive."

"*Mom*," I whine. "That's not fair. You know I'm trying to get used to other alternatives."

Mom lifts her fingers off the steering wheel as a mark of surrender. "I'm sorry, Josie. I don't mean to argue with you. I'm just anxious. I wonder how much it costs to park at the airport," Mom mutters to herself as she looks out at the road. "And have they already organized your flight home? We agreed to three days at the maximum, but if we can have you back sooner, it'd be ideal. But can they just fly back whenever they want? How much notice do you have to give a local airport that you'll be..."

"*Mom*," I cut her off. "You're doing it again."

Her hands tighten around the steering wheel. "Sorry, darling. You know I can't help rambling when I'm nervous."

"Well, it's not exactly helping. I feel like every vein inside me is jittering."

"I'll stop. I promise."

I side-eye her. "Do you think you can keep it together while I'm gone? You know the twins feed off your nervous energy."

She chuckles, wiping her brow. "I'll try to keep a handle on things for their sake."

"Good, because I don't want them hijacking phones and bombarding me with guilt-ridden text messages."

We pull into the airport parking lot, taking a ticket at the boom gate. Once we park, we make our way over to the departures lounge. As we approach the area where security scans everybody's luggage, a local hockey team streams in. Their big, burly frames crowd the small space, and my throat constricts as I watch them suck all the air with nothing to spare.

I back away from our space in the queue, gulping for any morsel of oxygen I can grasp. Mom hurries after me, grabbing onto my arm and tugging me back.

"Josie," she says firmly. "If you can't handle this line, I'm not letting you on the plane."

I shiver. "Wh-wh-what?"

She looks me dead in the eye, worry glossing her gaze. "You're about to walk into a world filled with Hollywood-types. If you can't handle our local airport and a hockey team, you won't survive."

I sniff hard as my eyes itch with tears. "Don't say that."

"Look at me," she says softly. "I can't let you go if panic will take you over."

I swallow hard and strain to say, "I need to see him."

Mom nods. "I know. But you're going alone. I'm scared for you."

I look back at the broad-shouldered team passing through security. "If it's just me and Wyatt, I'll be okay."

"Remember all the times you said you'd be okay because Wyatt was there," Mom whispers. "You never stepped foot in any of those concerts."

I sigh, heart falling to the pit of my stomach. "They're just too crowded."

"He's still a celebrity," Mom warns. "Are you sure you can do this?"

"Can't we just wait until they all pass through?" I plead. "I'll be fine. I promise."

I can tell by her expression that Mom doesn't believe me, but she lets me line up behind the team and their coaches. We finally move through the line, after my luggage passes through the scanner, and a security guard waves a scanner wand over our bodies.

We're given directions to the private boarding lounge, and on our way through, I grin in wonder at the sparkling white Learjet waiting on the tarmac. The Circle 8 logo is proudly displayed at the back end of the plane.

"Hello, Josie?"

I look to the side, and near the glass sliding doors is a familiar-looking man wearing a sharp suit.

I place a hand on my chest. "Yes, that's me."

We move over to him, and he holds out his hand. "Hi, I'm Randall, Erika's assistant."

"Nice to meet you," I say, shaking his hand. "I remember you from the video call last night."

Randall chuckles. "Yes, it's been a long night."

Mom shakes his hand, introducing herself. "Hi, I'm Rosa Bartlett. Did you fly in this morning?"

"Yes," Randall replies. "With everything we've been organizing for Wyatt's release from the Clearview Clinic, there hasn't been much room for sleep. I had to work on the flight here, and there's still more to do as we fly back." He smiles at me. "Speaking of which, are you ready to go?"

Nervousness cramps my stomach, and I shiver. "I guess."

Mom rubs my back. "Please, be careful, darling. Oh, *geez*, I'm having regrets. I really don't think you should go."

My blood runs cold. "Please, don't do this to me."

She eyes Randall and then sniffs as she looks back at me. "Am I really letting you board a plane with a stranger?"

"Mrs. Bartlett, I promise Josie will be safe." Randall gestures at a broad man dressed in black on the tarmac. "We have the best security with us."

Mom shudders. "Somehow, that doesn't put me more at ease."

I pull Mom into a hug. "I'll be careful. I know how to look after myself."

"I know, honey," she whispers. "You already look after all of us. I just can't imagine a night without you at home."

"We'll have her home sooner than you know," Randall says, beckoning me over. "Now, we must be getting back to Cherry Beach."

Mom sniffles, nodding as she lets me go. "Okay. Good luck, darling. Say hi to Wyatt for me."

I let out a soft giggle as I swipe at a tear. "I will. Thanks, Mom. I love you."

She clasps her hands near her face, smiling and nodding as her eyes well. "Love you, too."

With more adrenaline than I know what to do with, I follow Randall onto the tarmac. We're waved through by ground staff, and a broad man wearing all-black keeps an eye on us as we take the steps onto the Learjet.

"Whoa." I gasp at the interior. "Does Wyatt own this plane?"

"Nice, ain't it," Randall says with a wink. "And no, it's not exactly Wyatt's plane. It's Circle 8's plane. You'd probably know all the members of the crew. Like Portia, Simon McAlister, Theo Granger, and Maggie Silver."

"Oh, yeah. I listen to all the albums and watch all the movies."

"Nice. At Circle 8, we produce all the music and all the movies. It's a nice little machine we have going here. Each Circle 8 member has their own fans and careers, but when they collaborate, it's golden."

I nod, hugging my middle. "Like Wyatt and Portia."

Randall grins. "Exactly. Those two work magic together."

The pilot exits the cockpit and wears a welcoming smile. "Good morning, Miss Bartlett. I'm Captain Frank Ford. I'm honored to take you on this journey."

I jitter as we shake hands. "Uh, umm, thank you, sir."

Captain Ford nods at us. "Take your seats, folks. We'll be off in a jiffy."

We move into the body of the plane, and it's a lot to take in. Along the aisle, there's first a group of four chairs, two on either side of the aisle and facing each other. They're overstuffed and leather, like the most ridiculously comfortable armchairs. On each headrest, the Circle 8 logo is embossed.

"Good morning, Randall," a woman in a blue blouse, tight-fitting pencil skirt, and matching vest, says. She wears a navy blue scarf around her neck, and her hair is secured in a bun. If I didn't know better, I'd say she was a flight attendant.

She welcomes me further into the plane. "Welcome, Miss Bartlett. My name is Claire, and I'm here to serve you during your flight."

I choke on an intake of air, coughing. "You are a flight attendant?"

Claire chuckles. "You could call me that. I'm part of the Circle 8 staff, and I specialize in flight safety and service."

I follow behind her and don't know where I should look first. What I can only call a plush, three-seater couch is along one side of the plane. On the other side are two swivel armchairs and a beautiful mahogany desk. There's an incredible lighting design throughout the plane, along with more mahogany accents.

"Please, make yourself comfortable," Claire says, gesturing to the three-seater. Beyond our seating area is a wall with walkways on either side. "Behind here are the bathrooms and the refreshments area. Can I get you anything to drink? Coffee, soda, juice, water? Or any snacks? Pretzels, chocolate, jelly beans? Anything you want."

I sit forward. "Did you say jelly beans?"

Claire beams. "Mr. Hayes insists we keep them aboard."

I nod. "I remember him always eating them."

"May I bring them to you?" Claire asks.

I sit back with a boost of happiness. "Yes, thank you."

"And a beverage?"

I shrug. "Orange juice?"

"Certainly. Now, please ensure your seatbelts are strapped tight. The captain is getting ready for take-off."

As Claire radios the captain that we're ready for take-off, I fish between the throw cushions for my seatbelt. Once I'm buckled, the captain comes through the overhead speakers and gives us an arrival time of one p.m. at Cherry Beach.

Just like Dad taught me, I cross my fingers as the plane ascends, only relaxing when we level out.

"Okay, folks, enjoy your flight," Captain Ford says through the speakers. "I'll be back in touch soon when we're ready to descend."

Claire reappears from the rear of the plane with a small bowl of jelly beans in an array of bright colors.

"Wow, thank you," I say when she sits the bowl on the coffee table in front of my couch, alongside a tall glass of OJ.

"I'm happy to arrange anything for you, Miss Bartlett," Claire says.

"Please, call me Josie."

She beams. "Certainly, Josie."

Claire flicks a button by the partition wall, and from the base of the small mahogany table, a flatscreen TV rises up.

"Whoa," I breathe.

Claire grins. "Any requests?"

I shy away, shaking my head. "Ah, no."

Randall unbuckles, crossing his legs as he scrolls on his phone. "Pick anything you like, Josie. It's more than likely on the hard-drive."

I bite into my lip, remembering my out-of-this-world distraction from my movie selection last night. "'No Way, Goodbye.'"

"Excellent choice," Claire says, flicking through the movie options.

Randall grumbles, shifting in his seat. "I've not seen that movie a billion times."

"You don't like it?" I question, sinking in my seat.

Randall smirks. "My life revolves around Wyatt Hayes and the rest of the Circle 8 kids. I've seen every piece of media, and heard every song, way too many times."

I tilt my head at the flatscreen. "Do you have Wyatt's songs on there too?"

"Yes, of course," Claire replies. "Both the tracks and the music video versions."

"We can cue them up after the movie," I say, bouncing in my seat.

"Yay," Randall grunts.

I eye him with glee. "And, of course, we'll end our flight with 'Without You.'"

Randall lifts his palms in defeat. "Why not? It's a Wyatt-palooza, of course."

Claire chuckles, selecting 'No Way, Goodbye.' "Despite Randall's gripes, we're all wishing Mr. Hayes the very best. It's not the same without him around."

"I hope my visit does some good," I reply. "I don't really know what I'm supposed to do, or what to expect."

"From what I hear," Claire says, "he's dying to see you."

I clasp a hand over my rising chest. "Really?"

She gives me a kind smile. "I hope you enjoy your flight. Please, don't hesitate to ask me for any further assistance."

I sit back, hugging a throw pillow as my feel-good movie comes on screen. It still gives me the giggles seeing Wyatt as a jock. He was the complete opposite when I knew him. He wasn't sporty. He'd actually hide from footballer-types, fearing they'd bully him. Luckily, it gave us plenty of time to hide away together. My favorite memories ever. Him strumming on his acoustic guitar, singing covers of pop songs, and me reveling in every moment, writing a new story as we forgot the rest of the world.

When I encouraged him to audition for Talent Quest, I never imagined it'd mean we'd lose contact. He used to text me while on the set of the reality show, wanting to back out and come home. I'd call him and spend hours on the phone, giving him pep talks to stay. He didn't need to fear elimination because he was so talented.

I never regretted telling him not to quit. Yes, he would've come home, and we could've been together. But then the world would've been robbed of his talent. We wouldn't have the albums and movies. I've barely heard from him in two years, but that doesn't mean he ever left my heart.

I blink at the boy on-screen with the former child model-turned actress-turned popstar. Portia, so fancy she only uses one name. I blink harder and picture my face over hers, just like the images on my bedroom walls.

I'm on a private plane, destined to meet him.

Evidently, I haven't left his heart either.

Throughout the movie, I work on the poem from last night, adding another stanza.

Grateful for a touch,
Soulful in words,
In memories and such,
Spirited like birds.

I put the phone down, too overwhelmed to fix the phrasing, and zoned out with the movie. When it ends, Claire sets a plate of finger sandwiches and a fresh OJ on the table in front of me. She then plays tracks from one of Wyatt's live performances after he won Talent Quest.

As I eat a sandwich, I settle into listening to Wyatt's upbeat voice.

"There's something electric in the air," he tells the crowd. "Are you feeling it?"

The crowd cheers "yeses" back at him.

"Okay," he says, strumming his guitar. "Then let's get this party started. Sing along if you know it. This one's called 'Summer Glow.'"

The crowd goes wild for the song he released right after winning the reality show. He built his fanbase from playing covers, but 'Summer Glow' is one of his originals that's insanely popular.

I hug the throw pillow tighter, giddy at the prospect of seeing him in the flesh. There's only two hours left of the flight. A sweat bead rolls down the side of my face, while another tumbles down my spine. I release the pillow and unbuckle my seatbelt. As Wyatt plays the fun track, I stretch in my seat, trying to mellow out before our meeting.

I turn to Randall, who's neck-deep in work. "Umm, Randall?"

"Yeah?"

I point at the TV. "Is it true Wyatt doesn't remember any of this?"

His face droops. "Nope. It really freaks him out."

I suck in a sharp breath. "He's freaking out?"

Randall shifts in his seat, avoiding my gaze. "You'll see him soon enough."

I gulp, needing to see Wyatt's sweet face. "Claire? Can you play 'Without You' now?"

"Of course," she says, getting the movie ready.

I exhale slowly, taking another finger sandwich. Will I see this version of Wyatt? Or has the injury turned him into a completely different person?

Randall busies himself with work. He obviously doesn't want to tell me all the details. It must be bad if he's using work as an excuse not to discuss it.

I pout, rubbing the space over my heart as I watch the devastated boy on-screen, hatching a plan to get the girl of his dreams back. There's something so cute and innocent about his performance in this movie. It makes me gush every time.

My poor Wyatt.

I hope he hasn't spent the past few weeks scared about who he is.

If I have to, I'll spend all my time reminding him of how incredible he is.

Three

Throughout the flight, the only turbulence was inside me. The mixture of emotions sent me queasier than any motion ever could. When we disembark the plane, both Claire and Captain Ford ask me to give their best to Wyatt.

On the tarmac, the broad man in black, who spent the entire flight sitting silently in one of the armchairs at the front of the plane, walks us to a shiny black SUV. We're not in the regular terminal area of the large airport. We landed in a more secluded area that screams of celebrity secrecy.

I'm let into the car first, and recoil at the sight of another person. "Oh, umm, hi."

The man wears an impressive three-piece suit and sits with his back to the front passenger seat. He nods at me while having his phone glued to his ear.

Randall gets into the car beside me and motions at the man sitting opposite us. "This is Martin Gilmore, head of financial management. He's arrived this morning to meet with Erika at the hotel."

"Will I meet Erika?"

Randall grins. "Of course. She's excited to meet you."

The car ride into the city center is mostly silent. Apart from Martin's phone conversation and Randall hurriedly tapping on his phone. To ease my running thoughts, I stare out the window, hoping the emerging cityscape will be a useful distraction.

As the skyscrapers and oversized billboards come into view, it only serves to spike my anxiety. Instead, I take the opportunity to text Mom and Dad, letting them know I've landed in Cherry Beach. I also add, I'll call them later, because we're on the way to the hotel.

After the twenty-minute drive, the car slows and Randall announces, "We're here."

A doorman opens our car door. "Welcome to the Gran Palacio Hotel."

Martin nods at the doorman, exiting the car first.

My hand pauses over the seatbelt buckle, too frozen to move.

Randall chuckles at me, gesturing to the open door. "Come on, Josie. This is us."

I swallow hard and edge my way out of the car.

"This way, miss," the doorman says, gesturing to the revolving door at the hotel's entrance.

I thank him and enter the hotel with Randall following behind. The expansive foyer is floored with large sandstone tiles, marbled with veins of gold. Overhead, a large five-tiered chandelier hangs from the twenty-foot high ceiling. Red leather armchairs surround glass coffee tables with gold legs. And ahead, well-dressed and professionally welcoming front desk staff await behind a tall counter.

Randall motions at the front desk area. "Let's get you checked in."

We move over to the counter, and a man with slicked back hair greets us. "Hello and welcome to the Gran Palacio Hotel. Do you have a reservation with us?"

"Yes, this is Josie Bartlett," Randall answers. "We reserved the presidential suite for her."

My heart misses a beat. It wasn't a dream. I'm actually staying in a presidential suite.

The front desk clerk smiles at me warmly. "Hello, Miss Bartlett. We've been expecting you." He dings the counter bell. "Someone will be here shortly to show you to your suite."

"That's it?" I ask, glancing at Randall and then back at the clerk. "You don't need anything else from me?"

"Everything is taken care of, Miss Bartlett," he says, handing me a keypass. "We hope you enjoy your stay."

I nod, backing away. "Umm, yeah, okay."

An attendant in a red jacket approaches the reception area. The man at the desk gestures at me and Randall, asking the attendant to show us to the presidential suite.

"Certainly," the attendant replies, taking my bag. "Please, this way, miss."

We follow the attendant past the large winding staircase and into a gold elevator. After swiping his key pass below the elevator buttons, the attendant presses the button for the floor; second from the top. When we reach our floor, the attendant says, "The entire floor above belongs to the penthouse suite."

I let out a whistle. "Wow."

Randall nudges me. "We have the penthouse reserved for Wyatt when he's released from the clinic."

My jaw drops, and Randall chuckles, returning to his phone.

The attendant swipes a card over the lock on the door labeled 'Presidential Suite.'

"I can't believe this is my room."

He opens the door, welcoming me in. "Here you are."

I walk in, feeling like I'm stepping into an alternate universe. The opulence is out of control. The attendant continues to show me around, but he may as well be on mute. I'm too overwhelmed to take anything in. From the large dining area with beautiful bouquets of flowers, the spacious sunken living area, to the extensive bar area, I'm about to have a head spin. When he shows me to the bedroom, with a bed that looks like two kings pushed together, and into the bathroom with more marble and gold than I've ever seen, I'm ready to keel over.

He then tells me which number to press on the room's phone to order meals, and the other number for the front desk.

Randall thanks the attendant, tipping him with a few folded bills. I give in to the head spin, flopping down on the overstuffed sofa and sighing at the detail work in the ceiling.

Is this a taste of what life as Wyatt Hayes is like?

Whoa. He really is worth mega-bucks.

I shiver with a twinge of guilt as Randall comes back into view. "Who's paying for all this?"

"The team," he replies vaguely.

"Wyatt?"

"Don't worry about it. He wants you here. Anyway, you'll want to order your meals here," Randall says, texting on his phone. "The food is way better here than at Clearview."

"Clearview. That's the hospital, right?"

"Correct," a woman's voice answers, making me jolt in my seat.

I look over my shoulder and see a woman in a pale green pantsuit, walking into the living area.

She holds out her hand over the back of the sofa. "Erika Hartley, Circle 8 Management."

I shake her hand, awkwardly twisting and attempting to stand. "Nice to meet you."

"We're very glad you're here, Miss Bartlett," Erika says. "No one more than Wyatt."

I suck in an anxious breath. "Re-re-really?"

She smiles, nodding. "Of course. He's been stuck on you since waking from the induced coma."

I stand in alarm. "Coma? Wyatt was in a coma?"

Erika pushes a hand down. "Induced. It was a decision made by the medical staff in order to help him recover from the trauma of his accident. He was under for no more than two days."

"Oh, okay," I say and take a steadying breath. "I haven't really heard much about his accident. It's been so secretive in the press."

Erika pulls a document from her purse. "And that's how we wish it to stay. We're not thrilled about his memory loss hitting the news cycle, but such is life." She hands the papers to me. "We need you to sign a non-disclosure agreement."

My hands tremble as I reach for the papers. "Oh, really?"

"You're going to hear about Wyatt's medical history and condition. We need to ensure his protection."

"I would never spread information about him."

Erika smiles. "Of course, you wouldn't. This document just gives us peace of mind."

I swallow hard, glancing down at the papers in my hands.

"We need you to sign it before visiting Wyatt," Erika says, tapping the face of her wristwatch. "And we want to get you over there ASAP."

I frown. "It's five pages long."

"It's standard stuff," Randall says, glued to his phone. "Just scribble your signature on the last page."

"Umm. I don't get to read it?"

Erika sighs. "Of course, you can. But Wyatt wants to see you now."

Randall shows Erika the schedule on his phone. "He will have finished physical therapy by now. He'll be expecting her."

Tingles ripple through my veins, and I shift in my stance. "Wyatt's expecting me?"

Erika smirks. "That's why we've brought you all this way, dear."

Even though my distrusting father is in my head, urging me not to sign something I haven't read, I do it anyway. Whatever the fine print says, it pales in comparison to seeing Wyatt.

It doesn't take Erika long to take the document back from me. "Great. Thank you. Now, I have to meet Martin downstairs. Randall, can you make sure the presentation is ready to go in the business center?"

Randall nods. "On it."

Erika looks me up and down. "I suspect you'll want to freshen up before you leave to see Wyatt?"

I flinch, unintentionally sniffing for BO.

Erika peers at her wristwatch. "Lexy will be here in thirty minutes to escort you to Clearview. That should give you sufficient time to shower and change."

I wince. Change? I'm already wearing my best outfit.

"Problem?" Erika asks, taking in my twitchy mood.

"No," I rush. "I'll be ready in thirty minutes."

Erika points to the floor. "Lexy will meet you in the lobby."

"Lexy? Is she another assistant?"

Erika mumbles a laugh. "No, dear. Lexy is in public relations."

I swallow as the information sets in. I'm going to see Wyatt with a PR person? Why? Is she here to ensure there's the right spin on this trip?

Oh boy. I wish my dad and his conspiracy theories wouldn't leap inside my head.

"Good luck with your visit," Erika says, and then snaps her fingers at Randall, motioning for him to follow her out of the suite.

Finally alone in my hotel room, I exhale hard, looking down at my pink cardigan and skirt. Do I really need to change? I guess it was a long flight. But Randall took two flights and is still in the same suit.

Okay, I have thirty minutes. I can at least freshen up in the meantime. I move into the bedroom and find my bag on the bed where the attendant left it. I pull out my toiletries and unfold my clothes. I hold a green dress with purple flowers in front of me.

Hmm. Maybe this is cuter.

With a huff, I toss it back on the bed. No, I wanna wear pink. Heck, Erika's not babysitting me. This Lexy person hasn't seen what I was wearing on the plane.

Oof. But she is from PR. What does that mean? Is she going to spin a story about my being a bad dresser? Is this outfit bad? I sling my head into my hands and groan. Ugh. As if I weren't already nervous to see Wyatt, now I have wardrobe mind games to deal with.

Instead of making a decision, I scoop up my phone and call Mom. It rings out twice before she answers.

"Hi honey," she says in a rush. "Sorry, it's a madhouse at work. But I'm going on my lunch break now."

I sit on the edge of the bed, slouching forward. "I'm just in the hotel room, waiting to see Wyatt."

"Is it exactly like we saw last night?"

"Even better in the flesh."

"Then why is your tone low? Is it these people? Are they treating you..."

"It's fine," I cut in. "They're fine. I'm just nervous about seeing Wyatt."

"Darling, you'll be okay. He remembers you."

"I know, but so much time has passed."

"Not to him. Imagine how scared he must be feeling in that hospital."

A lump balls in my throat. "I know."

"I wish I could give you a big hug."

I exhale slowly and stand from the bed. "I'm okay. Just needed to hear your voice. I'm just going to get changed."

"But I thought..."

"Long flight," I blurt. "You know, I should probably freshen up."

"The hotel probably has a laundry service. I bet they could freshen your outfit overnight."

"Brilliant." I snap my fingers, feeling more upbeat. "Thanks, Mom. Talk to you soon. Love you."

Mom chuckles. "You sound better already. Good luck, darling, and love you too."

After I hang up with Mom, I move to the landline phone in the living area. I call the front desk and ask about their laundry service, and they guarantee my outfit will be cleaned and back in my closet by the evening. They instruct me to place the clothing items in a laundry bag located in the bedroom closet. I'm told to leave the laundry bag on the dining room table, and housekeeping will come in and collect it.

After a shower and dressed in my green dress, I place my pink outfit where instructed, and leave for the elevator. Inside the elevator, my nervousness grows exponentially with every passing floor. When the doors open on the lobby floor, a woman in a pinstriped pantsuit and silk blouse stands in wait.

"Josie?" she asks.

"Umm, yes."

She holds out her hand. "Lexy Davenport."

"Oh, hi."

Lexy grabs my hand, shaking it roughly. "Thanks for coming, Josie. We're really excited to have you here."

I hide my wince in a smile, scared she'll tear my arm off at the socket. "Thanks."

Lexy beams at me. "Shall we?"

I nod with a tight mouth, following her toward the revolving doors.

We are then shown into a black SUV. When Lexy and I buckle into the backseat, I ask, "Are you visiting Wyatt too?"

Lexy shakes her head. "No, it's just on the way to my office. With all the meetings going on at the moment, we're running short on drivers."

I breathe out, settling into my seat. "Oh, okay. Makes sense."

Lexy nudges me playfully. "Did having someone from PR in the car freak you out?"

I smile bashfully. "Just a bit."

"We're so thrilled at the prospect of Wyatt's recovery," Lexy says, bouncing in her seat. "We're really hoping your visit does the magic trick."

I tilt my head. "What do you mean?"

"You know, jog his memory. Seeing all of us just confuses him, but he remembers you." Lexy's zeal grows as her eyes widen. "What if he sees you and all his memories come back?"

I shrink in my seat. "That's a lot of pressure."

Lexy pats my knee. "Don't worry, hon. We're not expecting it to happen immediately."

Eep. But they are expecting it at some point.

Lexy's phone rings, and she lifts an index finger. "Sorry, hon, I gotta get this." She answers the phone with a boost of enthusiasm. "Richmond, darling, how are you?"

I look out the window at the bumper to bumper traffic spread across the three lanes as Lexy makes small talk. My ears prick when her tone gets more serious.

"Don't they understand Portia needs to get back stateside?" Lexy says into the phone. "She and Wyatt were in the middle of recording a collab. The two are very close."

I cringe, listening to half the conversation, and picturing Portia in 'No Way, Goodbye' with Wyatt. Sometimes it's hard to picture her perfectly plastic face because of how often I've edited myself into her place.

"Look, it's not good enough," Lexy says into the phone. "Do you realize how bad it looks that Portia hasn't visited him yet? Circulation of their relationship was peaking. If she doesn't get back here soon, we will have lost momentum."

My head spins. If Wyatt saw Portia, would he recognize her? How intense was their relationship?

"We need to put a rush on the European leg of her press tour and get her back here," Lexy says. "Okay, good to hear. Chat soon. Ciao." She puts the phone down, shaking her head. "Who said orchestrating a romance between two big-name teen stars would be easy?"

I look up, my jaw tensing. "They're not really together?"

"This is show business," Lexy replies with a chuckle. "Who's to say what's real?"

"Will Wyatt remember her?"

Lexy shrugs. "They can start over. It'll be quite cute, actually."

I pick at my fingernails, hating the thought of Portia comforting Wyatt throughout his recovery.

"We can't be selfish with his time," Lexy says bluntly. "Do you know how big his starpower is, hon? There's a lot of people counting on him. Think of all the fans."

"I'm aware of them. I might be his biggest fan."

Lexy chuckles. "Adorable." The car slows, and she taps on her window. "Here we are. Clearview."

I reach for my seatbelt, and Lexy presses on my hand.

I look up, and her expression is soft as she whispers, "We're all on edge, hon. Losing Wyatt was an insanely scary concept. We're beyond grateful he's in recovery. We just want him back in regular form."

I shrink, muttering, "I want that too."

She squeezes my hand. "Please, do all you can. He means so much to us. We need him back."

"But…" I falter. "He's still here." I look up at the building through the window. "He's right in there."

Lexy releases my hand, frowning. "Not the old Wyatt."

Oh boy. Just how much has he changed?

"Thank you so much for coming and helping him."

I smile. "Of course."

Lexy exits the car, and before I can catch up to her, a woman in a pale pink blazer and matching pencil skirt darts towards her with her phone angled in her palm.

"Lexy," the woman calls. "You're back in town? Can I only imagine this means Wyatt's getting back in front of the cameras?"

Lexy grins, eyeing the woman's phone, which displays an audiowave. Wow, she's recording this. "Harriet, darling, don't exert yourself. When we have news, we'll break it."

"By giving me exclusive access?" Harriet asks overzealously.

Lexy hums a laugh. "Hon, if you keep camping in front of this clinic, who knows what'll happen."

Harriet then turns to me, and her eyes widen with glee. "And who's this? Doesn't exactly fit the mold of one of your PAs."

"Harriet, what did I say about exerting yourself?" Lexy asks with an air of condescension. "Don't worry your pretty head with who this attractive young lady is."

I choke on a breath and my insides flip. Why the heck did Lexy describe me like that?

Harriet licks her lips like she's spotted easy prey. "Oh, a *friend* of Wyatt's?"

Crap.

Would she stop looking at me like that?

Why the heck are we even talking to this woman?

I don't want to be mentioned in an article for whatever trashy website she works for.

"Sorry, Harriet, we can't stay out here on the sidewalk all day like some people," Lexy says, placing a hand on my back. "We've got to be going."

Harriet lets us pass, whispering rapidly into her phone while her eyes stay steely on us.

"Who the heck was that?" I pant as Lexy and I enter the building.

"Just a gossip chaser from Celeb-Eze dot com," Lexy replies. "She'll absolutely love digging into the mystery of who you are."

I let out a nervous squeak. "But I'm nobody."

Lexy shrugs. "Won't stop them from keeping Wyatt on the front page. Now, come on. I'll introduce you to Dr. Fincher before I head downtown."

Inside the Clearview Clinic, we move through an impressive and sparkling foyer. Lexy takes me to an elevator, and inside she hits the number five button. The top floor of the clinic.

"I had him paged before we left the hotel," Lexy says when we step out onto the fifth floor. "Oh, there he is." She snaps her fingers, calling out, "Dr. Fincher, over here."

A man in blue scrubs and a white coat paces toward us.

"Doc, I know you're busy, but this is Josie," Lexy says, gesturing at me. "Wyatt's school friend."

"Ah, right, Josie." Dr. Fincher nods knowingly. "I'm Wyatt's neurologist."

"Nice to meet you."

"You too."

Lexy pats my arm. "Good luck, Josie. Hope everything goes well."

I wave her off as she takes the elevator back down to the lobby.

"Have you been given the rundown on Wyatt's condition?" Dr. Fincher asks.

"Just that has some form of amnesia," I reply. "I really don't know the details of how this happened."

"That makes two of us," the doctor replies, taking me off guard. "Yes, Wyatt has short-term memory loss after having severe emotional shock. He did suffer a head injury, but the extent doesn't correspond with his symptoms."

I nod, trying to take in the information. "Okay."

"He's preparing to go back home," the doctor continues, "but I haven't signed off yet. I haven't pinpointed the cause of his impairment. He's clearly suffering from a traumatic event, but no one has come forward with an eyewitness account of the incident. I'm worried about something undiscovered triggering him when he returns home."

"But didn't the accident happen on the movie set?"

"I've been given very vague information." He gives me a kind smile. "Your visit is a last-ditch effort to bring some clarity to the matter. We are hoping seeing an old friend will relieve some of the stress he's been feeling."

"How exactly can I make that happen?"

"Because Wyatt doesn't remember becoming famous. He remembers spending time with you."

Goosebumps flood my skin, and I shiver in place. "Okay," I breathe. "I hope I can make a difference."

Dr. Fincher squeezes my shoulder. "There's no pressure on you. I'm just concerned because he is suffering from a neurological issue; however, I can't define what it is."

"Is that abnormal?"

"It is common for neurological issues to form without clear prompting. However, his team has stated a traumatic accident happened on set. His scans just tell another story."

My brain hurts from the conflicting information.

The doctor motions to the end of the hall. "Mr. Hayes's room is last on the right. Just focus on visiting an old friend. Don't try to jog his memory; he doesn't need that right now. For the past few weeks, all he's had are scared and confused moments. All he needs now is a new, happy memory."

I smile. "I can work with that."

I thank the doctor and make my way along the pristine hallway and find another broad man in all-black, standing outside the last door on the right.

I clutch my elbows and sheepishly ask the man, "Umm. Is Wyatt in there?"

The man looks me up and down, folding his arms. "Who's asking?"

I gulp and my knees knock. "I'm... I'm Josie. Josie Bartlett."

He scrutinizes me, taking an excruciatingly long time to respond. He finally huffs and points a thumb at the door. "You can head inside."

I suck in a breath. "*Eep*. Really?"

The man crooks an eyebrow, clearly not into idle chit-chat. I hurriedly nod and turn the doorknob, despite the dread seeping through me.

In a shaky voice, I call out, "Hello?"

Four

I edge my way into the hospital room. There are a few machines obscuring my view, but diagonally across I manage to see the panoramic view of city skyscrapers facing the famous yellow beach and cerulean ocean.

Whoa.

Near the floor-to-ceiling windows are a couch and two armchairs, and then a kitchenette where a nurse stands by the sink. She looks over her shoulder at me and smiles.

"Looks like you have a visitor, Wyatt."

"Huh?"

Even though it was just a syllable, I'd recognize that voice anywhere.

I turn to the opposite side of the room, and there he is. Sitting on his hospital bed in a light gray T-shirt and black sweatpants, a movable table fixed over his bed with an array of playing cards displayed. His hazel eyes shine behind square-framed glasses, which he then rips off and tosses onto the moveable tray table.

Wyatt shoves the table away. "Josie!"

I move over to him as adrenaline courses through me. "Wyatt. Oh my gosh. I can't believe it's you."

He leaps off the bed, pulling me into a hug. "Were you expecting someone else?"

I tremble in his arms, taking a moment before hugging him back. "No, it's not that." I let out a nervous laugh. "I just... It's been so long. I never expected to see you again."

He frowns, his shoulders slouching as he pulls out of the hug. "Really?"

My smile twitches. "Only because you're such a big star now."

He gently brushes back my curls and whispers, "I've missed you."

My knees weaken. "I've missed you too."

His throat flexes as he looks me up and down. "You look so pretty."

The blush warms through my cheeks. "Oh, thank you."

Wyatt stumbles backward, leaning against his bed for support.

"Are you okay?" I ask.

He smiles brightly. "Of course. You're finally here."

"Wyatt," the nurse says, "maybe you should sit down again."

Wyatt shrugs and pulls himself back on the bed. I get tummy flutters when I glimpse the tattoo inside his arm. He mostly looks the same as the boy I knew, just the tattoo, the hairstyle, and muscles are new since the last time I saw him in the flesh.

He pushes his palms down on the mattress, shifting in place and wincing from the effort.

"You good?" I ask.

He nods. "I just have a sore neck and shoulders. They say I had some kind of fall, or something."

"Yeah, I heard."

"I have to do all this ph-ph-physical therapy to help with my posture and walk properly again."

"Did you have to relearn to walk?"

He smirks. "I was just super wobbly." He catches my hand, tugging me closer. "Boy, am I glad to see you."

Tingles run down my spine. "Erika only called me last night. I'll be here anytime you ask for me."

"I ah, ah, asked for you to come for like, uh, uh, ages," he stammers with an adorable grin.

I giggle and rub a circle on the back of his hand. "Oh my gosh. It's so good to see you."

"You too. It feels like no ti-time has passed. But, la-la-look at you. You're a knockout."

I giggle, blushing so much I'm almost not concerned about his level of stuttering.

Wyatt clears his throat, and as if on cue, the nurse sets a glass of water down on the table near his playing cards and reading glasses. He thanks her and then takes a sip. His hand shakes as he places the glass back on the table.

"I, I stutter sometimes," he says, keeping his gaze low. "Th-the doctor said it's normal with, umm, the, umm, memory loss."

I plant a hand on his shoulder. "I'm so sorry this has happened to you, Wyatt. I've felt sick over it."

He lifts his gaze, wearing a lopsided grin. "You've been worried about me?"

I bite my lip, slipping my hand down his arm. "Of course. You've never stopped being important to me."

The nurse finishes up at the sink and turns toward the door. "I'll give you two some privacy to catch up."

"Bye," Wyatt says with a wave.

"Are they nice here?"

He shrugs. "I guess. Pretty nice for med-medical staff. I d-don't love the fact I'm here."

"But you're out soon, right?"

Wyatt plants his hands behind him, sighing at the ceiling. "Yes, I can't wait."

"Do you know you're moving into a penthouse?"

He looks down at me with wide-eyed optimism. "That's real? I thought they were messing with me."

I giggle with eagerness. "No, it's true. I just saw my room, and it's drop-dead-incredible. I can't even imagine what they have in store for you."

He tilts his head, grazing his bottom lip with teeth. "So, we're moving into the same hotel?"

Shivers. "Umm, yes, I guess so."

His eyes stay locked on mine, increasing in heat. "Nice."

I turn away, needing to fan myself. I gesture at the playing cards, hoping for a breather from the intensity in the room. "What's going on here?"

Wyatt pulls the table closer. "They have me playing solitaire." He rubs his thumb and index finger together. "I have numbness in my fingers, and also my brain is really foggy."

I look at the cards. "And the game is supposed to help?"

He mumbles a laugh. "Yeah, but I suck at it."

I ease into a laugh. "Practice makes perfect."

"I guess."

"And the glasses? I've been keeping up with you for years—on stage and behind the scenes—and I've never known you to wear glasses."

"They're new," he says, picking up the pair and spinning it by the earpiece. "I have killer headaches and problems focusing. They're supposed to help."

"Oh, that's good then. They look cute on you."

He sets them back on the table and puffs a laugh. "Thanks." He then sits back and gives me a hesitant look. "Umm. I don't know how to ask you something."

I flinch. "What?"

He rubs the back of his neck, looking down at the mattress. "What happened between us?"

"Nothing."

He looks up with his eyebrows lifted. "But we're not friends anymore?"

"We don't have to talk about this," I rush, waving my hands. "I'm just so happy to see you. The past two years don't matter."

He sits forward. "Two years? Have we not talked in two years?"

I fidget in place, clutching my elbows. "There's an update here and there, but I wouldn't call them conversations."

He winces. "Don't tell me I became a star and was too arrogant to keep in touch."

"I'd never call you arrogant. You're the sweetest."

"Then, what happened?" He rubs the heel of his palm against his forehead. "After my headaches weren't so bad and I got my voice back, I started asking about you. All these people I don't know were visiting me. None of them knew your name." He leans forward, urgency in his eyes. "How could they not know you?"

"Well, they're people who work for you, right?" I reason. "They probably don't know your school friends."

"But you're not just a friend, you're..." He swallows hard, sitting back. "Well, you *were* more than that."

I rub the space on my chest over my heart. "It's okay. I've never held it against you. Heck, I'm the one who told you to go on Talent Quest."

Wyatt frowns, looking down as he kicks out his feet below the bed. "Why..." he stammers. "Why wouldn't I keep in contact?"

My eyes water and I hurriedly blink them clear. "Don't worry about it. You're busy. I didn't expect daily updates."

"But I've thought about you everyday I've been in here."

My heart palpitates with mixed emotions.

Wyatt winces. "We didn't have a fight?"

"No. You just got busy."

"That doesn't make sense."

"We texted after you left town," I explain. "And the more successful you got, the more time came between your replies. I was fine with that. One day, the texts stopped. But that was okay. I kept watching your career. I just thought... maybe one day, I'd get another reply."

"It doesn't make sense that I was never going to reply." Reflectively, he looks around our surroundings. "I don't have my phone because the screen hurts my eyes and makes my headaches worse. But I wish I had it and could prove there were texts that were meant for you."

"Don't beat yourself up," I whisper, letting the frown take me over. "I'm not in your league anymore."

Wyatt looks up with surprise. "You're always good enough for me. I'm the one who doesn't deserve you."

I smile, swaying under his gaze. "Not possible."

"To me," he whispers, "we spent yesterday in your treehouse."

I bite into my lip and then whisper, "That was three years ago."

"We haven't seen each other in three years?"

I nod. "After the TV show, you were supposed to come home. But then you got all these opportunities, so I was going to visit you. But you got so busy, the visit kept getting pushed back. And that's it."

"That can't be it."

"Wyatt, I'm here now, and I couldn't be happier."

"A bonk on the head had to give me sense, I guess." He tilts his head. "I won Talent Quest?"

I giggle with pride. "Yes, you were so amazing."

"A nurse asked me to sign a T-shirt with my face on it, and said she saw one of my concerts." He shakes his head in disbelief. "I've played concerts?"

"You're incredible on stage," I gush. "You played a small list of shows after the season wrapped, and then you played a bigger tour for the second album."

"I saw some of the titles on the back of her T-shirt. Did I write those songs?"

"I've read every tidbit of information about you. You have a partial writing credit on a few of the songs."

"I should have you writing the songs," he replies. "Are you still writing?"

I plant a hand over my thumping heart. "You remember that? Yes, I'm writing almost every day."

"I'd love to read what you're working on," he says with eagerness, and then shifts awkwardly. "Well, maybe you'll have to read to me. I'm not so good at the reading part at the moment."

He taps the space beside him, and with bashfulness, I sit up on the mattress next to him. "Is it your eyesight or the brain fog that's tripping you up?"

He shrugs. "Bit of both. Just like the stutter, the headaches come and go."

I rub his arm. "Then it means, eventually, they can go completely. Just a momentary setback from the accident."

He crosses his fingers. "Hopefully."

I gesture at the playing cards. "Did you want to get back to the game? Or we could play Go Fish?"

Wyatt mumbles a laugh. "Only if you want an easy win."

I giggle. "Well, that's okay. We don't have to play a game. We can just talk."

"I can't believe you haven't been in my life," Wyatt says. "It's crazy because everything about you came back. Everything from back home is clear as day."

"That's fantastic. I'm so glad."

He rubs under his chin. "I haven't visited you at home?"

I frown. "Are you sure you want to hear this?"

He grounds his hands against the mattress. "Yes."

"Wyatt," I say gently, "you don't visit Victoria Falls."

His expression is muddled. "Ever?"

"Not in the three years since you left for the TV show."

"My parents said they sold our home."

I nod. "They left town to support your career."

"But I have friends in Victoria Falls," Wyatt says in a small voice. "I don't bring them on tour?"

I smile, biting my lip. "You don't realize how big a deal you are these days."

He stares at me intently. "You're a big deal."

Tingles race up my limbs, and I rub warmth into them. "It must've been so scary forgetting the past few years."

He touches my hand and interlaces his fingers between mine. "It's a trip. People keep te-telling me how much my life has changed."

"Wyatt, you have an amazing career." I curl my fingers over his. "I always knew you could do it. I'm so proud of you."

He frowns. "But you haven't been with me?"

"Well, I've had school, and you've been making albums and movies."

Wyatt shakes his head, narrowing his gaze. "How am I in movies? I've never taken acting lessons."

I giggle with a shrug. "You must have a natural talent."

He looks at me with intrigue. "Are the movies good?"

"I love them. They're teen rom-coms I've rewatched a zillion times."

"Oh. So I'm not a gun-wielding badass?"

I giggle again. "Nope, you're an adorable love interest."

He laughs. "Boo."

"Well, isn't this just the cutest," a female voice says, followed by two sets of footsteps.

I look ahead and almost jolt. "Mr. and Mrs. Hayes," I beam. "Hi, how are you?"

Wyatt's parents walk into the room, and I almost don't recognize them. They're dripping in designer threads and their hair is perfectly styled. Something about their strides and the way they carry themselves is unsettlingly unfamiliar.

"Fabulous, now that you're here," Mrs. Hayes says, opening her arms to me. "How are you, Josie, darling?"

"I'm good," I reply, sliding off the bed and meeting her in a hug. "I still can't believe I'm here."

"We wouldn't have it any other way," Mr. Hayes says as I pull out of the hug. "Wow, Josie, you've become a pretty little thing."

"She's always been pretty," Wyatt pipes up.

Mrs. Hayes moves toward the bed. "How are you doing, sweetheart?" She kisses Wyatt's forehead. "How's the headache?"

"Bad," he says bluntly. "They already gave me painkillers."

"We'll buzz the nurse for more," Mr. Hayes says, reaching for a button near the bed.

Wyatt lifts a hand. "Don't. They'll kick in soon."

"Well, can we get you anything, sweetie?" Mrs. Hayes asks. She then turns to me. "Josie? Anything you need?"

"No, thank you," I reply. "I'm good."

She turns back to Wyatt. "Sweetie?"

Wyatt shakes his head.

His dad nears the movable table and gathers up the mess of cards. "How's the numbness, son?"

Wyatt rubs his fingertips together. "Still here."

Mr. Hayes shuffles the cards. "Maybe it's time your doctor and physical therapist came up with a better plan than cards."

Wyatt sighs. "It's not the doctor's fault I'm not better."

I suck in a breath, heartbroken by Wyatt's defeated tone.

"You're getting better," Mrs. Hayes says, caressing the side of Wyatt's face. "That's all that matters."

Wyatt gives a small smile in reply.

His mom looks back at me with a happy smile. "We heard the laughter on our way in. It's so beautiful to see you kids back together."

I hug my middle, smiling. "I'll be here anytime I get a call."

Mr. Hayes's eyes light with hope. "Did any of the fog lift? Have you remembered any more about your life?"

Wyatt groans. "*Dad.*"

Mrs. Hayes moves over to her husband and clutches his arm. "Don't be mad at your father, sweetheart. We're just so excited about your recovery. Forgive us."

Wyatt shrugs. "I d-don't know what I'm su-su-supposed to do. I can't f-force myself to remember. I've tried."

"It'll come back," I whisper, eyes fixed on Wyatt. "There's no rush."

His smile grows in appreciation.

"We're not trying to rush you," his dad says. "You've just worked so hard for the life you have now. We'd hate for it all to disappear."

"I don't care about it," Wyatt says with a shrug. "I don't re-remember what all th-the fuss is about. I just care about Josie being here."

"And that's all you should focus on right now," his mom says in a rush. "Dr. Fincher said that this meetup will be good for you. We don't want to do anything to jeopardize that. We just wanted to say hi to Josie and check in on you."

Wyatt grins, looking down at the floor as he kicks his feet out. "So, you'll leave us alone?"

His dad laughs under his breath. "Sure, son. We'll leave you two alone."

Mrs. Hayes wraps me in another hug, and Mr. Hayes looks me up and down for a beat too long, and then they both leave.

I slink back to Wyatt's side. "They were a little intense."

"Tell me about it." He sighs. "They're get-getting impatient about mm-my memory coming back."

"They just want the best for you."

Wyatt shakes his head. "They're getting antsy. Dr. Fincher said I, I shouldn't be stressed. It, it doesn't help with re-recovery. But, th-they make me feel stressed."

I plant a hand on his knee. "It's okay," I coo. "They're gone. And I promise to keep the stress to a minimum."

Wyatt breathes out slowly and smiles. "I, I already feel the stutter going."

I grin with giddiness. "I'm so glad."

Wyatt groans, falling forward and cupping the sides of his face.

I gasp, clutch his shoulder. "Wyatt? What's wrong?"

He grunts, lifting his head, but then folding forward again.

"Wyatt? Wyatt?"

Hurriedly, I reach across and hit the nurse buzzer.

He forces himself upright, muttering. "It hurts."

My vision blurs with water, and I blink hard before a tear falls.

Through gritted teeth, he murmurs, "It always hurts."

"It's okay," I whisper with a tremble in my voice. "You'll be okay."

Wyatt lowers his hands, taking me in with red-rimmed eyes.

There's surprise in his expression that takes me off-guard. "What is it?"

He smooths back one of my curls. "You're upset."

My eyes well again. "I hate seeing you in pain."

He grunts again, holding the side of his head. "I'm okay, see," he strains to say. "Nothing to it."

"Stop it." I laugh nervously as a tear teeters in the corner of my eye. "Don't put on a front. I don't want you hiding your pain for my benefit."

The nurse from earlier bustles into the room. "Is everything okay in here?"

I break away from Wyatt. "He's in pain. It's his head."

The nurse holds a small flashlight in front of Wyatt's eyes, asking him to follow the light. She then checks her wristwatch, saying, "It's only been forty minutes since your last dose of pain meds."

"I'm okay," Wyatt says, catching his breath. "It was just sudden and intense. It's going away now."

"But the dull ache is still there?" she asks.

He nods. "It's always there."

"I'll page Dr. Fincher and discuss your next round of painkillers. Perhaps he lowered the dosage too soon"

I hug my waist, barely able to keep the flood of emotions inside me. "Is he... is he going to be okay?"

Wyatt sighs, looking at me with a pout. "Joze."

"I'm sorry," I say, letting a tear fall and swallowing back a sob. "I just hate this. It's not fair. You don't deserve this."

The nurse gives me a kind smile. "He'll be okay. He's handling this like a trooper. He's lucky to have a friend as caring as you." She turns to Wyatt. "I'll chat with your doctor and then come back with new pain meds."

Wyatt nods. "Thank you."

She turns and rubs my shoulder. "My name's Liza and I'm on shift until eight p.m. if you need anything else."

I nod. "Thank you."

Wyatt reaches his arms out, and I shuffle toward him until he wraps me in his arms.

His chin rests on my shoulder, and his breath tickles my earlobe. "Don't be sad."

I wrap my arms around his shoulders. "How can I not be?"

"How about because we're together?"

I pull my arms around him tighter. "I never want to let you go."

He buries his face in my curls. "Then don't."

My giggle lacks oomph as I trace a finger along the back of his neck. "Okay."

"We used to be close like this, remember?"

"I've never forgotten."

His head lifts, and he plants a kiss on my cheek. "I woke up from a coma thinking about you."

I lose control of my knees and fall against him.

He laughs, holding me up.

I gather myself, pulling my weight off him. "Sorry."

"Don't be. I liked the extra closeness."

Butterflies disperse from my stomach, and heat rises from my neck up. I still feel the imprint of his kiss, and it keeps my knees weak.

"Umm," I stammer, backing out of his arms. "I should probably sit down."

Wyatt points at the couch and armchairs facing the panoramic view. "I never sit over there, but they do look ultra comfy."

I bite my lip and nod, watching him slip off the bed.

Five

A mixture of adrenaline and heightened concern courses through me. He was just doubled over in agonizing pain. He shouldn't be getting up just because I can't keep it together.

"Are you sure you're okay moving away from the bed?" I ask. "I mean, you were just in so much pain."

"Nothing new, Joze." He pulls his arms around me. "But can you help me walk over to the couch? I'm feeling a little shaky."

"Are you sure about this? Because we can just…"

"*Joze*," he cuts me off with the most adorable smile. "It's chill. Have you seen this view?"

I smile, helping him walk over to the sitting area. "It is pretty magnificent."

"How the heck do I afford this? It's insane."

"I met your financial manager," I say as we round the couch. "He must be making good investments for you."

Wyatt furrows his brow as we plonk down on the couch. "I don't know if I've met him."

"His name is Martin," I reply. "Or, maybe that was his last name."

Wyatt shrugs it off. "There's been a lot of people visiting me who say they're *on my team*. It's hard to keep track of them all."

"I guess they're all working in the background. They want to keep promoting you while keeping your recuperation upbeat in the press."

"The press?" Wyatt asks. "Do people really care about me being in the hospital?"

I nod emphatically. "Absolutely. So many of us were eagerly awaiting your next movie. Plus, your condition has been so secretive. The fact online commentators had so much to speculate on has kept you in the news cycle."

Wyatt blows out a hard breath. "Maybe that's why it's a secret. So people *do* talk."

I nod in agreement, remembering Lexy used the tactic downstairs with Harriet.

"Have people at home been gossiping about me?"

"The walls of Ashworth Academy hold a lot of gossip. But, generally, people gush about how such a big star came from our school."

Wyatt frowns, disbelievingly. "Do the Ashworth kids still go to school there? How does anyone care about me when fr-freaking billionaires roam the halls?"

I gesture at the view. "Umm, you're not doing too badly yourself."

Wyatt laughs, rubbing his forehead. "I guess."

"By the way," I pat the seat cushion, "this couch is ridiculously comfy."

He sinks into the seat beside me. "I know. Beats a hospital bed, that's for sure."

"There's this really plush sofa in my hotel suite," I tell him. "I can't imagine how the penthouse is decked out."

He grins, clutching my hand. "You'll have to check it out with me."

With bashful nerves, my hand trembles in his. "We'll be practically neighbors."

He leans in, whispering in a breathy tone, "I can't stop picturing us in your treehouse."

My pulse accelerates as my memory floods with images.

"You remember?" he asks softly. "How we..."

My chest constricts around my swelling heart. "Umm, how we... kissed?"

Wyatt silently chuckles, pink highlighting the sides of his face.

I look away, stealing a moment to settle my racing heart.

"Things with us..." He pauses until my gaze slips back in his direction. "They were heating up."

"Mm-hmm."

He sits back, but the intensity in his eye contact never wanes. "I don't remember how it ended. Or if it ended?"

I exhale slowly, my shoulders slouching forward as every timid cell in my body frazzles.

"It feels like we've never been apart," he says, running a hand over his hair. "Well, to me, anyway."

I rub the tightness from my chest and clear my throat. "But we have been apart."

He shifts nervously.

"I mean," I continue quickly, "I've been watching everything you've been doing. But, seeing you now... It feels like the same you I've always known."

He grins, rubbing a circle on my hand.

Beep, beep.

I slip my hand into the pocket of my dress. "That's my phone. It might be my mom."

"Is she back at the hotel?"

"No, she and Dad had to work. Plus, there are the twins. Long story short, I came solo."

"Wow, that's brave of you."

I smile, unlocking my phone. "I was coming to see you. Well worth the anxiety."

It's a text from Kylie. *"Are you with Wyatt? We need visual proof!"*

I cup a hand around my eyes and sigh. "Kylie and her boyfriend are pestering me about getting a photo with you."

"Kylie has a boyfriend?"

I nod. "They're cute together, despite the toxic start to their relationship."

"Sounds like there's a story there."

Beep, beep.

There's another text from her, wanting updates and selfies. Can I even send her a photo? I mean, I've signed a document, promising not to spread information about Wyatt. Did that include photos? Dang it. I should've read the NDA. Kylie would never share the photo, but who knows who else could see it and share it with the wrong people.

"Kylie wants a photo of us." I lift my phone in camera mode and frame myself with part of his shoulder and ear. "I'll just hide your face."

I snap the photo, and Wyatt says, "Hang on. Take it again."

As my hand presses against the shutter button, Wyatt leans in and kisses my cheek, perfectly captured in the frame.

I giggle, lowering my phone. "Well, I'm definitely not sharing that one."

As I touch the spot where the warmth from his kiss lingers, he whispers, "It feels like yesterday when I last kissed you."

"Umm..." it comes out of me shakily as I hesitate to respond.

Yes, he's the Wyatt I remember, but he's also a freaking movie star.

Wyatt frowns, pulling back. "But you must have a boyfriend."

Unintentionally, I laugh out loud.

He blinks, grinning apprehensively at me. "What?"

I press a hand to my lips, settling my laughter. "Umm, sorry. It's just me, having a boyfriend. It's laughable."

His brow raises in surprise. "How is it? Look at you. You were pretty before, but you're drop-dead-gorgeous now."

My chin drops as all my muscles seize. Wyatt Hayes thinks I'm gorgeous.

Sure, a few years ago, I might have bought it. But now? I've seen him with popstars on his arm and kissing super model-esque actresses in movies.

He scoops a hand into my curls and cups his hand behind my neck. "You're really single?"

"Yes," I whisper, breathless. "I've never been on a real date."

His teeth graze his bottom lip as he smiles. "Really?"

I blush and nod.

Whoa. He's so freaking close.

"A lot has happened to you since we last saw each other," I whisper, searching his lips that have been on other girls' lips.

His hand runs down my shoulder, and he collects my hands in his. "What we have isn't in the past tense."

I shiver and feel my stomach flip. "But we haven't stayed in contact."

"I was obviously an idiot," he replies. "It's a mountain of a mistake I need to make up for."

"I never expected to be back in your life. You're bigger than whatever was between us."

"Josie, I care more about fixing our relationship than fixing my memory."

I shake my head. "Don't say that."

"It's true."

"You need to get better."

"And then what? Never see you again? Nuh-uh, not happening."

"But, if you don't..."

Wyatt clutches my hands tighter. "Jo-Josie. Can you just let me w-work on making this up to you?"

I shiver with a wave of goosebumps, slumping forward. "But you... Okay."

"Wyatt?"

I sit back, air caught in my lungs, surprised by the intrusion.

Dr. Fincher blinks at us, holding his clipboard, and then breaks into a self-conscious chuckle.

"Oh, I'm sorry," he says, flustered, "I didn't mean to interrupt."

Wyatt clears his throat, sitting back with space between us. "It's okay."

The doctor approaches the couch, tapping his clipboard. "I just wanted to check in, Wyatt. Liza was saying you were experiencing stronger pain."

"It's not as bad now," Wyatt replies, sitting back on the couch.

"Scale?"

"Felt like a nine, but, I dunno, maybe it's at a four."

Happy surprise brightens Dr. Fincher's face. "Wow, that's a big drop."

I pivot between them. "What does this mean?"

"Wyatt rates his pain level out of ten," Dr. Fincher explains. "Ten is the highest level of pain on the scale."

"Wow, four's not so bad," I say with glee.

Wyatt chews his lip, his eyes dancing over me.

"Maybe you had a distraction from the pain?" Dr. Fincher suggests with a knowing smile.

Wyatt clears his throat, embarrassment tweaking his facial muscles. "Mmm. Yeah."

"And how was physical therapy this morning?"

"Savanna had me walking with the bars," Wyatt replies, "but I also tried walking on my own."

Dr. Fincher nods. "Good. And the cards? Do you feel like you're getting a better handle on them?"

Wyatt's head tilts to the side as he sighs. "I'm still not very good at it. Sometimes I can't work out what see-sequence the numbers sh-should go in. Erhm, other times I have trouble pi-picking up the cards."

"The dexterity will come. Does the numbness still come and go?"

Wyatt nods. "I don't have it all the time."

"Good. I'm confident it should be eradicated, but we'll keep monitoring it," Dr. Fincher replies. "I know it can be frustrating to relearn all these basic movements, but stay positive. You've got this."

"Thanks, Doc," Wyatt says with a small smile.

Dr. Fincher tilts his head, studying Wyatt with care. "I'm still concerned about what caused your memory loss. If you've suffered severe emotional shock, I don't want you returning to your life and becoming triggered."

"I, I need to go," Wyatt says with urgency. "Besides, I'll still see that psych, psych... therapist? Right?"

Dr. Fincher nods. "Right."

"So I'll be leaving soon?"

Dr. Fincher glances at me and then returns to Wyatt. "Yes, we will just have to perform a few tests before your release. The administration staff already has a list of appointments with your physical therapist, psychologist, and speech therapist. You're staying in the city for a while, correct?"

"Yeah, there's a hotel booked for me."

"Good. Of course, you can fly back for future appointments. But I feel it's important, initially, for you to stay close to the clinic as we monitor your release. We want you moving forward, not relapsing."

"How could he relapse?" I blurt.

"An increase in slurred words, or less mobility," Dr. Fincher explains. "Those sorts of things. I don't anticipate worsened memory loss, if that's your concern. But we will need to monitor the frequency and intensity of the headaches."

"I already feel better," Wyatt rushes.

Dr. Fincher smiles warmly. "And have you and Josie been able to recall the same memories?"

I raise a hand. "Wyatt brought them up first."

"She's filled me in on some of the present-day stuff," Wyatt says. "But, I swear, the past is clear as day."

"That's fantastic," the doctor responds.

Wyatt sits forward with eagerness. "So, I'm leaving the clinic?"

"You're improving in physical therapy, and with improved stress management your stutter will diminish," Dr. Fincher replies. "So, yes, you can leave after we conduct a few more tests."

"Anything you want, doc," Wyatt says with urgency. "I just feel like I'm broken when I'm stuck in this room."

Dr. Fincher smiles warmly. "I certainly don't want you to stay if you feel it's hurting your progress. Of course, you do realize this involves some memory tests."

Wyatt clicks his tongue. "Bummer. What if I fail again?"

Dr. Fincher chuckles to himself. "You've never failed one-hundred percent."

"Does he need one-hundred percent in order to leave the clinic?" I ask.

"Not at all," Dr. Fincher replies, clutching his clipboard close to his chest. "You still have a long recovery period, Wyatt, but I'm very optimistic for you."

Wyatt sighs out happily. "Thanks."

I sit up, a sinking feeling in my gut. "Dr. Fincher, is there anything I should or shouldn't be doing? I don't want to hurt Wyatt's progress."

"You're not tasked with anything, Josie," the doctor replies. "Remember, you're simply a visitor. I don't want you to feel any pressure or stress. Yes, it's hoped your visit has a positive impact on Wyatt's health, but there's a lot of factors that go into neurological issues."

Wyatt squeezes my hand, and I catch the tug in his smile.

"I would recommend not rushing Wyatt when he's stumbling over his words." Dr. Fincher makes sure to give Wyatt an optimistic look. "He's doing much better. But, on the times when he slurs or misplaces a word, give him the time to adjust. It'll help him to make the connections himself."

I inhale deeply and nod. "Okay. I can do that."

"Wyatt, remember you need to pause when you're stuck on words," Dr. Fincher says. "At least counting back from ten. Having Josie visit is a big thing for you. Of course, it would increase any anxiety you are already feeling."

Wyatt sits up. "She didn't cause..."

Dr. Fincher raises a hand to halt his sentence. "Excitement and anxiety can feel more alike than we realize."

At that, Wyatt blushes.

"How's the vision?"

"It's okay, I just had a really bad headache."

"I'll have another dose of painkillers administered on the hour." Dr. Fincher taps his clipboard against his chest and turns toward the door. "Keep up the good work."

"That sounded positive," I say, now that we're alone.

"Mm-hmm."

"So, memory tests. You've already had them?"

"Yeah, I've had a few. They seem like they should be easy, but, ugh... They're so hard."

"They'd probably be really hard for me too," I reply, "and I haven't had an injury."

Wyatt slouches beside me, misery coloring his face.

"Hey," I whisper, grasping his hand. "You okay?"

He exhales shakily. "I just don't want to be broken anymore."

"Hey," I coo, squeezing his hand. "You had an accident, that's all. You'll heal. It'll just take time."

"But you heard the doctor," he says, shattered. "I slur and forget words. I don't want you to see me like this."

"Wyatt," I say, bravery faltering. "I wouldn't be a very good friend if some stuttering was a turn off."

His smile is small as red lines his eyes. "I'm just scared."

I sniff and water builds in my eyes. "I know. Me too."

He pulls an arm around me. "Thank you so much for being here. I'd be going out of my mind without you."

I lean in and peck his cheek. "We can't have you stressing out. The doctor said that's at the top of the no-no list."

"I think if I get extra time with you, I'll be as mellow as a hippie."

I giggle, watching a dimple embed in his cheek. "I'll stay as long as they let me."

He swipes his thumb across my chin. "You said you'd never been on a date?"

I bite into my lip. "I guess I've always had someone else on my mind."

There's something so soft and sweet about the light dancing in his eyes. I can't help glancing at the shine on his lower lip. The hours I've spent imagining myself kissing this boy again are unfathomable. He was my first ever kiss at twelve-years-old, and there hasn't been anyone else since. Not that I ever put myself out there to date another boy.

As Wyatt tilts his head like he's about to lean in, I can't help imagining him in the movies I've watched over and over. How many times I envisioned myself as the girl in his arms. And then Portia fills my mind.

I push on his chest, reclining myself away from him.

His mouth hangs ajar, startled. "What is it?"

"Uh," I stammer. "I don't have a boyfriend, but..."

His eyes widen as I leave him hanging.

My stomach cramps, and I force out, "You might have a girlfriend."

Six

Wyatt scrunches his eyes closed, shaking his head. "I what?"

I clasp my hands over my mouth, too terror-stricken to respond.

He opens his eyes, his brow furrowing skeptically. "I can't have a girlfriend."

"But, I think..."

He sits back, unconvinced. "Why would I have a girlfriend?"

"Because I've seen..."

"No, why would I have a girlfriend and she's never visited?"

"Oh, umm..." Because Lexy said she's still in Europe. "She, umm..."

He sits forward. "What are you trying to say?"

"Well, you might not be official, but..."

He points at his chest, dumbfounded. "You think I have a girlfriend?"

I raise my palms as my vision blurs. "I... I..."

He catches my hands, pulling them to center between us. "Joze, you're st-starting to st-stutter worse than me."

I blink back my tears, but one sneaks out, leaving a wet trail down my cheek. "I'm sorry," I whisper hoarsely. "I just... I don't want to do anything when she might be..."

Wyatt frowns. "Who is she?"

I bite into my lip as my stomach spasms. "Your co-star. And, umm, apparently you were recording a song together."

He squeezes my hands gently. "Doesn't mean we were a couple."

I nod. "It might've been fabricated, but I don't know how real either of your feelings were."

He tugs me toward him. "The only real feelings are what I feel for you. This person obviously doesn't care about me. I've never heard from whoever she is."

"But..."

His thumb swipes over my tear-stained cheek, and he shakes his head to halt my sentence.

I frown. "But, what if..."

"What if I never hit my head, and we weren't sitting here together?" Wyatt says softly, cupping the side of my face. "Yeah, it scares the crap out of me that I, I have this whole life th-that is just blank in my mind. But I don't care about it as much as I care about being with you."

"But before your accident you didn't want..."

He cuts me off. "I can't believe that I didn't want to be with you. There has to be another ex-ex-explanation for me not keeping in contact."

I swallow hard over the lump in my throat. "Because of another girl."

"No way," he says firmly. "If I didn't always want you, I wouldn't have woken up from a coma thinking about you."

I clamp down on his hands. "I just want to be with you, Wyatt."

His grin lights up his face. "Then let's be together. There's no one standing in our way."

"But our lives are so different now."

"Let's worry about that later. For now, we've got this comfy couch and this wicked view."

I settle against him, still unnerved by Portia wreaking havoc in my thoughts. His hand runs over my curls and he gently nudges my head to rest against his shoulder.

As he runs a hand over my arm, he smirks at the inside of his bicep. "Did you know I have a tattoo?"

I smile at the Sanskrit inked into his skin. "Yes, I knew."

He stretches his arm out to view the design. "I don't even know what it means."

Giddily, I mumble, "Perception is reality."

"Huh?"

I lean my head against his shoulder as I run my thumb against the inscription. "It's what the tattoo means; perception is reality."

"How do you know that?"

I blush. "It was in an article I read online. It's written in Sanskrit."

"Oh, okay." He flexes his arm again, watching the tattoo. "You must know more about my life than I do."

"Well, I am a super fan."

He laughs. "Whatever."

I giggle. "Hey, I am."

He lets his arm flop and then reaches across to hold me. "Well, heck, at least I got a tattoo and can't remember the pain."

"You wouldn't have felt the pain. You're such a tough guy now."

"I dunno. At the moment, I'm feeling battered and bruised."

"But you're healing."

He kisses the top of my forehead and settles in beside me. We hold each other in silence, only breaking apart when Nurse Liza returns with Wyatt's new dose of painkillers.

At the kitchenette, Liza fills a glass with fresh water and presents it to Wyatt with a small plastic container with two pills inside, half blue, half white.

Wyatt breathes out slowly. "Thanks. It's been agony waiting for these."

My mouth falls open, and I gently whack his arm. "You didn't tell me you were still in pain. I said, don't put on a front."

He flashes a guilty smile. "Maybe agony was too strong a word."

I eye him. "Or, maybe it was the truth."

Wyatt avoids my eyes and quickly throws back the pills and chases them with three big gulps of water. He hands the pill container and glass back to Liza. "Thanks."

"Hiding your pain won't do you any good," Liza says, stepping away from the couch. "No matter how pretty the girl by your side is."

I sink lower on the couch as my blush rises.

Wyatt hugs an arm around my shoulders. "Can you blame me for wanting to soak up all this time with you?"

"Honestly, it's given me such a head rush. This is a trip, Wyatt. I've been dreaming about you for so long. It's almost like whiplash, actually being with you."

His lips press into a line, and worry flashes in his hazel eyes. "Is this not okay?"

I plant a hand on his chest, maintaining our closeness. "No, of course it is. It's just... For me, it's been a long time."

His bottom lip twitches, and he nods slowly.

"It's just hard," I whisper, "pretending like no time has passed."

"But... What am I supposed to do?"

I shake my head. "Nothing. It's not your fault."

He frowns, rubbing his forehead. "It kinda is."

I gently caress his jawline. "You can't help what you don't remember. I don't want you to stress about it."

"But you're uncomfortable."

"Not with you," I rush. "It's just the situation. This place. What I know about your life now. It's a lot to balance."

Wyatt slides back on the couch, his arm pulling away from my shoulders. There's a tug at my heart, and I clasp his wrist as he recoils.

My shoulders hunch forward. "I'm sorry."

He tilts his head. "You shouldn't be apologizing."

"I don't want you to feel bad about all this. You can't remember us being apart."

"But I'm the reason we were. I'm the reason you can't feel good being so close to me."

I press a hand over my chest as my chin drops. "I love being close to you."

"But you're thinking about all this other stuff. I don't want a career, or a girl I don't remember, to wreck what's happening between us. But it has, and I don't know what to do about it."

I exhale shakily. "Should we just take a minute?"

Hurt crosses his expression. "Do you want to leave?"

I frown, and it quickly morphs into a pout as the lump pulsates in my throat. "I never want to leave you."

He squints, circling his thumb between his eyebrows.

I wince in second-hand pain. "Your head's still hurting?"

"Yeah." He opens his eyes and points at the kitchenette. "Sometimes they get a washcloth. It helps."

I dash off the couch and move across to the kitchenette. Near the sink is a neatly stacked pile of stark white washcloths. I run one under cold water, wring it out, and take it back to Wyatt.

"Thanks," he mumbles, placing it on his forehead.

"Do you need anything else?" I ask, settling back on the couch, a space between us. "Should I buzz Liza again?"

"No, I'll be okay."

"Are you sure?"

He blows out a shaky breath, eyeing the early evening view ahead of us. "I don't want to hear about my life. But... Can, can I hear about yours?"

"What do you want to know?"

A small smile tugs at the corners of his mouth. "What you've been working on. Would you read to me?"

My heart eases to a slower pace, and I reach into the pocket of my dress. "Hmm. I'll need to find one of the stories I've put the most effort into."

"But I thought everything you wrote had maximum effort."

"I've gotten a lot more serious since you last read something of mine," I say, scrolling through the Docs app on my phone. "My editing process is a lot more ruthless."

"But you don't cut out the heart, right?"

"Never. I'm just more thorough with something before I let it out into the world. Plus, Casey is a really harsh critic."

"What, isn't she, like, four?"

I giggle. "The twins are ten-years-old now."

Wyatt sighs, shaking his head. "Whoa. They wouldn't even know me anymore."

"They do think I'm lying about knowing you," I admit. "Even when I show them old polaroids of us. Casey's a skeptic, like Dad, and she thinks I've doctored the photos."

Wyatt shakes his head, shifting uncomfortably. "Don't tell me anything about me not being in your life. It's fr-freaking me out. Distract me with a story."

I nod hurriedly, scrolling through my word docs.

Wyatt sits back, readjusting the washcloth as he stares up at the ceiling. "Which one has been given your tough seal of approval?"

My finger hovers over one. "Well, this one won the Courtney Prize last year."

Wyatt grins at the ceiling. "An, an award winner. Okay, I, I gotta hear this one."

I bite into my lip, fingers trembling as I sit back, ready to read to him. "Okay, here goes. It's called 'Marked Alone.'"

I read him the story of a man living in an isolated cabin in the woods. The man has everything he needs for survival, but he yearns for home. As the story progresses, it becomes clear he can never return home because he's now in the only place that is safe. I finish with a cliffhanger ending about how the world changed after chemical warfare.

"Whoa. That was intense," Wyatt says, pulling the washcloth off his forehead. "So many twists and turns. No wonder it won a prize."

I grin, taking his washcloth back to the sink. "Thanks, Wyatt."

"It was so sad how he reminisced about his home," Wyatt says, leaning his chin on his hands as he watches me over the back of the couch. "I wonder what'll happen when I go home."

"You'll be safe at home."

"I don't think I live with my parents," he mutters.

"You don't?"

"Someone told me that. Erin?"

I shake my head, walking back to the couch. "I don't know an Erin."

He sits back as I return to the couch. "Who called you?"

"Erika."

His jaw rocks, and he mutters, "Must've been her."

I bat a hand. "Erin, Erika, same difference."

"Hmm."

"You misplaced a name. No big deal."

He frowns, eyes drooping as he nods.

"I thought you didn't want to talk about your life."

He sighs. "I don't."

"Why don't we do something else to distract us?" I gesture at the table near his bed. "What about solitaire?"

"No, I don't wanna do that."

"There has to be something we can do."

"I kinda wish I could play my guitar," he says wistfully at the view. "That always pulled me out of my thoughts."

The idea of hearing him play sends a thrill through my veins. Eagerly, my eyes dart around the room. "Well, why don't you? Surely they've brought your guitar here."

Wyatt folds his arms across his middle, shaking his head. "I can't play it. My fingers aren't working very well."

"Oh, right." Duh, Josie. The playing cards.

He untucks his right hand from his side, opening and closing it. "My phys-physical therapist has me doing, erhm, hand exercises. They're supposed to help me g-get ready to play the guitar."

"What are they?"

"I have a band that goes around my fingers and I have to ster-st-stretch out the digits as far as I can." He looks over at his bed. "I th-think it's over there."

I get up and move over to the bed. "What am I looking for?"

"It's an elastic band. I don't know where I, I left it. It's not by the bed somewhere?"

I crane my neck, searching the area. "Umm, I don't see anything."

Wyatt huffs, and I turn around, seeing him flop back against the couch.

I edge toward him, clutching my elbows. "You look so tired. Maybe you should go back to bed?"

"I don't want to sleep," he mutters.

"Aren't you wiped?"

He pulls himself up to sit. "I don't want to waste any time while you're here."

I giggle, fidgeting in my stance. "But acting like a zombie because you need sleep won't be an effective way to spend our time. Besides, I don't mind if you sleep."

"I don't want to wake up and find out you're gone." He gulps. "Or worse, that you were never here, and it was all just a dream."

I move over to the couch and kneel on the floor in front of him. I slide my hands against the sides of his face and smile. "I'm not going anywhere. But I'm not letting you derail your recovery." I stand on my knees, and let out a soft chuckle. "Plus, I don't want to be around grumpy Wyatt. And I know he'll be gone as soon as he naps."

Wyatt lets out a quiet laugh. "I love having you here. You know me."

My hands rest behind his ears. "I'll never stop caring about you, Wyatt. You don't have to worry about me leaving you."

He bites his lip, almost looking queasy.

My hands slightly lift off him. "Are you okay?"

"You're worried about me leaving you," he whispers. "That I'll forget you."

"You woke up remembering me," I whisper. "That's all I need to know."

"But you…"

"I'm sorry I let my insecurities out," I cut in. "You said there was no other girl in your thoughts, and I believe you."

"I don't want you to apologize for telling me your feelings."

I nod, sliding my hands down to his shoulders. "Okay, thank you. Now, will you go back to bed?"

He nods. "I know my physical therapist will hate that I've been sitting here with terrible posture."

"Does your back hurt?" I ask, helping him stand.

"Yeah, but it's nothing new." He smirks. "This didn't help, but I'd have a dull ache either way."

"So, I have to play posture police with you now?" I half-joke.

Wyatt grasps my hand as he gingerly walks back to his bed. "Oh boy. I didn't realize how tired I was."

I stand by his side as he carefully pulls himself onto the mattress. "You should get some shut-eye." Unintentionally, I yawn. "Oh geez, think the flight is catching up with me."

"Are you going back to your hotel?" he frets.

I throw a thumb at the couch. "That seems like a good place to nap."

He grins. "Okay, good."

"Sleep well, Wyatt."

"Thanks," he says, eyes dazzling with bliss as he grins.

I stand upright, woozy from the pounding of my heart. Okay, now I really need to lie down.

Seven

The travel did it. There's no way I would've conked out otherwise.

Wyatt Hayes and I are in the same room, reminiscing about the past. How have I not been electronically charged this whole time?

I rub my forehead, staring up at the ceiling as I lie back on the couch. I just wish this could be paradise without the heaviness weighing down the situation. He has a whole life he doesn't remember. A whole life that doesn't include me.

Did he shut me out on purpose?

I sit up and view him asleep in his bed. Did the boy he turned into not want anything to do with me? If he had all his memories back, would he absolutely hate that I'm in this room?

Would he want Portia here instead?

My stomach churns with an ugly growl and I peel myself off the couch. I need out of this room before my thoughts truly spin out of control. On my way out, I can't help watching Wyatt sleep. Dang, he's so sweet looking. My stomach quivers with the conflicting emotions.

This boy acts like he wants me around every second.

But so did the boy that left town for Talent Quest.

I rub my hands over my face and amble out of the room. I double take at the broad man in all-black, still standing guard outside Wyatt's door. Why is he still here? Does Wyatt have a stalker or something?

Eep.

Was a stalker involved in his accident and that's why his team has been so secretive about it in the press?

As I move into the hall, I bump into a tall woman in a light blue uniform.

"Oh, I'm sorry," I say, straightening myself up.

"No, totally my fault," she says, steadying her footing. "I was just on my way to see Wyatt. I'm Savanna, his physical therapist."

"Oh, hi. Umm, he's asleep."

"Ah, no bother then." She eyes me questioningly. "Are you Josie?"

"Umm, yes. How did you know?"

The question disappears, leaving a twinkle in her eye. "Just our boy in there has mentioned you one or two times."

Is it possible to blush too many times in one day? "He did?"

She turns around, walking me down the hall. "He's been waiting like a kid on Christmas."

"Well, I have to admit, I'm pretty thrilled to be here with him."

"You're friends from school, right?"

"Yep, we were pretty close."

She nudges me with a wink. "I've heard you're more special than the other kids back home."

I rub behind my neck, peeling off the slick curls sticking to my skin.

Savanna moves toward the elevator, hitting the down button. "I won't need to see Wyatt tonight. I just wanted to check in with him before I clocked out. To be perfectly frank, he's my favorite client."

"He is? That's not hard to believe."

Savanna folds her arms, smiling as she falls into thought. "We get so many celebrity-types in the clinic. I never met any like Wyatt. He's so reserved, polite, and super sweet. It's refreshing not to have a diva attitude to contend with."

"That's totally how I'd describe Wyatt when he was back home."

"He seems like fame couldn't have changed him too much."

I bite my lip, contemplating the statement. Unfortunately, with his memory wiped, I have no idea how much he really changed since becoming a household name.

"Everything okay?" Savanna asks, holding the elevator doors open before she steps inside.

I jump out of my thoughts. "Yeah, totally. Oh, wait, before you go. Umm, Wyatt was asking about some kind of elastic. For his hand exercise, or something."

"Oh, I thought I left one in the room for him."

I wince. "I couldn't find it."

"That's okay. I have plenty." She beckons me to follow as the elevator doors ping open. "I'll give you one to take back with you."

I step inside with her. "Thanks."

"It's really important he keeps up his exercises," Savanna tells me, hitting the number three button. "I spoke with Dr. Fincher in the hall earlier. We want to release Wyatt soon, and it's important he doesn't get slack on his stretches and other therapy."

"I know he wants to get better."

"He does," she agrees, as the elevator slows to the third floor. "But it can be really hard for people to keep up momentum. Sometimes, small progress can feel like nothing to someone in recovery. It's common for people to give up and then backslide."

We move out of the elevator. "I'll help him however I can."

Savanna smiles kindly, showing me to her office. "That's amazing. I love that he has someone in his corner. Yes, I know he has a whole team around him. But he needs someone who sees him as a person. Not just a bunch of people who consider him a brand."

A whole flood of ick surges through me, causing me to halt before we reach her door.

She pats my shoulder. "It's up to him to stay on top of his exercises. But the support of a cheerleader never goes astray."

I smile and nod.

Savanna steps inside her office, and I wait in the doorway, clutching my elbows. My eyes wander across the filing cabinets and scattered exercise equipment, including exercise balls and resistance bands.

She plucks a red elastic from a drawer and sets it around her fingers. "This is all he needs."

I step toward her. "How does he use it?"

"He just has to make sure the band sits under the first knuckle on the three middle fingers," she says, demonstrating on her right hand. "It's fine if it sits against the nail on the thumb and his pinky."

"And does he do this every day?"

She nods. "Multiple times, if possible."

"What about when his head hurts? Can he skip them then?"

"Unfortunately, headaches and trauma go hand in hand. Besides, I think it'll do his mental health a world of good to be able to play his guitar again."

My heart bounces at the prospect. "Yes. Wyatt's not Wyatt without his guitar."

"Was he like that back at school?"

"Totally," I boast. "He's always been talented."

"The more I can work with him on hand-eye coordination," she says, "the faster I can get him back to feeling like himself."

I sigh, shaking off the mess of muddled feelings. "He just seems so confused. I mean, I'm confused too. This whole situation is so complicated. He remembers his life with me, but I know so much more about his current life than he does. I wish things could get more comfortable for him."

"Neurological issues can be so tricky," Savanna says with a tight mouth. "We can't rush him."

"I know. It's just hard."

She smiles sweetly and rubs my arm. "Just focus on having a nice visit. It's all he needs right now."

I nod, moving out of her office. "Thank you. I will."

"Will you be okay?" she asks, tilting her head with concern as we move into the hallway. "Do you wanna get a coffee at the café downstairs? I have sometime to chat, if you would like."

"That's okay," I say, grateful. "I might head back upstairs and call my friend. I haven't returned any of her texts since getting here."

"No problem. Maybe I'll see you tomorrow. Wyatt will be back in the gym with me in the morning."

"Is that to help with his walking?"

"Yep. Have you noticed him struggling?"

"Mm-hmm. He called himself shaky. He seems both tired and in pain."

"He's doing super well," she says optimistically. "Compared to where he was, he's improved exponentially in a short amount of time."

Tingles of hope burst inside me. "I'm so freaking glad."

"I hope you have a wonderful evening."

I wave, backing toward the elevator. "I will. Hopefully, I'll see you tomorrow."

She waves me off, disappearing down the other end of the hallway.

I get back into the elevator, squeezing the elastic band around my fingers. As I open and close my hand on my ascent, the resistance is tougher than I expected. Wow, this really is a workout.

As I step out of the elevator and pull out my phone, I can't help remembering Savanna's words. *"A bunch of people who consider him a brand."*

I can't imagine his team not being compassionate about his welfare. Heck, there's Wyatt's assistant Devon. I've seen him tons of times on Wyatt's social media. The two seem like genuine friends. It'd hurt so much to find out Devon didn't have Wyatt's best interests at heart. Their interactions online have always melted my heart.

I shake out of the thoughts and dial Kylie's number.

"Hi," she replies breathlessly. "How's everything going?"

"Are you okay? You sound panicked."

"No, no, it's cool. I'm just catching my breath."

I lean against the wall by the elevator, hugging my middle with my free arm. "Just what are you and Parker getting up to?"

She laughs into the phone. "We went for a run. I know, me, running. But Parker needed to let his emotions out, and playing the good girlfriend, I went along."

"Is he okay? I know he's dealing with a lot of family stuff right now."

"He's doing good, considering. Anyways, we want to know how you're doing. Have you actually seen Wyatt?"

I sigh dreamily. "Yes, we've been talking for ages."

"Wow, that's incredible."

"Kylie," I whisper. "I think he tried to kiss me."

"*What?*" she exclaims. "You almost kissed?"

"Like, I dunno, there were a lot of heightened feelings. It was like a rush, you know."

"*Soooo,*" she drags out the word. "Why didn't you go for it?"

"We haven't seen each other for years." My stomach cramps. "And, umm, I don't know what the deal is with Portia."

"Has he been talking about her?"

"No, he doesn't know who she is."

Kylie sniggers. "Then why are you worried about her?"

"Ugh. Because he's had a whole life that hasn't involved me."

"Okay, okay," Kylie replies defensively. "I get it. I'm just excited for you to be back with the guy who you're constantly drooling over."

"To him, no time has passed. He thinks about us, alone in my treehouse." I bite my lip as my grin stretches. "And you know my feelings have never wavered."

"This is huge."

"It's complicated. Ugh, and so messy."

"But it's good, right?"

"Being with him is heaven. But, ugh, he's in so much pain. And he's scared about his neurological issues. He can't even play the guitar." I sigh into the phone, pouting. "It's so tough."

"*Oof.* Sounds like it."

"I'd better get back to him."

"Tell him we say hi."

"I will. I was going to send you a photo, but he kissed my cheek when I took the picture."

"That sounds so cute! I wanna see."

"His manager is way strict about information getting out about him. They made me sign an NDA."

"Intense."

"Totally. Tell Parker I said hi."

"Hi, Josie!" Parker's voice calls through the phone.

"I don't have you on speaker," Kylie says. "He's just way too close to me."

"Why are you two so adorable? Anyway, I'll text you later."

"You'd better. Hope you have a nice night in your fancy hotel suite."

"I'm sure I will."

We hang up and I make my way back to Wyatt's room, my smile only waning when the man in black gives me a once-over. I cower under his scrutiny, pointing into the doorway as a nonverbal way of asking if I can enter. He gives me a grunt, which I promptly take as a *yes*, and I move inside Wyatt's room.

I edge my way inside, finding him sitting up and craning his neck at the couch.

"Hey," I whisper.

He snaps his head in my direction, immediately wincing and squinting his eyes closed.

My jaw clenches, and I'm careful with my approach. "Are you okay?"

"Mm-hmm." He grunts, opening his eyes and rubbing the side of his head. "I moved my head too fast. It always hurts when I do that."

"Do you need me to call someone? Or to get a washcloth?"

Tight-lipped, he shakes his head, sitting back on a mound of pillows. "No, I'm good." He lets out a soft laugh. "I was worried you were gone."

I smile, sliding my hand onto his forearm. "It wasn't a dream. I'm here."

His smile grows, and his chest eases with a swell of relief. "Who knew getting stuck in a hospital could be better than a dream?"

"Maybe we could've found a better scenario to meet up than this," I joke.

He lets out another faint laugh. "I know. My bad." He nods out at the view. "Must've missed the sunset."

"Yeah, it's about seven-thirty."

"Did you get some sleep?"

I nod. "Guess I needed it."

"Did someone bring dinner?"

I check the door and then the kitchenette. "Not that I saw."

He shrugs. "Usually someone brings it around six. They always bring a vegan meal. Did you know I was vegan?"

I grin and press a hand against my chest. "Yes. I'm trying to become vegan too. I eat mostly vegetarian food."

"That's awesome. I remember as a kid always feeling grossed out about eating animals. I'm really glad the part of me I can't remember did something so cool like this."

"I think it's awesome too."

"Are you hungry?"

I pat my stomach, thinking about the protein bar and two finger sandwiches I've eaten all day. "I could eat."

Wyatt hits the nurse buzzer. "Think this is supposed to be just for em-emer-emergencies. But, heck, I don't have a food button."

"Oh," I say, lifting my hand and showing off the elastic band. "I ran into Savanna in the hall. She gave me this for you."

He sits up, taking the elastic. "Is she still here?"

"No, she said she was clocking out, but she'll see you in the gym tomorrow."

"Yeah, she's working with me so much because I just wanna get outta here."

"She might hold you back though," I say teasingly, making him pout. "Because she said you're her favorite."

He lets out a sigh. "I thought you were being for real."

"I get the impression she's gonna miss you."

"I have to come back for check ups," he replies. "Plus, she said I'll need to keep up the phys-phys-physical therapy for a few more months."

"I'm sure she wants to spend more time with you."

He mumbles a laugh, giving me a wary look. "Savanna's like ten years older than me. Why are you acting like she's putting the moves on me?"

"Because a lot of women, young and old, have crushes on you."

Wyatt winces. "I don't wanna think about that." He reaches for my hand, and I awkwardly meet his grasp. "And I don't want you worrying about me and other girls. There's only one girl's opinion I care about."

"Wyatt," my voice shakes around his name. "I... I."

"What is it?"

"I've never stopped crushing on you."

He swiftly pulls my hand to his lips, kissing it gently and sending tingles up my arm.

"I'm just scared," I whisper.

He keeps my hand near his chin. "Because you don't know what will happen when I leave here?"

I sniff and nod.

"I don't know either," he murmurs. "I don't know where I live, go to school, or if I have any friends. It scares the crap out of me."

I squeeze his hand, feeling foolish for being scared when his reality is so much more up-ended than mine.

"But... if, if I can... can have you," he stammers, lowering my hand, "I, I think it'll be okay."

My eyes grow glossy, and I nod with a small smile. "I want to stick by you."

He pushes himself off the pillows, leaning closer to me near the edge of his bed. "I can't explain why I shut you out in the past. If I can get you an-an-answers, I will."

"I'll try to stop obsessing over it," I say, shifting my weight. "I just can't help feeling like I'm not meant to be here."

"But you want to, don't you?" he asks urgently. "I sure as heck want you here."

"All I want is to be around you. Even if it's just today."

The sleep disappears from his eyes. "It won't be just for today."

"I don't want you stressing about us falling out of touch. The doctor said it wouldn't be good for you."

"But I've upset you. I want to fix it."

"You can't. You don't remember." I rest my hands on his shoulders and sigh. "Besides, you can't change the past."

"Evening, Mr. Hayes," a nurse says, walking into the room. She abruptly clears her throat, eyeing our closeness. "Oh, sorry for the intrusion."

Wyatt hums a laugh. "It's okay, Liza. We just wanted dinner."

I jut my mouth open, looking at the nurse who clearly isn't Liza. I turn back to Wyatt, who doesn't seem to register the mistake.

"Dear, Liza has finished her shift," the nurse says gently. "I'm Ronnie."

Wyatt recoils, but I hold him close. "Oh." His frown is hard lined, clearly frustrated at himself. "Sorry."

Ronnie bats a hand. "Don't worry about it. This nurses' uniform has us all melded into one blob. Sometimes, I wish I'd forgotten our names too."

I cringe. Somehow, I don't think that is the best thing to say to someone suffering from memory loss. Wyatt's posture droops under my hands, and I give him an encouraging smile.

"I'll get the dinner service to come by soon," Ronnie says, scribbling something onto a chart. "Then I'll be back to give you a new dose of medication."

"Thanks," Wyatt mutters.

Ronnie leaves the room, and Wyatt huffs, hanging his head low.

"You just woke up," I whisper, combing my hand through his soft, sandy hair. "And Liza was here all day. Honest mistake."

He lifts his head, exhaustion returning to his face. "What happens when I'm not in the clinic bubble? People won't be so quick to blame the head injury. I'll just be the dumb guy who can't remember anything."

I cup his face earnestly. "You're not dumb."

"I've always been dumb. You know that."

"*Wyatt*," I scold. "Don't talk about yourself like that."

"We only met because I repeated a grade. Only dumb people are held back."

"You're more than your learning style. You're creative and talented."

"I'm dumb and I'm broken."

"Stop it. You're not dumb. You're not broken. You're beautiful." I pause, exhaling hard. "You just need time to recover. People will understand."

"I don't remember other people seeing me like you do." A glossiness covers the red lines creeping through his eyes. "You can't leave me. I can't do this without you here."

With deep purpose, I stare into his eyes. "I'll never leave you."

Eight

The only thing that pulled me away last night was Wyatt's obvious exhaustion despite his nap. Nurse Ronnie walked me out after dinner. She told me, seeing me would've given Wyatt such a thrill that he used up more energy than usual. I can't help feeling bad that my visit wiped him out. With a crushing amount of confusion running through his head, unable to remember how much time we'd spent apart.

I got back to my hotel after the man in black called for an SUV to pick me up at the clinic. After wiping off my makeup, I replied to the several unread texts from Kylie and sent her the cutest photo of me and Wyatt on my camera roll. I then called Mom and checked whether it was too late to read to the twins. She gladly put them on the phone, obviously exhausted from dealing with them solo. After our story session, I was out as soon as my head hit the pillow.

Waking up after the best sleep of my life, breakfast was brought to me in the presidential suite. Not only was the bed like sleeping on a cloud, but I was on a high from actually being in the same room as Wyatt.

I'll never get enough of it.

After conference-calling my parents on their respective commutes, I take a shower and dress in my freshly cleaned pink outfit from yesterday. With a final check of my curls in the mirror, I leave the suite to find Erika and Randall. They wanted to meet up before I leave for the Clearview Clinic.

When I step into the hallway, I stumble backward, awkwardly retreating into my suite. Ahead, Wyatt's parents are talking with Erika and Randall. Mr. and Mrs. Hayes's arm movements are wild, and there's aggression in their stances. I gulp, holding myself up with the door handle as I take in the heated intensity.

Randall gestures at the elevator, his eyes fixed on Wyatt's parents. "Let's get a coffee and talk about this."

"Why are you pushing us out?" Mrs. Hayes wails. "He's our son. We are entitled to more than this."

Entitled? Why does that word make my muscles cramp?

"No one's pushing you out," Erika's voice cuts through.

"This is just like before," Mrs. Hayes says, her arms flailing. "You're still playing games with us."

Games? Oh geez, I really shouldn't be listening to this.

"Wyatt is pulling through," Mr. Hayes says, clutching his wife's shoulder. "Soon, he'll be well enough to voice his opinion." He cuts a look at Erika. "His *real* opinion."

As sweat builds against my hairline, I swallow the jitters warping their way through my body.

"I don't like his limitations either," Erika says. "But we brought Wyatt here because Dr. Fincher is one of the best neurologists in the country. Working with him is the best way to ensure Wyatt's memory returns."

"The doctor said there are no guarantees," Mrs. Hayes says, shivering against her husband.

"Please don't fret," Erika says. "We aren't sparing a dime."

Mr. Hayes stands tall, and his voice is gruff. "Yet that's where you people always cut off the conversation, isn't it?"

"Josie?" Randall's voice halts their conversation as everyone in the hall turns and stares at me.

I stumble against my ajar door. "Umm. I wasn't eavesdropping. I swear."

Randall turns back to Wyatt's parents and gestures toward the elevator. "Please, Mr. and Mrs. Hayes, come downstairs to the restaurant and we'll talk this out. I understand your frustrations."

With huffs of defeat, Wyatt's parents leave with Randall. Before they board the elevator, Mrs. Hayes turns back at me with red-rimmed eyes, and it crushes my heart. I can't imagine what they're going through. First, their son becomes a star, and now he's in a clinic, struggling to come to terms with the person he's become.

"Josie," Erika says, storming toward me. "Open up your room. I need to light up, and your balcony is the closest place."

I flinch as she enters my suite. "You smoke?"

She *humphs*, taking out a cigarette pack and a lighter from her purse. "You would too if you had my life."

She makes her way over to the sliding door, leading to my balcony, and I fidget my way across the room. Am I supposed to join her or give her space?

After a few desperate drags, Erika holds the cigarette behind her, leaning back into the room. "How was your visit yesterday?"

"Really good."

"And he remembered you?"

"Yeah, he didn't miss a beat."

Relief fills Erika's face. "Thank goodness. The doc was worried his past might still be patchy. This is really good news."

"I agree. Maybe I should tell his parents. They seemed really freaked out."

"Don't worry about them," Erika says, brushing it off. "Randall's placating them downstairs. All we need you to do is keep Wyatt focused on remembering your past together."

We? Who exactly is *we*?

Gosh, could skeptical dad please get out of my head?

"Do you always stand like that?" Erika comments, judgment in her stare.

"Huh?" I stand upright in a flash, not realizing how bad my hunch had become.

"You know, if you want to be seen around Wyatt, you gotta act the part." Erika puffs on her cigarette, the cloud of smoke wafting into the room. "You know how the world sees him. You should want to act like you belong in the same space as him."

I hug my middle, willing myself not to lean or fidget. "I will."

Erika flings cigarette ash onto the balcony floor, and my mouth waters in the worst way. I swallow hard, suppressing the urge to retch at the putrid stench.

A throaty laugh hums out of Erika. "You'd better."

I stiffen. "Does that mean you could send me home?"

Her cackle unsettles me further. "Why would I do that? You're the most valuable tool I have at the moment."

Tool?

What the actual heck?

"Do you remember I had a meeting yesterday with our financial manager?" Erika asks and then takes another drag like her life depends on it. "We're in a very unpleasant limbo regarding Wyatt. We were in the middle of some changes for him, and this incident has come at the absolute worst time."

"I'm sure he didn't plan on ruining things."

"All I'm saying is, we are very hopeful of your influence bringing him back to form," Erika says, a smoke haze billowing past her face. "Wyatt will be released from Clearview very soon, and we can't wait for him to be back in meetings with us."

I bite inside my cheek as icy prickles embed themselves along my spine. "You don't plan to rush him, right? He still needs recovery time."

Heck, he doesn't even know your name, Erika! He called you Erin!

There's a metallic taste in my mouth as I bite down hard to keep those thoughts from slipping off my tongue.

"There's just a few things we need quick action on. Anything you can do to keep him in a stress-free headspace as we lead up to our meetings is greatly appreciated."

I try to rid the contempt from my face. The best way to make him stress-free is keeping him well away from Erika and the rest of her team.

"I'm just here for Wyatt. I don't plan on having anything to do with your business stuff."

Erika smiles, but I can't get a read on her. "Of course, dear."

"Besides, shouldn't his parents be the ones to help him get into that headspace? I mean, he's still a minor. Can't they act on his behalf?"

Something shifts in Erika, but it quickly dissolves back to her flat facade. "We're in the same talks with Mr. and Mrs. Hayes we've always been. No need to worry about that."

"But they looked so distraught. Shouldn't they..."

Erika cuts me off. "I really don't have time to talk about Wyatt's parents. Besides, you should be getting back to Clearview."

I back away slowly. "Maybe I should just speak to them before I go?"

Erika huffs. "Look, if you really want to chat with Wyatt's parents, I'm sure they'll be back at the clinic today. Or, if they don't show up, they're staying on this floor." There's an air of annoyance in her tone. "We've had to give them the royal treatment, of course."

"He is their son," it comes out of me wounded. I mean, why wouldn't they get a fancy suite if I did? They're the most important people in his life. I've been a ghost for nearly two years.

Erika stomps out her cigarette and shuts the balcony door behind her. "Come on," she says, marching past me. "I'll take the car to the clinic with you."

"Okay," I say, trailing behind.

Why do I get the sinking feeling she wants to make sure I avoid Wyatt's parents?

Downstairs, Erika beckons me to follow her toward the revolving front door of the hotel. As we near, loud chatter bursts in from off the street. I slow my pace as a hard wave of unease crashes over me. As Erika beckons me to hurry up, the distinct clicks of cameras prick my ears.

What the actual heck is going on out there?

Erika snaps her fingers. "*Today*, Josie."

I swallow the warning signs leaping up from my cramping stomach and force my feet forward. The chatter gets faster as people with phones and DSLR cameras get a glimpse of us exiting the Gran Palacio Hotel.

"That's her," someone yells across the mass of voices. "The girl who was with Lexy Davenport yesterday. Erika, Erika! Who is this mysterious girl?"

My chest constricts as the whole crowd sucks air out of the surrounding space. My knees clang together, and I shiver as lenses zoom in on me.

Security opens the back of our idle SUV, and Erika pushes past the onlookers, entering the car first. Barely keeping upright, I make my way across the sidewalk. With locked shoulders against my earlobes, I cup my hands around my face as strangers fire questions at me. Someone flashes their camera at me, and while I blink away the spots and someone else grabs my arm.

"Hey!" the security guard barks. "Get back and keep your hands to yourselves!"

I launch myself into the car, panting my breaths as security closes the car door. I shudder, still feeling the person's handprint on the top of my arm. My stomach jitters, and bile lines the back of my throat.

"Well handled, Josie," Erika says, scrolling on her phone.

I swallow hard, wincing at her disinterested face as my trembling hands fumble into my lap.

My dad's skepticism leaches through me once again. Was that all a setup? Is Erika using me to keep Wyatt's name in the gossip columns? Did they prep all those people outside, waiting for us to leave this morning?

I swallow hard again, sucking in a breath as the bile urges to be released.

"*Eww*," Erika mutters. "Are you going to be sick?"

Did she really just *eww* me?

"No," I murmur, folding my arms. "I'll be fine."

Throughout the entire car ride, Erika taps furiously on her phone as deep-set wrinkles harden on her brow. When we enter the Clearview Clinic, she still appears deep in thought as she marches to the elevator and hits the number three button.

"Wyatt's doing physical therapy in the gym," Erika says, checking a notification on her phone. "I just want to check in before leaving for my next meeting."

When we exit the elevator, Erika rattles off a list of tasks in a voice note and sends it to Randall. Her energy spikes have my head spinning, and it's hard to keep up on our way to the gym.

I gulp, finding a man in all-black standing in front of a closed door, arms folded.

He puts his hand up like a stop sign, eyes locked on Erika. "No way."

Erika guffaws. "Excuse me? Don't you know who's paying you?"

"I'm paid to do a job," he says, broadening himself in front of the doorway. "And my job is to keep you out of this room while he's in there."

I rub my lips together, suppressing the urge to smirk at hasty Erika being stonewalled.

Erika lunges for the door handle. "It'll just take five minutes."

In one swoop, the man grasps Erika's wrist and forces her backward. "You know the rules."

Erika groans, brushing back the loose hairs falling out of her no-nonsense bun. "He's already made all the progress he needs. For goodness's sake, he'll be released soon. We don't need these silly rules anymore."

The door opens from within, and Savanna emerges. "What the heck is going on? We can hear the squabbling from inside."

"I just need two minutes of Wyatt's time," Erika rushes, ready to mow down Savanna to get inside.

Savanna frowns. "He's walking and doesn't need the distraction."

My back curves with my slouch, and I back away, humiliated at the idea of being associated with Erika.

"Oh, Josie," Savanna says, mood lifting. "We've been waiting for you. Come on in."

I point at my chest, still hunched. "Me? Are you sure?"

Savanna beams. "Of course. Get over here."

I clutch my elbows tightly as I slip past Erika's steely gaze.

"Just Josie," Savanna says curtly.

"Fine," Erika says, straightening her blazer over her sheer blouse. "I trust Josie to help Wyatt with his recovery, anyhow."

A slimy feeling slithers over my spine at her words, and I duck into the room before catching another look from Erika. Savanna closes the door behind us, and it's a relief even before I lay eyes on Wyatt.

"That woman," Savanna mutters under her breath. She then nudges me, and her tone is upbeat. "Check out our champ."

He takes my breath away. Wearing a light gray t-shirt, black sweatpants, and white sneakers, Wyatt holds himself up between two parallel bars that are about twelve-feet long. On the floor, between the bars, is a rubber mat for him to walk along.

"Wow, Wyatt, you look so strong," I say, following Savanna across the gym.

"I think I work out," he jokes, holding onto the bars. "Look at my muscles. I still remember myself as being skinny."

"Ready to get moving again, Wyatt?" Savanna asks.

He nods, stepping forward as Savanna walks on the outside of the bar.

I tilt my head, watching his biceps flex. "Does it feel weird being stronger? Does it feel like your body?"

"I spend most of my days feeling exhausted," he says in a strained tone as he steps along the rubber surface. "It's nice that I have some strength."

"Well, I've seen you work out," I say, blushing. "You've posted them online."

"I have?" Wyatt turns his body to face me, and he slips, losing his balance.

"*Wyatt*," Savanna yelps, rushing to help him.

My hands clamp over my mouth as I gasp.

Wyatt grunts, pulling himself up. "Ugh. I'm good."

I lower my trembling hands. "I'm so, so sorry," I whimper. "I didn't mean to. I'm sorry, I'm not supposed to say anything…"

"Joze," he cuts me off as Savanna gives him the all clear. "You didn't do anything. I was just surprised. I shouldn't have turned so fast."

My hands clasp over my chest. "But it was my fault."

"You di-didn't trigger me, I was just int, int…" He huffs, shaking it off, and continuing stepping forward.

"Interested?" Savanna asks, watching his steps.

"Intrigued," he puffs out, wincing as he makes his way forward.

"I shouldn't just blurt things out," I mutter, folding my arms. "I should know better. I could hurt you."

"Josie." He sighs. "You… You can't hurt me."

"Wyatt, this is amazing," Savanna says, eyes glued to his steps. "You've been distracted, and you've corrected yourself. I'm so proud of you for pushing through and keeping your eyes on the prize."

His smile twitches. "I'm out to impress."

I look at Savanna for confirmation, and her grin is undeniable. My presence hasn't completely derailed his efforts. Maybe it's okay to cut myself some slack.

Savanna's head tilts as Wyatt approaches the end of the bars. "Posture, champ. I need you to keep that back straight."

He winces, stretching himself to walk taller.

It makes me giggle, catching both their eyes.

I bat a hand, saying, "Sorry, it's just he's already putting me to shame. Erika gave me a hard time earlier for slouching. Now Wyatt, who's in recovery, has better posture than I do."

Savanna fakes putting her fingers in her ears. "Don't alert me to your posture or I'll be forced to work on you."

Wyatt lets out a soft laugh as he stops at the end of the bars. "Don't you dare fix her. It's cute when she hunches."

Savanna chuckles. "Wow. There's not many people attracted to bad posture."

Wyatt wipes his brow, holding onto one of the rails as he meets my eyes. "I love when she hugs her middle and leans to the side. Gets me every time."

I chew my thumbnail, awkwardly trying to straighten myself as I fidget in my stance.

Wyatt grins. "*See.* Cute."

Heat engulfs my face as I swing my body away. "Stop. You're embarrassing me."

"I'm sorry, it just keeps making you look even cuter," he teases.

"Okay, you need to stop," Savanna says, "or I'm gonna feel like I'm third-wheeling with teenagers. It's adorable, but slightly uncomfortable. Okay?"

Wyatt laughs, looking down at the gym floor. "Okay."

"In all seriousness," Savanna says, wheeling over a wheelchair. "You are crushing this recovery. Do you remember when just sitting was an effort?"

Wyatt sighs, looking off to the side. "Yeah, when ab-abs-absolutely ev-everything hurt."

Savanna taps the wheelchair. "Take a seat. You need a breather before we move on."

Wyatt takes a seat and looks up at Savanna, asking, "Will you stick with me when I leave?"

"Of course," she replies. "I've already discussed out-patient care with your team, and I've organized all the correct gear to be installed in your home gym."

Wyatt's shoulders shake with laughter. "A home gym. Me."

Our eyes meet, and I nod. "That's where the videos of you working out were taken."

Wyatt rubs his bicep. "I guess I should be thanking the version of me I can't remember. Because he worked out, I'm getting through this recovery a lot faster."

I glimpse the tattoo on his arm, and tingles dance along my skin.

"I'll be with Dr. Fincher today when we conduct your memory tests," Savanna says. "I don't see any reason he won't approve your release."

Uncertainty shifts his expression. "But I could fail the tests."

"It's unlikely you'll pass with one-hundred percent," Savanna says. "Heck, I have trouble with some of those questions. All you need to do is express problem-solving skills. If you do that, it shows you can continue improving outside of the clinic."

"I'm ready to leave," he says.

"If you're serious about leaving, then we should take it up a notch." Savanna motions at a ramp, which arches in a hill formation with rails on each side. "Wanna give it a go?"

He stands out of the wheelchair. "I'll walk there."

I clasp my hands in front, afraid to breathe too loudly. I don't want to distract him as he slowly makes his way over to the apparatus. Savanna keeps a hand poised behind his back, ready to help him if he stumbles.

But he doesn't. He makes it the whole way on his own.

"Wow, Wyatt," I gush. "You're amazing."

He blushes. "Thanks, cheerleader."

"What am I, chopped liver?" Savanna jokes.

He winks at her. "You're the coach."

Savanna laughs. "Okay, I can deal with that. Now, ready to go? Or, do you need a moment?"

Wyatt takes hold of the grab rails. "No, I got this."

I hold my breath as he takes the incline.

"Okay, Wyatt," Savanna says, following on the other side of the rails. "Stop at the top. Going down a slope requires you to use those abs of yours."

His body tenses as he approaches the decline. There's a flex in his jaw, his biceps pulsate, and his sweatpants pull around his thighs.

"Okay, use those muscles," Savanna coaches. "You got this. Nice and slow."

With a grunt, Wyatt makes his way down the rubber ramp.

I join Savanna in applause as he holds onto the grab rail, panting.

"Need a seat?" Savanna asks, ready to haul the wheelchair over.

Through deep breaths, he shakes his head, determined to stand.

"We'll finish with your stretches," Savanna says, "and then we'll call it for the morning. Good job, Wyatt."

"Thanks," he says, settling his breath.

She turns to me with a wink. "And great job, cheerleader."

I keep my hands firmly clasped in front as I bounce onto the balls of my feet. "It was all him."

Nine

When Wyatt finished his session in the clinic's gym, Savanna made him get back into the wheelchair for the journey back to his room. Savanna asked if I wanted to help him back to the fifth floor, and I barely let her finish the sentence before blurting, "Yes!"

Wyatt is happy taking control of the wheelchair, and I hang close to the rear handles, just in case. We make it into the elevator without a hitch. Not much could go wrong when the security guard follows our every move. When he boards the elevator with us, my throat closes in.

Thankfully, security hangs back while we travel across the fifth floor, giving us some breathing room. Relief washes through me when we're back inside Wyatt's room, out of eyesight of the looming man.

"Umm," I falter, watching Wyatt climb onto his bed. "That guy... back there."

"You mean, the security?"

"Yeah, umm..."

"Why?" Wyatt asks, giving me a smirk.

"Yeah," I say, pacing toward the bed. "What the heck?"

Wyatt shrugs. "I dunno. They just said I have a high profile, and it was a precaution."

"It just freaks me out. Like they're waiting for something bad to happen."

"Something bad already happened," he says, tapping the side of his head. "Besides, he keeps the manager out. For all I care, he can stay indefinitely."

I smile at the thought. "Yeah, he really gave Erika the business outside the gym."

"Pretty great, huh? All those people are just noise. The security asked me if there was anything I wanted, and I said for them to do their best to keep the suits out."

I exhale an easy breath. "As long as you're not unnerved, it's cool."

"I get how it's weird, though," he says, propping his hand on the small table rolled over his bed. "If you're not comfortable, I can ask him to leave."

"No, it's fine," I rush. "I totally get the point of him being outside now."

With the elastic band wrapped around his fingers, Wyatt begins flexing his hand open and closed.

"I gotta keep this up if I'm going home," he says with heightened energy. "I can't wait to grab my guitar again."

"I sure hope it comes back to you," I say, settling into the chair by his bed. "But, it might take time."

"I know," he replies. "I'm trying to remember it might not be easy, but dang, I hope it is."

There's an itch in my eyes as I watch him concentrating on stretching his fingers out wide. My insides contort with nervous anxiety. It'll be soul-crushing to see him struggling with the thing he loves. The thing that made him famous.

Wyatt closes his hand, and the elastic springs off and lands at the edge of his table. He reaches across, pinching at the elastic in an attempt to pick it up.

I edge forward. "Want me to get it?"

"Savanna says I'm supposed to do it myself."

I sit back. "Oh."

He puffs a nervous laugh. "But I suck."

"You don't suck."

He finally picks it up and uses his other hand to wrap it around his fingers. "I hope Savanna's right and this does the trick."

"It's been so long since I heard you play something that wasn't recorded."

Wyatt mumbles a laugh. "I can't believe I've recorded music. That's so crazy."

"I still have a soft spot for all the covers you used to play on that old acoustic guitar."

He pauses mid-hand flex. "Don't I have it anymore?"

"I don't know. It's probably at your house."

"In Victoria Falls?"

"No, your parents sold that house. Remember?"

"Oh." He continues flexing his fingers. "Right."

"Sorry, should I not have..."

"No, it's fine," he blurts. "I just forgot."

"Sorry, just yesterday you said you knew, and..."

He winces, cutting me off. "Everything's still a little fuzzy. I forget stuff from the present."

I move forward on the edge of my seat. "Do you have trouble remembering things from the day before?"

"Mm-hmm." He stares at his hand, flexing his fingers in and out. "The headaches don't help."

"So, is the time we spent together yesterday patchy?"

He drops his hand, turning to me with rosy cheeks. "I remember every single time we got su-super close?"

Butterflies disperse within me, fluttering around my heart. "Oh, good. It's not a blur."

"It's almost like, my brain can't erase a single second I spend with you."

I giggle, shaking off the layer of goosebumps sprouting across my shoulders.

"Speaking of back home, how are your parents?" Wyatt looks at me with a wry smile. "How on earth did Mr. Skeptical let you come here on your own?"

I giggle, clutching the space over my bouncing heart. "You remember my dad?"

"Yes. I'm surprised he hasn't been texting you with a million questions and theories."

"He does a lot of traveling for work. Kinda holds him back from letting his mind spin out."

"Probably a good thing for the whole family."

"But, everyone's good. The twins are super annoying and think they know everything. Mom's still a basket of nerves. I seriously didn't think she'd have the strength to let me get on the plane."

"How was the plane? Super swanky?"

"And then some. You sure are living the high life."

"You've had more of a taste of it than I have."

I look out at the city view, framed by the dazzling beach. "I dunno. This view is pretty to-die-for. Not many people get to experience this."

"Maybe we can actually go to the beach sometime soon."

"That would be incredible. If you're up for it."

"Hmm. Maybe I won't want to leave the penthouse."

I giggle. "It's so crazy that's where you're headed after the clinic. I'm sure your team is ready to spoil you."

"Do you think that's who will help me get home? I don't even know my address."

"I guess. Your assistant will probably have it organized."

His lip upturns. "Randall?"

I ease out a soft laugh. "No Devon. *Your* assistant."

His eyebrows lift. "I have a personal assistant?"

"Of course. Who else would video you in the gym?"

He laughs uncomfortably. "*Eww.* That feels gross."

I giggle. "No, it actually seemed cool. Like, you two seem like actual friends. At least that's the impression I got from following you guys online."

"Oh, cool." Wyatt sits up, reflectively looking toward the door. "How come he hasn't been around?"

I shrug. "I've no idea. I would've assumed he was by your side this whole time."

"I don't remember him. Unless, he was only here in the beginning when I was still out of it. I don't remember much of the first few weeks."

"Hmm. Yeah, maybe."

Wyatt taps his knee, his shoulders locking as he mulls over a thought. "Should I ask my parents to move in with me?"

"Do you want that?"

He sighs, his eyes downcast. "I don't know."

"If it helps, they seemed really beat up this morning," I say. "I guess they're struggling with your recovery in their own way."

Wyatt runs a hand back and forth over his hair. "I just don't understand how my life has changed so much."

"Do you want to talk about it?"

"Ugh. I remember, after waking up, feeling so relieved the first time I saw my parents clearly." Wyatt frowns. "They were fussing about my speech and my vision, and I was trying to tell them I was okay, but the words couldn't come out."

I push for a smile as I gently touch his arm. "It's okay. You're doing so much better now. Your stutter is hardly an issue."

"It's such a blur." Wyatt winces, pinching the bridge of his nose. "My head pounded so hard that I couldn't see straight. Whenever someone talked to me, there was an intense ringing in my ears. It was like torture."

"Oh my gosh, I'm so sorry. That sounds awful."

"I remember days being crowded by people, but it's pretty foggy."

"Understandable. Dr. Fincher said you were in an induced coma."

"Mom and Dad looked scared." He swallows hard, keeping his stare low. "After going manic on the doctors, they were talking about me working. All these people were talking about my career and none of it made sense." Wyatt scratches the side of his head, dwelling on the memory. "The last thing I could remember was the summer before high school. My parents had to explain everything about fifteen times before anything registered as real."

"So, you don't remember attending Ashworth Academy?"

He bites his lip, his eyelids growing heavy as he gives a slight shake of the head.

"That's okay. Sometimes, I'd be happy to forget that place."

"Why? Are people not nice to you?"

"No, it's cool. Just high school drama."

"I hate the idea of anyone being mean to you."

"I'm mostly bypassed. I promise."

"Good. Man, I wish I could just rewind everything to where I remember."

"I'd live those times over if I could. Any extra time with you is a blessing, even if it's a do-over."

"It'd sure beat the way my parents look at me now."

"How so?"

"They look like their lives depend on me."

I suck in a breath, feeling the weight of his words.

"They uprooted their lives for me," Wyatt says with a strained jaw. "Right?"

My lips press together as I slowly nod in response.

"So, if I don't work," he mutters, "do they not have any money?"

I shiver from the chill sweeping the room. "I don't know."

"I mean, have you seen how they dress now? Looking at them is like looking at an alternate reality."

"That was one of the first differences I noticed about them. But I've seen you dress really well over the last few years."

He rubs the back of his head. "I guess a lot has changed. I dunno. Maybe I'm just projecting all these feelings onto them because I haven't seen how my life has changed on the outside. But I can't shake a bad feeling as to why I don't live with them anymore."

"Maybe because you're on the road? Like, recording or away on sets?"

"Yeah, maybe."

Nurse Liza is back on shift, and she brings Wyatt a new dose of painkillers at the same time an orderly brings our lunches. I remember Randall saying the hotel had way better food, but between last night's dinner and this meal, the Gran Palacio has a lot of catching up to do.

We move over to the armchairs, adjacent to the comfy couch, and eat together. Not long after, Savanna enters the room.

"Ready for your memory test?" she asks. She halts, panning around the room until she lands on us. "Oh, there you are. I've gotten so used to you hanging out on the bed."

I give her a wave as Wyatt says, "Josie found a comfier spot."

"So, I can see," she says, standing between our armchairs. "I'm here to help Dr. Fincher conduct some tests with you."

I crook my head to gain eye contact. "What kind of tests is he doing?"

"He'll need to recall some information and just easy stuff like writing down some prompts."

"Easy?" Wyatt says hesitantly. "My handwriting was terrible before I lost my memory."

I cover my mouth, stifling a laugh. "I remember that."

Savanna clutches her chest, pouting. "I just love that you remember things when it comes to your time with Josie. It's so adorable."

"Adorable is one word to de-de-describe me for-forgetting the past few years," Wyatt says, fidgeting in his seat.

Savanna pats his shoulder. "It just makes me enthusiastic. I've been watching you struggle, and seeing you two together warms my heart. You were adamant that you remembered your pre-fame life. We had no way of knowing how patchy your memory was until Josie arrived."

I want to ask if his parents had filled in some of the pieces, but I decide not to bring them up.

"Hi all," Dr. Fincher says, striding into the room. "Ah, would you like to conduct the tests over here?"

"Is that okay?" Wyatt asks.

Dr. Fincher wheels over the movable tray table and sets it in front of Wyatt. "Sure thing. Wherever you're most comfortable."

I push off the armchair, asking, "Should I leave?"

"No," Wyatt blurts.

I sit down, and Savanna mumbles a laugh.

"I would've said, you can stay if it's okay with Wyatt," Dr. Fincher says, sitting on the adjacent couch, "but clearly we have his answer."

Wyatt smiles, attempting to hide the pink hue on his cheeks. "It's painful when she leaves."

I blush. "Okay, I'm staying put."

"Wyatt, I'm going to give you three words, and you'll have to recall them at the end of this session," Dr. Fincher says.

Wyatt flinches. "How long is that?"

"Ten minutes tops."

Wyatt gives a doubtful look. "That's a long time."

"All you have to do is try," Dr. Fincher replies. "Now, remember these three words. Apple, table, penny."

"Apple, table, penny?" Wyatt says, lifting his brow like he's been asked a hard math question.

Apple, table, penny. Apple, table, penny.

Dr. Fincher hands Wyatt his glasses. I smile when Wyatt makes a face before putting them on. The doctor then places a sheet of paper on the table, along with a pencil. "Can you write your full name across the paper?"

Wyatt pinches the pencil between his thumb and index finger, but it drops back down on the table. He then uses both hands to help pick it up.

"Look at you," Savanna gushes. "You're problem-solving."

Wyatt leans over the paper, concentrating hard as he slowly scrawls his name. He pauses midway through, looking up at me with framed eyes. "I don't have a middle name, do I?"

I smirk. "Nope. You're good."

He shakes his head, returning his attention to the paper. "Didn't think I did."

"It's normal to doubt yourself over facts you know to be true," Dr. Fincher comments.

"I do it all the time," Savanna jokes.

Wyatt puts the pencil down. "Done."

I giggle, looking at the wonky lettering. "Wow, it's your autograph."

He slides the paper across the table toward me. "It's all yours."

I grasp the paper and check with Dr. Fincher. "Do you need it?"

He shakes his head. "No, all I need to do is make a note of his handwriting. You can keep it."

I smile at his written name. "I say it's an improvement from middle school, so give him a big check mark."

Savanna then plucks the deck of cards from the bedside table and brings them over to the sitting area.

Oh, wait. What were those words again? *Apple, table, penny.* Okay, got it.

Savanna takes three cards from the pile and shows them to Wyatt. "Can you read these numbers?"

He nods. "Yes."

Savanna then holds the cards face down against her chest.

Dr. Fincher taps the pile on the table. "Find the same numbers in the pile."

Wyatt's brow furrows as Dr. Fincher slides the deck across the table. They are shuffled in no particular order. Wyatt pushes the cards from side to side with his index finger. He slides the three of clubs toward him on the table and then leans forward, inspecting the other cards. After more searching, he pulls the ten of diamonds.

"Umm," he mumbles, scratching the side of his head.

Oh gosh. Has he forgotten?

Apple, penny... Oh, dang it. What was the third one?

As I struggle to recall the other word, Wyatt selects the six of hearts.

Savanna places her cards down by his. The three of spades, ten of clubs, and six of clubs.

"Excellent work," she says proudly.

Wyatt rubs his fingertips together. "It was hard enough getting the corner of the card."

"But you've been working on it," Savanna says. "You've improved so much by practicing. Keep it up, and you'll overcome the numbness."

Dr. Fincher then sets a new piece of paper on Wyatt's table. I lean forward, checking out the activities displayed. In one section, Wyatt has to match identical images in a cluster. In another section, he has to connect the dots to create shapes. And another he has to fill in the blanks of three sentences.

As he slowly works through the tests with Dr. Fincher carefully watching him, my mind draws blank.

Dang it. What were those words again?

Umm. Oops. I can't even think of one.

How the heck will Wyatt remember them after all these other tests?

Wyatt's hand shakes on the connect-the-dots, and he struggles with the sentences, wincing from a headache. He pushes himself through to finish, and Dr. Fincher retrieves the paper, thanking him.

"Okay, Wyatt," Dr. Fincher says with an optimistic smile. "Can you recall those words from earlier?"

He looks down as if the words will be written in front of him.

"Apple." He pauses, and after a beat, looks back up. "Table, and penny."

Savanna applauds. "Fabulous."

"Good stuff, Wyatt," Dr. Fincher applauds.

Wyatt's chest rises and falls like he's finished a mile run.

"Oh my goodness," I murmur. "I can't believe you remember those words."

Wyatt puffs out a laugh. "No faith in me?"

I sit up, shaking my head. "No, because I'd already forgotten them."

"Joze, you don't have to..."

I cut him off with earnestness. "No, I'm serious. Following along with all these different activities, I totally spaced."

Savanna squeezes Wyatt's shoulder. "See. Told ya you were a champ."

Wyatt shrugs, taking off his glasses. "I guess I paid attention because I really, *really*, want to get out of here."

Dr. Fincher shakes Wyatt's hand. "You did exceptionally well. I see no reason why we can't release you tomorrow morning."

Wyatt's eyes light up and his mouth falls open. "I'm leaving?"

Dr. Fincher smiles, releasing Wyatt's hand. "I wish you the best of luck."

When the doctor gets up and moves by Savanna, I launch off the chair and throw my arms around Wyatt. "I knew you could do it. You're so strong."

He sighs near my ear, and his body eases against me. "I don't want to live another day without you."

Ten

I left earlier last night than the night before. Wyatt had so much paperwork to fill out for his upcoming release from the Clearview Clinic. On this occasion, his team members were granted access to file into his room so they could assist with the release forms. The more they crowded, the less I could breathe. Every single one of my heartstrings tugged when Wyatt asked me not to go. But when he saw the anxiety crippling me, he asked for someone to arrange a car to take me to the hotel. On my way out, I passed his parents entering the room. I have to believe they were there with Wyatt's best interest at heart.

I had solace in leaving last night because I planned on returning as early as possible. No one gave me a clear answer on what time Wyatt would be leaving the clinic, and I wasn't about to let him venture back into the world without me by his side. I set my alarm for 6 a.m. and called a taxi to pick me up from the hotel. No doubt Wyatt will be asleep when I arrive, but I'm over the moon at the thought of being the first person he sees when he wakes up.

After last night's phone call with my parents, I need all the positive thoughts I can get.

They want me to come home.

Both Mom and Dad were on the line, repeating that today has to be my last day in Cherry Beach. They're concerned about me missing school, being without them in a big city, and they still mistrust Wyatt's team and their plans.

"We agreed to a maximum of three days because it was such a whirlwind," Mom said, unable to contain her concern. "But these two days without you have been beyond a struggle."

It didn't matter how many times I said Wyatt needed me. Besides his parents, I'm the only person in the room he remembers, and it scares him.

"Josie, these people are using you to get Wyatt on the mend," Dad told me. "I need them to arrange your flight home before they leave you behind, stranded and alone."

It didn't matter when I told them Wyatt would never let that happen to me. My parents are terrified, and I can't blame them. The fact I was plucked from home and dropped in this situation is surreal. Once the twins ambushed the phone call, any hope of convincing my parents to give me more time went out the window.

We said good night, ready to make further arrangements today. But I'm determined to put that ticking clock out of my mind. By 6:30 a.m. I'm in the lobby of the Clearview Clinic. A receptionist tells me I'm too early for visiting hours. I give her a polite smile and keep moving toward the café area. I don't think visiting hours really mean anything when I'm here for Wyatt. I've stayed pretty late, and no one has ever prompted me to leave. The fact he has security in front of his room kinda says he has a different set of rules to other patients.

However, to look like I'm playing along, I order a hot chocolate as an early morning pick-me-up. Heck, I order two, just in case Wyatt's awake when I get upstairs. Luckily, they make dairy-free alternatives.

With the two piping hot drinks nestled in a paper tray, I make my way to the elevator and reach the top floor for the last time. I jitter with excitement at the prospect of Wyatt being released from this place. He's one more step on the journey to being whole again.

When I reach the end of the hallway, the man in all-black is sitting in a chair and checking his phone. He glances up at me, gives a slight nod, and returns his attention to his phone. Feeling mild approval, I sneak into Wyatt's room. I tip-toe in, not wanting to wake him, but notice half the lights are on, giving a lamp-like effect.

Wearing his glasses, Wyatt reclines on his bed, stretching an elastic band around the fingers of his right hand. By his bed sits the small table with a mess of playing cards scattered across the top.

"Morning," I whisper giddily.

As if snapping out of deep thought, Wyatt looks my way. "Huh?" He sits up, grinning. "Hey, Joze. Wow, you're here early."

I lift the paper tray with the two to-go cups and place them on the table with the playing cards. "I wanted to be here when you woke up. I'm surprised you're not asleep."

He tosses his glasses onto the table and then opens his arms, welcoming me into a hug I gladly snuggle into. As he rubs a circle on my back, he says, "I was uncomfortable. Like, kinda cramped, but also thinking about what getting out of here means."

I pull out of the hug and touch the side of his face with concern. "You're happy to be leaving, right?"

He clutches my hand, sliding it from his cheek, and smiles. "Of course. I just... You know... I don't know what my life is."

I nod, taking a seat near his bed. "I get that. We'll find out together."

"You haven't seen the penthouse yet?"

Goosebumps sprout along my arms at the mention of it. "No way. Isn't it crazy you're renting out the entire top floor of a hotel?"

"And you wonder why I couldn't sleep?" he half-jokes.

"It'll be okay," I say, reaching for the hot chocolates. "It'll be overwhelming, but we'll work it out."

Wyatt sniffs the air as I pass him the paper cup. "Is that a hot chocolate?"

"Yes. It's from downstairs, so hopefully it'll be okay. I made sure it was vegan."

"Well, it's passed the smell test, so good start."

We both take sips, and simultaneously purr with satisfaction.

"Oh, yep," he says with a hopelessly adorable smile. "Definitely a winner."

"Kylie works at a place back home that does pretty epic hot chocolates," I tell him. "Maybe we'll have to sneak you back to Victoria Falls to try one."

His eyes light up. "I'd be down."

I tap the sides of the cup, letting the inside cool down. "Do you know what time you're leaving today?"

"Ten or eleven," he replies, reaching to put the cup on the table. His hand shakes as he slides the cup against a pile of cards, and I'm quick to help him place the cup down. "Thanks. Anyway, I'm just gonna let the suits work it out. There was way too much talking yesterday, and I zoned out."

I frown. "I'm so sorry that I left. This room got kinda suffocating."

"I get it. I would've left too if I had the option."

"Did you feel like I abandoned you?"

"No, I just hate when you're not here."

I lift my cup. "I thought showing up early might make up for it."

He grins. "It sure does."

I motion at the playing cards. "Did you decide to practice while you couldn't sleep?"

"Yeah. I feel a little more confident after doing those tests with Dr. Fincher yesterday."

"That's awesome."

"Yeah. I, I had to remind myself, I can just take my time and ev-eventually I can remember what number comes next."

"The brain fog must be so frustrating."

"Yeah, but wanting not to look dumb in front of you has me working harder."

"*Wyatt.* You're not dumb."

"Before you came, I'd wallow in not, ah, not knowing the numbers." He flexes his fingers. "Then there's the whole problem of picking up the cards."

"You found cards yesterday when Savanna and Dr. Fincher put you to the test. I'm sure it won't even be a problem soon."

Wyatt pushes his feet off the side of the bed, letting them dangle as he sits on the edge in front of me. "What if I pick up my guitar and I can't play it? What if I don't remember how?"

I sit forward. "Can you picture it in your head?"

He winces. "Not fully."

"Maybe muscle memory will set in? You played it before you got famous."

"So, it might come back, just like how my memories of you did?"

My heart swells. "Yeah, maybe."

He blows out a breath, appearing lighter in thought. "That makes me feel better."

Grinning, I rub the space on my chest over my thumping heart.

He tilts his head, smiling at me. "Geez, Josie, can you just stay with me forever?"

I lift off the chair, placing my cup on the cabinet by his bed, and toss my arms around him in a hug. "If I could, I would."

His arms pull around my middle. "Really."

"I love you, Wyatt."

His shoulders lock in my arms. "You love me?"

My stomach cramps with dread. *Crap.* It just slipped out.

The tension in his arms changes as he holds me, making me cringe.

Oh my gosh, this is so awkward. I shouldn't have said it. I didn't mean to say it.

But... it's true.

It's always been true.

As he holds me, I swallow hard and whisper. "It just slipped out. I didn't mean..."

I bite down hard as silence deafens the room.

His hands press against my lower back and he sighs into my curls. "You didn't mean it?"

I cringe at the thought of him thinking I don't love him.

Because I do.

I love Wyatt Hayes with every fiber of my being.

His breath patters against the nape of my neck as his head rests on my shoulder. I hug him tighter, easing into the comfort of our closeness.

"No, I meant it," I whisper. "I just... Didn't mean to say it."

My stomach eases, knowing I'll never regret saying those words to him.

His hands run against my waist as he pulls his head up. "You do love me?"

I swallow the tension and nod.

His voice is low as he says, "You know, I..."

"It's okay," I blurt. "I didn't say it so you would."

"It's not that..."

"I just want you to know I'm here for you." I clutch his hand, holding it close to my heart. "Forever. Always."

He blinks. "I... I, just..."

I lower his hand and gently shush him. "Don't stress," I whisper with a smile. "You don't need to stutter your feelings. I know you want me here. Believe me, it's more than enough for me."

"But... But I..."

I shake my head, lowering to kiss his hand. "It's okay."

He sighs in defeat. "I'm sorry."

I giggle and kiss his cheek. "Why would you apologize to me? You're letting me into your presence. I am more than fulfilled."

His hands brush through my curls. "Why are yuh-yuh-you cool with me acting pah-pah-pathetic?"

My nose bumps against his. "Pathetic is never a word I'd use to describe you."

His eyes close, obviously still warring within his head. I pull away, making him grab for me as I reach for his hot chocolate.

"Why don't you take another sip?" I say, giving him the cup. "It's impossible to be in a low mood when drinking hot chocolate."

He takes the cup but doesn't sip. "I'm not in a low mood. How could I be when I'm looking into your big beautiful eyes?"

I shiver and clutch my elbows. "Aww."

He smirks and rubs my arm with his free hand. "Cold?"

I blush. "Not exactly."

He keeps a hold of my arm and tilts his head. "Can I kiss you?"

I swallow hard as my stomach leaps toward my throat. "Umm, yes!"

He mumbles a laugh, tugging me close, and I ungracefully smack my lips against his mouth, feeling it ricochet against my teeth.

"*Ugh,*" it moans out of me.

Wyatt laughs, jiggling against the bed with a huge grin. He almost drops his paper cup, hugging his arm across his middle as he full-on belly laughs.

I take his cup and set it on the cabinet by the bed. "Geez. I'm glad I amused you."

He wipes his mouth with the back of his hand, struggling to stymie his laughter. "Sorry, Josie."

"Seriously, it wasn't that funny," I say, half-joking.

He reaches for my hand and gives it a gentle squeeze. "It totally cut through the awkward tension, and..." He starts laughing again. "Sorry, I..." Still laughing. "I..." Actually throws his head back, laughing. "That was... That was just so hilarious."

"Hey, quit it," I whine, hitting his arm. "I don't need you laughing at me when I try to kiss you."

His laughter softens to a mumble as he rubs his lips together. There's still a shine in his eyes, practically crying from laughter.

"Oh, brother," I mutter, rolling my eyes.

He grins, tugging me close again. "Do over?"

"No," I tease. "You don't deserve it."

"Oh, come on. You don't mean that."

"Nope. That's it."

His laughter simmers as he intertwines his fingers with mine. "You really gonna hold out on me?"

I sigh, leaning to one side as I let him tug on my hand. Unable to contain my giddy smile, I close in—this time without the frantic urgency—and let his mouth meet mine first.

Our kiss is gentle and sweet. His bottom lip slips against mine, and then he kisses me again with the right amount of pressure to make me moan. Oh goodness, this boy can make my whole body quake. His head tilts as he smiles in the kiss, and my fingers walk along his shoulders until my arms hook behind his neck.

His lips gradually pull away from mine with a breathy sigh. "Man. How could I ever be stupid enough to let you go?"

"I don't care about that," I whisper. "I just need this moment."

He kisses me again, pulling me close so my hips push against the insides of his knees. His hands stroke the length of my back, and then his lips move to my jawline.

"You should hop up on the bed," he mumbles between butterfly kisses.

"Maybe I should," I whisper, catching my breath. "My knees will give out soon."

Whoa.

Wyatt.

Hayes.

Kissed.

Me.

He mumbles a laugh, pulling back so I can move beside him. I grab our hot chocolates and sit them on the small movable table next to the playing cards. I sit up on the bed next to Wyatt, wheeling the table in front of us.

Wyatt waves off the table. "I don't need to sah-sah-see all that meh-meh-mess right now."

I shrug, lifting his glasses and offering them to him. "We have a while until you leave. Maybe we could mess around with them for a bit."

He waves them off. "I don't want to."

I set the glasses down and then collect the cards and give them a light shuffle. "You should practice. If you can pick these up, it'll make it easy to pluck the strings of your guitar."

He sits back, uninterested. "I don't need the pressure."

"It's not pressure," I insist. "You were practicing when I walked in, anyways."

He frowns. "I'd given up on the cards."

"Fine," I say, placing the pile on the table. "I'll play by myself."

He smirks. "What? Reverse psy, psy..."

I nudge him playfully with a goofy grin. "Yes, that."

Wyatt shrugs, reaching his index finger out and slipping the first card off the top of the pile. The card falls face down on the table, and Wyatt drops his hand.

I eye him. "Is that it?"

He shrugs again. "I touched it."

"What about your glasses?"

His nose scrunches up as his lip upturns. "I don't like them. They pinch my nose."

My eyebrows arch. "You're in one of the fanciest hospitals in the country with the top physicians. I'm sure they can provide you with the comfiest glasses imaginable."

He shifts away. "I just don't like them. Happy?"

A nervous laugh splutters out of me. "Happy that you're being such a baby about a pair of glasses? Not really. They seriously look cute on you."

He reaches forward and slides them back onto the table. "Don't get used to them."

"Okay, whatever. I'll let the lack of effort with the cards slide, considering it's so early in the morning."

Wyatt hooks a finger under my chin, turning me to face him and instantly meeting me with a kiss. I'm quick to lean in, pretty sure I'll never get enough of him.

He sends me a wink. "Can't we just keep doing this instead?"

I glance at the cards. "You wanna abandon your hands and do everything with your mouth instead?"

He bites his lip, zeroing in on my mouth. "Right now, yes."

I slide a hand along the side of his gorgeous face, unable to stop the swooning within. "I can't let you give up on these exercises. You're too talented."

"It might be all gone."

I shake my head and tap the space on his chest over his heart. "It won't be. I know it's still in you."

He relents with a small smile and reaches for another card. "I'll try. Only for you."

"You're doing it for yourself."

"Th-that didn't work," he says, moving another card. "I quit when I was by myself. But I sure as heck don't want to see you upset." He looks at me with a gleam of determination in his eyes. "You're my motivation, Joze."

I take him in, shakily moving cards around the table. He's slow and deliberate, and I find myself holding my breath. I don't want to move an inch, crack his concentration, and have him throw in the towel. His music means too much to him. It means too much to me. And it means too much to the world.

Eleven

Dr. Fincher had a final check in with Wyatt, plus Erika and Lexy have been in and out with their respective assistants. With all the chatter, Wyatt was glazing over as he rubbed the ache from his temples.

When he held my hand, he told me this morning's headaches were worth it.

It was all leading to him getting out of this place.

"Morning," Savanna says, pushing a wheelchair into the room.

Wyatt frowns. "What the heck is that thing doing in here?"

Savanna taps the brakes. "It's time for you to leave us."

"In that?" Wyatt winces. "Nuh-uh. No way."

"Please indulge me," Savanna says, patting the wheelchair. "Just to get you downstairs and into the parking garage. Once you're at the hotel, you can use either the frame or the cane."

Wyatt blows out a breath as his eyes roll upward. "Sounds *way* better."

Savanna chuckles under her breath. "I know. They have some geriatric connotations, but you're still in a stage of your recovery where you need the apparatuses. I don't want you overdoing anything and hurting yourself."

"I know. I won't."

Savanna gives me a knowing look. "Can I trust you to keep an eye on him?"

I nod. "I won't take my eyes off him."

Savanna grins. "Excellent."

"Wyatt." Erika strides into the room with Randall on her tail. "The cars are waiting downstairs. Are you ready to go?"

Wyatt slides off the bed, gingerly stepping across to the wheelchair in his white sneakers. "Let's do this."

"Easy, champ," Savanna says, watching his movements. "You got this."

He sits in the wheelchair, giving Savanna a questioning stare. "I really think I can walk out of here."

"Not happening," Savanna says, tapping the brakes. "If anything, I'd like you to stay in the chair until you get into your suite."

Wyatt clicks his tongue. "Ugh. You're changing the rules."

"Is that the best thing for him to do?" Erika asks Savanna. "We'll make sure he stays in the wheelchair if it helps him improve quicker."

"It just saves any mishaps," Savanna replies. "You never know when there's a spill on those tiled floors, or something else that could trip him up."

Erika gestures at Randall. "Got that. Wyatt's in the wheelchair until he's in the penthouse." She glances sideways at Savanna. "And what about when he's in the suite?"

"He should be fine," Savanna says optimistically. "He's been getting around this room without a walking aide."

"Uh, I don't..." Wyatt stops himself, slumping in the wheelchair with a sigh. "Never mind. Let's get outta here."

I step toward him, to ask if he's okay, but Erika gets between us.

"Randall." She snaps her fingers. "Help Wyatt to the elevator."

Wyatt lifts a hand, leaning away as Randall moves in. "I got it."

Randall gets behind the wheelchair and turns it toward the doorway. "It's no problem, Mr. Hayes. We're eager to get you out of here and back to your normal life."

Wyatt stretches out an arm. "Josie?"

I rush to his side. "I'm here."

Wyatt waves off Randall. "I have her."

Randall glances at Erika and shrugs, stepping away from the wheelchair.

Wyatt smiles up at me. "Having you by my side is the only thing that feels normal."

Sparks burst inside my chest. "Let's get you outta here."

Erika and Randall march ahead of us, and along with security, we move into the hallway.

Wyatt looks around the hospital floor. "Where are my parents? I haven't seen them all morning."

"We thought it was best that they wait for you at the hotel," Erika says, tapping the elevator button. "You didn't need any unnecessary distractions this morning."

As I stand behind the wheelchair, I watch Wyatt flinch as much as I do.

Unnecessary? Distraction?

They're his parents.

Shaking it off, we move into the elevator, exiting onto one of the garage basement levels. In front of us, three shiny, black SUVs lie in wait. As we move toward the vehicles, Lexy comes into view, along with her assistant, Thea, who I met earlier this morning.

"Okay, Wyatt," Erika says, moving toward Lexy, who yammers on her phone. "You'll ride with me and Lexy, and we'll prep you on..."

Wyatt winces. "Nuh-uh."

Erika deadpans him. "Excuse me?"

"I'm not sitting in a car with you two."

Erika blinks at him and Randall fidgets uncomfortably, waiting for Erika to explode.

Lexy lowers her phone, flicking her eyes between everyone. "What's happening?"

"Wyatt," Erika huffs, planting her hands on her hips. "We need to get you to the hotel safely."

Wyatt motions at the security team waiting in front of the SUVs. "I feel safe with them." He swallows hard and then glances at me. "And with Josie."

"Randall will ride with Jose," Erika says when Lexy goes back to her phone conversation.

"There's no way," Wyatt says defiantly. "I'm only getting in a car if it's me and Josie."

Erika huffs. "Wyatt, we…"

"I'm not going with you," Wyatt blurts with only the slightest of stutters.

Erika frowns, glances at Randall, and then throws her palms up. "Fine, it's your call. But I really think you should at least have Lexy by your side to prepare you for life outside the clinic."

"I-I'm going to a fan-fancy hotel," Wyatt says, pulling himself out of the wheelchair. "I think I'll be fine."

As he stands, Erika and Randall rush toward him, and Lexy snaps her fingers at her assistant to react. All just making Wyatt recoil.

"I don't need your help," he stammers. "I've got Josie."

I catch dagger-filled stares in my direction before they quickly dissolve. But as if I care about their jealousy. I'm the one getting the ultimate prize of being in Wyatt's company.

Wyatt motions for me to follow him when the security team shows him into the middle SUV. As he slowly slides into the backseat, I spy Erika and Randall taking the front car. Lexy and Thea move into the rear car.

When I get in the SUV with Wyatt, a security member gets into the front seat. "Ready to go, Mr. Hayes?"

"I, I guess."

I grin at him. "Now's the part where you get to be excited."

He smiles back. "I'm so glad we're away from everyone else. Once we're in the hotel, I'm giving them all the boot."

I sink in my seat. "But they're still paying for everything, right?"

He shrugs. "I dunno. Is it my money or theirs?"

I shake my head. "I really don't know. But I think they'll want to talk to you about money. Erika was saying something about her and the finance guy needing you to make some decisions."

"My first decision would be to get rid of them all. They've been getting in my head since I woke up in that clinic."

Our car pulls out of the parking garage, one black SUV in front and another behind us. The mid-morning sun breaks through the tinted windows, and I'm about to smile until we exit the garage to a swarm. Either side of the car, people with signs, phones, and cameras, crowd the three emerging vehicles.

"What the..." it tumbles out of Wyatt as his name is called between the camera flashes.

His hand grounds on the seat between us, and I'm quick to plant mine over it.

He turns from the tinted window and meets my eyes. He sucks in a breath and his chest squeezes as he exhales.

"It'll be okay," I whisper.

He takes another inhale and nods.

The SUVs pull onto the road, and car horns honk behind us. Through the rear window, we see Wyatt Hayes fans flood into the street with no regard for oncoming traffic.

"Holy crap," Wyatt murmurs, blinking at the chaos.

My hand plasters over my mouth. We were so close to seeing a full-blown calamity. Thank goodness there was security already on the scene, holding back the crowd. They manage to corral people back onto the sidewalk as our convoy of vehicles drive away.

Wyatt blinks at me. "They... They were... there to see me?"

I nod slowly. "You have fans, Wyatt."

He shifts in his seat, having trouble settling his gaze somewhere in the car.

I clutch his hand, and whisper, "It'll be okay. You'll readjust. It'll just take some time."

His mouth opens and shuts a few times before he's finally able to mutter, "How do they all know me? This is insane."

"I know it must be scary, but I'll help you get through this."

The corners of his mouth curl upwards. "I kn-know people have be-been saying I'm fa-fa-famous," he stutters as his grin spreads. "But I... I guess I never really believed it before seeing all those people."

"You're smiling," I say blankly. "Are you okay with this?"

He turns to me with bewildered excitement. "I, I mean... Who wouldn't get chills, finding out they're famous?"

My stomach flips, hoping he truly is adjusting to the idea of his celebrity life. "Well, I'm glad you're not flipping out."

He puffs out a laugh, hanging a thumb over his shoulder. "I still don't get why they'd all be into me. Es-es-especially don't get why they'd camp out in front of the clinic."

I mumble a giggle. "They might think they're superfans, but I think I've officially risen to the top. They'd all kill to be in this car with you."

Wyatt smiles, combing his fingers through his soft, sandy hair. "Never gonna happen. The space beside me only belongs to you, Joze."

My heart throbs as tingles send me into a toe-curling shiver.

Wyatt lifts my hand and kisses it softly. "I can handle my new life because I'll have you with me."

I nod with glee until realization twists and cramps my stomach.

My parents want me to come home. I won't be able to stay with him.

I just have no idea how to tell him we have an expiration date.

I give him a warm smile, suppressing the thought. I'm here right now, and that's all that matters. Even if we're not in the same room, the same town, or the same state, I'll still help him through this. No matter our separation, we can still be in contact. It won't be like last time. This time he won't wipe me from his memory.

"Hey, maybe Devon will be at the penthouse," I say with hope.

He tilts his head, recalling the name. "That's my, my assistant. Right?"

"Mm-hmm." I nod excitedly. "I can't wait to meet him."

Wyatt grins. "If he's as great as you say, then me too."

The convoy of SUVs pull into the rear parking garage of the Gran Palacio Hotel. Driving down the ramps into the basement subfloors of the hotel, the anticipation jitters through Wyatt.

I rub his hoodie covered arm. "You'll love it here."

"I'm nervous. Don't I have to act a certain way to belong here?"

I nudge him, giddy. "You already belong."

His eyes grow starry and the car slows near a series of elevators.

"Your stop, Mr. Hayes," the driver says, exiting the car.

He moves to Wyatt's door, opening it for him. By the time Wyatt carefully slips out of the car, Erika and Randall rush to his side, wheelchair ready.

"Seriously?" Wyatt grumbles.

"Your physical therapist said so," Erika says matter-of-factly.

I move around the car, and Randall moves out of the way so I can get closer to Wyatt. Lexy and Thea move into the elevator first, then Wyatt and I, followed by Erika, Randall, and security. It's a tight fight, which sends my anxiety sky high.

Seeming to sense my distress, Wyatt reaches up and caresses my hand. I melt from his touch, and soon, the elevator pings open to the top floor.

"He doesn't have to check-in?" I ask.

"Already taken care of," Randall replies.

We move out of the elevator and directly into the penthouse. Randall tells us, only those with the penthouse passkey can enter this floor. Wyatt gives me an uncertain look, which I immediately understand. Any of these people could barge into his suite any time they want.

I wonder if the security team will protect Wyatt's sanity at the hotel as much as they did at the clinic.

"*Soooo*," Wyatt drags out the word, rolling his wheelchair further into the suite. "This is all mine?"

To use the word opulent would be an understatement. With its elevated position and panoramic windows, this would be one of the most coveted spaces in all of Cherry Beach. The fact we're the only people on this floor screams privacy, which I hope puts Wyatt at ease after seeing that mob with their camera flashes.

We wander through the expansive layout, perfect for Wyatt to maneuver through with the wheelchair. He pulls himself up to standing near a sectional couch, using the back to hold on to.

"Wyatt?" Randall pipes up, edging close with a hospital grade walking cane.

Wyatt waves it off, still taking in the suite. Not only is the suite endless, the high ceilings accentuate the spaciousness with airy ambiance. Erika boasts about the multiple bedrooms, bathrooms, and living areas as she strides around the epic space.

"But you said my parents aren't here?" Wyatt questions. "Why do I have so many bedrooms if it's just me?"

Erika grins. "Because you're a star, Wyatt."

At that, Wyatt plonks down on the wheelchair, the overwhelm clear on his face.

"You haven't even seen the best part yet," Lexy says, striding over to a set of sliding doors.

In my suite, the sliding doors lead onto a balcony. Here, they showcase an impressive rooftop terrace, highlighting an infinity pool.

"Whoa." I gasp. "This place sure kicks butt compared to my room."

"Good morning, Mr. Hayes," say an older gentleman, in a suit that includes a bow-tie and jacket with tails, entering the living space. "My name is Hubert, and I'm the butler for the Gran Palacio Hotel penthouse suite. Anything you need, do not hesitate to ask me to provide it."

Wyatt's eyebrows lift, head moments from spinning. "Ah, hi... Thanks, I guess."

Hubert nods. "May I get you anything? Coffee, juice, a brunch platter?"

Wyatt shakes his head, having trouble taking it all in. "Nah, ah, nope. I'm good." Wyatt looks between Erika and Lexy. "Where are my parents?"

Lexy swats a hand. "They'll be around soon, hon. Don't sweat it."

I move close to Wyatt and scoop his hand. "This couch looks comfy. You wanna just chill for a bit?"

He looks up at me with thankful eyes. "Yeah, yes. Sounds awesome."

I help him out of the wheelchair, and we take it nice and easy, rounding the couch and carefully sitting with good posture. It's killing me not to snuggle up to him, but I need to be a good influence and keep my back straight. We're only just out of the hospital, after all.

Every time Erika and Lexy approach with some nonsense they read from their phones, Wyatt frowns, rubs his forehead, and grumbles at them to back up. Finally, they give us breathing room. In comfortable silence, we can gaze out at the rooftop terrace and take in the striking city view.

I'm almost dozy when Randall sheepishly sidles up, phone poised and ready.

"So, Josie," Randall starts and then clears his throat. "I've been in touch with your parents. We can either have you on a commercial flight tomorrow, or if we want to charter you a flight home, we need to..."

"What?" Wyatt blurts, grabbing onto my arm.

My mouth falls open, and apologies fill my eyes as I watch his shattered expression.

Wyatt's jaw tenses as the words strain out of him. "You can't leave."

I swallow the sickness spiraling inside me. "I know, but..."

"No," it comes out desperate as his arms pull around me. "No, Josie."

"My parents..."

"Bring them here," he's quick to reply. "The twins too, I don't care. Look how huge this place is. The whole family can take it. I'd move to a smaller room. Just don't leave me."

My eyes well. "Oh, Wyatt."

"Or, I'll leave with you." His grip on me tightens. "I don't care where I live, as long as it's in the same place as you."

"Umm," Randall pipes up. "Wyatt, you can't go to Victoria Falls. We need you well rested before we leave for Ferndale in a few days."

"Ugh, whatever," he groans. "Just don't separate us. Josie, please."

A tear drops onto my cheek and rolls down to sit along my jaw. "I don't want to go."

He leans in, urgent. "Then don't."

"But…"

His eyes widen. "But we can stay together."

My heart has taken a beating, only giving me energy to plop my head against his shoulder. As his stress-fueled breaths cause his chest to rise and fall, my limp body thumps against him. I creep my arms around him, embracing him because getting words out is near impossible.

"Ah, Josie," Randall says awkwardly .

Wyatt's arm tightens around me as he grizzles, "Go away."

Randall's footsteps hurry away, and Wyatt's body eases as much as mine.

Wyatt's hand smooths over my curls, and a choked moan slips out of him.

I scrunch myself against him, burying my face in the nape of his neck. "I'm sorry."

He kisses my forehead, stroking my hair. "Don't be. I g-get where your parents are coming from. But, there h-has to be another option. I-I'm not losing you."

I kiss his cheek, squeezing my arms by his sides. "I don't want to go, but they're scared."

"They can come here."

"They have to work."

"I'll make Erika give them money to cover their wages."

"I don't think it's that simple."

"None of this is simple. I'm in a fr-freaking penthouse and can't remember how I can afford it."

I wipe the wet from my face and sit up to look him in the eyes. "My parents won't listen to me. I already tried."

Wyatt hangs a thumb over the back of the couch. "We'll get Erika to call them. Why don't we use her motormouth for some good? Heck, she convinced your parents to let you come here, didn't she?"

I chew my lip. "I guess."

"You don't want me to ask her?"

"I'm just..."

His fingers plant under my chin. "What?"

"Well, Dad said, they might just be using me. That you might all leave, and I'll be stranded here. What if Erika..."

"Joze." He sits up, determination in his eyes. "I would never let that happen. You'll be protected. I promise."

"I know you wouldn't, but..."

Wyatt nods. "You don't trust them."

I nod, sniffing hard.

"Me either," he mutters. "But we'll use them to keep us together. We'll figure out how to shake them after we make sure we're not split up."

I exhale slowly, caressing the sides of his face. "Okay."

He grins brightly. "Okay?"

I nod. "Ask Erika to keep me here."

Hurriedly, Wyatt leans in and kisses me. As if he's giving me life, my lips suction to his. Only when I become very aware of other people in the room, do I break away.

Wyatt turns and looks over the back of the couch. "Erika, I need a favor."

Erika stands at attention, exhilarated by the thought of managing something for Wyatt.

Wyatt gestures at me. "I need Josie to stay. No excuses. You need to make her parents understand."

Erika's enthusiasm wanes. "I don't know if that's such a good idea. You know, Josie has a life to get back to."

"I'll never go back to work if Josie doesn't stay," Wyatt says bluntly.

Erika and Lexy share apprehensive glances, and then Erika nods, lifting her phone. "I'll make a call."

Wyatt slides back down onto the couch, but his eyes stay peeled on his management group.

"I might only be able to stay a few more days," I whisper.

"We'll g-get your schoolwork emailed," Wyatt says flippantly. "You'll go to school wherever I go." Wyatt catches Randall staring, and asks him, "Where do I go to school?"

"You don't. You have a tutor," Randall replies.

Wyatt turns to me with a smile. "See. We can share a tutor."

I giggle at his optimism. "I don't think it's that simple."

"I know, but we can work something out. Your family just needs to give us more time."

I nod. "Maybe they'll let me stay a week?"

Wyatt pecks my cheek. "Maybe a month."

"Let me just work out some logistics," Erika says, tapping on her phone, "Then I'll call Mr. and Mrs. Bartlett."

"Whatever," Wyatt mutters. He pans around the room, and out of the corner of his mouth, asks, "Do you think there'll always be this many people in this room?"

"I'm sure they're just here until you settle in." Can he tell my fingers are crossed?

Lexy notices Wyatt staring, and she smiles brightly. "Anything I can do for you, superstar?"

"There's a lot of people here," Wyatt remarks. "Where's Devon?"

Lexy, Erika, and their respective assistants all freeze. Gradually, they exchange puzzled yet alarmed looks.

Wyatt shifts uncomfortably. "Dang. Did I mess up a name again?"

"Wyatt," Erika says in a low tone. "Why do you know that name?"

Wyatt looks at me and then back at Erika. "He's my assistant. Isn't he?"

"Wyatt," Lexy says, trepidation dripping off each syllable. "Umm, we... He..."

Randall's face pales. "Do you remember Devon?"

"No," Wyatt replies. "Josie told me about him."

Every eye zeroes in on me, burning me with a blazing heat.

"What?" Wyatt drags out the word. "What is it?"

Erika sucks in a breath, edging her way closer to him. "Wyatt, honey, we had to let Devon go."

Wyatt shifts beside me. "Umm, okay?"

Lexy steps in. "He was with you when you had your accident. He's the reason you were in the hospital."

My hand rushes to my mouth as a gasp whooshes out.

"He..." Wyatt closes his eyes, shaking his head. "He hurt me?"

"We didn't want to bring it up and trigger you," Erika says. "We were hoping to keep him from you while you were recovering."

I can't help noticing the dig when Erika's eyes flash in my direction. I lower my hand and utter, "I had no idea."

"Why would you?" Lexy replies. "We were keeping it on the down-low."

I clasp Wyatt's hand. "I'm sorry. I didn't mean..."

"Don't be, be sorry. I don't re-remember him."

"Nothing has come back?" Erika asks, scrutinizing Wyatt's reaction.

He shakes his head, lifting his palm. "No. I don't remember anything from the accident."

Erika and Lexy release exhales, filling the space with shared relief.

Oh my gosh, what the heck happened? It's so bad they don't want Wyatt to know anything about it? Do they even know the full extent? Or, was it only Wyatt and Devon on the scene when the accident happened?

I squeeze Wyatt's hand, giving him another apologetic look.

Wyatt shrugs. "I guess I don't have a cool guy in my corner."

I frown. "I'm sorry. I never should've brought him up."

"You didn't know. You were excited. Can't blame you for that."

My insides slush with a gross, gooey feeling. Online, it always looked like Wyatt and Devon were friends. Best friends, even. But he did something to hurt him. Is he in jail? *Let go.* Does that mean fired? How responsible was he? Shouldn't he be held more accountable?

Wyatt notices the questions scrambling my expression, and he gains the attention of everyone in the room. "Hey, can you all leave? Josie and I need some time alone."

"Ah, Wyatt, we needed to discuss..."

He cuts Erika off. "Now."

"Don't stress him out," Lexy says to Erika. "Okay, Wyatt. We're off."

Erika relents, and the four of them leave the penthouse via the private elevator.

Wyatt's hands slip along my jaw until his hands cup around my ears. "Don't get upset. I can't miss someone I never knew."

I struggle against my frown. "He just didn't look like someone who would hurt you."

"But isn't everything altered online? Maybe, before the accident, I did know the real him and we got into it?"

I nod in his hands. "Yeah, maybe."

His fingers tremble against his face, and when they lower, I capture them in mine.

"All we have to do is focus on you getting better," I say.

"I'm already better since the day you arrived."

He leans in to kiss me, but my teeth chatter as fear takes over. I slide his hands away from my face, and his chin drops.

"Joze?"

"Wyatt, I..." I falter, teeth chattering harder.

He squeezes my hands. "Josie. What is it? You look, terr, terrified."

My eyes water with no hope of drying up. "I... I..."

He pulls me closer, running his arms around my waist and pressing his hands into my back. "You're shaking. What is it?"

"I don't... You can't..."

"Hey, hey," he coos. "Take a minute. Don't get upset."

"But I..."

He shakes his head. "Take the minute."

I swallow the lump in my throat and squeeze my eyes shut. Tears leak out, and I hold my breath, waiting for my heart to stop hammering against my ribs.

"Wyatt," I whisper, keeping my eyes closed. "I'm scared because..." I swallow another lump and open my eyes to a blurry version of him. "You're relying on me to get better. But I can't stay with you forever."

"You can because we can work it out."

I shut my eyes again as the tears overwhelm my sight. "No, you don't understand. You're a big star and have all these commitments. My life is back home in Victoria Falls."

He pulls me so tight our chests collide. "I'll quit. I'll move back home."

"Wyatt, you can't."

"I can. I don't care about it. I just care about you."

I open my eyes, blinking through the blur.

His lips meet mine before I can utter a word. The gentleness of his touch spread tingles across my lips. When he pulls away, his words vibrate against my lips. "All I care about is being with you. You don't need to be scared. I'll make this work."

"I don't think it's that easy."

"I already got everyone out of the room. Obviously, I have some kind of pull. I'll find a way. I promise. I'm not letting us get separated again."

His chest puffs with his words, and I pull my hand around the back of his neck and rest my face by his. When I sigh, his hand presses between my shoulder blades, guiding me to flop against him. All cried out of energy, I go limp against him as he rubs a circle on my back.

"Life would suck without you," he whispers. "I think a head injury is the best thing that's ever happened to me."

Exhausted, I puff a laugh. "Don't say that."

"It brought you back to me. I can't be ungrateful for that."

"I'd never see you again if it guaranteed you never getting hurt again."

"Not an option, Joze."

Twelve

It didn't take much convincing to let Wyatt make-out with me on the sectional couch. Heck, we're alone in a fancy penthouse suite, and he's the most drop-dead-gorgeous seventeen-year-old on the planet. I'm his whenever he wants me.

Ah, it's the *whenever* that's the problem. Erika's probably talking about me to my parents like a sleazy salesperson. I can just imagine the scenarios going through my dad's head. There's no fathomable way that my parents will let me stay here for a few more days. Maybe they'll fly over here? But they're always so panicked about work. I couldn't ask them to do that. I try to lessen the stress in our household, not bring it in.

Oh my gosh, what about the twins? How is Mom handling them on her own? Dad gets home so late these days, and Mom was already a bucket of nerves.

As I lie in his arms, Wyatt pulls away and views my face. "You stopped kissing me back. Where'd you go?"

I sigh, rubbing my forehead. "Sorry. Thinking about home."

He mumbles a laugh. "Killed the mood."

I smile up at him. "I must be crazy to let thoughts come in when I get to kiss you."

Wyatt lowers, connecting our lips with toe-curling pressure. I slide my hand along his jaw until it combs through his sandy hair. I kiss him back, begging myself to be with him. But with every caress, my siblings barge their way into my brain.

I rip my mouth away from his. "Ugh."

He pulls back. "Ugh?"

I exhale hard. "Not you." I rub my hands over my face. "I need a minute."

Wyatt sits up and pats my thigh. "Don't worry about it. Let's cool it."

I lower my hands and sit up. "I'm sorry, I didn't mean..."

"It's okay. You're not into it."

"I'm into you," I rush, clutching his shoulder. "Just... My family. They won't leave my head."

"Do you want to call them?"

An ache burrows into the back of my skull. "Not until I know Erika called them first." I push a hand into my uneasy gut. "I don't want to make things overly messy."

"Why don't we check out the rest of this pad?" Wyatt says, scooting to the edge of the couch. "It was too hard to look around without someone racing to my side with the wheelchair or walking cane."

"Maybe you should take the cane."

He side-eyes me.

"What? I don't want anything to go wrong. If you stack it, I can't exactly hold you up."

He pushes himself off the couch with a grunt. "Fine, I'll take the walking cane. Not that I need it."

"No, of course not."

"Sarcasm?"

I smirk. "Not at all."

Wyatt gestures at the walking cane, which leans against an armchair. "Just hand it over, would ya?"

I smile and give it to him. He then steps forward, putting his weight on the walking aide.

"I wanna check out these bedrooms," he says, making his way ahead of me. "I gotta pick the best one."

"You could sleep in a different room each night."

"Or my parents will move in. They should, shouldn't they?"

"It's up to you. Personally, I would move mine in, but it's not the same situation."

He halts, allowing me to step in line with him, and then nudges me. "You could move in here."

My face reddens. "Ah, what?"

"Why not?" he says, edging his way closer to the bedrooms. "The floor below me is too far away. We could be roommates."

Tingles dance under my skin. "Are you serious?"

He tilts his head, watching me with braced apprehension. "You don't want to?"

"Of course, I want to. I always want to be close to you. It's just..."

"Joze, I didn't say move into my bedroom. You'd have your own room."

I giggle nervously. "No, yeah, of course."

"Besides, kissing wipes me out. If we did anything more, you might put me back in the hospital."

At that, red blotches cover my chest and arms, eliminating any hope of hiding my flushed embarrassment. Has he been thinking about doing more than kissing me? Has he done more than kissing since moving away from Victoria Falls?

Has he and Portia...

"Hey, what's the hold up?" Wyatt asks, standing in a bedroom doorway. "I thought you were following me."

I shake out of my thoughts and quicken my pace. "Yeah, sorry, coming."

Wyatt leans against the doorframe, keeping his back straight. "This room looks pretty frickin' sweet. I might not have to check out the others."

I grin, leaning into the doorway. "Wow, it's huge."

We move into the bedroom, which has oodles of space around the California king bed. Behind the bed is a massive walk-in closet, which leads into the studio-apartment-sized bathroom.

"You should definitely take this room," I say, gesturing at the shower. "Everything is easy to walk through. Looks like they've already set you up with a shower seat and grab rails."

"Kinda kills the vibe."

"It's just to keep you safe." I smile and rub his arm. "No one wants you slipping and winding back in the clinic."

He forces a smile. "Yeah, I know."

"You're good?"

He nods, moves back through the walk-in closet, and drags himself over to the bed.

"Just think about how cool this place is, not the hospital-grade stuff they put in here."

He sits on the edge of the bed, rubbing his forehead. "Yeah, I know."

"You've got a headache? I can get your painkillers."

He drops his hand, patting the space beside him. "Can I get a hug instead?"

I bounce my way over to him, sitting and wrapping my arms around him. "I'll never deny you a hug."

A laugh whispers out of him as his mouth grazes my earlobe. "Thanks, Joze."

"I know it sucks, but you're so close to not needing this stuff. But your headaches," I falter as my voice cracks. "They come on so strong. What if you had to grab your head, and you didn't have anything holding you up? You could collapse."

"Why are you being such a downer?"

"I'm being a realist."

"I thought you Bartlett's only dell-dealt with con, con..."

"Conspiracies?" I say it for him. "Well, I don't mind being skeptical about your health if it keeps you protected."

He kisses my cheek and pulls out of the hug. "I told you, I'm the one protecting you."

"But I remember the last few years. You need me more."

"But I need to help you feel safe enough to stay with me."

I clasp his hands and brush my nose against his. "For now, I'm willing to soak in our time together. The logistics of us staying together are gonna be so messy. I can just imagine my parents flipping out on Erika."

Wyatt squeezes my hands. "Okay, then we won't think about it. We'll just live for now."

I brighten, sitting taller. "I love that."

"Wow," he breathes.

Intrigue has me smiling. "What is it?"

"In this light, you look even more beautiful than normal." His eyes wander across my face. "I couldn't have guessed that was possible."

My shoulders bunch high. "Aww, Wyatt."

He brushes the side of my face and plays with my curls. "You really are amazing, Josie. No matter what the suits tell me to do, I'm not letting them push us apart again."

I nod along with the beat of my heart. I bite my tongue, not letting myself say he'll get busy again. That I won't be able to keep up with his fast-paced lifestyle. We agreed to be in the moment. And, at this moment, he's not a jet-setting celebrity. He's not leaving for a movie set, or heading into a recording studio. Right now, he's the same Wyatt Hayes I remember. The guy I had to practically push into auditioning for Talent Quest. The guy who would call me at all hours of the night, anxiety-riddled from the television camera. The guy who would write me the most adorable emails on his off-hours.

I swipe my thumb across his bottom lip, letting a giggle slip out. "You're perfect, Wyatt Hayes. I'm keeping you locked in my heart forever."

He pulls his arms around me, making sure there's no air between us. "Move in here. You can have the second-best bedroom."

I giggle, doing my best not to lean my weight on him. "Okay. Should we go find it?"

He shrugs. "I dunno. I'm pretty comfy here. Do you really wanna move out of this position?"

"Is your back okay?"

His eyebrows wiggle. "You wanna lie down instead?"

Nervousness writhes inside me. "Ah, I..."

He pecks my cheek. "If it's all the same, maybe I will lie down. I'm kinda beat, and that headache is getting a little worse."

"Okay. I'll ask Hubert for your painkillers."

"Will you come back?"

"You want me to lie down with you?"

He sneaks another kiss onto my cheek. "That'd be amazing."

I giggle, pulling my arms from him. "Okay. How about you lie down and relax?"

I leave the bedroom, searching for Hubert. Where the heck do you even find...

"Yes, Miss Bartlett?" Hubert asks, meeting me in the living area.

Uh-oh. Is the bedroom bugged?

Hubert smiles kindly. "You look startled."

"Umm, yeah. Were you listening to..."

"Your pace sounded serious. I felt you needed some assistance."

Okay, time to switch off the skeptical part of my brain. "Umm. Yeah. You've got Wyatt's pain meds, right?"

He nods. "I shall fetch them for him. Where would you like them?"

I gesture toward the bedroom. "He's going to bed."

Hubert nods. "I'll be there in just a moment."

"Thank you."

I make my way back to the bedroom to let Wyatt know relief is on the way. When I get inside, I find the bed empty. "Wyatt?"

I search the walk-in closet and spy the bathroom door closed. I knock on it. "Wyatt?"

"Yeah?"

"Oh. Just checking."

"I'm good. Be out in a minute."

I edge away. "Okay. Hubert's coming in with the painkillers."

"Thanks, Joze."

Backtracking through the closet, I find Hubert placing a glass of water and a small dish, with two half-blue, half-white pills, on the nightstand. He then turns down the bed, turns the lamps on a low setting, and draws the curtains closed.

"Anything else, Miss Bartlett?"

I shake my head, clutching my elbows. "No, that's amazing. Thanks."

Hubert nods, making his way to the doorway.

"Oh, if Wyatt needs anything else…"

Hubert cuts me off, gesturing to an intercom on the wall. "Just call for me, and I'll be at your service."

Still jittery, I push for a smile. "Thank you."

Hubert leaves the room, and I sit on the edge of the bed. My foot bounces and my fingers tap against my knees. I keep my gaze fixed on the closet entrance and listen hard for noises from the bathroom. I'm well aware Wyatt was taking himself to the bathroom when in the clinic, but I still have this sinking feeling something could go wrong. My stomach churns at the thought of him tripping or collapsing.

Before I go into full meltdown, he makes his way back into the bedroom, walking cane in hand.

He notices my overzealous grin and looks down at the cane. "Yes, I'm being a good boy."

I giggle, standing to give him space to make it to the bed. "Savanna would be proud."

"I didn't want you to fr-freak out about me."

"Me? Freak out?"

He side-eyes me. "With Mr. Skeptical as a dad, and Mrs. Nervous as a mom, umm, yeah, you're known to freak out."

"I just like to make sure everyone's safe."

He smiles and slides under the covers. "That's what makes you amazing, Josie."

I hand him the glass of water and two pills. He takes them with an unsteady hand, and I'm quick to take them back when he's finished.

"Good?"

He nods after swallowing.

"Excellent." I round the bed, slipping under the covers beside him.

He snuggles close to me, draping an arm around my waist. "I want to say something."

"You can say anything."

"Well, no, I can't." His brow furrows. "I should say it, but I don't know what it means."

"Wyatt, you're not making sense."

"This morning." He pauses. "You said..."

I sigh. "Oh. That."

"Well, I... You know, well..." He huffs, looking up at the ceiling. "If my life were what I remembered, I wouldn't hesitate. But... it's not. And, you said..."

"That I love..."

"No," he blurts, looking back at me. "No, that, that, I might have... That there might be, be, someone else?"

My shoulders lock, and my insides turn to sludge.

"I mean, I haven't heard from this person, so we ca-can't b-be in love." He gulps. "But it just hits home that there's so many fr-freaking un, un, unknowns in my life. Even my parents. Th-they... I don't know if I'm okay being around them."

"Wyatt, you're stressing out. You don't need to think about this stuff."

"But...But, it's stopping me from telling you..."

"I told you, you didn't need to say it."

"But I feel it."

Instantly, the ick inside me dissolves into butterflies.

"Joze, it's only you. You're the only person I wanted to see when I was surrounded by people. Of course, I do. But when I don't know who I am, I just feel..."

I nod as he grapples with his words.

"There's just a big X over me." He sighs roughly. "When things become cl-clearer, I won't be so guarded."

I grin as my heart bounces with bliss. "Oh my gosh, Wyatt. You practically said it. That's totally enough for me." I giggle with overwhelm. "More than enough for me."

He smiles, tracing my chin. "You deserve more, though."

"You said you *feel* it."

He nods.

I grin. "That's mind-blowing."

He puffs a laugh. "Why?"

"Because you're a superstar and I'm just a normy."

He grins, clutching my wrist. "We used to spend so much time together." He tugs my hand up to his chest. I press my digits against him, feeling the thumping of his heart. "I'm not different."

"You're exactly how I remember." I then giggle before I add, "Just bigger and with a better hair cut."

He winks. "You're still the better looking one."

"I think you have a giant fanbase who would disagree."

"They don't exist right now."

I nod. "Right. It's just you and me."

He lifts my hand to kiss it. "Right."

"You gonna get some sleep?"

As if on cue, he yawns, making me chuckle.

His smile has sleepy written all over it. "Maybe just a few minutes."

"And you're sure you want me to stay?"

His eyes close and his smile stays dreamy. "Yes, please."

I giggle, flopping beside him. "Okay. No problem."

I don't care how creepy it might seem. I just can't pass up the chance to watch this beautiful boy sleep.

His hand grows limp against mine as he drifts into dreamland. I yawn from close proximity, but I don't feel like sleeping. I'm careful not to shift on the bed as his breathing grows heavier.

My gaze traces the lines of his face, until I'm interrupted by my phone buzzing in my pocket. The harsh noise causes creases to form across Wyatt's forehead as he moans and stirs in his sleep.

I lean forward and kiss the top of his head. "I'll be right back."

I slide out of the bed, hit answer on my phone, and leave the bedroom. "Hello?"

"You want to stay longer?" Mom's frantic voice yelps through the phone.

"Wyatt needs me," I whisper as I edge my way into the living area.

"No, you need to come home," Mom says adamantly. "I can't deal with the stress of worrying about where you are all the time."

"I'm with Wyatt," I say, plonking down on the couch. "He's in the hotel now, so I don't even have to go anywhere. Besides, there's a ton of security around. You should feel good that I'm so safe here."

"I should feel good?" Mom says sharply. "No, Josie. I don't feel good about you being hours away from us. You're only sixteen. I don't like this."

"Mom, please, don't..."

"I never should've let you go," she says the words I was hoping she wouldn't.

"I don't need the guilt trip."

"That's not what this is. I'm being a parent. Your parent."

"Mom, he's scared. If I leave, I think he'll fall apart. Do you really want him to get worse?"

"He has the best medical team in his corner. He'll be fine."

"You're being so flippant. He doesn't remember any of the people surrounding him. He needs me." I huff my frustration. "Can't you all come here instead?"

Mom laughs in shock. "Did you really just say that?"

"Look, I'm not coming home. I can't."

"Josie, don't you dare speak to me like this. Your father and I need you home."

"I know. I wish I could be in two places at once."

"You can't."

"I'm not getting on a plane."

Mom's sigh rattles through the phone. "Why are you making this so difficult? You know you need to come back."

"You didn't see him wig out when Randall spoke about arranging my flight home. He's not ready for me to go."

Mom doesn't respond for a while, making me wonder if she fainted or something.

"Mom?"

She sighs. "All I want is to cuddle you in my arms. I've been forcing myself not to think about Wyatt, because I just want you home. I can't even imagine what his parents must be going through."

"Neither can I. They haven't visited him since he left the clinic this morning."

"Why? Where are they?"

"No idea. Wyatt keeps asking for them, and they haven't turned up."

Outrage fires in Mom's voice. "What?"

"Besides me, they're the only people around him who he remembers. If I go, he'll basically be abandoned."

"Abandoned? I can't believe his parents would abandon him."

"They're not here. Whenever I do see them, they're using words like entitled, and wishing he'd get back to work."

"What? Already?"

"There's something really off about them. Wyatt can't rely on them. And it only makes things worse when his team is pushing for him to get better in an instant."

"Oh my..." her voice trails off, until another sigh puffs out of her. "Hmm, it's already Thursday. I guess the weekend is coming up soon. So, it's not like you'll miss out on much more school."

"Do you mean..."

"I'll call your father. We won't stop being nervous wrecks, but we'll handle you staying there a few more days."

I sit back on the couch, relieved. "Thanks, Mom."

"Are you with Wyatt?"

"He's asleep. His headaches take it out of him."

"Poor guy."

"I hate seeing him in so much pain."

"He's lucky to have you. The twins are completely jealous."

"Ah, I miss them. Maybe I'll read them a story over video chat tonight."

"They'd love that."

"Talk later?"

"Of course. Love you, honey."

I smile against the phone. "Love you, too."

I move back into the bedroom, finding Wyatt lying on his back, rubbing the side of his head.

"You're still in pain?" I ask, sitting on the edge of the bed.

He lowers his head, turning to view me like he didn't hear me come in. "You're back?"

"My mom called," I reply. "I had to talk her off a ledge. But she agreed to let me stay here with you."

Wyatt smiles weakly. "Awesome."

My heart hurts, and I scoot across the bed to sit beside him. "Are the painkillers not working?"

He grunts, eyeing the ceiling with glassy eyes. "I dunno. Just feels like something's pulsating in my head."

I wince in second-hand pain. "Do you want me to call someone? Maybe Erika could get your doctor on the line?"

He shakes his head and grabs my hand. "No, it'll be fine. It'll eventually stop. Just cuddle me."

"That I can do." I lie down beside him and wrap my arm around his middle. "I'm sorry if my phone ringing woke you up."

"No, it was the headache."

I lift my hand and massage his temple. His eyelids fall shut, and he exhales softly.

I smile. "Better?"

His lips curl and he gives a slight nod, keeping his eyes closed. I keep gentle pressure on the side of his head, rubbing concentric circles with my thumb.

Before long, quiet sleeping sounds purr out of him. I keep massaging his head, ensuring he falls deeper into sleep.

Gosh, he looks so freaking beautiful.

Unable to help myself, I press my lips against his, relishing every bit of his sweetness.

Thirteen

I'm sitting up in bed and tapping on my phone when Wyatt stretches awake.

"Hey, sleepy head," I say, reclining against two pillows.

He squints at me. "Hey. What ya doing?"

I lock my screen. "Just writing."

Wyatt frowns. "I thought you didn't hide what you wrote."

I bite my lip. "I don't hide stories."

He deadpans me. "You locked your screen."

I wince. "Because it's not a story."

"Then what is it? What are you hiding?"

I cringe. "A poem."

Wyatt sits up. "You write poetry?"

I press the phone against my chest. "It's just for me."

"You don't share the poetry?" he questions. "It could win awards, like the short stories."

I squeak, sinking against the pillows. "I'd be too embarrassed."

Wyatt chuckles. "Why? You're a great writer."

I fan my face, mortified. "They're about you."

Wyatt's eyes fill with glee. "Show me."

I hide my face behind my phone. "*Eep*! No!"

Wyatt doesn't push. "Okay, okay. Have your secrets."

I lower my phone, needing a subject change. "How's your head?"

He smiles. "Great. It feels clear."

I lean forward and kiss his forehead. "That's beyond amazing."

He reaches out a hand, patting my blanket-covered leg. "Best sleep I've had in ages."

"You wanna stay in bed a little longer?"

He throws off the covers. "Nah, I gotta get up."

I slip out of bed and watch him slowly pull himself up. "You good?"

He grunts as he pushes off the bed. "Yep. Good."

"You hungry?"

"I guess I could eat. You wanna check out the other bedrooms before we find food?"

"Yeah, sure."

His eyebrows wiggle. "Gotta find where you're sleeping."

I giggle as he shuffles toward the doorway with me. "You're still set on me moving in?"

"Ah, yeah." He gestures for me to leave the room first. "I'm telling Erika to get you checked out of your suite."

I giggle as I wait for him to join me in the hall. As he steps behind me, his hands grasp my hips and then slide around my waist. When his hands plant on top of my stomach, I blissfully move forward with him cuddled behind me.

We move into the second bedroom. It's slightly smaller than Wyatt's but looks super cozy. There are overstuffed pillows on the king bed, a chaise lounge, and a walk-in closet acting as an entryway into the bathroom.

"Umm, I could totally kick it in here."

He keeps me hugged close. "Yep, you need this one." He kisses my cheek. "It's the closest to mine."

"So, you'd say I'm staying in here, even if it were the worst room?"

"Well, maybe not if it were the *worst*."

I giggle and lead him out of the room. "Come on, let's check out the other rooms."

The third bedroom is similar to the second, and the fourth bedroom has been turned into a makeshift storage room. It houses an array of miscellaneous items, and my eyes lock onto something propped up on a black stand.

"Oh my gosh." I gasp. "Wyatt, it's your guitar."

"It doesn't look like my guitar."

"This is the one you play at concerts."

He doesn't respond, except for a gulp.

I clutch his hand. "It'll be okay. Do you want to hold it?"

"Nuh-uh." He doesn't budge when I tug on him. "I can't."

"You don't have to play it, but maybe it'll feel good to have it in your hands." I gesture at the bed. "Why don't you take a seat and I'll bring it to you?"

He runs a hand through his hair, apprehension paling his expression.

I frown, touching the sides of his face. "Are you worried you can't play it?"

Red lines frame his eyes, and he nods.

"Savanna's had you building up your hand muscles. You might need a refresher on the chords. But, after some time, I'm sure it'll all come back to you."

"Joze," it comes out broken. "Guitar is the one thing I love. Apparently, it got me famous. Who am I without it?"

"You're the same person. The same sweet and talented Wyatt Hayes."

He looks down at his hand, flexing it as if there's an elastic band around his fingers. "The talent might be gone."

"This morning you said, you were taking your time, remembering the sequences with the playing cards. Give yourself some credit. You're already improving."

He sucks in a breath and blows it out slowly. He edges toward the bed and gingerly sits down. "Okay. I'll try."

I mask my massive enthusiasm, forcing myself to move slowly toward the guitar. Tingles shoot up my fingers as I lift the iconic acoustic guitar. I can't even count the many live performance recordings I've watched.

I hand it over to him. "Ready?"

He takes it, resting the body against his lap, and holding the neck against his open palm.

I kneel on the carpet in front of him, keeping my focus on the guitar. "Does it feel okay?"

"Holding it isn't the scary part," he half-jokes.

"You don't have to play it. This can be enough for today."

His index finger brushes against the strings, light enough not to make a sound. His eyes move across the neck, and then around our immediate area.

"Is there a pick anywhere?"

My heart hammers with anticipation. I jump to my feet, searching the area around the guitar stand. Hiding my excitement has totally gone out the window.

On the carpet, I spy a black and purple guitar pick. "Got it!"

Wyatt mumbles a laugh as I take it to him.

"Sorry," I murmur. "I'm trying not to get overexcited."

"It's cool, Joze. I'm fr-freaking out about playing too."

I wince. "Your stutter's coming back. Are you too nervous to do this?"

He shrugs, the pick resting between his lips as he correctly positions the guitar against him. He plucks the pick from his mouth and says, "I think I'll stay stressed out if I don't play. You know, wondering if I could or not."

"Well, take it easy. Like, don't be hard on yourself."

His left hand moves along the frets, his fingers trembling as they fumble against the strings. He frowns and shakes his head, shifting his gaze to the sound hole and rubbing his thumb and index finger against the pick. Tentatively, he strums downward once.

He puffs a laugh. "Way out of tune."

My heart expands, and a massive grin stretches my cheeks. "You heard that. *See.* Told ya it would come back to you."

"But look at my hand."

"It's just nerves."

"It's a brain injury."

The swell in my heart deflates with a tear.

He strums again, keeping his head hanging low. He then strums two more times. And then three times, up and down.

He looks at me with a small smile. "Okay, that part isn't too scary."

I stand on my knees. "You feel okay?"

He nods and taps the fretboard. "Yeah, but I, I don't wan-wanna do this part yet."

"That's okay. You've taken a huge step just holding the guitar."

He tilts the guitar against his lap. "This is a nice one. You've watched me play it at concerts?"

"Not live." I cringe. "But I've watched the recordings over and over again."

Wyatt's eyebrows lift, and he sucks in a ragged breath.

I cringe, hoping I haven't triggered him.

He chews his lip, resting the guitar against him. "What kind of songs do I play?"

"You play pop songs, just like the old covers. Your second album had some electronic beats. Also had some cool blends with an indie folk sound."

Happy surprise lifts his face. "Oh, that's cool."

I slip my hand into my pocket, grasping my phone. "Did you want to hear one?"

He grits his teeth, too tense to use his words.

"You don't have to. I know you've been avoiding all this stuff."

He slips the guitar off, sitting it on the bed beside him. On the other side, he pats the empty space next to him. "If I'm with you, I should be okay to hear it."

I sit on the bed, nestled close to him. I open my phone to the playlist of Wyatt Hayes songs. It's filled with studio tracks, concert performances, and recordings from Talent Quest. I tilt the phone so he can see the list. "There are a few songs to choose from."

Wyatt's eyes widen, and he leans forward. Tentatively, he flicks a finger against the phone screen, scrolling through the playlist. "Dang. They're all my songs?"

"Everything you've recorded that I could get my hands on."

"Do you have a favorite?"

I scroll back up the list, landing on 'Summer Glow.' "This was the first song you released after winning the reality show. It still gives me chills."

He peels my thumb away from the play button. "Not yet."

I place the phone on my lap and curl my hands around his. "No problem."

"I-it's like I'm li-living in some crazy dream. Can you imagine wa-waking up and being told hun-hundreds of people know your name, and y-you've recorded albums, and been in, in movies?"

I stop myself from correcting him. It's not hundreds of people. It's millions. But I think that would only hurt his brain further.

I squeeze my hands around his. "No, I don't know how I'd deal with my life completely changing. Especially when it seems like it was overnight. But I don't have to imagine it, because I see you going through it. It's not fair."

He sighs, letting his forehead rest against mine. "I wish I'd never gone on that stupid show."

I gasp. "No, you can't..."

He lifts his head, and his red-rimmed gaze locks deeply with mine. "I wish I'd never left home, never left you, and didn't ruin my family."

"Wyatt, you didn't..."

"My parents aren't here," he cuts me off. "I, I don't live with them. I don't have a re-relationship with them."

"You travel a lot. You haven't ruined anything."

"But you don't know, Josie. You're not here." His eyes grow glassy as his voice wavers. "We aren't friends anymore."

Those four words hit me hard, like a dagger into the chest. My airway constricts, and I choke as I look away from him.

He lifts my hands, still clutched around his. "Because of me. I hate myself for abandoning you."

I whip my face back to look at him dead in the eyes. "Don't say that."

"It's true. I do."

I pull him into a tense hug. "You don't understand how happy you make me. I've never hated you, so don't let those thoughts enter your mind."

He's limp against me. "How could you not hate me? I don't even understand why you want to be around me."

I rub my hands against his back, trying to bring warmth into him. "Because I've never been without you. I've always had your music, and I was able to watch you online. Why do you think I pushed you to go on Talent Quest? I never expected to keep you all to myself."

He finally hugs me back. "Really?"

The tension slips off my back. "Yes, of course. I mean, yeah, it sucked when we stopped texting. But I knew you had film shoots and press tours."

"You're being too lenient with me."

"I can't help it. I'm obsessed with you, Wyatt."

He sighs against my shoulder. "I should've confided in you all along. Maybe if we'd stayed in contact, I never would've been hurt."

"Maybe, but we can't know. But we can get through these unknowns together."

"I just wish I woke up where I remember."

I brush my hand against his back and kiss his jaw. "What do you remember last?"

His hands settle against the base of my back, and his chin sits on my shoulder. "Your treehouse. Acting out a scene from one of your stories."

I giggle at the silly memory. "And you said you didn't have any acting experience."

He lets out an exhausted laugh. "*Ha.* Guess that was the clincher."

I run my hand up, resting it against the back of his head, and pull out of the hug. His back straightens, and he's quick to pat his eyes dry.

I pout. "You look exhausted."

"No, I'm okay. But, I could do with some food."

I stand from the bed. "Shall we find the kitchen?"

"Or, just the butler?"

"Last time I looked for him, he just appeared. I wouldn't be surprised if he turned up at the doorway right about now."

Wyatt smirks, standing and stepping away from the bed. "Not creepy at all."

I chuckle. "Nope, not at all."

We leave the bedroom and find Hubert making his way towards us in the living area.

"May I prepare dinner for you, Mr. Hayes and Miss Bartlett?" Hubert asks diligently.

"Read our minds," Wyatt says, his smirk lingering.

"Any requests?" Hubert asks.

Wyatt looks my way. "I haven't had pizza in forever."

My taste buds tingle. "I would love pizza." I turn to Hubert. "Can you do pizza?"

Hubert smiles politely. "I can organize anything to be brought up to the penthouse. Make yourselves comfortable, and I'll make the arrangements."

Wyatt staggers his way to the sectional couch and flops down. "I love how normal pizza sounds."

I sit down beside him, curling my feet up on the couch. "Reminds me of when we'd stay up late and watch movies."

"We should do that," Wyatt says, gesturing at the television on the wall. "Watch a movie and eat pizza."

I click my tongue. "You probably wanna watch one of those 'Wasteland Gang' movies. I haven't watched one of those shoot-em-up movies in forever."

"And, by your tone, I guess you still don't want to?"

"You know I always opt for rom-coms."

Wyatt sniggers. "I really don't care what we watch. As long as the plot is dead easy to follow."

I reach toward the coffee table and grab the TV remote. "I'm down for an easy watch. Maybe something we've already seen?"

Wyatt snaps his fingers. "What was that one, you know, with the kids? They find that bunker and pretend to be spies?"

I laugh, flicking through the movie options. "You mean, 'Super Secret Kids?' That movie is so bad."

"I know. I remember. I wanna watch something so bad it's good."

I type the title into the search bar, and we both crack up when the goofy movie poster appears on the screen. I hit play, asking, "You sure?"

Wyatt stretches an arm across my shoulders, relaxing against the plush couch. "I'm totally, completely sure."

I drop the remote on the armrest and snuggle into Wyatt as our childhood nostalgic movie plays. My shoulders jiggle as I cringe at the bad acting and terrible visual effects. Wyatt's hand strokes my arm, and his body language is more at ease than it's been my entire visit.

Oh my gosh. This is what he's needed all along. A true taste of home. Something simple and familiar. He's been surrounded by a team who want to spoil him with the best of everything; from doctors to accommodation. But that just puts him more on edge, feeling completely foreign in a life that's supposedly his.

"This is so bad," I say amid my laughter. "Excellent choice."

"I have no idea why this crap came into my mind," Wyatt says, grinning. "It's weird what my brain chooses to remember."

"At least it's a memory that's brought a boatload of happiness."

He kisses the top of my head. "Anything's a good memory if it includes you. I'm glad I don't remember the last few years without you."

I lay my head against his shoulder. "No, I hope those memories come back to you."

"Mmm. Me too. It's just hard to think about."

"I know. But I'm here for you."

"I think I'm supposed to see the shrink again soon."

"Psychologist?"

He smirks. "Yeah. I just still have trouble with that word."

"They help, though?"

He nods. "He's all right. He doesn't push me."

"That's awesome."

"He'll probably like hearing about my time with you. He's the one who suggested I ask Erika to get you here."

"I like your therapist already."

"I guess I'll see him again before leaving for wherever my home is."

"Ferndale."

"Huh?"

I lift my head off his shoulder, looking into his eyes as I repeat, "Ferndale. It's where you live."

"Oh."

"It's where all you Circle 8 kids live."

His eyebrows lift, and I quickly wave the conversation away.

"It doesn't matter. It's just the group of teens, who were either child stars in TV and movies, or from reality shows, and are under the same management."

He points at his chest. "And I-I'm one of them?"

I wince, hearing his stutter come back. "Yeah. Sorry, we should be flinching at this movie, not the stupid stuff I say."

"You don't say stupid stuff."

"I keep blurting stuff out about your life, and it rattles you. I call that stupid."

Wyatt tugs me close and lays a kiss on my lips, halting the spiraling thoughts in my head.

His lips gradually peel away from mine, and his voice is breathy when he says, "I don't kiss stupid people."

I giggle, brushing my nose against his. "Okay, got it."

Our vegan pizza arrives when we're halfway through our bizarrely entertaining movie. Oh my gosh, the pizza has an amazing pesto sauce drizzled over it, and the veggies are grilled to perfection.

After his second slice, Wyatt leans over me for the remote and pauses the movie.

"Everything okay?" I ask.

He lifts his palm. "Can I see your phone?"

I slip it out of my pocket and unlock it. "Yeah, sure."

It's still open to the playlist of his songs, and he taps on 'Summer Glow.'

"Wyatt," I breathe. "Are you sure?"

"I can't stop thinking about it," he admits. "It's your favorite, right?"

It's hard to hide my smile. "Yes."

He shrugs, hitting the play button. "Can't be that bad then."

Wyatt sets the phone on his thigh and closes his eyes as the song plays. Goosebumps sprout on my limbs, the way they always do when I hear him sing. His muscles flex, recoiling in anticipation. As the song moves into the chorus, his body eases and his eyelids slowly lift.

I smile at him with hope. "Are you okay?"

He taps the phone. "It sounds familiar. Like, I know that's me."

My heart bounces in my chest. "Do the lyrics sound familiar?"

He shakes his head. "No, I've never heard it before."

Excitement and anxiety tussle inside me.

Wyatt grins, mumbling a laugh. "How silly does that sound? I've never heard it before, but it's literally me singing."

I don't laugh with him, worried he's about to break. "Should we turn it off?"

"No, I like it."

"You're okay with listening to it?"

He grins. "Yeah, it feels normal."

"Wow." The anticipation bursts inside me, letting out a mess of jitters. "That's incredible."

He rubs my arm briskly. "Are you okay? You're shaking."

"I'm just overwhelmed. I was so worried you wouldn't be okay."

"Honestly, me too."

I peck his cheek, and he's quick to turn his head and find my lips. I slide my hand onto the side of his face and tilt my head as he applies heart-melting pressure into the kiss.

His hands dig into my waist as our kisses deepen, but then he rips himself away as the track changes. It's a live recording, starting with a crowd of people cheering. His eyes bug and his chest rises and falls with force as he hears himself addressing his fans.

Hastily, I snatch the phone and stop the song. "*Crap.* Sorry."

"It's… It's…" His chest continues to puff as he struggles to catch his breath. "It's not you."

I motion with the phone. "It's this. I'm sorry."

"I just…" He pauses, taking an inhale of air. "I wasn't ready for… *that.*"

I slip my phone back into my pocket.

He wipes his forehead and sighs. "Dang it. I really thought I wasn't gonna freak out."

I wrap my arms around his shoulders. "Don't do that to yourself. No one's ready to find out they suddenly have a ton of fans."

He blinks hard. "Just, ah, wow. Umm, that was me. At a concert? And talking to a ton of fans? That's legit."

I smile nervously. "One-hundred percent legit."

He blows out a hard breath. The same bewildered excitement appears on his face as it did earlier on the drive from the clinic. "*Crap.* I have fans."

"And you saw only a fraction of them outside the clinic today."

His fingers tremble as they reach for the sides of his face. "Whoa. Like, I know I've been told this is real... but, umm... just, wow."

I smile, placing a hand on his back. "It is wow. Who knew you'd kill it after auditioning for a national talent show?"

"Not me. I'd get so ner-nervous before middle school talent shows."

I nudge him gently. "But remember how you felt once you were on stage?"

His gaze falls into a dreamy state, and his smile softens. "It was magic. I felt untouchable."

"No matter what anyone said to you in the school halls, or in class, they all loved you when you were on stage."

"Yeah. For one song, I wasn't the dumb guy who got held back a grade."

I grunt, feeling the stabbing pain in the pit of my stomach. "Ugh. Wyatt, don't do that. You're not dumb."

"Either way, apparently I ditched that label." Wonder brightens his face. "I got freakin' famous. I get to sing for a living. This is so freakin' cool."

I cuddle into him and kiss his cheek. "It's so good to see you so happy."

"All I gotta do is mend things with my parents, then I'll be living the dream."

"I'm sure there's a good reason why they haven't visited yet. They want what's best for you. I'm sure any tension or animosity stems from them fretting about your health."

He nods, picking up the TV remote. "Yeah, you're probably right. Shall we watch the rest of this hideous movie?"

I giggle, resting my head against his chest and listening to the settling beats of his heart. "I was hoping you'd forgotten about it."

He hits play on the remote and envelopes me in his arms. "No chance, Joze."

Fourteen

After the movie and a belly full of pizza, it's late into the evening, and Wyatt encourages me to pack my bag and officially move out of the presidential suite. Let's face it, he's too ridiculously adorable to disagree with.

On the floor below the penthouse, I move along the hallway toward my suite, and I pass an opening door.

"Oh, Josie," Mrs. Hayes says frantically, grabbing onto my arm as she leaves her suite. "Do you know if Wyatt has been released from the clinic yet?"

I blink at her. "Huh?"

Her grip on me tightens. "He was supposed to be getting out today."

"Yeah," I drag out the word. "And he did. This morning."

She lets me go, stumbling backward. "He did?"

"Yeah. He's been waiting for you."

She clutches her chest. "He has?"

"He's been really cut up about it. He doesn't think he has a relationship with you or his dad."

"We were told we'd get a passkey to the penthouse when he arrived here." Her stare narrows and hostility hardens her tone. "You're telling me he's been here for hours?"

I raise my palms defensively. "I don't have anything to do with you getting a key."

"But you've been with him? You've been in the penthouse?"

"Yes. I went to the clinic this morning so I could travel here with him. You could've done the same."

Malice strikes through her glare. "Are you trying to guilt me? You don't think I love my son?"

I back away, crossing my arms in front for self-protection. "I didn't say anything like that."

She shoots out her hand. "Give me your passkey. I need to see Wyatt."

"I... I... I don't know if I can."

She snorts in contempt. "You guilt me for not seeing him, and now you won't help me get upstairs?"

"No, it's just I need the key. Once I get my bag, I'm going back upstairs."

"You can have Randall get you another passkey. Wyatt's father and I need to get upstairs now."

"But Randall could give you..."

"Now, Josie!" she snaps. "Hand over the key."

Her threatening tone chills my blood to ice. My knees knock together as I hand over the passkey.

Mrs. Hayes snatches it and turns on her heels. "Thanks."

My hand tremors as I pull out the passkey to my suite and unlock the door. I get inside and plant my back against the closed door, panting for breath. Her mood snapped so fast. I wasn't expecting such a severe reaction from her.

Instinctively, my eyes lift to the ceiling. *Crap.* What mood will Wyatt be met with? Will she tone it down with him and be gentle? Or will she rage about not being notified he was in the hotel?

Should I tell Randall? I have to ask him about getting another passkey, don't I? Or can I just call the front desk and ask for another key? Would they just hand it over to me?

Somehow, I doubt it.

I peel myself off the door, fanning my face as I walk further into my suite. I enter the bedroom to pack my bag, but I'm too flustered. There's a horrible mix of heat and ice inside me, so I decide to refresh with a shower. When I'm under running water, it's hard to gain the willpower to turn off the taps. The temperature and pressure is a renewing comfort, and I want to stay safe in this place. But when my mind shifts to Wyatt, the need to get myself back upstairs fills me with purpose.

Hurriedly, I pack my makeup and skincare products from the bathroom counter and dump them into my carry-on bag. With a brand new outfit on, I chuck the rest of my clothes into the bag without care of creases and wrinkles. Slipping the bag over my shoulder, I move to the landline phone in the living area.

"Hello, front desk," a male voice says on the other end of the call.

"Hi, it's Josie Bartlett in the presidential suite." Gosh, I sound so full of myself.

"Yes, Miss Bartlett. How may I assist you?"

"Umm. I need to get in touch with Erika or Randall. You know, the people who work with Wyatt Hayes."

"Yes, Miss Bartlett. I believe they're having drinks in the bar. I can patch you through and have the bartender notify them of your call."

"Thank you. That'd be great."

As I'm placed on hold, knots tie through my abdomen and twist around my spine. I hope Erika and Randall aren't super peeved I gave Mrs. Hayes my passkey to Wyatt's floor. Maybe they're well aware of her manic tendencies, and that's why they prevented her from visiting Wyatt today.

But that's no reason to keep Wyatt in the dark. He was left thinking his parents didn't care about him.

After ten minutes of on-hold music, someone finally answers. "Josie?" Erika's tone is matter-of-fact.

Dang. I was really hoping for Randall. He's less intimidating.

"Umm." Any confidence I had is completely shot. "Umm, I..."

"Spit it out, would you," Erika grunts. "I need to get back to my meeting."

"Wyatt wants me to go back to his floor, but I need a new passkey."

Erika pauses for a moment, filling me with dread. "A *new* key. Where is the key you had? Have you lost it? That would mean you've put Wyatt's safety at jeopardy. Is that what you're telling me, Josie? Anyone could be on their way up to Wyatt's floor?"

"No, it's not just anyone," my voice tremors. "I gave it to his mother."

"You did *what*?" Erika hisses. "Why did you do that? Who gave you permission to do that?"

"No one," I squeak. "She was upset, and Wyatt was asking about his parents."

Erika groans in fury. "This is not what I need right now. Okay, I'll meet you on your floor and take you up." She then yells away from the receiver. "Randall! Get to the penthouse and calm Mrs. Hayes down."

The line then goes dead and all my nerves frazzle. I shudder, lowering the phone onto the cradle.

Crap.

What have I done?

Crap.

Oh, I really hope Wyatt is okay.

I leave my suite with my bag and wait by the elevator for Erika. When the doors ping open, Randall isn't with her. She ushers me inside, telling me he dashed up to the penthouse while she tied things up with other associates.

"I'm sorry if I did something wrong," I mutter at my shoes. "She just... She was in my face."

Erika huffs and the elevator doors ping open. "It's fine. Wyatt's parents take a lot to handle."

Erika marches into the penthouse, and I trail behind.

"Why are we not being notified about our son's whereabouts?" Mrs. Hayes yells from the dining area. As we move through the living space, her wild arm movements come into focus. "We're left out of the loop, and for some reason,

Josie isn't. She's spent years without contact with Wyatt. Suddenly, she's back in the fold and with him every step. Explain to me how this makes sense!"

I stop dead, sick at the thought of making eye contact with the hysterical woman.

Erika steps in to help Randall diffuse the situation, and I pan the room for Wyatt. Since I left the penthouse, it's been close to forty minutes. I hate the idea of his mother berating him all this time. I'm so angry at myself for not calling Erika before my shower. How could I be so selfish? I should've made sure Wyatt got the help he needed before taking care of myself.

Clammy with nerves, my hands twist around the strap of my bag. Quiet and cautiously, I edge along the living area and toward the bedrooms. I keep my eyes peeled to where everyone stands around the dining area. My heart leaps into my throat when I see Wyatt. He sits at the dining table with his dad standing at his side. When his mother continues to go off on Randall, Wyatt's thumbs draw circles on his temples.

My teeth grit, realizing how deep the ache in his skull must be burrowing. I move toward the bedrooms and spot Hubert in the hallway.

I gain his attention, whispering, "How long has it been since Wyatt last took his pain meds?"

Hubert looks at his wristwatch. "He should be due again in about fifteen minutes. I'll ensure they're ready for him."

"Thanks." I gesture at the noise coming from the dining area. "Any way you can break that up?"

Hubert clasps his hands in front. "It's not my place, miss."

My shoulders slouch, and I nod in understanding. I then pull my bag off my shoulder. "Umm, I don't have many clean clothes left. Are there laundry bags here?"

Hubert smiles warmly. "Yes, Miss Bartlett. Just package what you need laundered in the bag located in your closet. If you leave it at the foot of the bed, I'll have it returned first thing in the morning."

"Thank you."

I dump my bag in my bedroom and then steal enough courage to return to the dining area. When I force myself out of the hall, Wyatt's eyes brighten at the sight of me.

He sits taller, willing me toward him. As I move closer to the table, his mother whips around, and steam sizzles out of her ears.

"Josie, darling," Mrs. Hayes says, swallowing her simmering rage. "We are so very grateful you've helped Wyatt get released from the Clearview Clinic. But we have a life to get back to, and so do you."

"Mom, she's not going anywhere," Wyatt says firmly.

"You can't live in the past," his mother replies. "The longer she stays, the longer she holds you back."

"Sh-she's th-th-the only one who..." He sighs out, pressing on his chest in frustration. "Jo-Josie mm-makes me better."

"Mr. and Mrs. Hayes," Erika says, stepping in. "Josie is here at Wyatt's request."

"Wyatt's had a brain injury," Mr. Hayes says. "He doesn't know what's best for him."

At that, Wyatt pales and shrinks in his seat. How could his dad cut him down like that? Wyatt has a functioning brain. He knows what he wants.

"We are stepping in," Mrs. Hayes says, raising her volume. "There's been too much decision-making by the Circle 8 team. It's time for his father and I to take care of him."

Wyatt winces, pressing his fingers against the side of his head.

Mrs. Hayes combs her fingers through Wyatt's hair. It makes him flinch, which only increases his pain-ridden wince.

"Wyatt, sweetie, tell them to leave. You're the only one who can end this now."

Wyatt lowers his head, cowering from his crowding parents.

"Wyatt?" his father presses. "Come on, son. We're just helping you get back in form."

"St-st-top," Wyatt stammers. "I-I-I can't t-t-take this."

"*See*," Mrs. Hayes yelps. "We need him moving forward, so he's not stuck in this horrible mess."

"Mrs. Hayes," Randall cuts in. "With all due respect..."

"Don't even think about telling me how to deal with my son," she spits. "You people all forget that he's mine."

Wyatt hunches further, hanging his head in his hands, despite the pain it causes to his back.

"You need to stop!" Fire burns in my gaze as I stare down Mrs. Hayes. "Can't you see what you're doing to him? He can barely talk. Haven't you worked out that his stutter gets worse under stress? My God, you need to back off!"

Mrs. Hayes sucks in a ragged breath. "How dare you..."

"Josie, this is a family matter," Mr. Hayes cuts in.

Wyatt's hands tremor as they cover his face. "What f-f-family?"

His dad leans closer to him. "What was that, son?"

"Wyatt, sweetheart, we love you and just want to take care of you."

A shattered sigh—littered with the effort to keep back tears—pours out of Wyatt.

"Don't let Josie hold you back," his mother whispers harshly. "You need better than this. That's why we encouraged you to stop contact with her."

Wyatt's brow furrows. "You did what?"

"You strived when you didn't have your old life weighing you down," Mr. Hayes adds on. "Without Josie's calls and texts distracting you, you were able to work harder."

"You had years of success, thanks to us," Mrs. Hayes says with wild desperation. "You can have it again."

"You..." Wyatt pivots between his parents, unable to fathom their words. "You're not my parents. Get out!"

At that, my heart shatters into a thousand tiny pieces.

Erika snaps her fingers at Randall. "Alert security. This needs to be over."

"No, this isn't over." Mr. Hayes glares at Erika. "We're not leaving things like this. We need to be alone with our son."

Wyatt's palms rub over his eyes as his head hangs low. All I want to do is hold him, but I'm scared. If I move one step closer, Mrs. Hayes might crash-tackle me to the ground.

"Wyatt, sweetie," his mother says softly. "You don't mean this. You're confused. Let us stay and help you see things clearly."

"I, I know what you want," Wyatt stammers, keeping his face covered. "Y-you just want me to g-go back to work."

"We want you to feel like yourself again," Mr. Hayes responds.

Wyatt sniffs hard. "You want me to get back to work so, so, so I can mm-make you more money. You don't love me."

Mrs. Hayes's expression shatters as she clutches her chest. "Sweetheart, that's not true."

His dad squeezes Wyatt's shoulder. "Son, we only..."

Wyatt bumps him off. "No, don't touch me. You're not making me do anything. That includes keeping me away from Josie."

"That's it," Erika steps in. "The room needs to be cleared."

At that, security moves in. As if they've been through this before, Wyatt's parents back away. My heart thunders in my chest as security escorts them to the elevator. With my pulse blocking my ears, I watch Erika and Randall close in around Wyatt.

I will myself back to life as Erika pulls a manila folder out of her large handbag. I can't stop blinking as she slips it in front of Wyatt.

Wyatt's hands still shield his eyes, but it doesn't stop Erika from softly saying, "This form is an emancipation document. Our legal team had it drawn up before your accident because it was something you wanted to sign. Wyatt, honey, dealing with your parents won't get easier. I'll leave this with you. If you want further information, I'll have someone from legal drop by and walk you through it." She snaps at Randall again. "Come on, let's go."

Erika and Randall leave the dining area, disappearing toward the elevator. I move closer to Wyatt as his hands lower from his face. Before he can reach for the document, I slide it away and wrap him in my arms.

"You don't need that right now," I whisper, cuddling him against me. "I'm so, so sorry. You don't deserve that kind of treatment."

His body shivers against me, and he lets out a shattered sigh.

I rub his back, standing as I hold him in his seat. "You can let it out. It's okay."

"I, I..." he stutters. "I hate this."

Before I realize it's happening, a tear drops from my eye and lands on the top of his head. I sniff hard, attempting to dry my eyes. His head shifts, but ultimately rests against me again.

"They..." He exhales roughly. "They kept us apart."

Unable to respond, I cling to him.

"How, how..." Tears morph his tone. "How did ev-everything get so, so, ruined?"

I grit my teeth, urging myself not to say it, but it slips out anyway. "Money?"

Wyatt tugs on my shirt, motioning me to crouch down. I lower and his face hides in my curls. "I, I never should've done what they said. I, I should give it all away. Just, go home with you."

I slip my hand to rest behind his head and shush him. "You don't need to dwell on this. They're all gone. We'll just work on lowering your stress levels."

"They won't, Joze. My parents won't stop."

His head turns away, angling at the table. I peer over my shoulder, spying the same document as him.

"I wan-wanted to sign it before..." He pauses, swallowing hard. "I, I didn't want an-anything to do with them."

"You don't really know what was happening before the accident."

"But it feels right." He grips the back of my shirt into a bunch. "It's like the only thing from the present that I can remember."

I massage his head. "Are you sure?"

He gulps and nods. "It makes sense to me."

"I'm so sorry, Wyatt. I hate that things have gotten so bad with your parents. I wish I'd known sooner."

He tilts his head, showing me his red and puffy eyes. "You didn't know, and that's the point. My parents got between us."

My heart pangs in angst, remembering the way Mrs. Hayes spoke about me. She accused me of stunting Wyatt's recovery. She believed my past influence would've stopped Wyatt from becoming famous.

She, along with her husband, are the reason my contact with Wyatt ended.

Hubert approaches the dining table and places a glass of water and a porcelain dish, with two of Wyatt's pills, down.

"Umm," Wyatt falters, wiping his face dry. "Can you ask security not to let my parents back in?"

Hubert nods. "Certainly, sir."

Hubert leaves as discreetly as he entered, and I gesture at the medication. "You should take them. You've been in pain for a while."

He hugs me close, kisses my cheek, and then reaches for the porcelain dish. I pull the water glass closer, knowing his hand will tremble and he doesn't need the trigger.

He swallows the two pills and sets the glass back down. "I love you, Josie."

I choke on an intake of air, kneeling beside his chair. His hand presses into my back, keeping me upright.

He smirks. "You okay, cutie?"

"What, what..." I shake my head, mumbling a laugh. "What did you say?"

He crooks a finger, lifting my chin. "Josie Bartlett, I love you so much. You're my only person and I never want to be without you."

I throw my arms around him and lay a kiss, filled with heightened bliss, onto his lips. His hands run up and down my back as I shiver with the thrill of his words.

He tucks one of my curls behind my ear, whispering, "Tomorrow, it's just you and me all day. I'll ask Hubert to arrange something where no one will find us."

I get tingles at how clear his words were spoken. "Really?"

His grin stretches. "Yeah. Too many people can make their way in here. I want to be sure we're alone. I hate looking over my shoulder."

I nod in overwhelming joy. "Okay, yes, let's do it."

He tilts his head at me. "You changed clothes?"

Guilt sours my happiness. "I had a shower after running into your mother downstairs. I'm so sorry. I shouldn't have wasted so much time before I told Erika. I was just overwhelmed, and..."

His hands lock around my wrists. "Joze, it's okay. It's not your fault."

"But they got up here because of me."

"It's okay. It happened. They're not getting back up here. I'm almost glad it happened so I know to keep my distance."

I pout. "I'm sorry."

He smiles, releasing my wrist and stroking my chin. "Don't be. It freed me to love you."

At that, I'm jelly.

Slowly, Wyatt gets up from his seat and he's wobbly. He's beyond tired, so I walk him back to his bedroom, where he says he'll take a shower. I leave him for my room and change into my pajamas. After brushing my teeth, my ears prick to the buzzing of my phone.

I round the bed and find the display saying, *'Dad Calling.'*

With a quick exhale, I answer. "Hi Dad."

"Josie," he rushes. "What exactly is going on over there? Your mother told me..."

"Oh, Dad," I say, mid-sigh. "It's so much worse."

"I was talking about Wyatt's parents. Is there something else that..."

My chest tightens. "No, it's them."

"I just can't believe his parents would abandon him," Dad says. "I want to get their number and speak to them about this."

"I don't think that's such a good idea." I wince. "A really chaotic scene went down in the penthouse."

"What happened? Are you okay?"

"Yes, I'm fine," I rush. "But Wyatt's parents went ballistic and put him in tears. They're pushing him to go back to work, instead of prioritizing his recovery. It's really sick and twisted."

"What exactly did they say? I can't believe that..."

"Dad, his mom was yelling at everyone. She didn't even care how bad she made Wyatt's headaches. Gosh, Wyatt is devastated. He had to ask security not to let them back in the penthouse."

Dad's voice turns raspy. "It was that bad?"

"Yeah, it's awful. Erika gave him emancipation papers. Apparently his team drew them up before his accident."

"This is bad. So there was already damage to their relationship?"

"Looks that way. It seems Erika was keeping them away for good reason."

"This is a mess. I don't like that you're in the middle of this."

"I'm okay. Besides, Wyatt told me I'm the only person he can count on. Dad, I can't leave him."

Dad sighs. "No, you can't. He's in a fragile state and doesn't have family support. We know very well that you're a wonderful caregiver. Even though I want you back yesterday, I'm glad he has you by his side."

"Are you giving me your blessing to stay?"

"On the condition that you don't fall behind on school. Wyatt has a lot of resting to do, right? During the downtime, you can do your homework. I'll make sure the school emails it all through."

"That's cool with me. I promise to get it all done."

"I know you will, kiddo. You were already ahead in half your subjects. Give Wyatt my best."

I sigh with happy relief. "I will. Thanks, Dad. I love you."

"Love you too, Josie."

Love.

Wyatt said that word to me.

Wyatt loves me.

I drop my phone on the bed and walk to Wyatt's room to say goodnight. I stumble in his doorway as he dries his hair with a towel, shirtless, and wearing gray sweatpants.

"Ah, hi," I stammer, reddening by the nano-second.

He lowers the towel, grinning at me as pale pink dusts his cheeks. "Hi. Dang, don't you look cute."

I giggle, smoothing a hand down my pink satin, button-down pajama shirt that matches my pink satin shorts.

Wyatt flings his towel over the chair adjacent to his bed, and grabs a charcoal T-shirt and carefully pulls it on. He winces as he pulls it down over his abs.

"Are you good?" I ask.

Wyatt motions at the nightstand, where a glass of water and two blue and white pills sit in a small dish. "Hubert already hooked me up."

"Well, I just wanted to say good night."

His eyebrow crooks. "Wh-where do you think you're going?"

I giggle. "To my bedroom."

He chucks a thumb at the California king. "This could fit five people. Are you really gonna make me stay in it all alone?"

My heart thumps with frantic desire. "You, you want me to stay with you?"

He rubs his chin, looking away with a soft chuckle. "Don't tell me the stutter is catching on."

I dab my forehead, giggling out of nervousness. "No, it's just, the thought of being with you always makes me nervous. But giddy."

Wyatt sits down on the bed. "Why are you nervous? It's just me."

I sit next to him, stroking the side of his head. "Because I've always been in love with you. For the last few years, I've been building you up in my head."

He hisses, frowning. "Am I not living up to what's in your head?"

"No," I rush. "Of course, not. You're amazing, wonderful, and incredible. But you're, like, mega famous. How could I ever…"

He plants a finger on my lips, muting the rest of my sentence. "Don't you dare say you're not measuring up."

My shoulders slump and I let out a heavy exhale.

"I love you, Josie. Nothing in this world could change that." He looks around the room. "I've seen how my world has changed, and it hasn't stopped how I've felt about you. If anything, it's made my feelings for you stronger."

I hug my arms around his neck, settling against him as his hands stroke my back. When we settle under the covers, sleep comes easy, snuggled next to the most beautiful boy in existence.

Fifteen

My forehead wrinkles as I shut my eyes tighter before I squint them open. What the heck is happening? What is that?

As I blink and take in his scent, realization sets in. Wyatt's kissing my forehead. Oh my gosh, what a magical way to wake up.

"Morning, princess," he says in a croaky tone.

"Mmm." I yawn and stretch myself awake. "Morning, my prince."

He mumbles a laugh, returning his lips to my forehead.

"Nuh-uh," I whisper and then tap my index finger against my lips.

Taking the instructions well, Wyatt's lips meet mine with the best good morning kiss of my life. Okay, granted, I've never woken in the same bed as a boy I'm crazy about before. But, it'll still be hard to top.

I kiss him back and then my body locks. Oh gosh, what if I have morning breath? I've been waiting for the other shoe to drop and for him to be completely turned off. *Crap.* Is this what will do it?

Wyatt pulls away, leaning on his elbow to look down at me. His expression is blank. Dang it. It's happening.

"What are you doing?" he says flatly.

My heart races. "Huh?"

"You froze. What's wrong?"

"Oh, umm, it's..." I cover my mouth, too embarrassed to admit it.

"Josie?"

I lower my hand and squeak. "I wanna brush my teeth."

Wyatt mumbles a laugh, sitting back against the pillows. "I did that before you woke up."

I sit up. "You did? So, I'm not the only self-conscious one?"

"You said you were building me up for years. I'm not letting some morning breath finally turn you off me."

I giggle and peck his cheek. "Oh my gosh. We've both gotta stop fixating on the other one leaving us."

He nods. "Agreed. You're just so pretty."

I sit up and click my tongue. "Uh, stop."

"You are!" He sits up against the pillows. "I don't want to do something stupid and push you away again."

"You never pushed me away."

"You're right. My parents told me to stop talking to you." He frowns hard. "The worst thing is, I can't believe I listened to them."

"I doubt they said it pointblank," I reply. "You were probably on tour or something, and they told you not to get distracted. Your mom was acting pretty manic. Maybe she took your phone while you were working or something."

"Me working is all they care about." He sighs, staring at nothing in particular. "It now makes sense why they never talked about home with me. They always tried to remind me of my new home and my new routine. They were desperate for me to remember."

"And I now understand why they weren't the ones to call me about visiting you."

Wyatt scoffs. "They weren't interested in you coming here. It wasn't until Dr. Fincher said it could lead to my release from the clinic, that they acted like they were onboard."

"They thought I'd only be here for a day."

"Well, they can suck it." Wyatt shifts closer and lassos me in his arms. "If having you in my life means having them out of it, so be it."

"No, don't say that. Your parents are more important than me."

"I agree, parents should be important. But mine aren't acting like parents."

"I really hope you can eventually make peace with them."

"Josie." He deadpans me. "They forced me to cut you out of my life. They don't deserve my time."

"You were focusing on your career. You should be proud of the success you've achieved."

He huffs, lowering his chin onto my shoulder. "Proud I have parents shoving me into work? Or proud I have a team organizing my life? It's so sad I should laugh. I don't have any friends. I have a team."

"You have the other Circle 8 kids. I'm sure you're friends with them."

"They're other kids who work all the time. I haven't seen any of them in the flesh."

"Wyatt, I don't want you to be sad. I wish you could see your life from my perspective. It's fabulous."

Wyatt lifts his chin and meets my gaze. "And I wish you c-could see how head over heels I am for you. I wish you'd understand that my re-re-relationship with you is the only thing I care about."

"But…"

I'm cut off when Wyatt's lips rush over mine. I lower my eyelids, delighting in every sensation tingling in our kiss. Wyatt tilts his head like a pro. Perhaps how to kiss is the one thing he remembers from his film star life. The pleasure skyrockets past anything I remember from our middle school dalliance. It's almost unfathomable, because I have romanticized the heck out of those past kisses.

Our hands stay clasped, and the connection gives me an extra thrill of electricity.

He breaks away from me, mumbling a laugh as he pants. "Sorry. Needed to come up for air."

I rub my lips together and bashfully raise a hand over my mouth.

His chest rises and falls and then he leans in again, head perfectly angled.

I press a hand on his shoulder, asking, "Are you good?"

"I can't stop kissing you this soon," he says breathily. "We have so much time to make up for."

"We have time," I whisper.

He grins. "Not enough."

I giggle, sliding my hand behind his neck, and he lays another kiss on me. His arms snake around my back and he tugs me closer. As his hands press into my lower back, his arms flex at my sides and pull me up against him. I hum a laugh against his lips, and my chest hits his as I'm cradled in his arms.

When our lips break apart, his nose brushes against mine.

"I'm not letting you go, Josie Bartlett," he whispers. "Not now. Not ever."

I giggle. "Not even to let a girl freshen up?"

He butterfly kisses my nose. "Okay, I'll unhand you for that."

After freshening up in the bathroom, I grab a robe from Wyatt's walk-in closet, and meet him in the dining room for breakfast.

As he sits in a dining chair, I creep up behind him. I wrap my arms around his shoulders, latching my hands against his chest. As he clutches my bundled hands, I kiss his cheek.

"I was missing you already," I admit, slinking into the chair beside him.

He kisses my hand. "Same."

"Do we call room service for food?"

"Hubert already came by. I didn't know what you wanted, so he said he'd come back to ask you."

"What are you getting?"

"Coconut yogurt and granola," he replies. "It's the only thing I want in the mornings."

"How health-conscious of you," I joke.

He smiles. "I guess so."

"Miss Bartlett," Hubert says, making his way into the dining room. "I trust you slept well this morning. May I get your breakfast order?"

I twist a finger around a curl, sensing the growl of my stomach. I know exactly what it's craving, but I can't exactly ask for it when Wyatt's getting muesli.

"Joze?" Wyatt asks, tilting his head. "You're on mute."

I laugh, cupping a hand over my eyes. "I have a craving, but I'm embarrassed about it."

"You are being too cute. Just say it."

I lower my hand and avert my eyes. "I really want waffles."

Wyatt turns to Hubert. "Can you make waffles happen?"

"Certainly, sir. Miss Bartlett, the kitchen staff can prepare many varieties. Do you have a preference in mind?"

I swallow hard, panning my gaze back to Hubert. I feel so ridiculous, asking a butler for a waffle stack. "Umm, just to drown them in loads of maple syrup."

Hubert smiles warmly. "It'll be here before you know it."

When Hubert leaves, Wyatt gives me a confused look. "Why were you embarrassed about that?"

"Ugh. Because you're getting muesli, and I'm being a glut."

Wyatt throws his head back, laughing.

I nudge him. "*Hey.*"

"Sorry," he mumbles, settling his laugh. "A glut is the last thing I'd call you. Heck, I'm the one who ordered pizza last night."

"And I ate it, and now I want more carb-loaded food."

"Relax, Joze. We're in a penthouse together. Let's fr-freaking enjoy it."

My grin matches his. "Okay. Can do."

Okay, my best friend makes some killer waffles, but these fancy hotel waffles are giving her a run for her money. They even enticed Wyatt to take a bite, until he realized they were made with buttermilk. I swear, I'm trying to go vegan. But, ugh, it's hard.

After breakfast, Wyatt reminded Hubert to make sure security doesn't let his management team, or his parents, into the penthouse today. Apparently, the front desk has already changed the coding on their passkeys to invalid. Gotta love technology, right?

On my way to my bedroom to change into a new outfit, Wyatt tells me to meet him on the terrace when I'm done. There's a stunning infinity pool and lush garden out there. Plus, I can't wait to take in that view.

Unfortunately, I'm way too in my head when picking my outfit. Wyatt told me he loved me. More than once. This is monumentally huge. I wanna look my absolute best, but I've already gone through all my outfits because I was only meant to be here for three days. Do I go with the green dress he first saw me in? Or the pink outfit I like the most?

My mind filters back to when he first saw me. He told me I was pretty after all that time apart.

No brainer. I select the green dress.

Before I leave, I check my phone, which I left on the bed before I went into Wyatt's room last night. There's a text from my dad. *"School's emailing you your homework assignments. Make sure you log into the student portal and get to work on them."*

Thank goodness he can't see my massive eye roll. *"Okay, no problem."*

Happily ignoring my schooling responsibilities, I make my way to the terrace with a spring in my step. For as long as I can stretch this out, I'm focusing on savoring every second with Wyatt.

I move through the balcony doors, and the rooftop terrace is empty. That is, except for the deck chairs surrounding the crystal blue pool, and the wealth of plants surrounding the comfy cabana lounges. As I make my way toward the balcony edge, the salty sea breeze hits me, and a wave of calm settles through my nervous system.

I plant my hands on the sides of my face and slowly inhale and exhale. "Oh my gosh."

"I could say the same thing," Wyatt's voice sounds behind me.

I whip around and find him making his way onto the terrace with the help of his walking cane.

"It's the ocean," I say breathily. "I can smell it from here, and it's gorgeous."

"I wish there weren't so much traffic and then we could hear the waves."

I eye his walking aid. "Do you think you'd manage getting closer to the beach sometime soon?"

"I'm sure we can get one of the security guys to drive us down there."

"Yeah, but," I pause, glancing at the cane again, "you can't exactly walk across the sand, can you?"

"It's not like my legs don't work," he says, scuffing his way past me. "I need everyone to relax about the fact I *might* fall over."

"Wyatt, I..." I trail off, watching him trudge toward the balcony edge. I shake off the coldness and follow him. "I'm sorry. I didn't want to suggest something that might not be the best fit for you."

"I know you're looking out for me," he murmurs, keeping his back to me. "But ev-everyone is either telling me to be ca-careful or blow off medical advice to g-get back to work. It's like whatever suits them at the time."

I rub his shoulder, and he turns to face me. "We're ignoring all those people today, remember?"

His smile is small. "Right."

I turn my gaze to the beach and slouch. "I'm not a water person by any stretch. My dream of walking along the sand is moot, anyway. It's Cherry Beach. It's famous for being constantly overcrowded."

"Then we should find a stretch of beach that's isolated." His eyes brighten, and he snaps his fingers, missing his thumb and making a faint whooshing sound. "That's what we'll do today. We'll have security drive us along the coast and find an empty beach. We wanted to do something where it was just us, right?"

"Oh my gosh, that sounds incredible." I plant my hands on cheeks, giddy. "And you'll have plenty of space and time to make your way across the sand."

"And no crowds to spike your anxiety."

I hook my pinky around his. "Let's do it."

Footsteps enter the terrace, and we turn as Hubert carries a silver tray toward us. It showcases two tall glasses of fruity deliciousness.

"It's some kind of fruit cocktail," Wyatt says, gesturing at the drinks. "I thought it'd be nice in this setting."

Hubert hands us the glasses, and I grin when Wyatt's hand doesn't tremor when he takes his glass.

"May I get you anything else, sir?" Hubert asks Wyatt.

Wyatt turns to me. "Do you want me to get security ready to drive us along the coast?"

"Only if you're feeling cooped up," I say, twirling the straw through the fruit cocktail. "At the moment, we have a rooftop pad completely to ourselves."

Wyatt clinks his glass against mine. "True." He nods at Hubert. "We're cool for now."

Hubert nods and then leaves the balcony terrace.

"It sure is dreamy out here," I say, eyes wandering along the pool. "And, heck, it is secluded."

Wyatt leans his walking cane against the glass panel of the balcony railing and rests his back against the rail. "This is cool. I'm standing outside. I haven't done this for weeks. I'm feeling good."

"It might be another slow day, but at least it's us choosing what we want to do. Nobody's here to boss us around."

Wyatt smirks. "And I've got that part handled. Learning I can threaten not to work has really come in handy."

I laugh, remembering Erika's deer-in-headlights look when Wyatt expressed his unhappiness with her presence.

Wyatt peels himself off the balcony railing and slips off his flip-flops. "Wanna sit by the pool's edge?"

"I can handle that."

I follow Wyatt over to the pool, carrying our drinks. Wyatt's in dark athletic shorts, making it easy for him to sink his legs into the water. I place our drinks on the tiled ground and shimmy my dress up so it doesn't touch the chlorinated water when I sit. The pool is heated to a delightful temperature, and we nestle together with our drinks in hand.

I take a sip of the most deliciously sweet drink I've ever tasted, and say, "A pool is more my speed than the beach, anyways."

"You always did opt for things with less people."

I bite my lip as I brush my arm against him. "With just one particular person was always the best."

"I hope you haven't been feeling alone since I left."

"It's okay. I mean, I have Kylie." I shrug, tapping the sides of the glass. "But she has a boyfriend now, so I see a little less of her."

"Do you like her boyfriend?"

I nod, liveliness thumping from my heart. "Yeah, he's great to her."

"That's good."

"He's tried to stop me from crushing on you. He was convinced none of us would ever see you again." I giggle, searching deep into Wyatt's eyes. "Guess I showed him."

Wyatt slouches. "So, no one thought I'd go back to Victoria Falls?"

I gesture at the cityscape and beach view. "Cherry Beach might beat Victoria Falls."

"I dunno. There are no mountains here."

"True. There's no place like home."

Wyatt hooks his pinky around mine. "I promise to visit home again."

I peck his cheek. "I believe you. But there's no rush."

He nods. "There's a, a lot of check ups lined up for me."

"Are you nervous about that?"

He rubs his knuckles against his chest. "I have th-this sinking feeling they're gonna ad-admit me back into the clinic."

I curl my arm around his. "Oh, Wyatt, that's not going to happen. You're making such good progress. You'll only go back to the clinic for routine check ups."

He pats my arm. "I, I just can't shake the feeling I'm gonna get thrown back in."

"Not possible. I didn't remember those three words during your tests, but you did. You've gotta give yourself more credit."

He sighs. "Without you, I make really dumb decisions."

"How can you say that?"

"Listening to my parents, for starters."

"You don't know what the other factors were in your life."

He clutches my hand. "I know I didn't have you."

I intertwine my fingers with his. "But you had your music. Remember how learning chords and lyrics helped you memorize things when you studied?"

Wyatt kicks his feet in the water. "It's the only thing I'm good at."

"Hmm. You're also good at kissing."

His shoulders jiggle with a laugh.

I squeeze his hand. "You're also in movies. You've remembered lines from a script. That's proof you're not dumb."

He waves off the subject. "I'm still weirded out by the idea of the movies."

"But you're cool talking about the music?"

"I like thinking about the covers. The stuff I remember practicing in front of you."

"That's my favorite stuff you've done. The new albums were great, but listening to the covers is like heaven to me."

"Did I record covers before I left for that show?"

I pull out my phone and open the playlist of Wyatt's songs. "No, but there are recordings from the show. It's like listening to you before you left town."

His eyes brighten with piqued interest. "Like the old covers I sang?"

"Yeah," I say, fidgeting in excitement. "Those covers are how you won the show. Don't you remember that I told you, you had a gift?"

He mumbles a laugh. "You always were my number one supporter."

"Still am." My finger hovers over a track. "Do you think you're up for listening to one? It could remind you of home."

"If I could handle a brand new song, I think I can handle an old one."

I play a cover he's guaranteed to remember. It's the one he'd practice the most whenever we'd hang out in his basement or my treehouse. As the song plays, his hand taps against the pool's edge. Thirty seconds into the track, Wyatt mumbles the words. Then the mumbles morph into a tune, and soon, he's singing along with his past self.

Goosebumps shoot down my arms, and my mouth falls open in awe. His voice is as incredible as ever. His eyes fall closed as his volume increases. There's not a hint of a stutter, and he doesn't miss a single lyric. A thrill races down my spine, and the need to pull him into my arms grows rapidly.

When the song finishes, I hit the pause button, and my mouth still hangs open.

"Wyatt, that was amazing," I stammer like the true fangirl I am. "My gosh, you didn't skip a beat. How did it feel?"

"Awesome." He gasps. "Truly, fr-freaking awesome."

I rub my arms. "Wow, my goosebumps aren't budging. Dang. It's like you're back to being concert ready."

He blushes. "I wouldn't go that far. Singing along is one thing, but playing to a cr-crowd. Hmm. I don't think I'm up for it."

"Can you imagine yourself playing sold-out shows?"

He blows out a breath, wonder dazzling in his eyes. "*Ha.* Umm, no. I still picture the school auditorium decorated for the annual talent show."

I nudge him, grinning. "So, do you believe me now that you're incredible?"

Wyatt's eyes sparkle. "I didn't miss a word. That's insane. Dr. Fincher should've been testing me on song lyrics and I would've been out of the clinic weeks ago."

My heart swells. "I'm sure he'll be super proud of you at your next check up."

I hate that Wyatt's been panicking about failing tests and being readmitted to the clinic. The trauma of repeating a grade in middle school has convinced him he's not smart. He's so much more than memorizing some words from a textbook. Once we figured out he learns best, he moved onto high school with me.

"You know, I can't stop thinking about your secret poetry."

I blush hard.

He gestures at the phone. "We've listened to me sing. Why don't we listen to your words?"

"I've never read my poetry aloud before."

Wyatt grins. "There's always a first time."

I set my phone aside and shake out my hands. "There are some lines I've been mulling inside my head. Sometimes I go over them a few times before writing them down."

"I'm cool with being a sounding board."

I close my eyes and take a settling breath.

"The space is big enough for me.

One hundred people fit here.

But I'm only happy if it's us.

Crowds will break my spirit.

But together, we bring the light."

I shake out my hands again, exhaling, and slowly opening my eyes.

Wyatt rubs his arms. "Wow, Josie. I got goosebumps."

I shy away. "Really?"

"I loved it."

"The phrasing still needs work."

He nudges me. "You should write song lyrics."

I cup a hand over my face and shake my head. "I don't think so."

"Okay, you're getting embarrassed." Wyatt tugs his T-shirt up his torso. "Wanna get in the water?"

"Uh." I gesture at my dress. "Not exactly pool attire."

He stretches his arms above his head, ripping the shirt off. "Did you bring a bathing suit?"

My mouth runs dry, eyeing the tattoo running along the inside of his arm. "Umm, no."

Wyatt slips into the water, and for a moment, my heart malfunctions.

Wading into the water, he beckons me in. "Come on in. You can have your dress washed afterwards."

Why is he being so irresistible right now? "Are you okay in the water?"

He nods, making his way through the water. "I did hydrotherapy at the clinic. As long as I can touch the bottom, I'm good."

"When I wanted to go to the beach, I had no intention of getting in the water. Chlorination doesn't exactly beat saltwater."

Wyatt moves closer to me and reaches for my thighs. "Come on, Josie-posey. The water won't hurt you."

He was already transfixing me before he was touching my legs. With a shiver, I gulp my fear, and nod at him. I slip into his arms, moving into the perfectly blue water, illuminated by the lighting hidden amongst the turquoise tiles.

A throaty laugh hums out of him, and his arms wrap around my middle. "Not so bad, is it?"

I plant my hands on his shoulders. "Experiencing anything with you isn't so bad."

His hands lower, and he hoists me against him. "Thanks for sharing a sneak peek of your poetry."

"No problem. I feel safe with you." I pat his arms. "Should you be holding me up?"

He tilts his head, smiling adorably. "You have an objection?"

Butterflies flitter through me. "No, of course not. I'm just checking if you're okay."

He carries me toward the side, resting my back against the pool's edge as his arms cinch around my waist. "I feel a lot stronger in the water."

I smile. "So we should make coming in here a habit?"

He looks through the water ripples at my dress. "You should probably get a bathing suit then."

"I need to get more clothes in general. I didn't pack enough to extend my stay."

"Were you planning on leaving right away?"

"To be honest, I didn't think you'd want me to stay. I thought it was just a trip down memory lane, then you'd get back to your celebrity lifestyle."

"Have I proven to you I can do both? I'm not bringing just anyone from school into my penthouse."

I giggle, running a finger along his tattoo. "I'm glad you have a sense of humor about this."

His eyes follow me, tracing the Sanskrit letters inked on his skin. "I get that you were on edge because we hadn't seen each other in so long. I don't know how I'd feel if you called me up after t-two years of radio silence."

"Well, we wouldn't have this view if you hadn't gone and become famous." I motion toward the majestic display over the clear drop of the infinity pool. "This is pretty special, Wyatt. There would only be a handful of people who get to experience this."

He leans in and kisses my cheek, making his way to my lips. He purrs near my mouth, "I'm so glad you're here with me."

I kiss him back. "Anytime you need me, I'm here."

Sixteen

After wringing out my dress several times, and wrapping myself in a towel, I still drip water inside the apartment.

"Sorry, Hubert," Wyatt says as we make our way into the living space. "We're making more mess for you to clean up."

"It's not a problem," Hubert says kindly. "I hope you had a lovely time in the pool."

"We did," I say, bundling the towel tighter around me.

"May I get you anything?" Hubert asks. "Some robes, perhaps?"

Wyatt slings his towel over his shoulder and steadies himself with his walking cane. "I'm gonna get in the shower. But, hey, is there anywhere close by where Josie can buy new clothes?"

"Yes, sir," Hubert says, standing with beyond perfect posture. "This hotel is on Royale Boulevard, surrounded by several boutiques."

I grit my teeth and then sigh. "Royale Boulevard boutiques don't exactly sound like they're in my price range."

Wyatt smirks. "Not exactly a mall, is it?"

Hubert clears his throat. "Many of the boutiques have chargeback facilities with the Gran Palacio Hotel. It won't be a problem for Miss Bartlett to charge the items back to the penthouse."

Wyatt's eyes brighten. "Awesome. Let's do that."

I lift my hands in unease. "No way. I can't do that."

"Joze, let the management team pay for the clothes," Wyatt says, careful to move slowly as he leaves a trail of water on the floor. "Besides, I'm the reason you're staying longer than you intended."

I grin. "Didn't take much convincing."

"Still, I don't want you paying for designer threads. Erika can do that."

"I don't want to take advantage."

Wyatt shrugs. "Your money's no good here."

"So, you actually wanna go clothes shopping with me?"

He grins. "Sure, why not? Wanna meet up after our showers and check them out?"

"It's a date."

After my shower, I slip my saturated dress into a laundry bag for another wash. My curls are flat after washing the chlorine from my hair, and I make sure my makeup is on point. Back home, the clerks at the boutiques can be ultra-snooty. So I can only imagine it's a level above on Royale Boulevard. Even if I'm shopping with Wyatt, I want to look a smidge like I belong.

Wyatt attempts a whistle when we meet in the living area. "Dang, Joze. Looking good."

My blush is lightning fast. "Thanks, Wyatt. You're looking dreamy yourself."

He's in a dark blue button-down, dark denim jeans, and navy trainers. His sandy hair is styled to the right, and something about it makes his hazel eyes pop.

He steps forward, leaning on his cane. His left arm bends into a wing. "Shall we?"

I hook arms with him, and we move toward the elevator. Two security guards stand by the elevator, and they step inside with us as we descend to the ground floor. On the way down, I can't help staring at the partial tattoo dipping below his shirt sleeve.

Wyatt chuckles. "What is it?"

I jolt, embarrassed. "I'm sorry. It's just seeing that tattoo in real life. Just reminds me of how much you've grown up."

Wyatt's eyebrow crooks, looking me up and down. "Could say the same thing about you, Joze. You're a knockout."

My blush intensifies.

Wyatt brushes a hand over the tattoo. "I think about the ink a lot. I really want to remember what it felt like."

"I'm sure it'll come back to you."

"No, I'm legitimately thinking about getting another tattoo."

I gawk at him. "What? Like, now?"

He smirks. "Soon."

"Whoa."

"And I know what I want." Wyatt turns the inside of his arm up, and traces the space above his wrist. "I'm getting a J there."

I jitter as his hand draws an invisible J over the space. "R-r-really?"

Wyatt lets out a nervous laugh. "I want something that reminds me of you, every second of the day."

"But it's so permanent."

He plants a kiss on me. "That's the point."

I shiver as my heartbeat pounds in my ears. "Oh my gosh."

The elevator doors ping open and security lets us enter the lobby first. We make our way past the front desk, and toward the front revolving doors.

"First things first." Wyatt squeezes my hand and grins ear to ear. "I haven't ventured out anywhere in so long. This place is supposed to be fancy, right?"

"Uber fancy," I gush. "Only the best for Wyatt Hayes."

The doorman tips his hat as we carefully descend the front steps of the Gran Palacio.

Wyatt cranes his neck, taking in the bustling traffic. "All this is happening so close to that epic beach."

"Yeah, it's so crowded. It's hard to believe the ocean we were checking out upstairs is so close."

Wyatt gestures across the pavement. "Shall we find you a new wardrobe?"

I giggle and curl my arm around his. "One new outfit will be more than enough."

He winks. "Maybe three new outfits." He then lobs his walking cane at one of his security guards. "Keep a hold of this for me. I don't need it right now."

I slip my fingers between his. "You sure?"

He kisses my cheek. "Positive."

I giggle again, blushing hard. "Okay, let's shop."

We edge our way across the sidewalk, letting the heavy foot traffic side step us. With Wyatt ditching his walking aid, I don't want him weaving between people and having a spill. I can already hear Erika's lecture if anything happens to Wyatt on my watch.

Wyatt's eyebrows wiggle as we approach a boutique. "This looks swanky. Wanna go in?"

"I feel out of place just standing in front of it."

He nudges me. "We're charging it to the room, remember? Let's just look around. If you don't feel comfortable, we'll leave."

"Okay." Heck, there's no reason to feel uncomfortable with Wyatt by my side.

As we move toward the entrance, something catches the corner of my eye. I lift my gaze and spy two girls pointing and whispering with looks of surprised glee on their faces.

Oh boy.

"What are you looking at?" Wyatt asks, reaching for the boutique's front door.

I motion behind me. "Those girls."

"What about them?"

I smirk. "They're checking you out."

He points at his chest with surprise. "Me?"

I giggle. "We've been clocked by Wyatt Hayes fans."

"Oh," he mutters.

He checks over my shoulder, and his smile grows. He waves at the girls and then laughs at their excited squeals.

Wyatt takes my hand and tugs me into the store. "C'mon, let's go in."

"You good?"

He sweeps his hand over his sandy hair. "Absolutely."

I watch Wyatt with curiosity as one of the security guards enters the store with us, and the other remains outside. The interior of the store takes my breath away. The display cases have gold accents, the walls are a rich cream, and the clothes hang like priceless pieces of art.

"Good morning," a salesperson says, making her way over. "Are you kids in the right..." Her tone suggests we're in the wrong place, until she makes eye contact with Wyatt. Her chin drops, and she utters a few indistinguishable syllables. "Excuse me," she clears her throat. "Welcome to our store. My name is Sonja, and I'd be delighted to help you today."

Wyatt gently swings my hand. "Josie's the one shopping today."

In reaction, my shoulders bunch up, and heat streaks across my face.

"Certainly," Sonja replies. "What are you looking for today?"

"*Ahhh,*" I stammer. "I need a new outfit, but I'm not really sure this is my style."

Sonja smooths down her blazer and turns to a nearby rack. "I wouldn't necessarily say that. You're a well put together young lady. Perhaps something from the new Aisha Karen collection would complement your features nicely."

The new Aisha Karen? She was about to kick us out for being "kids" mere seconds ago. Now, she wants to dress me in something from one of the most famous designers ever?

"Allow me," Sonja says, moving toward a rack of stylish items.

"Whoa," breathes out of Wyatt.

I follow his line of sight to the back of the store, and my skin prickles with goosebumps. Holy heck! Rachael Roman is posing in a sheer, blush-pink dress in front of a floor-length mirror.

"She's that movie star, right?" Wyatt mutters out of the side of his mouth.

"Mm-hmm," I reply, pinching myself.

Distracting us from our ogling, Sonja returns with her selection. Draping it against herself by the hanger, she displays a cream, scoop-neck maxi dress, cinched around the waist with a braided bronze belt.

Wyatt's mouth falls open as he smiles. "Joze, you'd look amazing in that."

Sonja's gaze slides left, double-checking Wyatt is real. No doubt she's been keeping up online about him, just like everyone else. This is the first time anyone from the public would've seen him up and about.

On instinct, I look over my shoulder at the front windows for fans or paparazzi. I sigh and turn back to the clothing when the foot traffic continually moves along the sidewalk as it did before.

Okay, there is an award-winning actress in the store. Maybe no one cares about a teen heartthrob entering the boutique.

"You okay?" Wyatt asks, rubbing my upper arm.

I shrug. "It's a beautiful dress, but I don't think it's me."

"No sweat," Wyatt says, hugging his arm around my lower back. "I said we'd leave if you weren't feeling it."

Sonja's chin drops. "But... but..."

Wyatt nods at Sonja. "Thanks for your time, but we're gonna check out another place."

Sonja's face flushes as she gulps and nods in reply.

Security follows us out as Wyatt's hand nestles on my back. Once we hit the sidewalk. Wyatt bursts into laughter.

I grab on to his arm, smiling. "What is it?"

"We, we…" He catches his breath as we move away from the storefront. "We bailed on a store that a real-deal celebrity was in. Seriously, what planet are we living on?"

"I know. It doesn't seem real."

"You were right. We didn't exactly fit in back there."

"Well, you did," I clarify as security follows us along the busy sidewalk. "Didn't you notice how Sonja kept eyeballing you?"

"Because I was some kid in her store."

"No, because you were *Wyatt Hayes* in her store."

"No way am I in the same league as Rach… Uh, what's her name again?"

"Rachael Roman. Ah, seeing her gave me goosebumps."

"She's one of the all-time greats."

I wrap an arm around him and lean my head on his shoulder as we walk. "I'd still rewatch one of your movies over one of hers."

"Because you like fluffy rom-coms over three-hour dramas."

"I bet you, Rachael knows who you are."

He puffs a laugh, his shoulders tightening. "There's no way."

I giggle, tugging on his arm. "Wanna go back and find out?"

"Are you crazy?" he lowers his voice, his face glowing red. "I'm not going back there. How embarrassing."

I giggle again. "I didn't know big-time celebrities got embarrassed."

"Rachael is A-list. She's big-time."

"I have a feeling I saw a video of her lip-syncing to one of your songs."

He scoffs. "Whatever."

"Don't you remember those girls who were ogling you earlier? You're famous, remember?"

He goes redder. "Joze, don't. Seriously, you're freaking me out. I mean, it's Rach, Rachael Freaking Ray-Ramon."

I grin wider and kiss his heated cheek. "Okay, cutie. I'll stop teasing."

Wyatt turns me toward a storefront. "Quick, let's go in here. I need a subject change."

I send him a wink. "I bet there will be another sales clerk who'll be going gaga over you."

Wyatt rolls his eyes, following me into the store. There's a funky techno beat playing overhead, the floor tiles have a high shine, and there's a dramatic lighting design highlighting the different sections of the store.

Compared to the previous boutique, this one has a more youthful, energetic feel. It's still a little too hyped for my liking, but I might be able to find clothes that fit my preppy aesthetic.

"Mr. Hayes," an enthusiastic voice calls out. A woman of about twenty-five dashes towards us, her shiny black pumps clicking against the tiles. "It's so incredible to see you again."

Wyatt reluctantly shakes her hand. "Ah, thanks."

She plants a hand on her chest. "My name is Marsha. You probably don't remember me."

Wyatt winces. "Ah, no, sorry. B-but, it's not because you're for-forgettable or anything."

Marsha sucks in a breath, her face growing a shade paler. "I've been following online about your recovery. I'm so sorry you've been out of action for so long. It must be killing you not to be performing."

Wyatt scratches the side of his head, trying to rid his discomfort. "Uh, yeah."

"Sorry, it's probably the last thing you want to talk about. I've been such a fan since Talent Quest, and it's such a thrill to see you again."

"And how do we...?"

"We actually worked together."

Wyatt's eyebrows lift. "We did?"

She cups a hand around her forehead and averts her eyes bashfully. "Umm, yeah, well, kinda, I guess." She shakes her head, lowering her hand. "Oh my gosh, sorry. I'm totally losing my cool. I mean, we get celebrities and high-profile clients here all the time. I should be able to keep it together. But, umm, Wyatt, you have me falling apart."

Wyatt glances at me and then back at her. "Oh, ah, sorry?"

She giggles, swatting a hand. "Don't apologize. It's my bad. I can't keep my fangirl in check."

"*Sooo*," he draws out the word. "How did we work together?"

"It was on the set of 'Without You,'" Marsha replies, composing herself. "I worked in the wardrobe department; fitting you, Portia, and Simon McAlister."

Wyatt nods, trying to act like it rings any bells.

"Anyway, I moved away from sets and found a place in retail," she says. "I actually feel more at home here."

"That's awesome."

"Do you and the other Circle 8 guys still hang out?" Marsha asks. "You all looked so close when I'd see you between scenes."

Wyatt glances at me again. "*Ahhh.*"

"Well, you haven't seen them in a while, right?" I say, hoping to help.

Marsha's eyes widen with intrigue. "They didn't visit you when you were in..."

Wyatt folds his arms, and his jaw flexes as he shakes his head.

"I think they're all busy," I tell Marsha. "Wyatt hasn't been working, so I think they've been working the other Circle 8 kids really hard."

She presses her lips into a line and nods sheepishly. "Sorry, it's none of my business. I shouldn't have asked."

"It's okay," Wyatt says. "You were being super nice about it. I, I just had no idea wh-what to say."

"Well, it's great to see you again. Are you staying close by?"

Wyatt hangs a thumb over his shoulder. "Yeah, in one of the hotels."

"The Gran Palacio?" Marsha questions. "I think you guys stayed at that hotel for the 'Without You' press tour. I remember the paparazzi kept trying to snap you and Portia together." Marsha covers her mouth, letting out a soft chuckle. "Poor Simon got no attention."

"Oh," it draws out of me. "I've seen those pictures. Oh my gosh, I think it was the same hotel. How did I never put that together?"

Wyatt shrugs, again having no answers.

Marsha extends her hand to me. "I'm sorry, I haven't caught your name yet."

I shake her hand. "Josie."

She smiles, glancing at Wyatt. "Are you Wyatt's new PA?"

I mumble a laugh. "Ah, sure."

Wyatt clicks his tongue. "Umm, no. She's my girlfriend."

My jaw drops faster than Marsha's.

Wyatt.

Freaking.

Hayes.

Called.

Me.

His.

Girlfriend.

He smirks, searching deep into my eyes. "That's okay to say, right?"

I nod eagerly, my grin stretching to reach my ears. "Ah-huh."

Wyatt smiles, curling his hand around mine and giving it a gentle swing.

"I'm sorry," Marsha rushes. "I just... You..." She clears her throat, regaining composure. "I just didn't realize you and Portia... Umm, never mind."

Queasiness ripples through my stomach.

Portia.

Everyone thinks Wyatt and Portia are together, despite them never having made it official in the press. And Marsha saw them together on the set of their rom-com. She has a first-hand account of their relationship.

Crap. I'm totally making out with some other girl's boyfriend.

No, not *some* other girl. A freaking model/actress/singer.

I swallow hard, resisting the urge to hurl onto the shiny floor.

Wyatt squeezes my hand. "I'm not dating anyone named Portia."

"I'm sorry," Marsha rushes, mortified. "I'll keep my fangirl in check. I've just been a touch obsessed with you and Portia. When I heard you were making another movie together, I almost called to get my old job back."

Wyatt's eyebrow raises. "But you're happy working here, right?"

Marsha nods. "Yes. I'm so sorry for being inappropriate. It's really none of my business who you date." She looks at me and smiles. "But you two do look awfully cute together."

Wyatt gestures at me. "Josie is the one shopping today."

Marsha beams. "I'd love to help you out today. Do you have a particular style in mind?"

"Nothing too flashy," I say, distracted by the lighting display in the corner of the store.

"And we're staying in the penthouse at the Gran Palacio," Wyatt adds. "Can you charge everything back to the room?"

"Not a problem. I'll just need your signature on the invoice before you leave." Marsha snaps her fingers and turns toward the counter. "I just got some new arrivals in, Josie, that might be perfect for you. Give me one moment."

When Marsha moves back to the counter to unwrap her new stock, Wyatt clasps my hand and waits for me to meet his eyes.

"I saw you get rattled," he whispers. "You know it's only you in my heart, right?"

I lift on my tippy toes and peck his lips. "I do. I should be over the moon that you called me your girlfriend. I don't want anyone else's comments to ruin things."

Wyatt eyes Marsha, muttering, "Does she make you uncomfortable? We can leave."

"No, it's fine. If we go to another store, there will just be another salesperson who'll bend over backwards to kiss your feet."

Wyatt mumbles a laugh. "*Eww.*"

I laugh with him until I catch discomfort in his body language. "Hey, you okay?"

Wyatt turns to me for clarification. "Circle 8 is my management team, right?"

"Yeah. I think they're Circle 8 Management, and the stars are Circle 8."

"Huh?"

"Circle 8 is the name of your group," I explain. "Like, all you teen stars who signed with them are called the Circle 8 kids. They're like your colleagues."

"Oh. So, Portia is Circle 8?"

"Mm-hmm. There's 8 of you. Hence the name."

"And if one of us leaves?"

I shrug. "They get replaced. You replaced someone."

He winces. "I did?"

"Yep. And someone else was replaced a few months ago."

"Sounds like a machine."

Marsha beckons me closer. She shows me a few new pieces, and also walks me along the clothing racks. We narrow down my style, and she helps select a few outfits for me to try on in the fitting room.

As I walk around with Marsha, I can't help keeping an eye on Wyatt. He's just so effortlessly gorgeous. His arms fold around his middle, and his gaze wanders the clothes with slight curiosity. When Marsha picks out a short-sleeve, white knit crop top and pairs it with a lilac and mauve tartan skirt, both my eyes leave Wyatt. The outfit is super cute, so I take it and two other outfits to the fitting room.

As I enter my stall, the giggles of two girls break my concentration. I pull back the curtain two inches and watch the girls link arms as they slink their way toward Wyatt.

"Umm, hi," one girl says, followed by a mass of nervous laughter.

Wyatt warily lifts a hand. "Hi."

"Oh my gosh," the other girl gushes. "It's really you."

Wyatt clutches his elbows, and his posture straightens. "Have we met?"

This sends the girls into another fit of giggles.

"Ah, no," one says, clutching her friend. "I can't believe this is happening."

"We're huge fans," her friend gushes.

Wyatt combs his fingers through his hair, and the girls almost collapse. "Well, thanks."

The girls raise their phones and ask in unison, "Can we get a photo?"

As if on cue, Wyatt's security guard approaches the three of them.

"It's okay," Wyatt tells the man in all-black. He then smiles at the girls and lifts his index finger. "One photo."

I grip the wall of the fitting room as my heart thunders in my chest.

One girl flings her phone at the security guard. "Take a photo of us, will you?"

The security guard presses his lips into a hard line, but obliges. The girls gather at Wyatt's side, pressing their bodies against him as they squeal, "*Cheese*," at the phone's camera.

Wyatt's grin grows, reveling in the adoration from the two girls.

The security guard gives the phone back. "Okay, ladies. Time to step back."

"Thank you so much, Wyatt," one girl gushes, as she and her friend step backwards.

The other girl sneakily lifts her phone and presses the side button. "Yeah." She giggles. "This was awesome."

As my stomach fights its way toward my esophagus, I pull the velvet curtain closed. With shaky hands, I force myself to try on the different outfits. I barely look at myself, emerging in my final look, the white knitted crop and purple tartan skirt.

Wyatt's jaw drops. "Wow, Joze, you look adorable."

I clasp my hands in front, hoping against hope I don't appear as awkward as I feel.

He takes my hands and notices the clamminess. "Whoa. What's up? Geez, you look so pale."

"It's nothing. I'm fine."

"Joze?"

"Really, I'm fine."

"Not buying it."

I sigh hard. "Those girls," I say, sliding helplessly into awkwardness. "Were you okay with them coming up to you?"

"You mean those two?" he says, looking at the door, signaling they've already left the store. "It was harmless."

"It's random people wanting a photo with you."

"You're the one who reminded me I'm famous."

"Yeah, I know, but it was your first real interaction with fans. It had to feel intense."

Wyatt smiles and shrugs. "I dunno. I kinda liked it."

I brace myself. "You did?"

"Makes sense." He shrugs again. "How else would I become famous if I didn't like the attention? I always imagined interacting with people when I used to practice my songs. It's wild that this is now for real."

I squeeze his hand, clamminess be damned. "As long as you're okay."

He leans in and kisses my cheek. "Well, I'm okay, but clearly you're not. I hate seeing you so shaken up."

I sigh again. "I'll be fine knowing you're not freaking out."

He grins. "I swear, I'm not freaking out in the slightest."

One of the many knots in my stomach unravels.

"So, I hope you're getting this outfit," he says, swinging my hands out to the side, "because you look gorgeous."

"Can I remove the tags?" Marsha asks, sidling up to us. "You can wear it out of the store."

"That'd be great," I reply. "And I'll take the other two outfits too."

"Excellent," Marsha says. "I'll wrap them up and have them delivered to the penthouse."

"Thanks for your help," Wyatt says to Marsha. "And nice to see you again, I guess."

Marsha hums a laugh. "The pleasure is all mine, Mr. Hayes."

As Marsha collects the clothes I came into the store wearing, plus my new clothes, Wyatt and I get ready to leave.

"Sir," the security guard says, raising a hand to stop Wyatt and I moving toward the door. "We have a situation."

"A sit-situation?" Wyatt stammers.

"Seems word has gotten out that you're on the strip," the security guard says. "A crowd of fans are outside."

Wyatt smirks. "A *crowd* of fans? Get outta here."

I gulp. "A crowd?"

"My associate has kept them back to make a clear path for you," security continues. "Or, if you like, I can ask the salesperson if there's a back entrance we can take."

Wyatt cranes his neck, checking out the people milling on the sidewalk. "Hmm, I dunno if I need to escape."

Security motions to the front door. "I can escort you out if you want to do a meet and greet."

Wyatt mumbles a laugh, shaking his head. "There's really a crowd? For me?"

I grab his forearm. "You really love this?"

He turns to me. "Huh?"

"The fame. You're into this?"

His eyes sparkle and his lips quirk into an electrified smile. "My dream really happened," he whispers. "I used to play covers at the school talent show, and now there's a crowd of people wanting to meet me. How is this real?"

My knees knock together. "You don't have to go out there, if you don't want to."

"Are you kidding?" he beams. "Meeting those girls lit a spark in me. Imagine the boost I'll get when I go out there." He gasps and clutches my hand. "What if my memory comes back?"

I shiver at the thought.

His smile wains. "Why don't you look happy?"

I squeeze his hand. "No, I am. Of course, I want your memory to come back. I'm just scared for you. It could be a shock or jarring for you."

Wyatt leans in and pecks my cheek. "I'll be okay, Josie. I promise."

I swallow hard and nod. "Then don't leave your fans waiting."

He shakes out his arms and blows out a breath. "Wish me luck."

I fake an elated smile. "You don't need it, superstar."

He clutches my hand. "You're coming with me."

I slip my hand out of his. "I'll follow behind. They're here for you, after all."

He frowns. "You don't want to come with me?"

I frown back at him. "You know I don't like crowds."

He fakes a smile, but not as well as I do. "Yeah, of course. Sorry, Josie."

The security pulls open the front door. "Ready, sir?"

Wyatt nods and moves toward the door. "Ready."

Seventeen

The adrenaline hits me, and I shiver as Wyatt greets the hyped crowd. I really thought he might shy away from all this. I remember all those late-night phone calls where he'd need a pep talk to film the next day's episode of Talent Quest. It made sense he'd be scared of the limelight when he's suffering from short-term amnesia.

But he clearly loves this. And now, with the thought of his memory coming back, he's ecstatic. There's nothing more I want than him being one-hundred percent healthy. *Ugh.* I just got the old Wyatt back and I'm terrified of losing him. He's already intoxicated by the fame, and I don't have the stomach to follow him into the spotlight.

My stomach cramps as I slink out of the store. I shimmy myself behind the security and want to hurl as Wyatt listens to his fans gush about how much they love him. This isn't anything new. I've seen footage of these interactions online. My heart melts for him, knowing his music and his performances have moved people. I want everyone to experience his talent. But...

The dry heaves won't stop.

"We heard you had some kind of memory loss," says one girl in the crowd.

"Yeah, is it true?" another girl asks. "Did you forget that you're famous?"

The question makes Wyatt smile, and he murmurs a laugh. "I'll tell ya," he says, scribbling his name on a piece of paper, "after being cooped up in, in a hospital room for weeks, th-th-this all sure feels new to me."

The crowd is circling him and I swear they're sucking up all the oxygen in the street. *Gah.* Is something tied around my throat? *Ouch.* I'm being strangled from the inside out. I press my sweaty palms against the wall behind me, propping myself up before I mutate into a ghostly white puddle on the pavement.

One girl collapses in tears. "Oh my gosh," she wails at Wyatt. "I can't believe you've been so sick. I hate this. It's not fair. I never want you to be sick!"

"Hey, hey," Wyatt coos, rubbing the girl's shoulder. "I'm good. See? Don't cry. I'm okay."

The girl sniffs hard and smiles as tears streak her face. "I just love you so much," she sobs. "I don't ever want you to be hurt. I'd full-on die."

Wyatt recoils. "No, no, you won't."

She smears wet mascara across her cheeks. "Yes, I will."

"I'm so glad you enjoy my music, but no one's dying over me."

The crowd pushes in tighter and I gasp for air. I trip backwards, as the shopfront wall ends, leaving nothing for me to lean on. I shrink, hunching forward and hugging my cramping belly. A rush of girls race into the crowd, knocking into me so hard I almost fall forward.

"We need you to finish your movie," another girl blurts. "I need to see it, like, yesterday."

Wyatt turns to this girl. "You like the movies better than the music?"

She shrinks under his eye contact. "Umm, yeah. I mean, I replay your first album, like, every day, but I live for the movies."

Wyatt tilts his head thoughtfully. "Huh."

I stumble backward, teary-eyed and shaken from the mass of voices and lack of space. I keep moving backward, feeling my heart being ripped away from the guy of my dreams.

"Okay, everybody," one of the security guards says in a no-nonsense tone, "time to back it up. You've occupied enough of Wyatt's time."

A collective "*Aww*," whines from the group.

Wyatt waves to them as he ducks behind his security. "Thank you so much for reaching out to me. This was really fun."

Local police officers join the scene, and the crowd disperses as Wyatt and his security make their way toward me, three shop fronts away.

Wyatt moves with a spring in his step. "What a rush."

I quickly wipe under my eyes and blink a few times before he can take me in.

"Maybe I should stop giving Lexy the brush off and actually do something to publicly address my fans," he says, his gaze off to the side as his thoughts carry him away. "That was such a rush. Like, addictively good."

"That's so good to hear."

Wyatt catches the tremor in my tone, and his eyes finally meet mine. "Crap. You're not okay."

"What? No, I'm..."

He cuts me off, pulling me into his arms with a tight embrace. "I'm sorry. I sh-shouldn't have left you."

"You were excited," I mumble into his shoulder. "It's so good to see you so alive."

"But you're scared."

"I have you." I pull my arms around him, pressing my fingers into his back. "As long as I get to be with you, everything will be okay."

He strokes my hair and kisses the top of my head. "You're ev-everything to me, Josie. I promise to get you to safety before ever doing that again."

"It's okay," I whisper. "It wasn't planned. I get it."

He pulls his arms away and tilts his head to view my face. "We should've gone out the back. You were sh-shaken up when it was just t-two girls in a store. I'm a dang idiot."

I caress his face. "Don't do that to yourself. You were excited. I didn't want to take that away from you." I suck in a breath. "Your memory. Did anything come back to you?"

He shakes his head. "Nope. It all felt new. But…" He bites his lip as he thinks about it. "It felt normal, if that makes sense. Like, comfortable. Like, I'd done it before. Does that make sense?"

I lift onto my tippy toes and squeal in delight. "That's amazing. So, in a way, something did come back to you."

He grins. "I guess."

I lean in and kiss him. "This makes it all worth it."

His eyebrow raises. "*All* worth it? I think we could do without any Josie panic attacks. Don't you?"

I bite the inside of my cheek, lowering onto my heels like a limp balloon. "Yeah, I agree."

"Let me make this up to you." He smooths his hands against the sides of my face. "You're looking fab, so why don't we turn this into a real date and find a nice restaurant?"

"I could go for something to eat. Why don't we check out the restaurants back to the hotel?" I suggest. "Randall said they had some of the best food."

Wyatt winces. "The hotel? I don't want to risk running into Erika and the other suits. This is supposed to be our day away from them, remember?"

I sigh. "Yeah, you're right."

"We'll just get a nice, quiet table in a cozy corner," he says, hooking an arm around my shoulders. "What do you say? We'll find somewhere romantic."

I shiver with delight. "Romantic?"

"Sure," he beams. "I want to spoil you, and this is our first time out as an official couple."

"Well, okay. If we find somewhere not too overcrowded, it sounds good to me."

He wiggles his eyebrows. "Just good?"

I giggle and peck his cheek. "It sounds stupendous."

He laughs. "Now that's a top-tier word."

"Sir," one of the security guards pipes up. "If you want to dine somewhere your fans won't bother you, there's an Italian restaurant up the block you and the Circle 8 crew like."

"How do you know the fans won't be there?" Wyatt asks.

The security guard smirks. "They're priced out."

I wince. "Can we afford it?"

"Like I said," the security guard replies, "the Circle 8 crew are regulars. All the bills go straight onto the account."

Wyatt wriggles his eyebrows. "What do you say, Joze? Wanna get spoiled?"

I hesitate to smile. "We aren't just taking advantage?"

"C'mon," Wyatt coaxes. "You just went through hell. Why not take advantage of the fame perks you'll actually enjoy?"

I look over my shoulder at where the fans had flocked. I really don't want to wait around for round two.

With a shrug, I reply, "Why not?"

Security takes us to the restaurant, and inside I'm immediately relaxed by the soft piano music, cozy lighting, and lack of wandering eyes ogling my boyfriend.

My boyfriend.

Still can't get enough of that.

"Do you have a reservation?" the hostess asks the couple in front of us.

"No," the man says. "We were hoping you'd have room to fit us in."

"I'm sorry, sir," the hostess replies. "We are booked solid. I can offer you a seat at the bar."

As the couple in front weigh up their options of a bar stool or leaving the premises, Wyatt gives me an uneasy look.

"Oops," he mutters. "Looks like we walked into the wrong place."

As the couple in front of us turn and leave, Wyatt gestures at the door, signaling for us to follow them out.

"Oh, Mr. Hayes," the hostess says, stopping us in our tracks. "Welcome back."

"Oh, umm, hi," Wyatt says with a wave.

She beckons us over. "Would you like to dine with us today?"

"We were hoping to, but you're booked…"

"Give me one moment," the hostess cuts in. "I'll have a server get your table ready."

Wyatt and I share bewildered glances.

The hostess nods at Wyatt's security. "I can give you gentlemen a space at the rear of the dining room."

The security nods in approval.

The hostess has a server show us to a table for two, where security can keep tabs on us. After we're seated and handed menus, we thank the server, who gives us a few moments to look things over.

Wyatt lowers his menu. "I didn't take any notice of prices in the clothing store, but have you seen the ones here? *Cha-ching.*"

"What are you worried about, Mr. Hollywood?"

"Hey, it's just a bit different from getting burgers back home," Wyatt jokes. "That's all I'm saying."

"I know. I'm trying to act like I belong." I clear my throat and put on a phony posh accent. "Ah, yes. Forty dollars for a salad. That seems right."

Wyatt snorts a laugh, composing himself as a server approaches our table.

"Hello, my name is Diana, and I'll be your server today," she says, hands clasped in front of the waist. "My management would like to welcome you back to our establishment by comping your bill today. Please, order to your heart's content. It's a pleasure to have you here, Mr. Hayes, and your companion as well."

My chin drops as I look at Wyatt with wonder.

"Oh, thanks, but we can…"

Diana demurely waves a hand. "No need, Mr. Hayes. You're our valued guest. We're glad you're on the road to recovery and want to celebrate this with you. Now, may I start with your drinks?"

"Ah, yeah, sure," Wyatt splutters.

Diana grins. "Shall I bring over your usual bottle of champagne?"

Wyatt chokes on air. "Uh, uh, what?"

"We have your usual order chilled on ice," Diana replies.

Wyatt shares my apprehensiveness. "Uh, I don't think we want champagne."

"Not a problem. Come to think of it, the champagne was only ordered when you were with Miss Portia."

Ugh. There's that name again, like a stab in the gut.

Wyatt tilts his head, sighing as he takes in the hurt on my face. I force a smile for his sake. It's not his fault he has a past. Obviously, he and Portia have spent a lot of time together because they work together. I've seen all the event photos. Heck, some of them are on my walls. But I hate that everyone brings her up in front of me, like I'm completely invisible.

Diana fidgets as if she's reading the awkwardness growing from the table. "Or, would you like me to suggest a nice bottle of wine?"

I clear my throat, wading in discomfort. "Uh, you give alcohol to minors?"

Diana splutters some syllables, pivoting between me and Wyatt as a sheen coats her forehead.

"Well, I'm on medication," Wyatt says, shifting in his seat as the awkwardness grows. "And I feel very seventeen right now. So it's no alcohol for me."

"Certainly, sir," Diana says, composing herself after finally getting the hint. "We have a range of non-alcoholic drinks. Perhaps you and your companion would like a mocktail?"

A nervous laugh splutters out of me. "Like a Shirley Temple?"

Diana smiles. "Absolutely. Would you like one?"

I shrug. "I've never had one. No time like the present."

"And for you, sir?"

"Just a diet coke, thanks."

Diana nods. "Not a problem. I'll have them brought over."

Diana hurries away, and I can't help smirking. "I think she wants you to be an out-of-control teen celebrity."

"I don't want to talk about that." Wyatt mutters, struggling to meet my eyes. "I saw that look in your eyes."

"What? About the wine?"

Wyatt frowns. "No, not that. I wish you wouldn't get jealous over a name."

"It's not just a name. You two have history."

"But we don't have a present," he replies. "She's never called or visited. And I don't miss her."

"You don't remember her."

"I didn't remember meeting fans, and I felt like I found something I'd been missing."

I slouch in my seat. "What if it's like that when you see her? What if she's the missing link to you getting your memory back?"

"There's no chance," he says firmly. "You're the girl I woke up thinking about. You're the only one who makes me feel better."

"But everyone…"

"I don't care what everyone says," he says wholeheartedly. "All that matters is what we think."

My heart swells, and I reach across and find his hand. "I'm yours no matter what happens."

He lifts my hand and kisses it. "You're beautiful, Josie. I don't want you to ever think you're second-best."

Our drinks arrive, and we instinctively clink our glasses together. Diana talks us into the Alfredo pasta, where the sauce is made from cashew nuts, which we share with a side of mushroom and truffle arancini balls. It's officially one of the best meals I've ever tasted. How will I ever be able to go back home and eat diner food?

As our plates begin to clear, I enjoy the safety in Wyatt's presence. Being amongst that mob of fans was terrifying, but being stripped away from Wyatt's company was worse. I lean into our closeness, sharing with him three more poems stashed in my Notes app.

"My goodness, Josie," Wyatt says in awe. "You have a real talent. Your words make me feel things, like my favorite songs do."

I'm giddy with his praise.

"They top a fantastic meal." Wyatt lowers his cutlery. "Diana was right. That's the best thing on the menu. I don't need to try anything else."

"What about the desserts?"

"Oh, we are *so* getting dessert."

I giggle. "I'm not sure I can fit it."

"Oh, c'mon. I'm here to spoil my beautiful girlfriend."

My heart flutters as I stare at him adoringly.

We're not just collage clippings on my bedroom wall anymore.

I'm finally his girlfriend.

Wow.

Wyatt loves me.

"Get used to it," Wyatt says, his hazel eyes sparkling. "You're back in my world, and it's only the best for you."

"Well, I like all this stuff when it's just us," I say, fingers trembling against the linen napkin. "But I can't see myself fully being part of your world. You saw me cower from all those people. I can't be around anything like that."

"But no one's asking you to." He reaches across and catches my hand. "The fact I have fans doesn't have anything to do with us. I would never ask you to stand among them all."

"But how can we ever just hang out if everywhere we go, someone wants an autograph, or a photo, or reaches out and hugs you?"

"I'll tell security to keep everyone back while I'm with you."

"So you never look approachable? That won't help your image. And if word gets out your girlfriend is banning you from interacting with fans, I can just imagine the hate online."

"Is that what you're doing?" He side-eyes me. "Banning me?"

"No, I'd never tell you not to do anything. I'm just saying, it'll come out I'm the reason you're shutting yourself off. And I can't do that to you. I saw how much you enjoyed being around everyone. You lit up."

He squeezes my hand. "Not as much as when I'm around you."

"It's a different kind of electricity. You have to admit it. You want to experience it again, don't you?"

He sighs, averting his eyes. "Well, yeah. I get how I became famous. I liked being around all those people. It made me want to pick up my guitar and start playing. I want to perform in front of a crowd."

I grin. "That's amazing. I want that for you. I've been telling you all along there are millions of people who want to hear you play again."

He winces as he meets my eyes again. "They want the movies more. I still can't picture myself in front of a camera like that. It doesn't compute."

"Do you want to check out a scene from one of your movies? It could help, like how listening to one of your songs helped you relax into this whole celebrity image."

He sits up, planting a hand against his stomach. "Nuh-uh. I can't just yet."

I squeeze his hand back. "Okay, then it's off the table."

"You like the movies, though, don't you? They're good?"

I grin and nod eagerly. "The best."

"Those girls in the crowd said the same thing. I just don't get it."

"I'm sure it'll all come back to you."

He frowns. "They don't like my new music. *My* music. The stuff that's not covers." He sighs, sinking back down in his seat. "I practiced the covers to become good enough to do my own music. But I'm not good enough on my own. I'm only good at pretending to be other people."

"That's not true. The record company gave you songwriters without heart. You just need to find the passion behind the music."

He swallows hard. "Is that what people think about my music? That it doesn't have heart?"

I fidget in my seat, finding it hard to look into his beautiful hazel eyes. "People enjoy the music because it's from you, but... but it just underwhelmed. That's all." I grit my teeth hard. "Sorry."

He shrugs, sitting back. "Don't be sorry. I asked the question."

"Maybe this new life experience will bring out the songwriter in you."

The corners of his mouth tug upward in a weak smile. "Or, maybe this experience brought a songwriter back into my life."

"What are you talking about?"

"Your poetry has more than heart. You could easily be the best songwriter I could find."

My heart expands, thumping to a heavy beat. "You, you want me to be your songwriter?"

"Why not? There's no one in my life I trust more than you."

I chew my fingernail, staring at the tablecloth. "I wouldn't know where to begin."

"Sure you do. You've been writing for as long as I've known you."

I fidget with the beige napkin again. "Your team would already have someone for you to work with."

"So? They already put me in movies because the music didn't work. What if it worked with you? What if you help me get out of the movies?"

"What if you give the movies a try, and you like it?"

"Why aren't you even giving this idea a try?"

I sit back with a huff. "Because the idea is terrifying."

His head tilts. "Why?"

"I already told you, being in this world makes me feel closed off from you. I won't survive."

"It's just writing. Heck, you've already won awards for your writing."

"But I don't need to show my face or deal with any people. I just write at my desk and submit the work to be judged. I didn't even have to go anywhere to collect my award."

"You don't have to be around anyone to write some songs."

I click my tongue. "I've met Erika and Lexy. They like to control everything. Have everyone in their bubble. I'm happy to be here as your friend, but I can't work with you. I couldn't stand the pressure."

"Okay," he says in a defeated tone. "You don't have to be around me anymore."

"I didn't say I didn't want..."

"I don't want to force you to be in my world."

"Wyatt, I want..."

"And, look, I'm sorry for springing the gi-girlfriend line on you," he says, fidgeting. "It's just, we, we said I love you, and all the ki-kisses, I just..."

"*Wyatt,*" I raise my voice, cutting him off. People at the next table turn and stare. I hunch forward, lowering my tone. "I love you, and I want to be your girlfriend."

"I love you an unreal amount," he whispers. "I just want you around all the time."

"I know."

"I want you to be all mine, Josie Bartlett."

I lift off my seat, leaning across the table to kiss him, soft and slow. I pull away gently and brush my nose against his. "I'm yours, Wyatt Hayes."

He caresses the sides of my face. "I'm sorry for getting defensive. I just hate the thought of you not being with me."

I sit back down, acutely aware of his fear of me leaving him.

"And, I really meant it when I said you should write lyrics," he says, brightening. "I think you'd be amazing at it."

"Thanks. But maybe I'll just pass some poetry your way, and you can pass it off as your own. I think I'd feel more comfortable not taking the credit."

"Seriously?"

I nod. "I'm much more at home in my short story world."

He shrugs. "If you're sure. I'm keeping the offer on the table, though."

I blow him a kiss. "It's appreciated."

Eighteen

Security escorted us to the penthouse after we were stuffed with delicious food, topped off with a to-die-for almond cannolis. The decadent meals were almost enough to rid the thoughts of inadequacy from my head.

Last night, Wyatt and I had just enough energy to curl up on the sectional couch. We wrapped ourselves in a shared blanket and watched another movie from our childhood. This time one not so cringe-worthy. Despite feeling drained, Wyatt's mind was whirring. Meeting fans had him buzzing, and all he could think about was performing again. As we watched the movie, he used the elastic he got from Savanna to strengthen his hand. He kept muttering about how he'd be playing his guitar in no time. Unfortunately, by the time the movie ended, Wyatt was hit with an excruciating headache, which sent him to bed early.

I told him I'd make a start on my homework, but my brain my crippled by negativity. I pushed the emotions into a short story as much as I could, but all I really wanted was a group hug from my family. Keeping the tears at bay, I video called Mom and asked her to put the twins on. I read them the new story, and they were both so rocked by the emotive language, they went to sleep without a fuss.

Mom probed me to tell her what was wrong, but I couldn't admit I'm not measuring up. I mean, everyone else can already see it. I'm not cut out to be the girlfriend of a teen celebrity. It was thrilling when Wyatt labeled us an official couple, but all the romance was dashed once the mob of fans surrounded him. There's no next time that I will be okay with that situation. I will run every time.

I rub my growling stomach, surprised I'm hungry after yesterday's Italian feast. I'm really feeling peanut butter on toast for breakfast. It's simple and reminds me of home. Ugh. I just want to be home right now.

I change into one of my new outfits, and after I fix my hair, I pick up my phone from the end of the bed. There's a text from Kylie.

"Umm. Have you looked online?"

My stomach flips. *"What are you talking about?"*

"You and Wyatt are all over social media. Don't look."

I press the back of my hand over my mouth, forcing myself not to hurl. *"Why did you tell me then?"*

"I didn't want you to see what they're saying."

"I'm gonna puke. What are they saying?"

"Well, it started by people trying to figure out who you are, but then, well, it's online. Things always turn nasty."

My hands tremble around the phone. *"I hate this."*

"Sorry! It's mostly positive. Like, people are loving seeing Wyatt out and about. I guess it's just fans seeing you being jealous."

Sweat beads around my hairline. People hate me. People, who don't even know me, hate me for being with Wyatt.

Kylie texts again. *"You two looked super cute. How was the date?"*

Is she serious right now? She just told me people are saying nasty stuff about me online, and now she wants me to gush about my date?

I drop the phone, backing away as my mind clouds with clashing thoughts.

Another text comes through, and I stare at it on the carpet. *"I'm sorry this has happened. I'm just trying to look at the positives."*

I breathe out slowly and lower to the carpet. I pick up the phone and text, *"I know. Don't be sorry. Being with Wyatt is amazing, but all those fans scared the crap out of me. I can't do this."*

"Can't do what? Stay in Cherry Beach, or be with Wyatt?"

I don't know how to answer, so I leave it with, *"It's all going to come to an end."*

I toss my phone back on the bed and pick myself off the floor. With my arms cinched around my fragile stomach, I scuff my way along the hallway towards Wyatt's bedroom.

Apparently, everything about him online is positive. I'm the negative holding him back.

I can't hold him back when he's preparing to go back into the spotlight.

I can't help shuddering as I approach his doorway.

I retch, folding forward. Is this really it? Am I going to call it quits with him?

Tears flood my eyes, and when I blink, my vision continues to blur.

No, I don't want this. I don't want it to be over.

Ugh. I wish this was easy. I wish we could be together without all the cameras and the speculation.

I just want him.

"It was like getting a piece of myself back, doc," I hear Wyatt say in his bedroom.

Doc? Is he talking to Dr. Fincher from the Clearview Clinic?

"I don't know how to explain it," Wyatt continues. "But when all those people wanted to talk to me, something about it felt normal. It's weird. How can so many strangers knowing who I am feel normal?"

I sigh and lean against the wall, listening to half his phone conversation.

It feels normal because his innate talent means he was born for fame.

"If some of the missing pieces are coming back," Wyatt says with growing anticipation, "does this mean my memory is coming back?"

I suck in a breath and hold it, waiting for Wyatt's response.

A despondent huff comes out of him. "Oh really? Then what's the point of this th-therapy? Isn't this supposed to help?"

There's a long pause before Wyatt huffs again.

"Yeah, I guess you're right," he says with a sigh. "The stutter is going away. Does make me feel better about myself."

At that, I smile as my heart bounces to a happier beat.

"Oh, yeah, that's the best," Wyatt says, more energetically. "Josie is the best thing in my life."

I hold another breath, only breathing out when my heart starts racing.

"So, when do we do another one of these therapy calls?" Wyatt says into the phone.

I pull myself off the wall, alarmed I'm listening to a therapy session.

"Okay, thanks, Dr. Maxton," Wyatt says. "Talk soon."

I shake out my hands, pacing a circle in the hallway, unsure whether to backtrack or actually enter Wyatt's doorway. I'm about to retreat, when a beautifully melodic sound stops me in my tracks.

Euphoria sets in as Wyatt hums a tune. Before I can pick the song, Wyatt's singing the lyrics. His perfect pitch has me shivering with goosebumps in the best way.

I make my way to the doorway, practically floating, as he sings a cover of an eighties pop song. He turns, meeting my eyes, slipping out a laugh as he finishes out the chorus.

"That's a different song to yesterday," I gush. "You remembered it on your own?"

Wyatt rubs the back of his head, an ecstatic grin lighting up his face. "I've been stopping myself from thinking about music. I was so scared I'd forgotten everything. Yesterday cured my fear."

I plant my hands over my chest, bouncing on bended knees. "Oh, I'm so happy for you!"

Wyatt scuffs towards me, reaching his arms to pull around me. I walk into his hug and he says, "You didn't join me last night?"

"Yeah, my homework was a struggle," I say, resting my head on his shoulder. "And then I called home and read to the twins."

"Aww, they would've loved that."

"Yeah. It made me homesick."

He pulls out of the hug and caresses the side of my face. "Are you okay? Oh no. Your eyes are all red and puffy."

I suck in a breath and pat under my eyes. "Dang it. Hoped I'd blinked the tears away."

"Joze, I don't like seeing you so sad. We shouldn't stay here if it's making you miserable."

I can't shake my frown. "I wouldn't say miserable, it's just..."

"You miss your family," Wyatt says, a shine of sadness in his eyes. "We need to get you back to Victoria Falls."

I bite into my lip. "You'd be okay with me leaving?"

He smirks. "No. I'd go with you."

My chin drops as I puff out an air of surprise. "Are you serious?"

His thumb rubs under my chin. "Then I get to see you happy."

"I'm happy when I'm with you, it's just..."

"We could be together in the same town as your family."

I grin. "That would be amazing. But would your team be okay with that?"

Wyatt shrugs. "I haven't said I'm going back to work anytime soon. And it's not like I have a school to go back to."

"But I do."

"Exactly. Let's hang out where you can get back to your life."

"Oh my gosh. This is amazing. But what about..." I stop myself from asking about his fans. I don't want to admit I was eavesdropping.

"There's no buts," Wyatt says gently. "I just want to be with you *and* feel like myself again."

I shouldn't, but I can't help myself. "But didn't you feel like yourself yesterday? With the fans and the special treatment?"

"You make me feel more like myself than any of those people do."

My heart balloons at the thought of having Wyatt back in Victoria Falls. However, it deflates when I remember people online are already talking about me being around him.

I frown. "I can't take you away from this life. You have people counting on you."

He lifts my hands and kisses them. "You're my person, Josie. You're the only one who matters to me. Reuniting with your family is gonna go a heck of a lot better than it has with mine."

"Will you be okay with that? It won't be triggering?"

"Are you kidding? I can't wait to see your family again."

"So, you're doing okay? You seemed wiped after that headache last night."

"I'm good," he says with a nod. "I took one of the sleep aids they'd given me at the clinic and slept like a log."

"Awesome. You're well rested then."

He smiles. "Sure am. I'm ready for another date with my girlfriend."

"You are?" The thought of being talked about online again makes my back cramp. "Maybe we should stick to the penthouse."

"Why? Don't you wanna check out the beach? Or there's still a section downstairs we didn't wander through."

"I dunno," I say coyly. "Other people are down there. You know I'm not a fan."

"Aww." He chucks my chin. "Are you getting anxious? Once we got to the restaurant, it was chill, wasn't it?"

"Yeah, of course, it's just..."

His eyes widen as he stares at me, waiting for me to finish the sentence. "What?"

"Nothing, I..."

"Joze?"

I groan, hunching forward and rubbing my hands over my face.

"What is it?" he asks, rubbing my back. "You're sc-scaring me."

I lift myself up, lowering my hands, and swallow hard. "People will talk if we go back home together."

His eyebrows arch. "What people?"

"*Hello, hello,*" Lexy's voice calls out from the living-dining area.

Wyatt rolls his eyes and groans.

"Wyatt?" Erika's voice calls out. "Are you up, hon?"

He then pinches the bridge of his nose and sighs. "Great. They're both here."

I clasp his hand. "I can tell them you're in bed with a headache if you don't want to see them."

Wyatt gives me a weak smile. "No, it's okay. I'll get it over with so they leave sooner." He lifts my hand and kisses the back of it. "Then the sooner we can go on another date."

I try for a smile, but end up with a weird quirk at the corners of my mouth.

I hate that the word date now conjures up images of crowds encircling us.

"Wyatt?" Lexy calls out again.

"Ugh." Wyatt groans and tugs on my hand. "C'mon, let's get out there."

"Can't we say I have a headache?" I half-joke as I trudge behind him.

Wyatt mumbles a laugh. "No. You're my safety net. I need you beside me."

"You did just fine yesterday when I bailed on being by your side."

"You mean with the crowd?"

"Yeah. Wouldn't you say you were in your element?"

"Oh my gosh, Wyatt!" Lexy cheers, throwing her hands into the air triumphantly as we enter the open-plan space. "I can't believe you did a public meet and greet without your publicist."

Wyatt stops dead, concern coloring his face. "Sorry? Was that wrong?"

Lexy giggles ecstatically. "No, hon. You did fantastically. You're blowing up online."

There goes my stomach again.

Wyatt squeezes my clammy hand. "Blowing up? That's good?"

Erika grins. "You did better than we could have hoped. With all the difficulties and setbacks you've had to deal with, we didn't know if you'd be able to interact with fans again."

Wyatt shrugs. "It felt right."

Lexy squeals in delight. "Ah, I'm so thrilled. We now have so many options to get you back in front of your fanbase. If you can do this well without our help, you'll be magnificent when we move forward with a strategic approach."

Wyatt stumbles on his footing. "Wh-what does that mean?"

Randall steps in from the side with Wyatt's walking aide, which he reluctantly accepts.

Erika beckons Wyatt closer. "Take a seat, Wyatt. Let's chat about this."

Wyatt creeps toward the dining table, which is covered with tiered platters of breakfast items. As he carefully takes a seat, he finds me over his shoulder, and I take my cue to sit beside him.

"Wyatt," Lexy begins, sitting across from him at the table. "You've been trending online since your accident. There's been loads of speculation as to what happened and what treatment you were undergoing."

Wyatt sits back, wincing. "Yeah, people were asking me yesterday if it was true I had memory loss."

"We tried to keep it under wraps," Erika says, "but these things inevitably get out when you're on so many people's radars."

"My point is," Lexy says, steering the conversation, "after the public saw you yesterday, you're tracking as high as you did when you won Talent Quest."

Wyatt turns to me and then back to Lexy. "I don't know what that means."

Lexy beams. "It means you're extremely popular."

"And it's all happening online?" Wyatt questions. "Like, are people just talking about me? Or is it photos and videos as well?"

"Maybe it's time you got back into the real world," Erika says suggestively. She pulls a phone from her oversized handbag and offers it to Wyatt. "Here, it's yours. Why don't you take a look for yourself?"

Wyatt flinches, frowning at the phone.

Lexy hums a laugh. "It won't bite, Wyatt."

I retch, thinking about Wyatt looking at us online.

His mouth falls open as he turns to me in concern. He then winces, holding the side of his head. "*Ouch.* Dang it. Turned too fast."

I clutch his shoulder and hiss in second-hand pain. "Ugh. These headaches."

"Are they still as bad as ever?" Lexy asks, leaning in.

Wyatt rubs the heel of his palm against his head. "I keep hoping they'll get better."

"He had a bad one last night," I tell Lexy and Erika. "So, don't rush him into doing too much. It'll wipe him out."

Wyatt lowers his hand and grasps the phone. "This might be too much," he mutters. "I'm only just getting my confidence back."

"You mean by meeting fans yesterday?" Lexy asks.

Wyatt rubs under his chin, holding back a smile. "And singing."

Erika and Lexy lean in with elation. "*What?*"

He combs his fingers through his hair, shying away as his cheeks brighten with a light pink. "Umm, yeah. Just a few covers."

"A few?" Lexy says, sitting up with stars in her eyes. "Like, more than one?"

I squeeze Wyatt's shoulder, grinning. "He didn't miss a beat. It was like hearing the old Wyatt again."

"Marvelous," Erika cheers. "And do you remember any of the songs from your albums?"

Wyatt's teeth grit. "No, my memory hasn't come back."

"Ugh, who cares," Lexy says, scooting her chair backwards. "Remembering the covers is a game changer. It's what the fans love the most."

Erika turns to Lexy. "What are you thinking?"

"Well, we can capitalize on the interest in Wyatt," Lexy says. "We could record a clip of him singing and post it to his account. Show he's back online."

Wyatt slides the phone away from him. "I never said I was going back online."

Lexy bats a hand. "Oh, don't worry, hon. We have people to manage your accounts for you."

Wyatt sits back. "Oh."

"If we get a clip of you singing an old classic, your audience will be absolutely gaga," Lexy says. "Maybe the track you performed on the grand finale."

Wyatt folds his arms, shifting uncomfortably. "Umm, I don't know what that is."

I bite my lip, a smile pushing at my cheeks. "Yes, you do," I say, rubbing his upper arm. "You were singing it in your bedroom."

Wyatt splutters a laugh. "No way. I won with that song?"

My grin expands as I nod emphatically.

"I love this idea," Erika says. "We'll be highlighting his roots. Back to basics as he gets back into action."

Lexy looks around our immediate area. "We just need to stage somewhere in the apartment."

"I-I-I've just been singing to myself," Wyatt stammers. "I don't kn-know if I-I'm performance ready."

"We're not talking about anything professional, Wyatt," Lexy says, tapping on her phone. "It would just be you practicing and showing your fans how well you're doing."

Erika picks up Wyatt's phone and opens an app. "Your fans are eager to get more from you." She scrolls through posts and reposts about yesterday's Wyatt-sighting. "Those who weren't on Royale Boulevard yesterday are extremely jealous of those who were. If you post a public video of you singing and strumming on the guitar, it'll show the fans you love them all equally."

Overwhelm scrambles Wyatt's expression as he watches the posts scroll by. "Ah, umm, yeah, okay."

"There's a ring light in the fourth bedroom, along with his guitar," Randall pipes up. "Should I get it?"

Erika grins at Wyatt. "You up for it?"

Wyatt stretches his hand open and closed. "I was practicing my hand exercises last night because I feel ready. Yeah, let's do this."

Erika claps loudly, only stopping when she stares down Randall. "What are you waiting for? Get moving."

At that, Randall jumps and then dashes up the hall in search of the light and guitar.

Lexy's thumbs hover over her phone, blissfully sighing. "The timing of this could not be greater."

Erika nods, stifling a happy laugh. "I know. Is that Thea with an ETA?"

"Yeah. They're just checking her in," Lexy replies.

"Oh good," Erika chirps. "Traffic must've been light this morning."

Footsteps hurry down the hallway, and Randall emerges with a guitar in one hand and a standing ring light in the other.

"Where do you want these?" he asks, lifting them in the air.

Lexy looks around the space, framing areas with her phone. "We should utilize the natural light coming from the terrace. If everyone can clear away from the dining table, we'll use the space between the dining area and the couch."

Erika snaps her fingers at me to move. When Wyatt stands from the table, he ditches his walking aid. Getting myself out of the way, I watch as Lexy stages the area, and Randall hands the guitar to Wyatt.

"Wyatt, why don't you just strum and get a feel for the guitar," Lexy says, angling the phone at Wyatt. "Take it nice and easy. We just need some candid clips, and the fans will eat it up."

Wyatt strums the guitar and glances around at us watching him. "You sure anyone will care enough to watch me practicing some chords?"

Erika gestures at me. "What do you say, Josie? You're a super fan, aren't you? Would you be into seeing this on your feed?"

I hug my waist and giggle, my eyes wandering up and down Wyatt. "Oh, yeah. I'd totally be into this."

Wyatt laughs nervously and then attempts a wink. "Okay, Joze. This one's for you."

Lexy taps the side of the phone as she records Wyatt. "Just imagine all the fans as Josie. You're doing it for every one of them. Every version of Josie out there. Got it?"

Wyatt nods, changing chords as he strums. "I got it."

Wyatt continues to strum, and soon he's singing like he used to. Tingles run up my spine, and I'm grinning from ear to ear. Wyatt performs like he has in all the videos I've rewatched, over and over again.

I can't believe this is real.

I'm no longer in my bedroom, swooning over the boy who got away.

I'm standing here as my boyfriend serenades the world.

The elevator pings, and heavy footsteps enter the penthouse. I turn toward the elevator entryway, and extra security guards appear first. My eyebrows knit together in confusion, and then a man in a sharp suit enters behind security.

Soon, Lexy's assistant Thea walks in with a wondrous look in her eyes. "My gosh, Wyatt." Thea gasps. "You're playing again. Awesome."

"I'd recognize that song anywhere," a voice says from behind Thea. "Only you could play it that well, baby."

Oh crap.

I'd recognize that voice anywhere.

But it can't be.

Can it?

Oh my gosh, it is.

Nineteen

Thea steps aside, and my jaw won't get off the floor.

From her sleek dark hair, falling below her ribs. To her flawless makeup, plastered over her olive skin tone. Wearing a high-priced wardrobe, accessorized with premium jewelry, I know exactly who she is.

Portia.

The child model, turned teen popstar, turned actress.

A member of Circle 8. The girl on my wall with my face plastered over hers.

My stomach plummets.

She's here. Not only in the building, but in the penthouse, and she's aimed at Wyatt.

Following her across the floor is a girl, who's about a foot shorter than statuesque Portia. She has wavy chestnut hair and wears oversized, thick-framed glasses. I'd take a stab and guess she's Portia's assistant.

Portia stops a few steps away from Wyatt and applauds with demure claps. The guitar hangs off Wyatt by the straps, otherwise, I'm sure it would've hit the floor by now. His eyes are round, and his chin drops low, absolutely awestruck by the beauty standing before him.

"Wyatt," Erika says, motioning at Portia. "This is Portia. She's your co-star and duet partner."

"Oh," Wyatt mutters. "Uh, umm, hi."

"Hi." Portia then sighs and throws her hands out wide. "I don't care if you don't remember me. I just want to hug you."

As Portia flings herself around Wyatt, he almost loses his balance before embracing her back.

She giggles, awkwardly hugging him with the guitar between them. "Hi baby."

Baby?

Ugh. This is not good.

Wyatt mumbles a nervous laugh. "This isn't awkward."

Portia pulls out of the hug, fixing her hair behind her ears. "Good to see you still have your sense of humor." She sighs again, trying not to frown. "My gosh, I've missed you."

"People have told me we were close," Wyatt says, pulling the guitar strap off him. "But I haven't he-heard from you."

"I tried calling a few times," Portia says as Randall takes the guitar from Wyatt. "They told me you haven't had your phone on you."

Lexy waggles the phone in her hand. "He's back online now."

"I guess it could've been triggering to be online when you don't remember becoming famous," Portia says, fidgeting with the gold bracelets around her wrists.

"Yeah, sometimes it's hard to recognize myself in the mirror," Wyatt admits.

Portia bites into her lip. "I've been in Europe since before your accident. They wouldn't let me stop working."

"You had commitments," the man in the sharp suit pipes up.

"Everyone has had to work harder with Wyatt out of commission," Erika adds on.

Wyatt folds his arms. "So, you've been working overseas this whole time? That's why you never visited?"

Is he upset she never visited, now that he's seen she's a beauty queen?

Portia's facade cracks, and her eyes grow glossy. "If we were regular kids, who didn't have to work all the time, I would've been by your side every chance I got."

Wyatt rubs the back of his neck, averting his eyes. "I, I've heard we work a lot. I don't kn-know when I'm gonna get the energy to do all that."

Portia gestures at the guitar, her expression brightening. "You're back playing and singing. You sound as wonderful as ever. I'd say you're on the right track."

Wyatt smiles. "Yeah, I'm feeling like things are getting back to normal."

"Normal?" Portia questions. "Like, you're remembering your life?"

"I don't exactly remember, but I get these feelings like I've done something before. Almost like déjà vu."

Portia beams. "I saw videos from your little meet and greet yesterday. It could've been at one of our premieres. You looked totally back in form."

"I don't know about that," Wyatt says, the corners of his mouth twitching into a smile. "But it was fun."

"Since we have you two together," Lexy says, still angling the phone at them, "why don't you try a song together?"

"That would be okay with me," Portia says, her eyes wandering up and down Wyatt. "I mean, you do have your guitar right there."

Randall hands the guitar back to Wyatt, and I notice his hand tremble as he takes it. "I've only just started singing and playing again," Wyatt says softly. "So, sorry if I'm a bit rusty."

"I just got off a long flight." Portia smirks. "My voice will probably be garbage."

Wyatt starts strumming and asks her, "What are we singing?"

"The George Michael cover you were just playing is a good place to start."

"Okay, let's do it."

Alongside Lexy, the girl with the oversized glasses, who walked in with Portia, films with her phone as well. Wyatt strums the recognizable beat of the eighties pop song, and he and Portia launch into the chorus. Portia taps the beat on her thighs and she swings her shoulders, harmonizing perfectly with Wyatt.

I shiver, watching every little interaction between the two, and listening to every note they hit. Every time their gazes meet, it's like a knife to my heart.

I knew it.

I knew when he saw her, I'd become invisible.

This is why we never stayed in contact.

Why would he call the girl back home when he was in the same vicinity as this stunningly talented girl?

As they sway to the music they're making, my body doesn't know what to do. It's always exhilarating hearing Wyatt sing, but sharing a song that means so much to him with *her*.

To say there's havoc inside me would be an understatement.

Just when I'm about to keel over, Wyatt misses a line and fumbles into laughter.

The room erupts in applause as Wyatt and Portia end the song with the most cutesy laughter you'd swear you were watching their rom-com.

"I'm so proud of you for getting back into singing," Portia says, curling her arm around his. "Jenna, bring my phone over."

The girl with oversized glasses hands the phone to Portia.

"You wouldn't remember Jenna," Portia says to Wyatt. "She's my PA."

"Hi, Wyatt," Jenna says with a kind smile and small wave.

"That was fantastic," Erika says, clapping as loud as usual. "Lexy, did you get some good clips?"

"Oh, it's a gold mine for sure," Lexy replies.

"We should get these two back into the studio ASAP," the man in the sharp suit says, stepping forward. "Wyatt, I'm Richmond Salinger, Circle 8 Management. I've been managing Portia for the past nine months. Even though it's been some time since you and I have worked together, I think it's time you got back to Ferndale."

Wyatt reluctantly shakes Richmond's hand. "Ah, okay?"

"Ferndale is where our recording studio is located," Randall explains. "And your loft."

Wyatt's eyes brighten. "My loft?"

"It's moody and artistic," Portia says, nudging Jenna. "It's totally his vibe, right, Jenna?"

"Oh, yeah," Jenna says, timidly making eye contact with Wyatt.

Wyatt clears his throat. "You've both been there?"

"It's near the studio," Portia says, playing with her hair as she eyes her phone. "Plus, my place is nearby."

"You could say Circle 8 has made Ferndale very neighborly," Richmond says with an offbeat chuckle.

"You two did great work back there," Jenna says. "Devon and I would always say..."

Jenna is cut off by the gasps whooshing out of those around her.

"*Jenna*," Portia grunts through gritted teeth.

I can't help staring at Jenna as her eyes water. She blinks them clear, taking a breath and standing taller. "I'm so sorry," she mutters.

Wyatt's brow lifts, and his bottom lip drops, but he falters on a response.

Portia sighs and strokes Wyatt's arms. "We heard about what Devon did. I'm sorry. It's so unbelievable."

"*Really* unbelievable," Jenna blurts. Portia glares at her, and Jenna swiftly squeaks. "*Sorry.*"

"Devon's the bad guy," Portia scolds her PA. "You need to stop pining for him."

Pining?

With intensity, I watch the million emotions crossing Jenna's face.

I'm in the same camp. I can't fathom Devon doing anything bad to Wyatt.

Here's a girl who actually knew Devon.

I need to know what Jenna knows.

My attention is pulled from Jenna when I hear a groan. Sucking in a breath, I turn back to Wyatt.

Clutching his forehead, Wyatt doubles over with a grunt.

"*Wyatt?*" Portia shrieks, clasping her hands by her face.

Randall helps get the guitar off him, and Wyatt uses the back of the sectional couch to keep himself upright.

Gritting my teeth until my jaw stings, all I want to do is get near him. Sirens blare in my head as everyone else crowds around him, ripping oxygen from the room. All I can do is stare as I hold myself so tightly my ribs ache.

"Hubert!" Erika shouts. "Get Wyatt's pain medication."

Wyatt's hand lowers, displaying his creased forehead and squinting eyes. "It's all right," Wyatt strains, pinching the bridge of his nose. "It's just... just..."

"Wyatt, hon," Lexy says, getting in his face, "what is it?"

Wyatt stands taller with another grunt. "It feels... It's like... Like I can remember."

Portia squeals, bundling her hands under her chin. "Your memory? It's coming back?"

I lose my breath, barely able to muster the strength to edge myself closer.

"No, ugh, yeah, umm." Wyatt rubs the side of his head, closing his eyes. "It's right there. Like, the memories are behind this fog, but I can't clear it."

Portia, Lexy, Erika, Randall, and Richmond crowd around Wyatt. They talk over each other, fighting to take control of how to fix Wyatt's headache.

My heart pounds heavy like a mallet, pumping my hot blood so fast, it's all I can hear. With my vision vibrating, the anger sweeps me up, and I stamp my foot. "Can you all just back off?"

Everyone in the room spins in my direction. The shock wears off, and I realize how deep my fingernails are embedded in my palms.

Portia puffs out a laugh. "Excuse me, who are you? I never even noticed you in the room before."

"This is Josie," Erika introduces. "Wyatt's friend from school."

His girlfriend.

I want to say it.

Dang it, I want to scream it.

But my lips may as well be glued shut.

With Portia staring me down, I'm shrinking into oblivion.

"Oh, you're the friend the team told me about," Portia says, wearing a movie star smile.

I shift my weight awkwardly as she towers over me. "Yeah."

"You must be loving the five-star treatment, being back in Wyatt's life all these years later," she says, sizing me up.

"I, I, I," I stammer under the weight of her intimidation, until something snaps inside me. I stand taller and click my tongue. "Look, just stop crowding him. He's not the same guy you remember."

Portia smirks, popping a hip. "I could say the same thing to you, honey."

"Joze," Wyatt croaks, rubbing the side of his head. "Thanks for sticking up for me, but I'm okay."

I stumble on my footing, disarmed by my boyfriend.

Portia turns to him, rising on the balls of her feet and grinning at him.

I huff in deflation. The smugness oozing from Portia makes me want to gag. Wyatt basically made her feel in the right, and me in the wrong.

I shouldn't have dared open my mouth in her highness's presence.

Hubert moves in with Wyatt's pain medication and a glass of water. Erika suggests he take a seat on the couch, and I breathe a sigh of relief when he's off his feet.

Portia clasps her hands in front as she looks me up and down. "Everyone says how incredible your visit has been. Oh my gosh, you have no idea how grateful I am that you were here while I was stuck overseas."

I rub the back of my neck, slouching under her height atop stiletto heels. "Ah, yeah, sure."

She gives my arm a slight pat. "At least you don't have to feel guilty about leaving now. I'll be by his side as he gets back to work."

My mouth falls open, but before I can muster a single syllable, Portia has moved over to the couch.

"How you doing, baby?" she asks Wyatt as he sets down his glass of water.

He rubs the side of his head. "I'm okay."

Portia sighs, sitting beside him. "I hate that you're in pain. It physically hurts me."

"Really?" Wyatt asks with an air of doubt.

"Yeah. You don't believe me?"

"It's not th-that. It's just... I-I don't..." Wyatt shakes his head and sighs. "I'm sorry that I don't remember you."

"Why would you be sorry?" Portia rushes, caressing the side of his face. "Ugh, baby, I hate that you've been going through this alone."

Wyatt's body angles toward me as he says, "Well, I'm not alone. I have..."

"I know, I know," Portia cuts in. "You have a whole team. I just hate that I wasn't here. I've missed being with you."

Wyatt winces. "Being with me? Does that mean... It's just... Umm, you keep calling me..."

Portia deadpans him, trying to read where he's going with this.

My stomach plummets and oozes an excruciatingly gross feeling throughout my abdomen.

"You know," Wyatt wipes his brow, fidgeting uncomfortably. "Calling me baby. Is that a girlfriend nickname?"

I retch quietly, hoping no one notices me dying inside.

Portia giggles, wiping a crooked index finger under her dark eyelashes. "We never wanted to label our relationship."

Wyatt sucks in a breath. "Oh."

"We're just very close," she says, curling her hand around his wrist. "We're always at parties together, and we work so well together. You'll always be baby to me."

Wyatt looks down at her hand on his. "Okay?"

"Does it bother you?" Portia asks, releasing him. "It never used to."

"Like I said, I don't remember you."

Portia swallows hard and nods. "I get it. I need to pump the brakes. I'm just so excited to see you again."

"It must be weird for you too," Wyatt says. "We had a relationship, but it's gone now."

"Not necessarily," Richmond says. "If we get you two back in the recording studio, it might be the magic fix that brings everything back to you."

"I... I..." Wyatt looks up at Richmond and then pans around to the others on his team. "I don't kn-know if I'm ready."

"Your voice is exceptional as always," Erika encourages.

"And what about that magic moment?" Lexy cheers. "You sang with Portia, and then it was like your memory was coming back. It's like you're getting pieced back together."

"Portia's the key to getting your life back," Richmond says. "You two can pick up where you left off."

How am I still standing?

Wyatt flinches. "But, I... I..."

"You should do it," I blurt.

Wyatt turns to me with surprise.

I nod, giving him a smile. "You've got to. What if it brings your memory back?"

"But we..."

I cut him off. "You're so close. You said it yourself. Don't you want to clear the fog?"

"Yeah, but we were..."

"It's okay," I say, pushing harder for a smile. "This is important. You've got to try."

It's agonizing, but this is the life he chose for himself before the accident. The fame and the popstar by his side. I need him to know he can forget about going to Victoria Falls with me. I'm not going to hold him back.

His parents were right all along.

I'm an unwanted distraction.

Portia curls her arm around Wyatt. "*Yay.* We're going back to the studio, baby."

Wyatt looks down at her arm around him, and then he gasps. "Wait, I remember you."

All the team members angle themselves closer to the couch, waiting with bated breath for confirmation Wyatt's memory has finally returned.

"You were on that TV show," Wyatt says, furrowing his brow to recall the information. "What was it called, 'Boy Crazy,' or something? You were the one who sang, right?"

Portia lets out a giddy laugh, flicking her long, sleek hair over her shoulder. "Yeah, that was me. I played Heather on the show, but left after season two when my concert tours blew out."

"Yeah, I remember watching you after school."

"That's so cute," Portia gushes. "Did you ever imagine back then we'd end up singing together?"

"Ah, no, not at all."

Portia giggles and traces her index finger under his chin. "We've done a lot together."

Seemingly hypnotized by her dark, almond eyes, there's only slight hesitation from Wyatt as he tilts his head back.

"Right before your accident, we were in the middle of working on a song together," Portia says.

"And you can get right back to your duet in Ferndale," Richmond says, driving his point home.

"You and Portia starred in 'Without You' together," Erika explains. "And she had a role in your latest film."

"It was only a small role," Portia says. "I'd already wrapped so I could get back to Europe for my music."

Wyatt winces, turning to look at Erika. "The movie you want me to get back to making?"

Erika beams. "When you're up to it."

Portia squeezes Wyatt's shoulder. "Getting back into the studio with me might feel more like home. Once we finish the song, I can help you run lines from the script. It'll be like old times."

Lexy squeals with glee. "You'll be back to your old self in no time, Wyatt."

Randall checks an alert on his phone, and then says to Erika. "Savanna from the clinic is due soon for an assessment with Wyatt."

"Okay, that gives us some time to figure out this week's schedule before going over it with him." Erika then turns to me. "And we'll need to get Josie organized if we're all headed to Ferndale."

My heart plummets to the pit of my stomach.

All I wanted when I woke up this morning was to go home.

Now, the thought of leaving Wyatt makes me want to puke.

Portia's wrapped around him. It's only a matter of moments until I'm completely wiped from his memory.

Randall starts suggesting options for my travel arrangements, but it only makes the blood pump louder in my veins. As it thunders in my ears, I find myself backing away. I mutter something to the effect of, "Needing a minute," and escape into the hallway.

With a weight on my chest, and oxygen barely getting through, I collapse onto my knees on my bedroom floor. It takes a few moments before my gasps subside and I finally hear a different ringing in my ears.

Through blurry vision, I find my phone lighting up on my bed, a call coming through.

I gulp the need to sob, and my trembling hand reaches for the phone.

It's Mom.

Twenty

My heart constricts, and I hit the answer button.

"Hello?"

"*Josie.*" Her voice is frantic. "I've been calling you all morning. What is going on?"

I wipe my eyes dry and notice the dull headache building at the base of my skull. "Huh? I was in a different room. Why are you calling? Aren't you at work?"

"Precisely. Where everyone is asking me why my daughter is gallivanting with a movie star?"

"Huh?"

I rub my head, shutting my eyes. This isn't computing.

"Josie, you're all over the local news. I almost swerved the car into oncoming traffic when the breakfast radio hosts were using your name."

My fingertips dig into my chest. "What? Why are they talking about me?"

"Because you were walking on Royale Boulevard with Wyatt, surrounded by a mob of people."

"But, how do they know who I am?"

"Apparently people were asking about you online, and people from your high school identified you."

"Ugh." I groan, folding forward. "I've done so well, staying invisible at that school. I don't want those people talking about me."

"I'm sure they have a million questions. Darling, *I* have a million questions."

"Did you see the videos?"

"I had a panic attack just hearing about it. Marcy showed me something on the way to my cubicle, but it was such a blur."

"Well, I was on the street with Wyatt, but I wasn't in a mob."

"People were saying…"

"Wyatt wanted to speak with his fans, but I couldn't stomach it. I hugged a wall so tight until his security moved us away."

Mom breathes a sigh of relief. "You had security with you?"

"Yes, they're always with Wyatt."

"Josie, I don't like the sounds of this. You get so scared in large crowds, and now you're in a big city, with a celebrity who has loads of fans, and you…"

"*Mom*," I blurt. "Stop. I'm already wigging out. I don't need any help spiraling."

"Darling, I just want you home."

Tears well in my eyes, and I swallow hard. "I want that too. But… But, Wyatt…"

"If mobs are forming around him, this won't get easier."

"I know. They're already talking about him going back to work. They want to send me home."

"I think it's for the best."

"Were the twins in the car when they were talking about me on the radio?"

"No, it was after school drop off." Mom huffs. "I now know why that group of moms was eyeballing me by the school gate."

"I'm sorry the news about me scared you."

"Oh, darling, I'm just scared about your safety. I want you home where I know you're safe."

"You could tell last night there was something wrong," I say, cradling the phone by my ear. "I'm not cut out for this. Oh, Mom, I love Wyatt so much. It'll hurt so much when we're pulled apart again. I'm already in pain."

"Oh, Josie." Mom sniffs back tears. "Maybe we shouldn't have let you go in the first place."

"I just wish he wasn't famous. I wish he could come back to Victoria Falls, and everything would be normal."

"I don't think that'll ever happen."

A sob breaks in my throat, garbling my words. "He said he'd come home. This morning, he said he wanted to come back, see all you guys again, and just be with me."

"But Josie..."

"But he loves this life. He got a taste of it yesterday, and it lit him up. He's so excited to record again and play his guitar. He'll go back to his life and forget he wanted anything to do with me."

"Oh, darling."

"I just hate this, Mom. He's so perfect. I don't want him giving up on his music or his movies. But I don't want to let him go."

"But your anxiety..."

"I know." My heart squeezes and pain ripples through my chest. "I know. I have to let him go."

"Do you need me to call Dad to arrange a flight home?"

"No, Randall will do it."

"Okay, let me know as soon as it's booked."

I nod against the phone. "I will."

"Love you, Josie-posey."

I crack a tear-stained smile. "Love you too."

After I end the call, I stand and shake out my hands. Without looking in a mirror, I make my way into my bathroom to freshen up. I don't even want to know how bad my mascara is running.

When I turn off the water, and dab my face dry with a hand towel, my nose scrunches up at a foul smell. I turn toward the bathroom window and sniff the air.

Eww.

It's cigarettes.

Unable to help myself, I step on the closed toilet seat, and soon hear the unmistakable sound of Erika's voice. As I peer out the half-open window, she and Randall are out on the terrace as Erika drags on a cigarette.

"We're so close," Erika says, gesturing with the cigarette between her fingers. "We get him back into the studio, then he's back at work."

"But he hasn't shaken that stutter."

"I know, and the headaches are going to derail production."

"The director will have to keep cutting if Wyatt's holding the side of his head through a scene."

"Bright side, he doesn't stutter while he sings." Erika takes another drag. "Bad side, his music underperforms. We only keep Wyatt signed because the movies do phenomenally well. What are we supposed to do with him if he can't keep it together on set?"

"Hopefully Portia can get him back on track."

Erika sighs. "Lord, I'm hoping so."

Erika butts out the cigarette, and she and Randall walk out of view.

I lower myself off the toilet seat and onto the tiled floor below.

I'm in the way.

I was brought to Cherry Beach to help him get released from the Clearview Clinic and adjust to his lifestyle. I've done that, and I can't help anymore.

Circle 8 has brought Portia back from Europe to help Wyatt. They're a dream team when together. I can't be selfish. I need to let Wyatt get back to what he does best.

Portia's here to step in.

I need to bow out.

Carefully taking in my mirrored reflection, the damage isn't as bad as I thought. With a quick touch up, I ready myself to join the others.

With a deep breath, I force myself out of the hallway.

"Huh?"

The open-plan space is empty.

Until, someone steps into view.

"Oh, hi," Jenna says with a friendly wave. "They took Wyatt to the hotel's gym to meet his physical therapist. Portia's gone to her suite to freshen up, and she told me to take you down to the day spa."

It takes me aback. "Excuse me?"

Jenny giggles, fixing her oversized glasses. "Yeah, as a thank you. She meant it when she said how grateful she is that you've been by Wyatt's side. I've organized her regular treatments for you downstairs at the spa."

"Oh, that's really nice of you, and her, but it's really not necessary."

Jenna clasps her hands in front. "Well, I won't force you, but the offer still stands."

There's something different about Jenna. She's not pushy and in a rush like the other Circle 8 team members. I'm reminded of her sweet and apologetic reaction at the mention of Devon.

I glance around the room, and whisper, "So, is *everyone* gone?"

Jenna nods. "Mm-hmm. Umm, if you want me to leave too, I can..."

"No," I blurt. "Actually, I wanted to talk to you."

"Me?" She smiles kindly. "Why's that?"

I edge toward her and whisper, "Devon."

Jenna recoils, frowning with a mixture of embarrassment and shame. "I shouldn't have said... Especially in front of Wyatt. It was so stupid."

"No, it wasn't," I rush. "I'm with you. I can't believe Devon would hurt Wyatt."

Her eyes grow larger behind her frames. "You do?"

I nod, gesturing for her to follow me to the couch. When we sit, I continue in a hushed tone. "They looked so close. Like best friends."

"They were," Jenna whispers back. "We all were."

"So, you and Devon were close too?"

She nods. "That's what I was going to say earlier, before everyone freaked out. Devon and I would always hang out whenever Wyatt and Portia were working together. We'd always comment on their friendship-that-could-be-more status."

I recoil, yet have to ask, "Were Wyatt and Portia ever more than...?"

She shakes her head. "Not more than I saw on set."

"And you were overseas with Portia when Wyatt's accident happened?"

"Mm-hmm. We were devastated. I can't believe they never gave Portia anytime off to see him."

"She wanted to come back?"

"Desperately. They didn't even tell her the status of his medical condition."

"Why not?"

Jenna's hands ball into fists, and she grunts in frustration. "Because of how high Wyatt was trending when his condition was kept a secret. They didn't tell Portia, Simon, or any of the talent what was wrong with Wyatt. That way, when they were in interviews and asked about Wyatt, their answers were vague, and it kept the mystery going online."

My jaw drops. "They really did that?"

Jenna rolls her eyes. "It's nothing new with Circle 8. Manipulating the talent is what keeps the cogs in motion. Heck, Simon was in town and ready to visit Wyatt. Portia texted him to ask how it went, and Simon told her his visit was canceled at the last minute."

"Why?"

"Because when Portia couldn't answer questions about Wyatt and speculation went through the roof, Erika and the rest of them couldn't risk the spike dropping. They wanted to keep Simon and everyone else in the dark."

My hands ball into fists. "I can't believe this! Wyatt thought he wasn't friends with any of them because they didn't visit him. He was alone in that room for weeks."

"Yet another reason for Erika to have kept hold of his phone all this time."

My blood boils, remembering her proudly revealing his phone from her handbag. "She's the worst of all the suits."

Jenna blinks at me. "The what?"

I bat a hand. "Oh, it's just what Wyatt calls the management team."

Jenna's mouth forms an 'o.' "Get out."

"Huh?"

Jenna latches onto my wrist. "That's what Devon would call the managers. Do you know what this means?"

I stare at her wide-eyed.

Jenna taps the side of her head. "Wyatt remembers Devon. He's in there. Why would he use an inside joke from the person who supposedly hurt him? Doesn't this sound like proof Devon didn't do it?"

I suck in a deep breath. "Like, maybe, somewhere deep down Wyatt can remember what happened to him. The truth."

Jenna rubs the ache from her chest. "I knew it. I just knew it."

"Can you get in touch with Devon?"

Jenna frowns. "No. All our phones are Circle 8 property. He's been totally cut off and all his social media was deleted."

"There has to be a way to find him."

"I kept thinking he'd reach out to me. Like, he'd still have my number, and he'd tell me the truth. Or at least what he knows. But it still hasn't happened."

Realization hits me hard. "Wyatt needs to get back to Ferndale. What if Devon's waiting to see him at his loft? Like, at a time when he'd be alone and the suits couldn't interfere."

Jenna nods along. "It's a possibility. Thea filled me in on Wyatt's trauma. About how the doctor said, Wyatt has memory loss after suffering severe emotional shock. There's obviously something big he's blocking out."

"And if it's not Devon betraying him, then what? Something that happened on the movie set?"

"Tensions were high before Portia and I left, but I don't remember Wyatt saying that anything was wrong."

"Could he have told Portia, and she didn't tell you?"

Jenna shakes her head. "She tells me everything."

It takes me aback, remembering how Portia snapped at Jenna. "Really?"

"Yeah, she needs someone to confide in. I wouldn't have stuck by her side all this time if we weren't friends."

I swallow uncomfortably. "It's just, earlier she seemed bossy or, umm, grumpy with you."

Jenna bats a hand. "That's just because we're both on edge about being around Wyatt. Portia's trying to put on a brave face, like everything's back to normal. And me, ugh, I was so anxious about seeing him again and not putting my foot in it. Portia was just worried. If I do something wrong, it's the same as her being in the wrong."

"That's not fair."

Jenna half nods. "It is. It works for us. We're a team, and she's the face of it."

"So, you and Portia are as close as Wyatt and Devon were?"

"Absolutely. I'd be crushed if I were cut out of her life."

I sit back with a thud. "Huh."

Jenna's eyebrow arches. "Didn't look that way?"

"I just had an impression of her. That she was high-strung. But you did just get off a long flight."

"Well, she is high-strung." Jenna laughs. "But she's kind-hearted above all. She really helped Wyatt navigate life with fame. Without her, I don't know if he'd have stuck it out this long."

I press a hand into my stomach. "Really?"

My eyes shut, and my mind contorts, imagining Portia as kind. Nope, can't do it. I concoct images of Wyatt's hand in hers, and I retch.

"Whoa." Jenna gasps. "You okay?"

I open my eyes and force a smile. "Peachy."

"Are you sure? Because you look green."

My stomach twists, realizing Portia's the girl Wyatt's parents prefer him to be with.

The girl, so famous she goes by one name.

Jenna pats my knee. "Come on, let me take you down to the spa."

I wave my hands in front. "No, really, I'm good. I just want to see Wyatt again. Maybe I can go to the gym? I already know Savanna. She'll let me join them."

Jenna winces, shifting in her seat. "I dunno. Erika gave me the impression Wyatt would be in a meeting after his session." She sits taller with a perky smile. "Come on, spa time. How could you say no to a free pamper session?"

"Why don't you take my spot instead?"

Jenna frowns. "Because I need to be available for Portia."

I sit forward. "But it's a free treatment. Why don't you take it?"

Jenna sighs. "Okay, I get it. You want to be around for Wyatt."

"He is my boyfriend. I want to know he's okay."

Jenna's mouth falls open with an air of surprise. "What? Boyfriend?"

I nod. "I'm not just his friend. I'm his girlfriend."

Jenna blinks at me. "No offense, but since when?"

I sit back, hunching as my courage deflates. "You expected him to be available for Portia?"

"Uh, umm, I..."

"He didn't remember her." I blow out a shaky breath. "Wyatt officially labeled us yesterday, but we were a thing before he got famous." I rub the space over my heart. "I'm the one who encouraged him to go on Talent Quest. Without me, he wouldn't be famous."

"So, in a way, Portia took the torch from you, helping Wyatt through all of this."

I sigh and smooth back my curls. "Yes. I've been watching my stolen kisses in 'Without You.'"

Jenna touches my forearm. "That's just acting. It's not real."

"Maybe what they did on screen wasn't real."

"They were never a thing."

I arch my eyebrow. "Are you sure about that?"

"Are you backing off if they were?"

"My head and my heart are currently at war over that."

"But what's the plan? If you and Wyatt are dating, are you moving to Ferndale?"

My nerves frazzle. "No, I can't. I'm only sixteen. I have school, and I need to get back to my family."

Jenna lifts her arms out wide. "You can be sixteen and move away from home. All the Circle 8 kids have done it. Surely you have a talent you can live off."

Instinctively, I shift away from her. "Ah, no. I'm not a singer or an actor. I'm a writer, but that's not a profession that screams for the limelight. And thank goodness for that."

Jenna mumbles a laugh. "You don't like the idea of being in front of cameras?"

I deadpan her. "I hate it."

"Then being with Wyatt might prove difficult. I'm sure you've seen the papped images of him and Portia."

"Mm-hmm. I already experienced part of that yesterday." I sigh, sinking into the couch. "Wyatt was such a natural. All I wanted to do was flee."

"Hey, maybe long-distance will actually work for you guys," Jenna says in an upbeat tone. "They all work so much, anyway. Even their friends in the same city barely see them."

"Long-distance is our only option." *Ouch.* My heart aches. "I'm just scared he'll forget about me."

"He's not that kinda guy."

I frown, having difficulty looking her in the eye, as I mutter, "He's done it before."

Jenna's eyes grow cloudy, and she chews on her lip. "You're worried about him and Portia being together once you're back home."

I can't stomach the answer. Thankfully, I'm spared by the ringing of Jenna's phone. She lifts it and I see the caller ID: "Randall."

"Hey," Jenna answers. As she listens, she quickly responds with, "Hmm... Mm-hmm... Yep... Uh-huh... Okay, no problem. See you soon."

Jenna ends the call, bouncing off the seat to stand. She looks down at me, saying, "I've got to dash and get Portia ready for a meeting."

I scoot to the edge of the couch seat. "Will Wyatt be there?"

Jenna taps her phone in her palm. "Ah, Randall didn't say. I just have to go to Portia's suite."

"Well, where's the meeting? Is it here in the penthouse?"

"No." Jenna rubs her lips together, like she's about to dodge a probing reporter's questions. "He didn't say, exactly. Richmond will be meeting us and will have the information for Portia." She backtracks away from me. "I'm sorry, I've really got to get going. So, downstairs at the spa, ask for Natalia. She's Portia's..."

I raise a palm. "Save it. I'm not going down there."

Jenna raises her hands in defense. "Suit yourself, but I hope you change your mind." She then waves. "I'm sure we'll catch up later."

As Jenna dashes off to the elevator, I fling myself back against the couch with a huff.

If Randall's involved in a meeting, then so is Erika, which means so is Wyatt. I doubt they're just talking about him now. They want him fully involved.

I sit up. Am I throwing in the towel?

Back in my bedroom, I'd basically quit my relationship with Wyatt.

I stand up. But I don't want that.

Whether I'm here or back home, I need to let him know I'm a part of his life.

I march to the elevator. I'm not bailing on him.

I impatiently press the elevator button too many times. Jenna only took it to the floor below to meet with Portia, but it feels like time stands still. Finally, it pings open at my level. I need to get to the hotel gym before Wyatt leaves for this meeting. I want to be by his side, showing him how much I care.

Twenty-One

I rush out of the elevator, hurriedly following the signs along the hotel floor, pointing me towards the gym. Seriously wish I were more coordinated, or worked harder in PE, because I'm out of breath as I race to find Wyatt.

Puffing and red-faced, I make it to the gym. I swipe my keypass against the glass door and stumble inside. One person is running on a treadmill, and another is in the corner using the weights. There's no one else in the gym.

I fold over with a huff. Dang it, I'm too late.

I straighten myself out, take a steadying breath, and leave the gym. Geez, I really hope this meeting is somewhere in the hotel. I remember Lexy mentioning an office downtown when I first arrived in Cherry Beach. If that's where they've gone, I have no hope of reaching them.

I wander the hotel floor, my mind flooded with thoughts of Wyatt. Wow, I really am lost without him. He's my every waking thought, and when we're apart, it's like I'm no longer whole.

Oh, I really hope he's okay. He mentioned the fog lifting from his mind. I hope they don't use that as an excuse to overload him. Lately, he's been looking to me for reassurance. Ugh. I hate that I'm not there for him right now!

I move into the elevator and press the button for the lobby floor. Maybe, just maybe, someone at the front desk will know where they've gone. Perhaps they called a car or made a reservation on their behalf. All I can do is bundle up every smidge of optimism left inside me.

As I walk across the lobby, I have my eyes peeled for anyone I recognize from Circle 8. I move toward the line of people waiting to be served by the front desk clerks. My eyes continue to wander as I wait in line, and my ears prick to a booming voice.

I spin and view over my other shoulder, and my enthusiasm kicks into action. Richmond, the manager assigned to Portia, talks loudly on his phone, and paces the small space in front of the hotel's restaurant.

Freaking yes!

I slink away from the front desk line, not too eager so I don't gain Richmond's attention. We don't know each other yet, and I don't want him to flip out and ban me from entering.

As I carefully approach the restaurant, Richmond continues to pace as he yell-talks into his phone. His back is turned, and I quickstep into the restaurant, still winded from my lame athleticism upstairs.

"May I help you?" a server asks, stopping me before I pass the small counter with a plaque reading, 'Please wait to be seated.'

"Umm, I..." I drag out the syllable, craning my neck to spy Wyatt and his team. "I'm here with Circle 8." I cringe, hoping I don't look like a hopelessly adoring fan. "I'm here to meet Wyatt Hayes."

The server gives me the once-over. "I'm sorry, miss, I was told the entire party had already arrived. That table has already ordered."

"That's no problem," I overzealously rush. "I'm not here to eat, just to join them." A brilliant detail strikes me. "I'm Mr. Hayes's PA, and I'm late. Please, I don't want to lose my job."

The server gives a slight nod, probably recalling the number of assistants already at their table. "Okay, miss, please follow me."

I look up at the ceiling with a relieved sigh. Oh, thank you, Lord, it worked.

I follow the server through the crowded restaurant, filled with boisterous conversations, clinking of glasses, and clanking of utensils on porcelain plates. Soon, my world feels right again when I lay eyes on Wyatt.

He sits back in a dining chair, at a long-stretched table, grinning and laughing as the suits surround him in conversation.

It stops me in my tracks.

He's happy?

I zero in on the empty seat beside him, and my heart bounces happily. He saved it for me. Oh my gosh, how cute. He knew I'd be coming.

The clip-clop of stilettos approaches from behind me. I turn and find Portia walking back to the table, Jenna on her heels.

"Oh, Josie, you're here already?" Portia asks, checking the time on her phone. "Seems a little soon to be finished with a treatment."

"*Uhhh*," I draw out the sound as I glance at Jenna.

Portia looks at Jenna. "You said you took her to the spa."

Jenna's mouth opens, mind whirring to come up with an answer.

It then dawns on me Jenna told Portia what she wanted to hear. Plus, Jenna did spill a lot of info up in the penthouse. I'm sure she's using the spa as a cover for spending so much time with me.

"Sorry, I had to bail on the spa," I blurt, lifting my phone. "My mom called, and it was a super important conversation. I didn't want anyone waiting around for me."

"Oh." Portia pouts. "What a shame. Well, you can still go. It's a standing appointment."

I wave a hand. "No, it's fine. Really."

Portia shrugs. "Suit yourself. I just thought you might enjoy it as a last treat before you go home."

I double-take at her. "Home?"

She nods. "We're all headed back to Ferndale, and I overheard Erika telling Randall to arrange your flight home."

My heart sinks. "Oh, they've done it already."

Portia's eyes round and her tan slightly pales. "You did know, didn't you?"

I fake a smile. "Yeah, I'm prepared to go home. Just, leaving Wyatt, it doesn't make things any easier."

Portia sighs. "I hear that. Every moment I was overseas was like agony. I just wished someone had told me he was okay."

I watch the genuine agony in her eyes. "That's really rough. I can't believe they kept you in the dark for publicity's sake."

Portia pats dry the corner of her eye. "It's fine. It's the business we're in."

My emotions bubble up, watching her turn on a brave face. "You still have feelings, though."

Richmond walks up behind Portia, landing a hand on her shoulder. "There's my hard worker," he boasts. "You'll never find a more dedicated popstar than Portia. I wish all our talent cared as much about their careers as she does."

Portia pushes for a smile. "Thanks, Richmond."

"Uh, hi, Josie," Randall says, stepping up beside me. "We weren't expecting you."

"Umm, yeah." I clear my throat awkwardly as I turn to him and Erika. "Just had a feeling you guys would be down here. Hope that's okay."

"It's fine," Erika says plainly. "We've wrapped up most of the details we needed to go over. Why don't you have a bite to eat? We're happy to still treat you while you're with us."

I gulp. "It's my last day with you all, isn't it?"

Portia motions to Jenna, and they take their cue to return to the table. I watch them out of the corner of my eye. Portia takes the seat next to Wyatt.

It wasn't for me.

I seriously need to get a clue.

"So, Wyatt has agreed to go back to Ferndale to work on his music," Erika says, swirling a glass of mineral water with three slices of lemon. "You really have helped us out with him. We can't thank you enough."

"We booked you a commercial flight home," Randall says, "and I thought a first-class seat might show you how much we appreciate you."

I puff out a breath, my airway constricted from emotional whiplash. "Oh, umm, yep. Thank you so much."

"You are happy to be going home," Erika says. "Aren't you?"

"Yeah, but I don't want to leave Wyatt. My family is the reason I'll be apart from him."

"Not to mention school," Erika replies. "Weren't you the one who encouraged him to become a star? You always knew you'd be apart."

"Yes, but..."

"He's eager to get back into performing," Erika continues to dig. "You wouldn't want to stand in the way of that?"

"Of course not," I blurt, breathless. "I've never wanted him to quit."

"Good," Erika says with a clap. "We'll give you some time to say goodbye. This trip down memory lane wasn't going to last forever."

I sigh, hunching forward in sadness and resolve. "Okay. I guess this is it then. I was just hoping for more time."

Randall grins. "You already pushed back your trip by a few days. Aren't you grateful for that?"

I nod at the carpet. "Yeah, of course. Thank you."

"Josie!" Wyatt calls from the table.

I look over and he's craning his neck and waving me over. I wince when he swiftly winces and rubs his neck.

Oh, this boy. I wish he wouldn't put himself in pain just for me.

"Please," Erika says, gesturing at the table as she makes her way over with her bubbly liquid. "Join us one last time."

Wow, she's being so nice. It really is over for me.

Wyatt taps Thea's shoulder, who sits on his other side. "Do you mind moving for Josie?"

Thea promptly complies, moving to the other side of the table.

I mumble a thank you, and shrink into the dining chair.

"Hey, I've missed you," he says, leaning over and kissing my cheek. "How was the spa?"

"Umm." I look over at where Portia and Jenna sit. I then lower my voice to say, "Actually, I had an interesting chat with Jenna instead. I'll tell you about it later."

Wyatt's eyebrows lift. "Oh, okay. All good, I hope."

I nod. "It was hopeful, to say the least."

"Okay, I guess you'll explain later. I met up with Savanna. She says hi."

"I'm sorry I missed her."

"She gave me her seal of approval to fly and get back to work."

It takes me by surprise. "Wow, really?"

"I know. First, they didn't want me to leave the clinic. Now, I'm improving like crazy."

I interlace my fingers with his. "I'm so happy for you."

A man wedges between me and Wyatt, places a document in front of Wyatt, and says, "You just missed an initial here."

"Oh." Wyatt picks up a pen and scribbles a WH by the man's index finger.

"Thank you." The man takes the document back. "I'll get this processed immediately."

Erika lifts her lemon-wedged sparkling water at the man. "Thank you, Raymond."

Martin, the finance guy, gets up from the table. "Raymond, I'll walk you out."

The men shake hands and leave the restaurant.

Portia watches Raymond leave, turns to Wyatt, then back to where the men left, and then lands on Erika. "Why was Raymond here?" Portia asks. "You had Wyatt sign something?"

Richmond leans over and pats Portia's hand. "Nothing to concern yourself with. Wyatt's just getting back to work, that's all."

I swallow the lump in my throat and meet Wyatt's eyes.

There's only one document I know Wyatt was mulling over signing.

Emancipation papers.

I murmur under my breath, "Was it?"

He nods slightly.

I blow out a breath.

Whoa. This is huge.

Erika keeps her glass lifted, cheering, "To Wyatt getting back in the studio."

Richmond lifts his glass of dark red liquid. "And to Portia being by his side."

Everyone around the table cheers. Portia sends Wyatt an encouraging look, and he replies with a small, hesitant smile.

As everyone else clinks their glasses together, Wyatt shrugs, lifts his water glass, and tilts it toward me. He then turns as Portia raises her glass toward him.

"Congratulations, baby," she says sweetly. "You're becoming you again."

As they clink their glasses together, my stomach sloshes like a half-empty water bottle, rolling around the backseat of a moving car.

Erika looks down her nose at me with a wry smile. "We need to get Josie a glass. She's not looking happy."

Wyatt looks back at me, his budding enthusiasm dwindling as he views my frown.

I can't help panning around all the faces and feeling a heavy dose of ick. "Wyatt's still in recovery," I say in a small voice. I sniff and gulp down the sourness lining the back of my throat. "You're not going to push him, are you?"

Wyatt's eyes shine, and he smiles at me with appreciation.

"We had meetings with his physical therapist and speech therapists, who are both onboard with Wyatt pursuing his singing career," Erika states. "Savanna will have a conference call with the guys at the studio to work out the ergonomics. All that's to say, Josie, you don't need to worry about Wyatt's health and safety. We have it at the forefront of our minds."

"I'll be okay, Joze," Wyatt says, brushing back one of my curls. "Portia says she'll help me get reacquainted with all the studio equipment."

Portia leans forward to make eye contact with me. "You don't have to worry, Josie. I'll protect our boy."

My teeth grit and I bite the inside of my cheek. *Our boy?*

I force myself to smile. "Thanks."

"It would be so nice to hang out with you before we leave," Portia continues. "Did they put you on the same floor as me? I'm in the presidential suite."

"Oh, my old room," it blurts out of me before I can catch it.

Portia blinks at me. "Excuse me?"

Wyatt mumbles a laugh, clutching my hand. "Yeah, I stole her. Once I got out of the clinic, I insisted Josie take one of the bedrooms in the penthouse. I mean, there's four of them and only one of me."

Portia flashes a smile. "Aw, cute. You've got some company."

"Portia," Richmond interjects across the table. "Have you given Wyatt the song lyrics yet?"

Impatience streaks across Erika's expression. "Yes, he needs that. Get in some practice tonight before the recording studio tomorrow."

Portia turns to Jenna. "You've got it, right?"

Jenna plucks a folded piece of paper out of her bag. "Here it is."

Portia takes it, unfolds it, and places it in front of Wyatt. "These are the lyrics to our song."

Wyatt blinks at the stanzas before him, and his jaw flexes. "Oh, thanks."

"Don't worry, you'll pick it up," Portia says. She then unlocks her phone and taps a few buttons. "I have a few soundbites from when we were working on it during breaks on set. Do you wanna hear it?"

Wyatt shrugs, bracing himself. "I guess."

A snippet of 'Summer Glow' plays from Portia's phone before she stops it. "Sorry," she mutters, becoming flushed. "It's one of your songs. I was listening to it while freshening up in my room."

"I know that one," Wyatt tells her.

Portia brightens. "You do?"

Wyatt nudges in my direction. "Josie played it for me."

Portia bobs her head as she scrolls on her phone. "Oh, that's nice. So you're okay with hearing some of your new stuff?"

"Took sometime." He squeezes my hand under the table. "It was easier once I had Josie by my side."

Portia smiles, leaning forward to look around at me. "That's great. I mean it."

Richmond clears his throat. "Hmm, Portia? The song?"

Portia goes back to her phone. "Ah, yeah, right."

Jenna reaches for the phone. "Do you want me to find it?"

Portia waves it off. "No, I got it."

We listen to the snippets from Portia's phone, and their voices sound as good as always, but something is just... off. Wyatt glances at me, and we share the same look. I rub my thumb in a circle on his hand. He feels it. Like there's no soul in his voice.

Wyatt takes the piece of paper and folds it up. "I'll get it. But right now, I wanna get upstairs." He nods at me. "Ready to go?"

I nod vigorously, standing from my seat quicker than he does.

Portia looks up at him. "Did you want me to come up to your apartment and help run through the lyrics with you?"

Wyatt shifts awkwardly. "Uh, no, umm. Josie's going home soon, and I kinda just want to spend more time with her."

Portia sits back. "I totally get that. How about I send these samples to your phone? You've still got it right."

Wyatt pats his pocket. "Got it."

Portia taps on her phone. "Sending them now. That way, you can listen to them when you're going over the lyrics. Hopefully, it helps you get the rhythm."

"Thanks, Portia." Wyatt then moves away from the table, waves to everyone and then clutches my hand. "I'll see you all tomorrow."

"Remember, we need to leave the hotel by eight in the morning to catch our flight," Erika says as we pass by the table.

"Yeah, yeah," Wyatt says, directing me away from the table. "I got it."

Just before we leave the restaurant, I stop so we can talk in private. "I can't believe you actually signed those forms."

"I know. I'm just sick of everyone fighting about what I do." He sighs, looking off to the side. "That's why I signed it. I want to be in charge of my life."

"Okay," I reply, placing my hands on his forearms. "I get it. It's been a lot."

Wyatt takes both my hands in his and shakes them as he talks. "Hey, so I know I said I'd go home to Victoria Falls with you."

"It's okay," I rush. "You need to go back to work."

His eyebrows push together as he shakes his head. "No, I don't *need* to. It's just..."

"It's okay," I insist.

He sighs. "Joze, just let me get this out."

I squeak in embarrassment. "I'm sorry. Go on."

"It's just." His jaw rocks, and he shifts his weight. "I just feel... Ugh, this is so tough. It just feels like I've got momentum. Like, things are coming back to me. I can't risk losing this shot."

"I get it," I reply. "I don't want you to miss the chance to get your memory back, no matter how slim the possibility is."

"I just hate disappointing you."

"*Wyatt.*" I squeeze his hands tighter. "You're not disappointing me. You never could."

"I just don't want to lose you."

"You never will." I raise our bundle of hands to the space above my heart. "You'll always be in my heart, no matter what."

There's a gleam in Wyatt's eyes, and he sniffs hard. "I don't want to just be in your heart. I want to be in your life. I hate the idea of going back to a life that's apparently mine, and not having you as a part of it."

"I get it. It's scary."

"I was wondering." He shifts awkwardly again, and his gaze drifts away. "Umm, it feels like a lot to ask, but would you come to Ferndale with us?"

"Oh." My turn to fidget. "Well, I would, but my parents..."

"Just for the day," he rushes. "Like, a layover?"

I giggle at his hasty suggestion. "What do you mean?"

"Well, we're taking the Circle 8 plane to Ferndale. What if it's gassed up, ready to take you to Victoria Falls later on?"

I lean into him. "You really want to squeeze in more time with me, don't you?"

The cutest smile graces his face. "Can you blame me?"

"Well, would that even work? I mean, Randall already booked my flight."

Wyatt bats a hand. "He'll cancel it. Wouldn't be the first time."

My heart thumps at the idea of extended time with Wyatt. "You really want me to come to Ferndale with you? What about Por—"

"Have I not been obvious enough with my feelings?"

I squeal and peck his lips. "I am really looking forward to going home. But once it hit me that I'd be apart from you, I was really dreading going on that plane."

Wyatt grins. "So, you'll come to Ferndale?"

"It's just delaying the heartache, but yes. I'd love to."

Wyatt cheers. "*Yes.*" He then backtracks. "I'm going to tell Randall."

"Now?"

"Yeah, then we don't have to worry about seeing them again until eight in the morning."

I send him a wink. "Good luck."

Twenty-Two

After promptly telling Erika—through Randall—that he refuses to work if I don't go home via Ferndale, Wyatt then walks me out of the restaurant, his security waiting idly by.

Before I can ask him how he felt about the confrontation, we're interrupted by a voice.

"Wyatt?"

We both turn toward the voice and spot his mother hurrying our way with large shopping bags in each hand.

"Here we go." Wyatt grunts and then rubs my upper arm. "Just wait here while I take care of this."

My gut tells me not to leave him. "Are you sure?"

Wyatt steps forward, leaving only a few feet between us. He huffs and folds his arms. "Hi, Mom. Have you been hitting up the boutiques?"

She places the bags by her high heels and brushes her bangs to the side. "Just a little retail therapy to clear the mind." She leans in towards Wyatt, motioning for a hug. "I've missed you so much."

Wyatt grimaces, pulling away.

Mrs. Hayes flinches, pulling back. "Sweetie? Are you okay?"

He glares at her. "Am I okay?"

His mother sighs, her eyes turning glassy. "Look, I've been wanting to see you since the ugliness the other day. We're just scared for you, Wyatt." She holds her middle, and her expression is tight. "Tensions got high, and your dad and I lost our cool."

I stare at her, too dumbfounded to blink.

"We don't need to talk about this," Wyatt says, taking a step back. "I hope you enjoyed your shopping trip. It'll be your last one on my dime."

Her mother chokes on air, confused by his words. "Huh? What was that?"

"Mom, you and I don't have a re-relationship," Wyatt says firmly. "Stop acting like you care. You just want to be cl-close to me for the cash."

Her mother stomps her foot and bundles up her fists. "That's not true!"

"There's no point arguing about this," Wyatt says, turning away. "I've already got everything in mm-motion."

Mrs. Hayes grabs her son's shoulder. "Wyatt, don't do this. Don't turn your back on your family. Ugh, this team. They controlled so much of your life before the accident. Now it's worse. You're in a much more vulnerable state."

Wyatt shuts his eyes, wincing as keeps his face turned from her. "Just stop."

Mrs. Hayes squeezes his shoulder tighter. "Your dad and I don't want them taking advantage of you."

An ache sizzles behind my forehead, and I grit my teeth as I rub the tender area. Erika and her team have painted a bad picture of Mr. and Mrs. Hayes and how they've acted over the past few years. If it's giving me a headache, I can't imagine how much worse it is for Wyatt. Ugh. They've all got to stop fighting over him and just let him heal.

"Oh, they didn't," a despondent voice says behind me.

I turn around and find Portia standing there, staring at Wyatt and his mother with mournful eyes.

"It was the emancipation papers," Portia says weakly. "I can't believe they convinced him to sign them."

"What are you..." I pause, taking a moment to really hear her. "What do you mean?"

"The team pushed for over a year to get him to sign." Portia shakes her head. "He always said no. He didn't want this."

My hand rushes over the space on my chest, as my heart thunders with overwhelm.

Portia steps forward. "Wyatt, don't you..."

"Portia!" Richmond calls, stepping out of the restaurant.

Portia's shoulders fall, and she turns with her head drooped.

I notice Mrs. Hayes's eyes light up. "Portia!"

Richmond beckons Portia over as he strides into the lobby. "Portia, you've got a job to do."

Portia nods and follows Richmond toward her security, who escort her to the elevator.

Before I can process Portia's commentary, I turn back to Wyatt and his mother.

"We just want to be the ones to help you through this," his mother says with desperation. "You're our child, sweetie. We don't want to be shut out of your life."

Wyatt pushes her hand off him. "Can't you see how hard you've made things for me?"

"We were trying to get our points across before the team shoved us out of the room. Wyatt, we remember all their tactics and manipulations. We can help you."

Wyatt winces again, rubbing his temples. "Just stop. It's not happening."

I step in and take Wyatt by the hand. "Come on. You need to get upstairs."

"Josie," Mrs. Hayes says my name in a forceful way. "Would you want your parents around if you were going through something like this?"

My heart thumps inside my chest as she stares me down. "Yes, of course. But Wyatt..."

"Wyatt thinks we don't have a relationship," Mrs. Hayes blurts, picking up her shopping bags. "But this no-good management company is filling his head with lies."

It's not that I completely trust Erika and the rest of the management team, but Wyatt feels a gut reaction to his parents. He feels like their fractured relationship is the only part of the last few years he can remember.

There's no way I'm letting his mother continue to attack him in the foyer. I tug on his hand, and he gladly steps away with me.

"Wyatt, your father and I want to see you again," she says, making one last-ditch effort. "We want to make things right. Any way we can."

Before Wyatt can contemplate answering her, his security approaches and escorts us to the elevator.

I can't help myself and take one last look over my shoulder before we leave the lobby. Mrs. Hayes stands alone, shopping bags in her hands. She blames the management team for her fractured relationship with her son. But they're not the ones who have been yelling and hurling accusations around.

Ugh. This is such a mess.

Inside the elevator, Wyatt wraps his arms around me. "I'm sorry you had to see that."

"Are you kidding me? I'm the one who's sorry. You shouldn't have to go through that. Especially with your parents."

"I just need to move on from them. Maybe, with a little distance, we can work things out in the future. But I can't be around them when they're so fixated on me working and providing for them."

I suck in a breath as an ugly thought strikes me.

Wyatt jolts. "What is it?"

I glance at the two security guards. They're standing tall and facing the closed elevator doors as we ascend the floors.

"Joze?"

"What if..." I whisper. "Umm. Your parents... Umm. The accident. What if..."

"They're somehow involved?"

I gulp. "Yeah."

"I don't know," he whispers. "There's something deep in my gut, te-telling me to keep a barrier between me and them."

"So, you feel good about signing the papers?"

He nods, holding me closer. "Yeah. It was the right thing to do."

When we get to our floor, and move into the living room, I tell him, "Portia said something back there when you were talking with your mother."

"Yeah?" He flops on the couch. "What's that?"

"She said you never wanted to sign the papers."

Wyatt grabs a throw pillow, hugging it against him. "Huh?"

I curl up beside him. "She said she saw the team ask you to sign the papers over the past year, but you didn't want to."

Wyatt shrugs. "Yeah, and I didn't want to now."

"What do you mean?"

"I don't want to divide my family. I want ev-everything back to normal. But it's never going to happen. Th-this was my only option."

I sit back, mulling over his words.

Wyatt grunts, rubbing the side of his head. "I don't want to talk about it anymore." He looks over the backrest of the couch. "Hubert?"

Hubert enters the living area. "Yes, Mr. Hayes?"

"Can you get my pills for me?"

"Right away, sir."

I massage the side of his head for him. "I wish these headaches would go away."

"Once I get my life back on track, I'm sure they will." He takes my hand and kisses my palm. "Getting you back in my life is the best thing I've done."

"Do you still feel that way after meeting the fabulous Portia?"

His eyebrow crooks. "Are you trying to compare her to you? No competition, babe. You've got her beat on every level."

I giggle, taking his throw pillow and bonking him on the head. "You goof."

"Hey." He ducks away. "Guy with a brain injury here."

I smirk. "And I'm sure a pillow is gonna make it worse."

He grins. "If only this were a cartoon and I could hit my head again, and all my memories would come flooding back."

"Too bad this is real life, and all you'd achieve is even worse headaches."

He frowns. "Yeah, not a good trade."

I slink down on the couch as Hubert brings his pills. "So, Ferndale tomorrow. Are you excited?"

Wyatt washes back the pills, and Hubert leaves discreetly.

"I d-don't know if ex-excited is the right word. But I'm hoping it feels like home."

I sigh at the possibility. "I really hope it feels like you get a missing piece back. It felt that way when meeting Portia, right?"

He gives me a startled look. "Yeah, but not like she was my..."

I cut him off with a laugh. "Wyatt, you've made it clear you're not interested in her."

He smiles. "It was like my work life, I guess. All the dark spots in my memory."

"And your parents never did that for you?"

"They just brought negativity around the blank spaces." He hugs the pillow again. "Portia brings brightness. Like, maybe this work thing won't be so bad after all. She makes it sound fun, doesn't she?"

"Well, sure. It's all very glamorous, being a celebrity."

Wyatt sighs, combing his fingers through his hair. "I guess so."

I tap his arm. "You're slouching. Savanna wouldn't be happy."

Wyatt grunts, pulling himself up on the couch. "I forgot. Hunching is your thing."

I giggle. "Shut up."

He grasps my hand. "Are you really okay with going to Ferndale with me?"

"Yeah, but my parents won't be. My mom is already panic-stricken and wants me on the next flight home."

"It's just a little detour."

"Yeah. I'll just tell them this is the quickest option to get me home. One more night away, and then I'll be home."

"Ugh. How am I going to survive without you?"

"There are always video chats. We won't really be apart."

He shakes his head. "It's not the same."

I lean in and kiss him softly. "That's why we need to get all our kissing in before I leave."

He caresses the sides of my face, hungrily kissing me back. As I reposition myself against him, I feel him shift. A soft moan pours out of him, and then he grazes my bottom lip with his teeth as he pulls away.

His hands stay locked on the sides of my face as he sighs. "All I want right now is to be kissing you. But I really should take a look at this song."

I slump against him and huff. "Okay."

He mumbles a laugh as he plucks the folded paper from his pocket. "Sorry to disappoint you."

"It's okay," I murmur, fanning my face. "We have all night."

Wyatt flattens the paper out and stares at it blankly.

I nudge him. "Where are your glasses?"

He shrugs. "I dunno. I haven't used them since I left the clinic."

My chin drops. "*Wyatt.* You just signed a legal document. Why the heck wouldn't you have your glasses with you?"

He shrugs again, purposefully turning his face away from me. "I dunno. Raymond explained it all to me. Felt like I didn't need them."

I click my tongue. "No, you didn't *want* to use them. What's with the vanity?"

Wyatt groans. "Ugh. They're just another thing wrong with me. It's bad enough everyone keeps tossing that walking cane at me. I don't need them shoving reading glasses on my face too."

I rub his arm, hoping to ease his tension. "Hey, they're not a mark of failure. They gave them to you to help with your headaches and strengthen your focus. It's okay if I go look for them?"

Wyatt shrugs. "They're in the bedroom somewhere. Hubert unpacked my stuff."

I stand from the couch and crane my neck toward the butler's quarters. "Hubert?"

Determined footsteps march our way. "Yes, miss?"

I smile at him with gratitude. "Do you know where Wyatt's reading glasses are?"

Hubert nods and moves toward the bedrooms. "I'll retrieve them at once."

"Joze, I really don't need them."

"Would you stop? The clinic wouldn't have given them to you if you didn't need them."

He frowns. "I used them while I was in there."

"So, why stop? I don't get why you're being so fussy."

He huffs. "I'm not being fussy."

Hubert returns with the glasses, but Wyatt doesn't make an effort to take them.

As the room oozes with awkward tension, I take the glasses from Hubert and thank him. He leaves, telling us to call him if we need anything further.

I hand the glasses to Wyatt. "Stop being a baby and put them on."

Wyatt groans. "You know I hate them. They pinch behind my ears."

I smirk. "I thought it was your nose they pinched?"

Wyatt rolls his eyes, sliding them on. "Either way, they suck."

I kiss his cheek. "No, they're adorable."

He gives me a disagreeable look.

I grin at his framed eyes and clap. "*Yay.* Now you're ready to learn your lyrics."

He fiddles with the earpiece of the glasses and glances at the paper. "Why do you love me?"

Like a vacuum, his words suck the air from my lungs. I bang on my chest and cough, searching for oxygen. Blinking hard and refilling my lungs, I then croak, "What?"

He sighs, lifting the paper. "We only met because I was the dummy who had to repeat sixth grade. How did I not turn you off?"

I curl my legs onto the seat of the couch and sit on my knees. "Because you're wonderful."

"You were stuck tutoring me."

"So? You're more than your reading age or how quickly you solve a math problem. You're creative and soulful. You're my other half."

"But you're so much better than me. You're intelligent, caring, and…"

I press my finger against his lips. "*Hush.* Don't you dare say a bad word about yourself."

His shoulders droop, and his eyes are glossy. "These glasses are basically a big sign on my face saying, I'm behind."

I drop my hands to his shoulders. "No, they're not. Don't you realize how many crazy-smart people wear glasses?"

"But I already have a history of trailing behind everyone else."

Tears prick my eyes. "Stop it."

He lifts the paper again. "You heard my voice on Portia's phone. My heart wasn't in it. All I've ever wanted was to be a musician and somehow it happened. And I'm blowing it. No one wants to hear an original song from me. I'm not good enough."

I cup my hands against his jawline. "Don't say that. Wyatt, you've lost your memory because you suffered emotional shock. Recording those soundbites was one of the last things you did on the film set. Maybe your heart wasn't in the song because other things were going on in your life." I lower my hands, sigh, and take the piece of paper from him. "You have a clean slate now. We're back together. Maybe we can put some soul back into these words."

Wyatt sucks in a breath and combs his fingers through his hair. "I don't want to mess it up."

I give him a gentle smile. "Isn't that why you wanted to come up here and practice? I mean, you stopped our make-out session for this."

He blushes, and the glasses slightly droop on his nose. "Okay, the worrying is over."

I graze my thumb against his chin. "I'm so glad you can be honest about your feelings with me. But don't ever doubt my love for you. Why you're still into me is another matter."

"What?"

A nervous laugh simmers out of me. "Portia would've locked lips with you if you'd let her."

"I'm not gonna let her," he replies firmly. "Your lips are the only ones I want."

My heart swells. "Really?"

"The girl got off a long flight," he says softly. "I wasn't gonna reject her immediately. Fi-firstly, she took me off guard. Secondly, I didn't want to be mean."

"See. Told ya, you're the sweetest."

"I've told you all along, you don't need to be jealous of some other girl." He grasps my hand and kisses it. "And, I don't doubt you love me. I just think you can do better."

A belly laugh rolls out of me. "You're a literal superstar." I wipe the tears of laughter from my eyes. "And I loved you before the fame. How could you think I was punching under?"

Wyatt's eyebrows raise. "You loved me before?"

I bite my lip. "I never said anything. It seemed too soon, and I figured we'd have more time." I pull my arms around his waist. "I felt so lucky when I was asked to tutor you when you repeated sixth grade. I was obsessed with you, right from the start."

Wyatt smirks. "Obsessed?"

"Big time. Those big eyes, luscious lips, and sweet attitude. You are everything to me, Wyatt."

Wyatt grins and kisses my forehead. "Then I'll be glad I got held back. Otherwise, I might not have you now."

"Exactly. Second chances happen for a reason."

"You still got the lyrics? I think I'm ready to practice now."

I pull my arms from around him and lift the paper. Wyatt gets up and rounds the couch. I'm about to ask where he's going when, from behind the couch, I see him pick up the guitar that sits against the dining table from earlier today.

He lifts the guitar strap over his head and plucks the pick from between the strings. "Can you hit play on the song Portia sent?"

"You sure you want to hear it again?"

"I just want to hear the music."

I hit play, and Wyatt bops his head as he listens to the tune. He begins to strum, and he picks up the rhythm as their voices come through the phone.

His eyes are closed as he still wears the glasses, strumming the guitar. He starts murmuring the lyrics, having heard them in the recordings. He focuses on playing the guitar, nailing the chords better than the words he needs to memorize.

The more he practices the lyrics, with me standing by him holding the sheet of paper, he tries putting emphasis on different words. His brow furrows, and he shakes his head. I'm worried another headache is building, but he sighs, showing it's just utter frustration.

He moves away from the dining table, pacing as he strums.

"Maybe you should take a rest?" I suggest.

He has his back to me as he continues to pace. "Just a minute," he mumbles.

More lyrics sing out of him, but I don't recognize them from the song. I look down at the paper, assuming I hadn't read the stanza, but the lines blur as realization sets in.

I gasp and drop the piece of paper. "What are you doing?"

He continues to sing, and my heart hammers into overdrive.

Holy cow.

Wyatt turns to face me, smiling as he sings the words with soulful power.

"The space is big enough for me.

One-hundred people fit here.

But I'm only happy when it's us.

Crowds break my spirit.

Together, we bring the light."

He's singing the words from my poem.

And, his voice makes them better.

"How..." I stammer. "How do you remember those words?"

He stops strumming so he can tap the space on his chest over his heart. "They're your words, Joze. They'll always be in here."

"I just... I never... I never expected anyone to sing one of my poems."

Wyatt's eyes light up behind his frames. "This is what I was talking about, Josie. Your words have heart. There's no way anyone could diss a song written by you."

I gesture at the lyrics on the floor. "But your team wants you to learn *this* song."

"But we can fix it. *You* can fix it." Wyatt folds his arms around his guitar. "Those guys have to know the song isn't working. Imagine how grateful they'll be when you Josi-fy the song."

I giggle. "*Josi-fy?*"

"Yes, make it amazing. Like everything you write."

"I don't think I'm allowed to just change a song."

Wyatt motions to his phone on the couch. "Call Portia and get her take on it."

My stomach somersaults. I'd rather walk on nails than chit-chat with the popstar.

I scoop the lyrics off the floor. "Why don't we try rewriting it first? Then we'll know whether we should bother Portia with the question."

Glee fills Wyatt's expression. "You'll do it?"

I inhale a large breath, hoping to boost my bravery. "I'll do it."

Twenty-Three

We stayed up way too late, working on the song. It was fun writing with pen and paper again, since I've grown so attached to typing on my laptop. Hubert supplied us with more sheets of paper as our work got underway. I crouched by the coffee table, scribbling away, and Wyatt sat on the couch, strumming, and singing the new hooks we came up with.

I actually feel a little hungover from all the brainpower used. I squint my eyes open, and my smile grows when Wyatt shifts beside me. He rolls onto his side, flings an arm across my middle, and attacks me with butterfly kisses up and down my face.

I squeal and giggle, half pulling away from the sickly sweet blitz.

"Ah, last night was amazing," he mumbles, flopping his head back down on his pillow. "It reminded me of the times we'd spend in your treehouse. Me playing my guitar, and you writing these wild stories."

I roll onto my side, blinking the last sleep from my eyes so I can take in his beautiful face. "It really was. I've held all those moments, just you and me alone and being creative, so near to my heart. Ah, I'm so happy we got to recreate it."

He lifts his head. "But it won't stop there, will it?"

My heart bounces to a blissful beat. "I'll always be on the other end of a video chat whenever you want to brainstorm lyrics." I lift my head and peck his lips. "Or anything else for that matter."

He brushes back my curls. "Thanks, Josie. You're one in a million."

It didn't take much convincing, after we dragged ourselves off the couch last night, to say yes when Wyatt asked me to sleep in his bed. Once he rolled on his side, I was out like a light. But waking up next to him is the cherry on top. This could very well be the last time we're together, and I want to soak up every second with him.

Wyatt sits on the edge of the bed and hisses a breath, rubbing the side of his head.

I get onto my knees and rub a tight circle on his back. "The headaches?"

Wyatt exhales slowly. "Not as bad as usual," he mutters. "Just a dull ache."

"You'd better take your pain meds, anyway."

"Hubert will have them ready." Wyatt stands from the bed. "Man, I'm gonna miss that guy."

"He was always around when we needed him." I get off the bed and move toward the bedroom door. "I guess I'd better get my bags ready."

Wyatt kisses my cheek as I pass him by. "I'm gonna take a shower."

I leave Wyatt's bedroom for mine, feeling lighter than expected. I'm beyond relieved I'm flying to Ferndale with him, or packing my bags would be torture. At least I won't unpack again, and the bags will be ready for my last flight home. Then the only excruciating part will be finally saying goodbye to Wyatt.

After a shower, styling my curls, and brushing on a fresh face of makeup, I dress in one of my new boutique outfits. I grab my carry-on luggage by the straps, and take one last look around the room. With mixed emotions, I move out into the hallway.

"Ready, cutie?" Wyatt asks, running a hand through his hair as he smiles at me.

The way his arm crooks, the sleeve of his T-shirt rides up, and reveals his tattoo.

I'm a pile of goo as I gaze at him. "Ready as I'll ever be."

"Allow me, miss," Hubert says, meeting me in the hall and taking my bag. "A porter will take all the luggage downstairs."

I look over my shoulder. "Oh gosh. Yeah, there's all that stuff in the last bedroom."

"Not our problem." Wyatt shrugs. "I just care about the guitar."

Hubert nods. "I'll ensure the guitar and all other property is taken down to the cars with Miss Bartlett's luggage, sir."

"Thanks, Hubert," Wyatt replies, "for everything."

"It was a pleasure," Hubert says. "Hope to see you again at the Gran Palacio Hotel."

Wyatt pulls his phone from his pocket. "It's a text from Portia." He squints at the screen. "It says, uhh..."

I deadpan at him. "Where are your glasses?"

Wyatt grunts and backtrack to his bedroom. I follow him and he snatches the glasses off the nightstand. He fixes them on his face, and checks the screen again.

"Oh," he says with a nod. "It says to meet on her floor. That's just one level down, right?"

"Right. It's the floor I used to be on."

"Good to know they gave you the second best room in the place," Wyatt says, pocketing the phone.

"I'm guessing I would've moved if I were still down there when Portia arrived."

Wyatt winks behind his frames. "I wouldn't have let them downgrade you."

I gesture to his pocket. "Aren't you gonna reply to her."

He bats a hand. "We'll see them downstairs in two minutes."

I take a breath for bravery. "Okay, so we're leaving."

Wyatt takes my hand. "I'm so glad you're going with me. The thought of going to where I supposedly live makes me sweat."

I squeeze his hand. "You didn't stay up all night thinking about it, did you?"

"Thankfully, the sleep aid knocked me out. I'm sure I would have st-stayed st-stressing all night otherwise."

Wyatt hands me his glasses, and I place them in their case and slip them into the strappy bag Marsha at the boutique talked me into getting. Just in case, I also get Wyatt's current pill bottle and sit them inside. Wyatt really needs extra relief during the flight. With Hubert organizing the arrival of our luggage, Wyatt and I take the elevator a level down to meet the others. I can only imagine it'll be a tight squeeze when we already have security riding with us.

When the elevator doors ping open, we're hit with a wall of noise. Besides the wall-hugging security, Erika, Randall, Richmond, Lexy, and Thea buzz in the hallway around Portia.

Jenna stands off to the side, holding a tray of to-go coffee cups. She brightens with a smile at the sight of us and we leave the elevator to join her.

"I did a coffee run," Jenna says, gesturing with the tray of cups. "I still have your order memorized, Wyatt. Oh, and Josie, I didn't know how you take your coffee, so I got you the same as Wyatt. Hope that's okay."

"Uh," I falter. "Yeah, of course. Thank you."

I glance at Wyatt, who squints like he's solving a riddle. "You got me a coffee?"

Jenna takes a cup from its cardboard holder. "Sure did. Your caramel mocha on almond milk."

Wyatt shrugs, taking the cup. "Doesn't sound too bad."

Jenna tilts her head, eyes widening. "You didn't remember your order?"

Wyatt puffs a laugh. "I don't remember ever drinking coffee."

Jenna's chin drops. "Oh... Well, I hope you like it."

Wyatt lifts the cup in a cheer. "Apparently, I did."

Jenna gives me my cup, and then makes her way over to Portia, who's still deep in conversation with Richmond and Lexy. Erika's talking on her phone, and Randall stands next to her, busily typing on his phone.

Wyatt lowers his voice, asking me, "Do you drink coffee?"

I cup a hand over my mouth as I jiggle in a silent laugh. "Nope. But it has caramel and chocolate in it. How bad can it be?"

Wyatt lifts the cup to his lips. "Let's see."

He turns with his back to the others and takes a small sip. He drinks, and everything seems fine, until he grits his teeth.

"Uhh, don't like that aftertaste."

I smirk. "I'm guessing that's the coffee part."

Wyatt taps his cup against mine. "You try it."

I've had coffee when I'm in a bind. Like, swiping my mom's morning brew when I'm not awake enough for school. I wouldn't say I love it.

I tip the cup toward my lips and take a sip. Sweetness glides over my tongue. The coffee blends with the nutty caramel and thick chocolate in a surprisingly delicious way.

"Mmm," I purr, pulling the cup from my lips. "Not bad."

Wyatt's eyebrows lift. "Not bad?"

"I've tried coffee before. This is better than anything I've ever tried." I tap my cup against his. "The you-you-don't-remember had good taste."

He grins. "That I can believe."

With blackout sunglasses atop her head, Portia walks over in a tight-fitting black jumpsuit and silver pumps. She holds a venti coffee cup in one hand, and a black Hermès bag sits in the crook of her other arm.

"Mornings never get easier, do they?" she says in a soft voice. "Did you sleep okay, baby?"

Wyatt clears his throat, his eyes averting to the floor. "Ah, yeah, fine."

"Good. We need to be in tip-top shape for the recording booth."

"Everyone ready to go?" Erika's voice booms over everyone crowded in the hallway. "Wyatt and Portia, you take the first trip down."

Portia steps onto the elevator with security and Jenna following closely behind. Wyatt nods at me, and we join them inside. When the elevator doors close, I smile with relief at the silence. Thank goodness, we'll have a few minutes without Erika's booming voice.

"You look happy," Jenna says to me.

"Oh." I blush, realizing everyone's reading my expression. "Just enjoying the quiet."

"You're really not in this business," Portia says with a subtle laugh. "If you can't deal with everyone talking at once, this lifestyle isn't for you."

I nod, finding it hard to look her in the eyes. I know Wyatt's a celebrity too, but Portia is a big-name star. And she's right here. Talking to me.

"Yeah, it's one-hundred percent not for me," I mutter at my shoes.

Wyatt takes my hand. "She's just here for me. Everything got easier once Josie came back into my life."

Portia awes. "That's really sweet. It's so good to have someone in your corner."

Wyatt glances at Jenna, and then back at Portia. "Just like you guys. You and Jenna seem like close friends."

Portia smiles at Jenna. "Yeah, we are. I'd be lost without her."

Wyatt clears his throat, shifting his stance. "Is that what me and my assistant were like?"

Portia's eyes turn into saucers, and I peek at Jenna and find her squirming.

Portia places a hand on Wyatt's upper arm. "You don't have to worry about him anymore. He's out of your life."

"But we were close, weren't we?"

Portia swallows hard, glancing again at Jenna, and then back at Wyatt as she takes her hand off him. "Yes, you were. Like brothers."

"Then why..."

She cuts him off. "That's what makes the whole thing so tragic."

Wyatt folds his arms, looking down at the floor as he nods his understanding.

The elevator doors ping open at the parking garage, and security walks us toward the black SUVs, which are waiting in a line.

Wyatt and Portia leave first, and I take my opportunity to clutch Jenna's wrist and tug her backwards.

She stumbles on her footing, turning to face me. "Josie? What's wrong?"

"You know what's wrong?" I whisper. "Wyatt wants to know about Devon. I saw Portia falter. Deep down, she knows Devon couldn't hurt Wyatt."

"Don't put words in Portia's mouth."

"You need to help us find him. He's the only one who has the answers."

"I can't."

"I just need a phone number. You don't have to contact him."

"I already told you, his phone is disconnected. Blocked, gone, *finito*."

"There has to be some way to trace him. Where would we find him in Ferndale?"

"Look, I can't go there."

"Where?" My heart pulsates with hope. "Tell me where we can find him."

Jenna slips her wrist out of my grip. "I can't do this, Josie. You need to drop it."

As she dashes away, a pit grows wider in my stomach.

Something is definitely up.

Yesterday, she divulged so much information about Wyatt and Devon's working friendship.

What's changed?

Did someone get to her?

Did Portia warn her not to talk to me about Devon?

Or was it someone else? Someone from management?

"Josie?" Wyatt calls from the open car door.

I hurry across the concrete landing to meet him. "Coming!"

The trip to the airport is mostly silent. Our three-vehicle convoy stays closely together, and once we get through the heavy Cherry Beach traffic, the SUVs pull up on the tarmac near the Circle 8 Learjet.

As we approach the boarding stairs, the managers talk loudly on their phones, seemingly needing to get all their calls in before the one-hour flight to Ferndale.

"Wow," Wyatt breathes as he grabs the staircase railing. "It's a private plane, Joze."

Tingles electrify my veins, watching the wonder in his eyes. "*See.* Told ya you were big-time now."

Wyatt laughs, and I follow him onto the plane.

"Mr. Hayes, it's an honor to have you aboard once again," the flight attendant says, placing a hand on her chest. "My name is Claire, and I'm here for anything you need. And hello again, Miss Bartlett."

I wave. "Hi Claire."

Claire shows us into the cabin, giving Wyatt extra attention. We find our seats, and she still hasn't fussed over Portia, who's sitting two rows away from us with Jenna.

Claire hovers a hand over her mouth as she chuckles. She lowers her hand and leans in to whisper, "I should never admit this, but you're my favorite of the Circle 8 members to have aboard."

Wyatt snorts at her admission.

"It's true," Claire insists. "It's rare to find someone who hasn't let fame go to his head, and still uses his please and thank yous."

"Oh, well, you're welcome."

"Please, let me know if there's anything I can do to make your flight more enjoyable," Claire says sincerely. "I can't fathom how difficult things must be. Dealing with a life that doesn't feel like your own. Can I get you anything?"

Wyatt tugs me close as he leans over to ask Claire, "How soon are you taking this plane back to Victoria Falls?"

"We'll need to refuel and clean the cabin. We'll have a few hours before our next flight."

Wyatt sits back with an exhale. "*Phew.* You're not taking her away too soon."

Claire's eyes land on me with warmth. "Are you nervous about your next flight?"

I snuggly wrap my arm around Wyatt's. "Only about leaving him."

Claire smiles and nods. "Anything else, you two?"

I grin. "Jellybeans. We need jellybeans."

Wyatt laughs. "Do they have them?"

"We always have them, waiting for you," Claire replies. "I'll return with them soon."

Wyatt kisses my cheek. "What made you ask for jellybeans?"

"Claire gave them to me on my flight over," I reply. "Maybe if we get a sugar rush, we won't think about not being together."

"Hope it works. I want to stretch out our remaining time together."

Captain Frank Ford greets everyone in the cabin, making an effort to shake Wyatt's hand. Wyatt is awestruck from all the attention, still reeling from the fact the private plane is a real thing. Captain Ford lets us know he's about to take off, and everyone gets settled in their seats.

Once we're in the sky, there's a bowl of jelly beans in front of us. People begin unbuckling, and there's a relaxed air inside the plane.

Wyatt sinks into his seat, his arm resting across my shoulders. I cuddle into him, needing so badly to forget this is our last day together.

Wyatt fidgets against me, and bats his hand in the direction of the aisle. "Nuh-uh. Keep going."

I look down the aisle and find Randall approaching. He lifts a finger, saying, "But I..."

Wyatt's face is stony as he shakes his head.

Randall continues along the walkway, and in his place, Portia comes into view.

She laughs to herself and takes a seat across from us. "You know, everyone says you think you're just a normy, Wyatt, but that was some celebrity attitude I just saw."

Wyatt's arm hugs around my shoulders, and his fingers stroke the top of my arm. "I don't need him ruining the time I have left with Josie."

"I get it," she says, making herself comfortable in her new seat. "Sometimes, flights are the only time I get to breathe. Once we hit the ground, they'll work us to the bone to get this track recorded."

With his free hand, Wyatt taps on the table. "I was practicing a lot last night. Hope I'm up to scratch. Your vocals are insane on the recordings you sent us."

Portia bounces in her seat. "Thanks, baby. But, after all this time, I only hear the areas I need to tighten up. Do you remember any of your vocal exercises?"

He nods. "Sure. All the stuff my music teacher from back home taught me."

Portia twirls a shiny lock of hair around her finger. "I still want to meet that teacher one day. You taught me some of his exercises, and nothing has helped open up my range like those have."

I sit up and ask, "Are you talking about Mr. Taveski?"

Portia giggles. "I just know him as Mr. T."

Wyatt relaxes beside me. "He thought that nickname was such a crack up."

Portia dreamily stares at Wyatt, and I feel myself becoming invisible. "We should fly him out on one of our recording days. We always talked about it."

Wyatt's grip around me loosens. "We did?"

"Yeah, we've talked about a bunch of stuff," she says, swatting a hand. "And with all the time you've been out of action, doesn't it show how precious our time is? Why not be a little spontaneous? We've put off enough things over the years. We never know how much time we really have."

Wyatt smiles, meeting Portia's almond-shaped eyes. "Sounds like a good idea for a song."

My stomach flips, watching Portia's eyes search deep into Wyatt's while his arm is around me. I fidget beside him, unable to help feeling bad for her. I was worried they were a couple when she wasn't in the picture.

Now she's here, calling him baby with an adoring stare. What if she thought they were a couple? What does she think of me, cuddled up beside him and stealing his attention from her? She must hate me.

It's not her fault. They were so close before his accident. She didn't do anything wrong. I just don't want Wyatt taken away from me. But they obviously share a history too. Ugh, I feel terrible.

"Are you excited to meet up with everyone else?" Portia asks.

Wyatt's hand jerks against my arm. "Everyone else?"

"You know, our peers," Portia elaborates. "Some of the gang are in Ferndale. Maggie's between shows, and Theo's in town for contract negotiations. Oh, even Simon's back in town."

Wyatt takes in the news, staring blankly as none of the names register.

"Simon just wrapped filming his latest project." Portia giggles, shaking her head. "We were texting last night, and he wanted me to tell you that you need to finish your movie."

At that, Wyatt squirms.

Portia smirks. "Apparently, they've approached him to take over the role if your speech doesn't improve."

Wyatt sinks further down in his seat.

Portia reaches a hand across to him. "Don't be nervous. I'll run lines with you."

Wyatt frowns. "Mm-hmm."

Her grip on him tightens. "It'll be okay. I've helped you tons of times in the past. You'll get back up to speed."

His jaw rocks, and uncertainty wavers in his stare. "I just... I don't see myself on a movie set."

Portia gulps, pulling her hand back toward her. "You will," she murmurs.

The discomfort radiates off Wyatt. I badly want to tell him everything will be okay. But with Portia watching us, I'm paralyzed.

She wants to be the one holding him. When she tells him it'll be okay, she wants him to believe her.

Portia takes a handful of jelly beans and then stands up. "Well, I'll leave you two alone. We all need to conserve our energy before we land."

"Thanks. Bye, Portia," Wyatt says as she moves back to her seat beside Jenna.

"That really unnerved you, huh?"

Wyatt's fingers tap along the table's edge. "The movie talk?"

"Yeah. You know, there's no rush."

"I think there is. Movies cost a lot, and I'm probably holding everything up."

"But you got hurt on set. It's their duty not to rush you back there."

Wyatt hugs me closer. I can't help but pout.

"Hey, what's wrong?" he whispers.

I motion toward Portia's seat. "Does she seem sad to you?"

"Portia?"

"Yeah. It's like she came over here to say something, but didn't actually say it."

"Like what?"

"I dunno..." I trail off, not wanting to say what's on my mind.

That Portia wishes she were in Wyatt's arms. That she wants to pick up where they left off.

I shake it off and hug my arms around my boyfriend. "Nothing. I just want to forget everyone else is here with us."

He rests his head against mine. "*That* I'm onboard with."

It doesn't take long before the plane is ready to land in Ferndale. Wyatt massages his temples as the plane descends. After we hit the tarmac, he promises me he's feeling okay.

We watch everyone else unbuckle before we budge an inch. It's like we both realize how much our time is running out once we leave this plane.

"Thea, can you hand me my sunglasses?" Lexy calls out to her assistant. "I can't deal with all those flashes. I don't want to be seeing spots for the next hour."

Flashes?

As Wyatt and I join the others in the aisle, Thea hands Lexy a pair of aviator sunglasses. Ahead, Claire opens the passenger door for us to exit the plane.

Through the hum of the usual airplane sounds, a louder rumble mixes into the surrounding noise.

The management staff vacates the plane with security watching over them. As I wander behind Thea, I peek through a window, and a gasp shoots out of me. The tarmac is littered with people. A huddled mass of cameras, microphones, hand-painted signs, and excited cheers. The crowd is held behind loose ropes, and I don't believe for a second they will hold back the mix of press and adoring fans.

"Joze?" Wyatt's voice brings me back into my body, and his hand grasps my shoulder. "You okay?"

I purse my lips and hold my breath, unable to communicate my fear of leaving the plane.

"Wyatt," Portia says, grabbing onto his forearm. "We're wanted outside. It's time for everyone to see us back together."

He chokes. "Ex-excuse me?"

She giggles. "This is what we do. We have our photo taken together, and there are clips filmed. It's how we stay relevant."

Wyatt checks the exit. "There's a crowd here for us?"

Portia nods. "Why don't we head out? They'll be preoccupied with us, and then Josie can sneak out after. I mean, look at her. She's obviously freaked."

Wyatt looks at me with heightened concern. "No, I can't leave Josie behind. Joze, are you okay?"

I shiver and force myself to nod. "Go with Portia," I stammer, chilled with fear. "I'll be okay."

Wyatt's worry increases. "But I..."

Portia gestures at a security guard. "He'll escort Josie out. She'll be safe."

The roars and screams from the crowd intensify, and when I shudder, something comes over me and I shove Wyatt away.

He stumbles, shocked. "Joze?"

"*Go,*" it comes out of me hoarse as my vision blurs and my insides quiver.

Portia helps Wyatt stand upright, and I internally yell at myself to apologize, but I'm frozen.

Wyatt leaves the plane with Portia, and the cheers raise an octave.

Jenna follows after them. Inside the plane gets so quiet, I realize I'm left all alone. That is, until the security guard steps forward.

"I'll walk you to your car, miss."

I clutch my elbows, fixated on the noises outside.

"Miss?" the guard works to gain my attention.

My stomach wobbles like a plate of jelly, and I swallow the urge to hurl the contents.

The only reason I want to go outside is Wyatt. But in order to do that, I have to walk out in front of all those people. The cameras. The judgmental eyes.

The general public already hates me for walking on Royale Boulevard with him.

What will they think when I'm walking out of the Circle 8 Learjet? Will all the online commentators call me a man-stealer? That I'm trying to take Wyatt away from Portia? That I'm just *some girl* who's constantly following them?

Like some kind of stalker?

Twenty-Four

I retch hard, my eyes blurring.

"*Oof.* You don't look so good," the security guard says bluntly.

Claire joins me in the aisle. "Josie? Do you want to take a seat? I could get you a glass of water."

Goosebumps prick my skin as a layer of sweat coats my entire body.

"Josie?" Claire asks in alarm.

I clear my throat roughly and blink the tears away. "I'm okay." I cough, wiping my brow. "Crap... All those people. Ugh. I just need to get out of here."

Claire motions for me to follow security. "He'll get you out of here. They're trained to be as discreet as possible."

My stomach flips so hard it might turn inside out.

He might get me out of here, but I still need to descend those stairs. Those people are still corralled around the stairs.

Holy cow.

Ouch! My stomach.

I wipe away the new layer of sweat.

Dang it. Maybe I should've just flown home. I've gone right into the Circle 8 hub. The homeland of the celebrity kids and their superfans. I'm spending a few hours here. I don't know how my nervous system will remain functioning.

The security guard snaps his fingers at me. "Okay, look alive. We're going down these stairs and straight to the car. Are you with me?"

Despite everything in front of me having a red haze, I nod. Claire's voice is garbled as she bids me farewell. My feet vibrate as I take my first step off the plane. Hot blood pumps thick in my veins as the deafening cheers hit me harder outside the plane.

The security guard keeps a hand on my back as he walks every step down with me. Wishing I'd swiped Portia's blackout sunglasses, I blink hard against the morning sun mixed with the camera flashes

Now, I hear her demure giggle break through the crowd noise. I gulp for air as a weight presses heavier against my chest. Through my blurry vision, I spy Wyatt and Portia, mingling with the crowd as Lexy controls when and who they speak with. I spy a marker in Wyatt's hand, and he scribbles his name against posters, T-shirts, and fan's flesh.

I'm almost steady until a group of girls spot me, pointing and yelling in my direction.

When the words, "The girl from the video," are hurled my way, I'm ready to topple over. Thank goodness, the security guard still has a hand anchored behind me. He keeps me moving, and soon I'm out of view of the crowd. I pant, feeling dehydrated after the sweat drained from my pores.

"This is your car," the security guard says, and I lean against it with a lack of energy.

I shiver my understanding, knees knocking so hard I'm sure to have bruises.

He opens the car door, encouraging me to take a seat inside. Embarrassingly, he has to help me into the car, as my coordination has left my body.

He closes the door on me, and thankfully, the outside noises are muffled.

Left with my own thoughts, my knees jerk a little less, and I remember how I left things with Wyatt.

I shoved him.

I shoved my boyfriend, who is finally walking without an aide.

I shoved the boy I love, who was only acting concerned for me.

How could I shove him?

Drowning in my thoughts, it feels like an eternity until the door finally opens.

"Hey, Josie," Wyatt says, getting into the car beside me. "Are you okay?"

"I'm sorry!" I rush. "I never meant to push you. I would never want to hurt you."

"I'm okay," he coos, brushing back my hair. "Are you okay?"

I swallow hard, but a retch breaks through. "I was selfish. I shouldn't have pushed you away."

"No, you weren't. I could see you were terrified. I only left with Portia so we could get out of there sooner. I knew if the crowd saw me, then you'd be safe from anyone looking at you. I know masses like that scare you."

I exhale slowly, chilled by every small bump sprouting on my limbs.

"Oh crap," he murmurs as the car hums to life. "You're shivering like crazy. Come here."

He wraps his arms around me, but I don't deserve his comfort.

"Wow, I feel your heart racing." He rubs warmth into me. "I'm so sorry you had to face all of that back there."

I clutch his sides, forcing myself to inhale a breath. "Were you okay?"

"Yeah, I'm fine," he says, his voice upbeat.

I ease into his embrace. "Really?"

He chuckles softly. "Joze, it was exhilarating."

I gulp, leaning my chin on his shoulder. "Really?"

He brushes his hand over the back of my head. "Yeah, this fame thing is pretty addictive."

My chest tightens. "Wow, you're really okay with the whole thing."

"It's an unreal feeling, having all these people call your name and say, they love you."

"I'm glad you'll be able to get back to your life. You might not have the memories, but there's a gut feeling."

Meanwhile, my gut is still in knots.

Our car travels away from the airport. The view outside our windows becomes more suburban.

"I mean, it'd be better if I could remember everything that got me this level of fame," he says, bemused. "But, no harm in taking in the adoration, right?"

I smile, happy for him, and pull out of the hug. "Of course not. I told you, you're loved by many."

His hands plant on the sides of my face. "There's still only one person I care about loving me. It was fun at the airport, but I'd still give it up to be with you."

"Even if you could stay and have Portia on your arm?"

He presses a kiss on my lips. "Portia's a nice girl. I see us being friends, but there's nothing more than that."

I mumble a laugh, rubbing my lips together. "I can't believe you still want to be with me after meeting her. Haven't you seen how she looks at you?"

Wyatt tilts his head and crooks an eyebrow. "How could you say that?"

I sit back, and my heartbeat races. "Huh?"

He lets out a breathy laugh. "That you doubt my feelings for you. Joze, you're my soulmate."

Tears automatically brim in my eyes. "Soulmate?"

His teeth graze his bottom lip as his smile grows. "It's how I feel."

My hands plant over the space above my booming heart. "I... I've been so worried about letting myself love you on such a grand scale. You know, in case I never got the chance to be with you again. But..." I pause, catching my breath and letting my heart slow down. "Oh, Wyatt, you're everything to me. I'm not whole when I'm without you."

He places his hands over mine. "Then we shouldn't let anything stop us from being together."

I interlace my fingers with his. "Even if you're on tour, or on a movie set, I'll be waiting for you. You can still be a star and be with me. We'll make it work."

"I don't have to…"

"But you got such a kick out of the limelight. Don't rob yourself of that joy. That's not how relationships thrive."

"But you won't be a part of anything involving big crowds."

"It's okay. We'll be together during the quiet moments. It can work, Wyatt."

"Except we won't be physically in the same place."

"It's just until I finish high school. Then nothing can separate us."

"Then you'll be off to college and I'll be too dumb to get in anywhere."

"*Wyatt*," I scold. "Stop calling yourself dumb."

"It's true."

"Ugh, stop it. Besides, you don't need college. Your career has already started. And I can take classes virtually. I want to be a writer, and I already do that."

"I don't want to wait years to be with you."

"We'll work it out. It's only been a week that we've been back together. It won't be over tomorrow."

He huffs. "Honestly, I don't know how I'll ever let you go. Even after the high back there, I don't think I can bear it."

"It won't be easy."

"How did you deal with it last time?"

"I had faith I'd hear from you again."

He lifts my hands and kisses them. "So, just have faith?"

"I've been waiting all this time. I'll always be waiting for you. I won't disappear on you."

He frowns. "But what if I do it again? I'm scared of what'll happen when I start working again." He looks out the window, on route to our new destination. "Throwing myself into work is the reason we stopped talking."

"You heard Erika. You work long hours. Then there's all the press and events. The job keeps you busy."

He looks me square in the eye. "I promise never to be too busy for you. It won't happen again."

I lean forward and softly kiss him on the lips. "I believe you."

"I don't have my parents in my ear this time." He squeezes my hands and lets out a weighted exhale. "I know you need to go back home today. I'll be okay."

"Somehow, we'll both be okay. I have faith."

He smiles and nods. "Right. Faith."

The car stops outside a trendy row of industrial buildings turned into dwellings.

"Welcome home, Mr. Hayes," the driver says.

Wyatt blinks out the window. "This is my home?"

My mouth falls open, and excitement bubbles over my previous nerves. I tap his arm, bouncing in my seat. "Let's go inside and check it out."

Twenty-Five

"Whoa," it breathes out of me as I take in the industrial-chic aesthetic of the loft apartment.

Wyatt grins, scuffing his way into the apartment. "This is my place?"

"Cool, huh?" I say, following him into the airy space.

The apartment is lined with exposed, weathered bricks giving it a dark yet romantic feel. A mix of retro and contemporary furniture fill out the living space, and large warehouse-style windows bring excess light into the apartment. Above the stainless steel kitchen, is the loft. It's lined with a glass wall and a black railing, which continues down the wooden stacked staircase.

Wyatt tilts his head, taking in the stairs. "Savanna would not be impressed with those steps."

I gesture to the right-hand side. "There's a hallway. Maybe there's a first-floor bedroom."

Wyatt wiggles his eyebrows. "But that loft does look pretty swanky."

I giggle. "Yeah, it does."

Wyatt takes my hand and shuffles toward the hallway on the right. "Let's check downstairs first."

We move through the hallway and find a guest bedroom, a bathroom, a home office, and a home gym.

"Okay, this has Savanna written all over it," Wyatt says, smiling as he sighs with gratitude.

"She definitely wanted you to be supported with a good setup when you left the clinic."

I fiddle with the strap of my handbag as we wander through the industrial-chic kitchen. The exposed brick and stainless steel mix has a very alluring, masculine vibe. Everything has a place and is well-organized. This leaves me to believe, Wyatt has someone who cooks for him.

We move back into the living area and Wyatt gazes up at the loft space. "I want to brave it and go upstairs."

"Are you sure you want to exert the energy before leaving for the recording studio?"

He swings my hand. "Come on. Aren't you curious?"

I melt, thinking back to all the videos I've watched on social media, filmed in this apartment. "Of course, I am."

Wyatt tugs me toward the stairs. "Then let's go."

Despite his budding enthusiasm, I make Wyatt take every step up the timber-stacked staircase with caution. The carefulness pays off when we're awestruck by the open-planned space. It's a huge master bedroom, with a computer and recording equipment piled on a desk, and a walk-in closet that leads into the ensuite bathroom. Unlike the spaces below, upstairs looks untouched by Circle 8's health team.

"This must be exactly how you left it," I say, edging my way through the space, feeling Wyatt's authenticity highlighted in every aspect.

Wyatt gasps, moving past the cluttered desk. "It's my guitar."

Wyatt picks it up, and I'm goo. It's his guitar he played back in Victoria Falls. At all the talent shows. All the times we spent in his basement. All the escapes in my treehouse.

Seeing him hold it against himself, this is the real-deal Wyatt Hayes.

"I knew you'd still have it," I gush.

He strums the strings. "I'm so relieved I still have this."

Wyatt places the guitar back on its stand and moves further around the space. We look at the books sitting on his nightstand, the large abstract painting on the wall, and the general untidiness of the space.

"Geez, Wyatt, I thought you'd have a housekeeper."

Wyatt crooks an eyebrow. "Did you notice how insanely neat downstairs was? If I didn't know better, I'd guess I told whoever cleans for me to leave this space alone."

"It must be where you're most creative."

Wyatt moves his fingers and thumb in a snapping motion, but due to the numbness he's still dealing with, he misses. His eyes still wander with purpose.

"What are you looking for?"

He intently takes in the large space. "Somewhere there has to be..." He zeros in on a shelving unit and plucks out a black vinyl notebook. "Got it."

I move over to him. "Got what?"

He flicks through the pages. "If this is where I'm creative, there had to be someplace I was working out lyrics."

My heart skips a beat. "*Ooh*. I wanna see."

Wyatt moves over to the desk, leaning against it as he thumbs through the pages. I stand close by, eyeing the hand drawn pictures and messy writing. He's written diagonally, in a spiral, and downwards against the edge of the page. Every page is like a work of art I would happily frame and hang on my wall. Every pen stroke was a piece of his heart, forming a permanent mark.

I sigh, wrapping an arm around him. "Wow. This is so cool." I then pluck his glasses out of my handbag. "Do you want to take a closer look?"

Wyatt takes the glasses and the journal and moves over to the bed, sitting on the edge.

The large OJ from the plane hits me, and I excuse myself for the bathroom. I leave Wyatt to read his journal, moving through the closet and into the black and white-tiled bathroom. Thankfully, the housekeeper has cleaned this space.

When I move to the sink, I take a while to cool down with the running water. Melancholy washes over me as I realize my last moments with Wyatt are here. I get to see the recording studio with him, but then I return to the airport.

And that's it.

The storybook is over.

Time for my regular life to resume.

After too long alone in the bathroom, I leave before Wyatt starts asking if I've collapsed or something. I move back into the bedroom and find him pacing the carpet.

"What's wrong?"

He rubs his forehead. "I need a pill."

I swiftly retrieve the pill container from my handbag and give it to him. "Here."

Wyatt takes the container and breezes past me and into the bathroom.

That didn't seem like a usual headache. I've seen them hit him enough times over the past week. If anything, that seemed almost like an anxiety attack.

Before second-hand anxiety pulls me under, I force myself to take a seat on the bed. Beside me, Wyatt's journal lies open on his bed, and his glasses sit beside it. I can't help becoming entranced by the page, littered with Wyatt's handwriting. It's not like the random scribbles of song lyrics or doodles that we flipped through earlier. This is an emotional dump onto the page. I don't mean to read it, but when I catch my name, my heart skips a beat.

He wrote about me?

While he was famous, and we hadn't spoken in years, he was still thinking about me?

I gingerly sit on the edge of the bed and lift the notebook onto my lap. I take a deep breath and read the journal entry.

'The worst part is that Josie isn't part of my life anymore. Who am I kidding? She'd probably hate the guy I've become. What even am I? A sellout? A pushover? A product to sell?

I don't know. I just know I'm not the guy she used to know. Dang, I wish I could just be that guy again. That I could just hit rewind and never step foot into this circus. I don't even know how everything spiraled this badly. How did I get here? Why do I keep letting them force me into being seen with certain people? My stomach hurts at the thought of Josie seeing me with Portia.

I don't know how Portia does it. She doesn't even bat an eye when we're told to act like a couple at some event. How could someone be so comfortable being so fake? I tell her I'm okay with it. I play along, because heck, we're both stuck in this mess. It makes me sick, but what can I do? There's this stupid contract hanging over my head. I'm trapped.

I JUST WANT OUT.'

The bathroom door opens, and I put the journal down as Wyatt walks into the bedroom.

"You read this?" I ask, my heart straining to pump blood.

He clutches his elbows. "Mm-hmm."

I stand from the bed and move over to him. "You know, I never thought anything bad about you."

He nods at the journal left open on his bed. "B-but you didn't... Wh-what I wrote... Sounds like you don't know who I became."

I caress the sides of his face, rising on the balls of my feet in an attempt to meet his melancholy eyes. "That journal entry sounds like you were struggling. You were giving yourself a hard time. Outside your team, people love you. I don't think you ever became fake."

His jaw flexes. "But we can't know."

"Yes, we can. There was the salesperson at the boutique, the server at the restaurant, and Claire on the Learjet. They all had such wonderful things to say about you. They only knew the famous version of you."

He looks away, struggling to believe my words.

I turn his head back to face me. "Wyatt, you are loved. You're a good person, and that's why you were struggling. The Circle 8 management is already asking too much of you. They were most likely too intense when you were well."

Wyatt gestures at the journal. "It confirmed my worst fears. I had a bad feeling I was some kind of sellout. And, that's exactly what I called myself."

My heart sinks. "Oh, Wyatt."

He plonks onto the bed, lifting the journal onto his lap. He flips through it and lands on a two-page spread of his handwriting. He gulps and hands me the journal. "You gotta read it to me."

I take the journal, and my stomach cramps. "You sure?"

"Looks like I wrote it in a rush. It's all slanty." He rubs the space between his eyebrows. "My headache's burrowing, but I gotta know what it says."

"Okay, I'll decipher your crooked writing," I say, trying to lighten the mood.

I sit beside him and read the journal entry aloud. "'*I never thought the second album sales would tank this badly.*'" I gulp and look up at him. "Are you sure I should read this?"

He rests his chin on my shoulder and kisses my jaw. "Please."

I exhale and continue. "'*I guess I should be grateful they're making enough money that the team still wants to work with me. I'm not being shoved aside like they did to Marcus.*'"

"Marcus?" Wyatt questions. "Who was Marcus?"

"Maybe Marcus McGregor?" I suggest. "He used to do the kind of movies you do."

Wyatt furrows his brow. "Wait, that sounds familiar."

"Yeah, he was in..."

"Oh, is that guy from '*Love Switch*'?" Wyatt says with recognition. "I remember you making me watch that movie. Ugh. Are my movies as lame as that one?"

I smirk. "'*Love Switch*' isn't lame. And I love your movies."

"I'll take that as a yes," Wyatt mutters.

"I guess you replaced Marcus when you joined Circle 8." I continue reading. "'*All I want to do is play music, but they keep forcing me into movie roles. I've never felt more uncomfortable. I hate playing a role and having a director tell me to be more believable. None of this is believable.*'"

Wyatt sighs. "Dang it. I'm already sick to my stomach at the thought of acting. Now it says I didn't even like it at the time?"

"Should I continue?"

"Yeah, go on."

"'*Plus, they're low-budget, streaming movies, so what happens when they run out of appeal? Will I just be out, anyway? Do I even want to stay in at this point?*

'*The only future I see is playing romantic leads in teen movies until I age out. Who knows if I'll be believable as I grow older? There's no way I could stomach making a bedroom scene. I gotta get out of this before it comes to that.*" I drop the journal and turn to him with an open mouth. "Oh my gosh. You really wanted out."

Wyatt turns ghostly pale and taps the page. "There's one more paragraph. What does it say?"

I swallow the sickness swirling in my gut and look down at Wyatt's messy handwriting. "'*Playing along with Portia is the only shot I've got. We can be seen at parties and all that stuff because it gets me into the recording studio with her. She's a bankable star. Movies, modeling campaigns, and albums. Everything she touches turns to gold. If this duet can get me back on the charts, it's worth the shot.*'"

Wyatt recoils. "Am I using Portia?"

I pull back. "No, you wouldn't do that."

Wyatt winces. "Sounds like I am."

I shake my head, placing the journal on the bed cover. "No. You Circle 8 kids always collaborate. That's what this duet is. A collaboration. Mutually beneficial."

Wyatt's lip upturns. "I guess that's a better spin on it."

"Portia genuinely seems excited to be singing with you."

Wyatt shrugs. "Yeah."

"And everyone lit up back at the hotel when you two sang together. You need to stay positive about this opportunity."

"The me-I-don't-remember really wanted to record this duet with her," Wyatt says tentatively. "Like, this is my last big shot at making my music work."

I squeeze his shoulder. "Remember the fun we had last night, working on the lyrics? You've gotta focus on that energy when you go into the recording booth."

Wyatt presses a hand into his stomach, his expression growing queasy. "Okay. We'd better get downstairs and back in the car."

I brighten, hoping his mood is lifted. I can't leave him slumping into anxiety. "You're okay, right?"

He nods, forcing a smile. "I can play the guitar, and I can sing. Everything has to be okay."

I help him down the stairs, my confidence in his words at an all-time low.

Twenty-Six

Wyatt and I hold hands for the ten-minute drive over to the recording studio. We're shown inside, and Wyatt is ushered forward and introduced to a music producer. Portia stands by his side, and the management team surrounds them.

I edge backwards, feeling claustrophobic in the small space. Behind me are two couches, and Randall stands in the corner, staring at his phone. I fold my arms, tapping my elbows with awkwardness.

As I take note of everyone crowding the space, I clear my throat and ask Randall, "Where's Jenna?"

Randall barely looks up from his phone. "She'll be around later. Apparently she had something important to take care of."

Dang it. If I could sit next to her, I might feel less on edge.

Wyatt and Portia are shown into the recording booth. It has a glass wall so we can watch them perform. Wyatt's given the guitar he had in the penthouse back at Cherry Beach.

"You've played so many live performances with this guitar," Erika tells him. "We're getting the real you back."

The comment makes me feel beyond icky. However, I plaster a smile on my face for Wyatt's sake.

I wall-hug as Wyatt and Portia begin the song. Wyatt doesn't miss a beat with the guitar, but there's apprehension in voice as he sings. Ugh. He can't try the new lyrics. I don't blame him. It would be daunting, having everyone stare at him like he's a zoo animal.

I watch Portia tackle the bridge, and she sounds a little rusty. No doubt struggling with jet lag and burnout from her European trip. Wyatt's voice melds with her, and soon, tingles race down my back.

Oh my gosh, he's doing it. He's singing the words I wrote.

I glance around at everyone watching, waiting for them to lean forward in wonder.

I swallow hard, only spotting confusion everywhere I turn. My heart leaps into my throat as I spy Portia in the booth. She continues to sing her lines, but her eyes slit as Wyatt's words take her off guard.

"Wait, Wyatt," the producer says, tugging at his headphones. "What was that?"

Wyatt fumbles with his guitar and says into the microphone, "Umm, the song?"

The producer snaps his fingers. "Someone get him the right lyrics. The boy keeps forgetting things."

Wyatt lifts a hand. "No, it's not like that. I changed the lyrics."

Erika leans over the producer's shoulder. "Wyatt, hon. This isn't a time for improv. We've gotta get this in the can."

"If you listen to it, you'll see that..."

"Wyatt," the producer cuts him off. "Just go with the lyrics as written. Yeah?"

Wyatt presses hard into a frown and then replies with a nod.

"Okay, let's take it again," the producer says. "Portia, lead us off."

I can't help feeling a little rejected when Wyatt and Portia try the song again. Without even giving the new words a chance, the suits cut them off immediately. I'm about to sink into the floor, when my heart lifts me up again.

My chin drops, and pigment comes back into my skin.

Wyatt's changing the lyrics again. He's going back to the words we stayed up all night working on. My gaze drifts to Portia and I note the corners of her mouth curling upward. There's a different inflection in her words and she bops to the music as she sings.

There's more edge in how Wyatt strums his guitar, and his voice is more powerful than any other time he practiced. People in my surroundings shift, not knowing how to act. I can't help sensing some agitation in the room.

Erika nudges the producer. "Cut it."

Wyatt and Portia stop singing, blinking at everyone in the room.

"This isn't working," Erika says bluntly.

"How isn't..."

Erika lifts a hand, cutting Wyatt off. "We know what works, Wyatt. We've been with you for years. We have the market research."

"But, if we try this," Portia speaks up, "and then you test it with..."

The producer gets up from his swivel seat with a grunt. "Take five, everyone. I feel a massive headache coming on."

Randall gains my attention. "You have to get going. Your car is out front."

My stomach drops. "Oh, okay."

"I'll let Wyatt know so you can say your goodbyes."

I back away from the others as Randall moves closer to the booth to let Wyatt know my car has arrived. Wyatt's complexion dulls, and he leaves his guitar in the booth. When he makes his way toward me, he nods at the rear door, signaling for us to have a moment alone.

"I tried," Wyatt says, leaning against the exterior brick wall.

I caress his cheek. "It sounded really good."

"Is it just me, or was Portia sticking up for the new lyrics?"

"She seemed into it," I say with my heart lodged in my throat. "Hopefully after I leave, she stays on your side."

Wyatt huffs heavily, running his hands down my arms. "This can't be real. It's really time for you to go?"

My eyes grow itchy as I stare into his hazel eyes. "Unfortunately, yes."

"Pull it together," Lexy's voice says harshly from around the corner.

It takes me aback. I edge myself backward, seeing her and Portia leaving the studio on the other side.

"Ugh. I just hate this," Portia complains, balling her fists. "I hate lying to him."

I suck in a breath, turning to Wyatt, who stands stiff against the wall and stares blankly ahead.

"You know it's for his own good," Lexy says. "Sure, when you both knew you were playing parts, it was easier. But you can't expect Wyatt to play along when he can't remember your partnership."

Portia moans. "But we never lied to each other before."

I rub the space over my heart, hearing the sincerity and heartbreak rattling through Portia's tone.

"I liked looking at our relationship as a game," Portia admits.

At that, Wyatt tenses beside me and a soft retch echoes from his throat.

"We'd laugh about everyone assuming we were a couple," Portia continues. "It made it easier for us to pursue the people we actually wanted to be with. Well, at least I was dating. I don't know about him. He hardly opened up about it. I guess he was always holding onto Josie."

I suck in a breath and make sure I'm securely hidden behind the wall. Wyatt clasps my hand and I breathe out slowly. So they do all see it. Just how magnetically Wyatt and I are attached.

And Portia's not jealous? She's just playing a role?

"Portia, hon, you can't back out now," Lexy says matter-of-factly. "You've done so well. You've made Wyatt believe there was something romantic to your relationship. You've made him relax and get back to work. We need you, hon."

A shattered sigh pours out of Portia. "But it feels so wrong. I just want to sit down and talk to him. Like we used to."

Wyatt drops my hand and marches back into the studio. I hurry behind, careful not to call out to him. I don't want Portia and Lexy discovering we were eavesdropping.

Back inside, I manage to clasp his hand. "Wait," I hush. "Talk to me."

"They're using me," Wyatt snaps. "Portia led me on, thinking I was cheating on her with you. And they're all in on it."

I hold the sides of his face, hoping to calm him down. "Just breathe. Remember your journal entry? You knew Portia was being fake."

His face grows hot in my hands. "But I didn't know management was behind it all."

"Wyatt?" Erika questions. "What's going on?"

"I know you're all manip-manipu..." Wyatt grunts at the floor in frustration. "You're using Portia to make me work. I'm not playing these games anymore."

Richmond closes in on him. "Wyatt, no one is using anyone. We're all here to keep your careers moving forward."

"No, you made Portia talk me into coming back to work!"

Portia enters the studio, her mouth ajar. "Oh my gosh," she utters. "You heard us out there?"

Wyatt tugs on my hand. "I'm taking Josie to the airport. You all better back off."

We rush out of the recording studio, and I'm beyond dizzy as we hit the pavement.

"Come on," Wyatt grunts. "Let's get in the car."

"Are you okay?" I ask, stumbling behind him. "Do you want to talk about it?"

"No, I want to leave."

"But what about when I get on the plane? Will you be okay, coming back to face all this?"

He stops and turns around to me. "I'm not coming back."

I choke on air. "What?"

His hands land on my shoulders. "I'm going with you, Joze. I'm going home."

I gasp for air. "Are... Are you sure?"

He smiles. "Will you take me with you?"

With the emotions bubbling inside me, I frantically nod.

Wyatt mumbles a laugh. "Can you breathe, Joze?"

I squeak. "*Just.*"

"Come on, beautiful. Let's get out of here while we still can."

As we move into the car, a garbled jingle starts to play. I look at Wyatt as he fishes inside his pocket and then hands me his phone. "Can you make this thing stop ringing?"

I show him the screen. "It's Portia."

Wyatt frowns. "Don't answer it."

I lean forward as our car joins the rest of the traffic. "Maybe you should. They might chase after you otherwise."

Wyatt's lip upturns. "I don't want them stopping me from leaving."

"Then talk to her."

He motions at me to press the buttons. "Put it on speaker. I'm not talking to her alone."

I hit answer and the speaker button, even though I have no intention of using my voice in this conversation.

"I'm sorry," Portia rushes through the phone line. "They made me do it. I didn't want to lay it on so thick, but my career is on the line too."

"You lied to me," Wyatt says.

"I embellished," she replies. "I'm sorry. They wanted me to pretend we were more than friends. They said it'd be easy because there was always speculation we were a couple. I was just supposed to make it seem real."

Wyatt's brow furrows. "Why?"

"To motivate you. Ugh, it's so icky, I know. It was out of desperation."

"I don't need head games, Portia. My head hurts enough."

"I'm so sorry, baby." She huffs through the receiver. "Sorry. Honestly, we do call each other baby, but it was never serious. We did it as a joke. The managers always wanted us to pose for photos like a couple. We'd call each other baby, making the whole thing one big game. A charade."

"But this time I wasn't part of the game," Wyatt says, the hurt shaking his words. "I was the one being played."

"Wyatt, I didn't mean to hurt you. I was trying to get the old you back."

"The old me is back. The old me is the ver-version that never left Josie."

"You still have a contract with Circle 8. You still have a career to come back to."

"Maybe I don't care about it anymore."

I reach out and grasp his hand as Portia says the words I'm feeling. "You don't mean that." Wyatt opens his mouth to rebut, but Portia continues with, "I saw first-hand how you work a crowd. You're into this. And you lit up when you went into the booth today."

"Only when I wanted to sing Josie's words."

"Our song is locked," Portia says with a heaviness to her words. "But, I wanted to let you know, I really did like the lyrics."

Wyatt squeezes my hand back. "Really?"

"They were beautiful and packed with emotion." A sorrowful sigh comes through the speaker. "Oh, I hate that I've ruined things. Wyatt, I promise, we were really good friends. I wish you could remember us."

"I can't. I remember you as you are now."

"I'm the same person. I got scared and forced into this mess. I should've refused, but they threatened my career. I'm sorry, but it's the one thing I'm not willing to give up."

"So our friendship wasn't that important then?"

"That's not fair. It's not what I meant. My career is my identity. Without it, I don't know who I am." Her voice cracks. "Except when I had someone like you in my life. You kept me real. Grounded. You're special, Wyatt."

Wyatt sighs, rubbing his forehead. "Portia, we've gotta go. I'll leave you to tell Erika and the others that I'm not coming back."

Portia gasps. "Ever?"

"I just need space. All I've had is people in my face, telling me who I am and what I have to be. I need time to figure it out for myself."

"Okay, Wyatt. I owe you that much."

"Bye, Portia."

Her voice cracks again. "Bye."

"Whoa," I breathe out when the call ends. "That was intense."

Wyatt sits back, hitting his head against the headrest. "What a mess."

I ditch Wyatt's phone into my handbag and clutch his hand. "You're really serious about going home with me?"

"Dead serious."

"Then we should make a detour by your loft."

Wyatt shakes off the suggestion. "Nah, I can get anything I need in Victoria Falls."

I squeeze his hand. "What about the journal?"

His eyes brighten, and he leans forward to gain the driver's attention. "Can you swing by my place?"

"Sure, no problem, boss," the driver says and changes lanes.

Thankfully, Wyatt's loft is close to the studio. I volunteer to go inside for him, wanting him to avoid using extra energy. I dash into the first-floor bedroom, which appeared setup for him, and realize my handbag is still hanging over my shoulder. Rolling my eyes at myself, I search the closet for an overnight bag. I pull out a light gray duffle bag and stuff it with clothing items Wyatt may need.

I throw the strap of the duffle bag over my other shoulder and hightail it upstairs. I snag his journal from the bed and zip up the bag. I then retrieve his acoustic guitar and smuggle it inside its case. With a mixture of awkwardness and caution, I make it down the stairs with my handbag, the duffle bag, and the loaded guitar case.

More of Wyatt's things were left in the living space for him, and I spy his walking cane leaning against the couch. I cross my fingers and collect it just in case. While I'm evaluating how to get out the door with all this gear, the driver enters the apartment to help me. I hand over the guitar case and walking cane, ready to follow the driver out with the duffle bag still hanging over my shoulder.

I leave the loft apartment, and Wyatt's phone rings through my handbag. My gut tenses, imagining its Portia again or worse.

"Please, please, please," I wish as I take out his phone. "Please don't take him away from me."

My mind is a flurry with Erika and Lexy making wild plans. I imagine them stopping us at the airport and dragging Wyatt back to the studio. My hand trembles as I stare at the unknown caller ID.

High on adrenaline, I hit the answer button instead of decline, and lift the phone to my ear. "Hello?"

"Oh, uh..." a male voice splutters. "Hi... I..."

I move toward the car, and the driver takes the duffle from me. He puts it in the trunk with Wyatt's guitar and cane.

"Are you the new PA?" the guy on the phone asks.

It takes me aback. "Huh?"

The voice grows quiet. "I'm... I'm looking for Wyatt."

I blankly move into the backseat, trying to work out whose voice this is. The driver gets back into his seat, and Wyatt tells him to take us back to the Learjet.

Wyatt then turns to me, mouthing, "Who is it?"

I bite my lip before asking, "Who is this?"

"It's... It's..."

He's hesitant to reveal his identity, which makes my heart surge more adrenaline throughout my body. "Devon?"

Wyatt stares at me in shock as the voice on the line continues to fumble.

Traffic whooshes past us, but at this moment, it may as well all be in slow-motion.

Finally, he clears his throat and answers, "Yeah, it's Devon. Who is this?"

"Josie," I blurt. "I'm with Wyatt. Where are you?"

"I can't tell you. Jenna has reached out to me and…"

"Jenna?" I cut him off. "She told me she couldn't contact you."

"It's not important right now. I need to explain what happened to Wyatt."

"Where have you been?" My palm sweats against the phone. "He's needed answers for weeks, and you bailed on him."

"Can I talk to him?"

I take in Wyatt, who's turning a pale tinge of green, and lower the phone. "Do you want to talk to him?"

"I…" He shakes his head. "I wouldn't know where to start."

I gesture with the phone and suggest, "Speakerphone?"

When Wyatt shrugs, I hit the speaker button, and say, "Okay, Wyatt's here."

"Wyatt?" Devon asks.

Wyatt opens his mouth, but his words don't budge.

After a few moments of silence, I ask, "Can you let us know what happened?"

"Can I meet you guys somewhere in private?" Devon asks. "I can explain everything. I just want to do it somewhere secure."

"We're about to get on a flight to Victoria Falls. Why don't you meet us at the airport?"

"No. No way. I can't have Circle 8 knowing where I am. Look, I'll meet you guys there."

"In Victoria Falls?"

"Yeah."

"It's a long drive. Over twelve hours by car."

"Just wait for me, okay? It's important."

Wyatt gulps and leans closer to the phone. "We will."

There's a long pause on the other end until Devon's voice shows a shred of happiness. "Wyatt. Oh man, it's so good to hear your voice."

"You know who caused my accident?" Wyatt asks, bracing himself.

Devon sighs. "I do."

Wyatt swallows hard. "Was it you?"

"No." Devon pauses before adding, "I'll explain everything. I promise."

"I live on Hamstead Avenue in Victoria Falls," I tell Devon. "Number thirty-seven. Come over as soon as you get to town."

"I will." Devon replies. "And, Wyatt... It's really good to hear your voice again, brother. See you soon."

And with that, the line goes dead.

"Holy cow," Wyatt mutters. "He actually reached out."

"Jenna actually came through," I say in wonder.

"You asked her to find him?"

"She didn't believe Devon could hurt you," I reply. "Even Portia didn't believe it. You saw her face back at the hotel. It pained her to talk badly about Devon."

Wyatt rolls his eyes. "That girl can fake anything."

When the car pulls up on the tarmac, I'm quick to leave the car. I dart around to Wyatt's side, knowing he can't move at a hurried pace like me.

Perhaps he got an extra dose of adrenaline after the events we went through. Wyatt bolts toward the Circle 8 Learjet, leaving me in his dust.

He turns around, laughing. "Come on, Josie. Don't you want to go home?"

"I was trying to be slow for you. I didn't think you'd ditch me."

"I'll carry you up the stairs if you want."

"Despite how Disney-romantic that sounds, I'll have to say no. You're gonna have to do extra physical therapy after sprinting across the tarmac."

With a lightened mood, we board the plane and are greeted by Claire.

"Oh, Mr. Hayes," Claire says, startled. "You're back?"

Wyatt nods. "I'm going to Victoria Falls with Josie."

"Okay, I'll update the manifest," Claire replies. "Anyone else joining us?"

"No," Wyatt and I are quick to respond.

Claire jerks from our abrupt reply, and swiftly composes herself. "Not a problem. Please, make yourselves comfortable, and we'll get ready to take off."

Wyatt and I take our seats, and while the driver brings our belongings onto the plane, I take the time to call my mom with an update. The pilot comes out to speak with Wyatt, and I frantically tap on my armrest, hoping Mom answers before I need to set my phone to flight mode.

The dial tone stops, and I'm quick to blurt, "Mom?"

A gasp whooshes through the phone. "Josie, what's happened?"

"Mom, don't panic," I rush. "I just want you to know I'm on the plane to come home."

She cheers. "Oh, yay! I'm so thrilled."

"Will you pick us up at the airport?"

"Yes, of course, I'll come and get you."

"*Us*, Mom. Wyatt's coming with me."

The line goes quiet.

"Mom?"

"I heard."

My back stiffens. "Is this okay?"

"I just... What does this mean?"

"There's no team coming with us. It's just me and him. So you need to keep it on the down-low."

"You make it sound like he's running away from home."

"Essentially, he is."

"Is Wyatt okay? He's not in any danger, is he?"

I sigh and lower my voice. "We need to get him away from these people. It's totally toxic."

"Do his parents know he's coming with you?"

"Oh, I haven't filled you in on the emancipation document, have I?"

"Oh, dear." Mom gasps. "This does sound like a mess. Ever since you told us about the broken relationship with his parents, your dad and I have been concerned about him." Mom takes a minute, composing herself. "Look, if Wyatt needs to get away, to feel safe and supported, then yes, he can stay with us for a few days."

"Thanks, Mom."

"I don't know what this means long term. If he's not working, what's his plan to support himself? Or is he going back to work after a certain amount of time off? Or..."

"*Mom*," I cut her off. "Please don't spiral. I'll text you our arrival time. I can't wait to get home."

"Me too, darling. We've missed you too much."

Twenty-Seven

"Mom!" I cry out, running toward her in the small arrivals lounge.

I drop my overnight bag onto the floor, and she wraps me in a tight embrace. "Oh, darling, I'm beyond happy to have you home."

I sigh out in her arms. "Me too."

She smooths a hand over my curls. "How was the flight?"

"Long. Wyatt slept most of the way, and I wrote to pass the time."

Mom pulls her arms from me and there's a distinct shift in her stance. I follow her gaze over my shoulder, turning to find Wyatt walking over to us.

With his duffle bag hanging over his shoulder, he waves. "Hi, Mrs. Bartlett."

Tears spring in Mom's eyes. "Oh, Wyatt. Look how you've grown. It's so good to see you."

Wyatt awkwardly combs his fingers through his hair. "Ah, that's good to hear. I really appreciate you letting me stay with you."

"It's really no trouble," Mom says, scooping an arm behind Wyatt's back. "We have a lot to discuss."

Claire brings Wyatt's cane and guitar into the arrivals lounge, and wishes us a safe trip home. Mom takes the items, anxiously muttering about whether

Wyatt should be walking without the cane. I give her a stern look, wishing for her to cool it as we walk to the car.

I offer Wyatt the front seat, but he opts for the back. Probably a good thing, the way Mom is already spiraling. On the drive home, I stare out the window, and the knots in my stomach ease.

I'm home.

I'm really home.

I look over my shoulder at Wyatt and we exchange smiles.

Wyatt's finally home.

We pull up at the house and I'm relieved Dad and the twins aren't waiting out front. It's Sunday afternoon, so maybe they're at the park.

I cross my fingers. Please be at the park.

As I open my car door, the house front door opens.

Dang it.

Callum races out of the house, bolting toward the car.

I stand in front of the car, holding out a hand like a stop sign. "Slow down or you'll hurt yourself."

"Callum!" Dad's voice calls out like a warning shot.

I buzz at the sound of it, watching the doorway until Dad appears. I squeal at the sight of him, and then Callum latches onto my middle. I hug my little brother back, walking him backwards as I move toward Dad on the porch.

"Hi Josie, darling," Dad says, beaming. "So good to have you home."

"So glad to be home."

He moves off the porch, giving me a hug while Callum is strapped to me.

I giggle at the beautifully awkward exchange, and pat Callum's head when Dad releases me. "How you doing, bud?"

Callum hugs me tighter. "Good, now that you're home."

My heart bounces with glee. "Where's your sister?"

Callum clicks his tongue. "In a mood, as usual."

Dad has moved past me, and I turn to see him shaking Wyatt's hand. "Good to see you, Wyatt. I hope you're doing better."

"I am, thanks," Wyatt replies. "Getting less headaches, walking better, and not st-stumbling over my words." Wyatt frowns at himself. "Dang it."

Dad chuckles, patting Whyatt's shoulder. "You're human, son. Good to see that fame hasn't changed you."

Callum unlatches from me, eyes bugging at Wyatt. "I can't believe you actually know the famous guy. I really thought you were making up more stories."

I scoff at him. "Where did you think I was all week?"

Callum shrugs. "Living in make-believe."

"You think Mom and Dad let me have a week off school to play pretend by myself?"

Callum stares at me blankly. "Casey said you could have psychological issues."

Wyatt laughs, planting his hand over his mouth.

I eye him, holding back a laugh. "Don't encourage him."

Wyatt lowers his hand, laughter still simmering. "Sorry. It's just funny because he can say that word and I still can't."

I look back at the house. "Seriously, where is Casey?"

Mom pulls the guitar case and Wyatt's duffle out of the trunk of the car. "Probably still punishing you, Josie. She wasn't too pleased when you extended your trip."

I hold my hips. "But I came home."

Wyatt moves over to Mom, taking the items. "Let me take those inside."

"Nuh-uh." Mom motions for Dad to take them instead. "I'm not having any issues before you even step inside the house." Mom hands Wyatt the walking cane. "You can take this instead."

"Mrs. Bartlett, I'm really okay. I don't need..."

Mom smiles at him. "End of discussion."

Wyatt smiles back and nods. He uses the walking cane to make his way into the house. Mom and Dad carry our luggage, and I take Callum's hand as we go inside.

"How come he needs a walking cane?" Callum asks, watching Wyatt move. "His leg doesn't look broken."

"It's not broken," I reply.

"Sometimes when people get hit on the head, it causes all kinds of neurological issues," Dad says once we're all inside. "Wyatt could've had part of his brain hurt, which meant he needed to relearn to walk."

"How long did it take to relearn to walk?" Mom asks Wyatt.

"I didn't com-completely fo-forget how to walk," Wyatt replies. "I just had balance and co-coord-ordination issues."

Callum pulls a face. "Is he having an episode?"

My gut drops and I whack Callum's shoulder. "Do you have no filter?"

Wyatt mumbles a laugh. "It's okay, Joze."

"Casey!" Mom calls up the stairs. "We're home!"

"So!" Casey calls back.

I move over to the bottom of the stairs with Mom. "Come down and tell me you missed me!"

My little sister is definitely in a mood. Loud stomps echo from the upstairs hallway. She appears on the top landing with a grumpy face and crossed arms.

Mom points at the floor by her feet. "Now, missy."

Casey trudges down the stairs, and stops on the last step in front of me. "Finally."

I arch an eyebrow. "That's all you have to say?"

"Yes. You were gone forever."

I open my arms out wide. "And now I'm back."

Reluctantly, she hugs me. I rub a circle on her back, hoping to deflate her sour mood.

When I pull out of the hug, I check her expression for something brighter, but she's quick to move past me.

Casey stomps in front of Wyatt with her arms folded across her chest. "So you're the guy who kept my sister away?"

Wyatt blinks at her, startled. "Ex-excuse me?"

"*Casey*," Mom scolds. "Don't be rude."

Casey huffs, keeping her stance rigid. "I want to hear what he has to say for himself."

I step between them. "Listen, you little monster. I told you, Wyatt was in the hospital. He doesn't have to answer to a snarky ten-year-old."

Casey rolls her eyes at me. "I didn't realize how much I'd miss you."

Her agitated exterior and the vulnerability of her words make me melt. "You're so annoying, but I love you."

She drops her crossed arms. "Don't get too sappy, but I love you too."

"I'm sorry for keeping your sister away," Wyatt offers.

Callum points at Wyatt. "Now he's not stuttering. What's up with that?"

Casey looks at Wyatt sideways. "You stutter? You don't stutter in the movies."

"Okay, kids," Dad says, placing his hands on Casey's shoulders. "Let's give Wyatt some space. He and Josie have gotten off a long flight."

"I'm sorry to say, Wyatt," Mom says, turning a shade of pink, "we only have the pull-out couch as a spare bed. If I had more notice, maybe I could've worked something else out. I know it's nothing fancy but..."

"It's fine, Mrs. Bartlett," Wyatt interrupts. "I don't need anything fa-fancy."

I gesture at the walking cane, leaning against the couch. "Probably a good thing he won't be using the stairs."

Casey wriggles her eyebrows. "You wouldn't want him going upstairs. Would you, Josie?"

I deadpan her. "Huh?"

Callum's shoulders jiggle as he laughs. "Your bedroom is full of pictures of him."

Wyatt grins. "What's this now?"

A mess of self-loathing embarrassment writhes inside me.

"Stop teasing your sister," Dad says, having difficulty holding back his laughter.

Wyatt turns to the twins. "How many pictures of me?"

I lunge at the twins, shoving my hands over their mouths before they can speak. "Don't you dare!"

Mom pats Wyatt's shoulder. "Let's just say, Josie never stopped being a fan of yours."

Wyatt edges toward the staircase. "You don't think I need to see this, do you?"

It takes me way too long to decide. Should I remove my hands from the twins' faces, or grab onto Wyatt instead? While my brain malfunctions, Wyatt moves onto the staircase.

"Take it easy up those steps," Mom says with brewing panic.

With bone-chilling despondency quaking throughout my body, I unlatch my hands from the twins' faces and edge forward.

"They're all over her walls!" Callum calls out.

"She's got problems," Casey adds on.

Nausea swirls inside me and I grit my teeth. "Quit it, you guys."

I follow Wyatt up the stairs, ready for the horror on his face when he calls me a crazy stalker.

Wyatt laughs to himself. "I don't even know which bedroom is yours."

"You can't miss it," Mom says, moving away from the staircase with a snigger.

I send a glare her way, and then hear Wyatt utter, "Oh my..."

The nausea vortexes.

I find him in the doorway of my bedroom with his mouth ajar. He takes in the wall plastered with his images, and even worse, my face taped over Portia's.

"Holy crap," whispers out of him.

I jitter behind him. "I swear, I'm not crazy."

Wyatt splutters a laugh, turning around to face me. "You don't think I heard you when you called yourself a fan?" He turns back to the room. "I just can't believe there are this many pictures of me in existence."

I cringe as he makes his way into my bedroom.

He points at an image of him and Portia, my face over hers. "*Ha.* This I like."

I press into my feeble stomach. "I seriously never thought I'd see you again. It was a harmless fantasy. I know it looks creepy."

"Creepy?" he questions. "Creepy is thinking about someone I don't know having this on their walls. At least you and I have a history."

"So, wait... You don't find this creepy?"

"It's somewhat off-putting," he quips. "But I can't diss your level of en-enthus... Eh, excitement."

"I've enjoyed following your career."

Wyatt gasps and zeroes in on the polaroids stuck to the wall. "Wow. These are awesome."

I brighten. "They're definitely my favorite thing in this room."

He smiles at the sixth grade versions of us in the treehouse. "And the treehouse is still standing?"

"Yes. We should leave this cringe-inducing room and go check it out."

Wyatt chuckles. "You really can't stop squirming, can you?"

I yank on his arm. "Besides, my dad will come up here and enforce his no-boys-in-the-bedroom rule."

Wyatt's eyebrows lift. "How often do you have boys over?"

I smirk. "Never."

"Then why is it a rule?"

I lift my palms questioningly. "Because I'm sixteen?"

As I pull Wyatt across the carpet, he tugs me back, glancing at the albums lying on my desk. "Whoa. These are mine?"

"Pretty cool, huh?"

He lifts up the cardboard covers, flipping them over and examining both sides. "Really fr-freaking cool. I didn't even know they still made these."

"I have every Wyatt Hayes collector's item imaginable."

Wyatt grins looking around the room. "That I can believe."

"Come on." I beckon. "Let's get out of here."

"Okay, I'll let you stop squirming," he teases, following me out of the room.

When we make it back downstairs, Mom calls out that she's getting dinner ready. Meanwhile, Dad is arguing with the twins in the living room. I encourage Wyatt to take the opportunity with me to sneak outside without them following.

Wyatt gasps as we move across the backyard. "It's just as I remember it."

I love seeing the nostalgia pour glee into his expression as his eyes wander the treehouse.

"We should've brought your guitar out here."

Wyatt carefully climbs into the treehouse. "It's okay. I'm a bit wiped. I'm happy to just sit out here."

I crouch beside him as we smile at crude artwork on the walls, board games piled in the corner, and childhood costumes in a busted crate.

"The twins are so blunt," Wyatt says with a nervous laugh. "They took me off guard since being around the suits, who kept trying to kiss my butt."

"Yeah, lucky I'm related to them, or I might not love them," I joke.

"It's really nice that your family has welcomed me here," he says. "It's a lot to ask when you've just gotten home."

"They adore you."

"No, I think I'm the consolation prize. They only took me so they could get you home."

"No, you're the bonus prize. Having you here is better than just having me home."

He takes my hand and kisses my cheek. "There's no *just* when it comes to you."

I awe. "Well, that was positively sickly sweet."

He laughs. "No good?"

I giggle and wrap an arm around his.

He pats my hand and reclines against the pine wall. "I love how quiet it is here. Life's happening, and your family is busy, but I don't feel pressure."

"I'm glad you don't feel the pressure."

He looks at me sideways. "Are you okay?"

I blow out a breath. "Yeah, of course. I'm so happy to be home, but there is a lot of pressure here. Mom and Dad are busy, trying not to show their stress."

"Oh, I'm sorry."

"It's okay. It's not your problem."

"But I care about your problems."

"They both work a lot, and Dad has crazy long commutes. I don't know how they managed the twins without me."

"Oh."

"I help a lot with them before and after school."

"It's easy to see how much you were missed. I feel like a jerk for keeping you away for so long."

"Why would you say that?"

"Because your family needed you."

I rub warmth into his arm. "You needed me too."

"I didn't have any clue about your home life." He sighs at the floor. "I'm sorry."

"I don't want you to feel guilty. I'm happy to be back with my family, but even happier that you're here too."

He rubs the side of his head. "I wonder how long we can make this last."

"Our pull-out couch is certainly no California king bed in a penthouse."

Wyatt smirks. "I bet it'll be the closest thing to home I've slept on for a long time."

I nestle into him. "I'm so glad you're here, Wyatt."

His hands press into the middle of my back. "Me too. I was so sick at the thought of you coming here without me."

"But you'll be okay when you go back?"

"I have another therapy call coming up soon," he replies. "I'll need to ask the doc how to survive my new work and home life."

"If it's stressing you out, you should take a step back. I'm sure if you told Dr. Fincher, you weren't coping, he'd tell Circle 8 you're not fit for work."

"Especially after them using Portia to manipulate me back into the studio."

"You really need some time away from the suits. They're rushing you."

"Well, like I said, the pressure is already off."

I smile and trace a finger under his chin. "That's so great." I peck his lips, and then say, "I hope my mom's panic doesn't trigger you."

"Your mom genuinely worries about everyone. It's sweet."

"We'll see how long *sweet* lasts before it becomes grating."

"Considering who I've been exposed to for the past few months, I think it'll last a while."

"She'll love having someone around who doesn't roll their eyes at her."

Wyatt chuckles. "I get an ache when I do that, so I'll keep her happy."

"How is your headache?"

"*Really* dull. I feel really good, Joze. Truly."

Before I can respond, the distinct slide of the back door sounds and then the racing of ten-year-old feet hit the backyard.

I hunch in my seated position. "Ugh."

Wyatt mumbles a laugh as Callum and Casey bustle their way into the treehouse. They plant themselves directly in front of us, forcing Wyatt and me to break apart.

"So what's it like making movies?" Callum blurts.

"Ah, I don't..."

Before Wyatt can get through a response, Casey talks over him. "Is Circle 8 a cult?"

Wyatt laughs in astonishment. "Huh? What?"

"Circle 8 all work together. You only make movies and music with people in the group," she elaborates. "Sounds like a cult to me."

I click my tongue, unable to look at her. "What would you know about cults?"

She crosses her arms. "I have the internet."

"I'm going to tell Mom and Dad to cut your connection."

"As if." She pokes her tongue out at me. "Dad's the one who showed me where to find the videos."

I huff in exasperation. "It's so annoying how he encourages you to question everything."

"I'm sorry I don't think everything is sunshine and rainbows like you and Callum," Casey argues.

I smirk at her. "I don't think everything's full of hope. A lot of things really suck."

Callum pouts. "Like Wyatt getting hurt?"

I pat Callum's knee. "Yeah, like that."

Wyatt opens his arms wide, smiling. "I'm getting better."

"A cane and a stutter seem pretty bad," Callum reluctantly replies.

"I read online that some neurological issues never heal," Casey says flatly.

I glare at her. "No one needs to hear that, Casey."

She shrugs. "I'm just saying, he might never get his memory back."

Horror sweeps over Callum's face. "*Never?*"

Wyatt sits taller. "I'll remember. It already feels like it's coming back."

"How?" the twins say at once.

Wyatt rubs the side of his head. "It's hard to explain. Inside my head, it feels like there's a fog over part of my mind. Now and then, it feels like it's lifting, but never quite does."

Callum beams. "So, one day all the fog will disappear?"

Wyatt nods optimistically. "Exactly."

I nudge Casey. "See. Sometimes there is sunshine and rainbows."

Casey watches Wyatt skeptically. "Maybe."

"Kids!" Mom calls from the back door. "Come on in for dinner."

"Thank goodness," I mutter, and follow everyone out of the treehouse of interrogation.

Back inside the house, Callum races ahead. "Can I sit next to Wyatt?"

I nudge Wyatt. "I think you have a fan."

"I'll take it," Wyatt replies. "It's nice compared to the third degree from Casey."

"She can't help it. Dad programmed her as a little cynic."

We move into the dining room, and Wyatt and I sit opposite each other. Callum next to him, and Casey next to me. Dad takes the head of the table, and Mom sits opposite him after serving our dinner plates.

"Mmm," Wyatt purrs. "Smells amazing."

"I hope you like it," Mom says with rosy cheeks. "I know you've been used to fine dining."

"The best meal I've had was when Josie and I watched old movies and ate pizza," Wyatt says, eyeing me while wearing the cutest smile. "But your home cooking might have that beat."

"They're black bean and squash enchiladas," Mom says. "I've never used vegan cheese, but it looks like it held together."

Casey screws up her face. "Vegan-what-now?"

"You won't even be able to tell the difference," Dad tells her.

Casey grumbles at her plate. "Tell that to Mom's face."

"It was just something new to try," Mom says, frazzled. "You know I get nervous when I try something new."

Callum cracks up, nudging Wyatt. "Mom gets nervous no matter how many times she tries something."

Wyatt takes a bite and smiles. "It's awesome, Mrs. Bartlett."

While Mom thanks Wyatt, Callum quickly shovels in a mouthful of food. "Yeah," Callum mumbles. "It's good."

"Don't talk with your mouth full," Dad tells him.

Mom laughs to herself. "It's good to see Callum trying something new. We need to have Wyatt over for dinner more often if it actually gets this boy to eat."

I smile, ignoring the fact my family is now onboard with vegan eating, despite my prior efforts to bring it into the dinner rotation. My heart is just too full, watching Callum's adoration. Yep, definitely a mini superfan.

"Are we just glossing over the vegan part?" Casey asks, gesturing with her fork. "What the heck is this cheese made from?"

"Soy," I say matter-of-factly.

She deadpans me. "Soy?"

"Yes."

"As in, the stuff we put on fried rice?"

I stifle my laugh. "Yes, it all comes from soybeans."

Casey pulls a face, which Mom and Dad are quick to tell her to drop.

Callum speaks with another mouthful of food. "It's good, Casey. Try it."

Casey huffs, rolls her eyes, and stabs her fork into her enchilada. "Should I say my final words?"

Everyone at the table huffs in frustrated annoyance.

Casey's eyes widen. "What?"

"Just eat it," we all say at once, erupting in laughter when Casey's eyes slit as she takes her first bite.

"Not so bad, huh?" Dad says, bouncing in his laughter.

Casey grunts a response, keeping her eyes fixed on her plate.

I happily take another bite of my dinner, satisfied we muted the mini skeptic.

The chatter throughout dinner is light and breezy, but when Mom starts clearing the dinner plates, I notice a shared look between her and Dad. There's a definite shift in the air when she returns from the kitchen.

"Casey and Callum," Mom says, somewhat on edge. "Why don't you two go watch some TV before dessert?"

Casey wriggles her eyebrows. "Why don't you give us dessert now?"

Dad points toward the living room. "It's not a debate. Just go."

The twins grumble as they scoot their dining chairs backward and leave the room.

Wyatt and I share a look, having not been excused from the table.

"So, we think we need to discuss something," Dad says, lacing his hands together on the dining table.

The way he looks at Wyatt makes me squirm. Is he going to say we should cut off all contact? That he doesn't approve of us being together when Wyatt's so famous?

Dad shifts in his seat, and says, "Wyatt, we're really concerned about your relationship with your parents."

My stomach flips inside-out. First, squirming at the word 'relationship' and going on a rollercoaster of emotions by the end of his sentence.

Wyatt gulps. "You are?"

"You're so young to have such a fractured relationship with them," Mom says, eyes growing glassy. "We were hoping there was some way we could help."

"We're happy to talk to them," Dad offers. "If that's something you would like."

"Uh, th-thanks, Mr. and Mrs. Ba-Bartlett." Wyatt clears his throat, his brow furrowing. "But it's really complicated. Like, they changed at some point when my career took off."

"Doesn't mean things can't be mended," Mom says gently.

"I don't want to put my parents behind a wall," Wyatt defends. "But they're not the same people. I don't like being a bank for them."

"You're more than a bank," Dad says.

"They were desperate for me to get b-better and go b-back to work."

"I'm sure they were desperate for you to get better," Mom says. "Going back to work would've been the cherry on top."

"I appreciate what you're saying," Wyatt says, bracing himself. "But you haven't seen them in three years."

Mom sighs, wiping the tears from her eyelashes. "It's just so sad," she murmurs. "I hate the idea of you being divided from them. Family is so important to us. We just want to fix it for you."

Wyatt smiles at her. "Th-thanks, that's really nice. Considering the adults around me have been en-encouraging me to sever ties with them."

"Josie mentioned emancipation." Dad grows rigid in his seat. "I don't think it was a great idea for you to sign documents when you're recovering from a neurological issue. I'm worried they're taking advantage of you."

"I signed it because it felt like a relief at the time."

Dad leans forward. "And now?"

Wyatt twists his lips and shrugs. "I dunno."

"We were thinking we could invite them here," Dad says.

I wriggle uncomfortably in my seat. "*Dad.*"

Wyatt swipes the clamminess from his brow. "Look, I really app-app-appreciate this, but..."

"It was just a suggestion," Mom rushes. "Something for you to think about."

Wyatt nods. "I will."

"We're just concerned, that's all," Dad says softly. "We want to help you make things better."

Wyatt forces a smile. "Thanks."

I finally take a breath. "Can we drop this now?"

Dad leans back and shares a look with Mom. "Sure. Sounds like it's time for pie."

Mom gets up from the table at the same time as Dad. "Yes. We picked up a lovely key lime pie when we heard you were coming home. It's vegan."

"That's awesome, Mrs. Bartlett."

When Mom and Dad leave for the kitchen, I reach a hand across the table and latch onto Wyatt. "I'm so sorry they put you on the spot like that."

"It's fine. They were only trying to help."

"But like you said, they don't know the real situation."

"But they care. That's all that really matters."

"I'll make them back off, if you want."

Wyatt lifts my hand and kisses it. "No. I like them just how they are."

Casey and Callum race back into the dining room.

"You get to read to us in person tonight," Callum cheers.

"You'd better have something amazing prepared for us," Casey says with an eager grin.

Wyatt smiles at me. "You do bedtime stories?"

"They're my critics," I reply. "They're first to hear all the stories I write."

"Oh, I'm jealous," Wyatt says.

Callum loops an arm around Wyatt. "You can come upstairs and listen to the story too."

"Thanks, little man."

Casey huffs, folding her arms. "As long as you don't talk through it."

Wyatt laughs and draws an X over his heart. "I promise I won't."

Twenty-Eight

Just like the night before I flew to Cherry Beach, I lied in my bed overnight, barely sleeping a wink.

Wyatt's in my house.

Wyatt is back in our hometown.

Amidst the excitement, there was still loads of cringe. I stared at the shadowy posters on my walls, mortified that Wyatt has seen my extreme level of obsession with him.

I came downstairs for breakfast in jeans and a T-shirt, and Mom turned me back around. Despite my complaining about how unfair she was being, she maintained her argument. I've missed four days of school, and she's not letting me miss a fifth.

It's not like I can pretend to go to school and then skip out in regular clothes like at a public school. I go to the elite Ashworth Academy, which comes with the quintessential private school uniform. After changing into the layers of clothes, topping it off with the school blazer, I trudge back downstairs.

Seriously. Wyatt's home. I should be able to skip one more day.

And however many more days he's in town.

"That's a cute look," Wyatt says, looking me up and down.

"Shut up," I hush, trying to hide my smile. I gesture at the pull-out couch. "How'd you sleep?"

"Pretty good," he says, half-convincingly. "Needed to take a sleep aid. My mind was kinda spinning?"

I give him a hug. "Everything okay?"

"Yeah, I'm just a little confused. Like, how long can I stay here? Is being here going to bring my memory back? And, I keep thinking about Devon's random phone call."

"Right, I'd almost forgotten about that. Will you be okay if he comes while I'm at school?"

"Umm, I guess?"

I stretch out breakfast as long as I can, but the twins are being fussy and distracting me from Wyatt. And like a gut punch, it's time to take the school bus.

Ugh. I haven't missed the bus.

I zombie my way from the bus into the school building. I don't know how many times Kylie says my name until I finally register her presence.

"Huh?" I snap awake.

Kylie yanks me into a hug. "I'm so glad you're back."

I sink into her hug. "Me too."

She whispers, "Where's Wyatt?"

"At home," I whisper back.

Kylie pulls out of the hug. "Your home?"

"Yeah. Where else?"

"I dunno. He's got money. Maybe he secretly bought a home in town and has it on the down-low."

"No, there's nothing secretive like that happening. It's just a secret he's back."

Parker races up to us, panting. "Where is he?"

"*Shoosh!*" Kylie and I whisper harshly.

Parker blinks at us. "What?"

Kylie whacks his arm. "Of course, he's not here."

"I dunno." Parker shrugs. "Maybe he wanted to come here and kick-start his memory."

"He remembers living here," I reply. "It's the becoming famous stuff that's foggy."

"Besides, he was barely even at this school before leaving for Talent Quest," Kylie says.

Parker bounces in place. "We get to meet up with him, right?"

"I'm sure he'll be cool with it," I reply.

Excitement ripples through Kylie. "I don't know how I'll be able to sit through an entire day of school, waiting to meet him again."

I sigh. "You and me both. It was agony coming to school this morning."

Parker wriggles his brow. "We could play hooky."

Kylie gestures between us. "You know who you're talking to, right?"

"If I get caught skipping class, my parents will flip," I say. "They're already not happy about how many days I skipped last week."

Kylie bats a hand. "I'll share my notes and get you caught up."

"I'm not worried about the homework. I'm trying to minimize the stress levels in my home."

"Can we at least skip out during our lunch period?" Parker asks, his enthusiasm bursting.

"He told me he'd be catching up on sleep," I reply. "I'll text him before lunch and we can make a game plan."

Parker grins and lifts his car keys. "I'm so ready to go whenever you say the word."

Kylie presses down on Parker's hand. "Cool your jets. We've gotta actually get through some classes first."

I nod, thankful. "I need some calm to stop my mind spiraling with thoughts about Wyatt."

My first two classes actually forced Wyatt out of my central focus. My teachers were on my case about the classes I've missed and what textbook chapters I need to read by tomorrow. I was so busy catching up with work, by my third class, I'd almost forgotten there's a high-profiled star hanging out in my living room.

"*Psst.*"

I turn behind me and find resident school gossip, Yvette Anderson, staring at me.

I jolt back and point at myself. "Me?"

"What was with that video?"

My stomach cramps. "What video?"

"You walking around with a celebrity."

The people at the surrounding desks turn my way. "Uhh, uhh... I..."

"Hey, what the heck?" Yvette asks, leaning forward against her desk. "Like, everyone saw you in Cherry Beach with Wyatt Hayes. What was that about?"

I shrink away from her, weighed down by all the eyes on me. "I don't know what you're talking about?"

"Yes, you do. How did you meet him?"

"He went to our school."

"Not in, like, forever."

I huff, knots tying over my spine. "That was last week. I'm back at school now."

"So?"

"So, my fifteen minutes of fame are over."

Yvette laughs to herself. "You got dumped that quick, huh?"

A fire grows in my stomach, but I bite down, ignoring it best I can. I'm not about to blurt to one of the biggest gossips in school that a teen heartthrob is currently chilling in my living room. I have to lean into the satisfaction that he's mine, and someone like Yvette will never have him.

The satisfaction wanes when people continue to fidget in their seats and send glances my way. The back of my neck coats in sweat. The thought of being Ashworth Academy headline news has me sick to my stomach.

When the lingering looks and harsh whispers continue throughout my next two classes, I pull my phone from my pocket and text under the desk. *"I gotta get out of this school."*

My knees bounce, and my fingers twitch around the phone. Seconds feel like hours until I get a response.

Kylie texts back. *"What's wrong?"*

"Gossip queens want to know why there's a video of me and Wyatt together in Cherry Beach."

"Vultures!"

"I just can't deal with hiding my relationship with him while he's literally in town."

"Meet me by our lockers after class."

I quickly send her a thumbs up emoji and sneak my phone back into my pocket.

"Are you okay?" Kylie asks, wide-eyed as we meet in the hallway.

I pant my breaths, leaning against my locker, and shake my head.

Kylie frowns. "They were giving you the second-degree?"

I frown harder. "Third-degree."

"Wanna get out of here?"

"Yes, but there's still two more classes after lunch."

Kylie shrugs. "So? You've just had a huge week amongst Hollywood-types. You should be allowed an adjustment period."

"There's no way my parents will sign me out."

"That's why I texted Parker." Kylie nods down the hallway, where her boyfriend approaches us. "He'll drive us out of here."

I give her a dubious look. "And what kind of adjustment period are you two going through?"

Parker reaches us and he pecks Kylie's cheek as she responds with, "My best friend just had a week with Hollywood-types. It's mental overload."

The comment makes me puff a laugh. "And what about Parker?"

Kylie shrugs, throwing an arm around her boyfriend. "He has a car."

Parker nods at me. "You wanna get out of here? Now's the time to do it."

I swallow the nausea. "What if we get caught?"

"We won't if we take the south wing exit," Parker replies.

Kylie motions for Parker to take the lead. "Shall we?"

I wince, looking between the two. "Can we not mention to Wyatt that I'm leaving because people were asking about my involvement with him? I don't want him thinking I can't handle it."

Kylie frowns. "Are you sure?"

"I'd rather we just hang out and have some fun," I reply. "I'll tell him about school another time."

Hesitancy creeps over Kylie's face. "Okay, if you're sure."

I nod and let them lead me out of the school. "I'm sure."

Kylie lets her smile break through and she whispers to her boyfriend. "I can't believe we're about to hang out with Wyatt Hayes."

Parker nods, grinning. "I know."

Somehow, the nausea subsides and I'm in Parker's car, and in another flash, I'm unlocking my front door.

"Wyatt?" I call out, leaving the door open for the others to follow me in. "I got out of school early."

I move into the living room as Wyatt stands from the couch.

"Hey, what are you doing here?" Wyatt asks, pulling his arms around me.

I hug him back. "I brought some friends who couldn't wait to say hello."

"Oh my gosh," Kylie says, shivering as she takes Wyatt in. "It's really you."

Wyatt waves, and then realization takes over his face. "Oh, Kylie, hey."

Kylie giggles, waving back. "Hey."

Wyatt turns his head between me and Kylie. "How come you came home early?"

"I told you," I murmur. "We couldn't wait."

Kylie flashes a smile. "I've been waiting to meet you again since Josie got the call to fly to Cherry Beach."

"Oh, that's nice," Wyatt replies. "Josie told me you're a crazy-good baker now."

Kylie blushes. "Oh, yeah, thanks." She throws a thumb over her shoulder. "We could head over to the café where I work if you want to try something."

Wyatt glances at me. "Could we?"

I nod. "If you like."

Parker jingles his keys. "I'm happy to drive us over."

Wyatt tilts his head. "Parker?"

Parker beams. "You remember me?"

"Umm, Jo-Josie said Kylie had a boyfriend."

"Oh," Parker falters. "Well, that's me."

Wyatt nods. "I'm pretty sure I remember you."

Parker grins. "Awesome."

Wyatt folds his arms. "Yeah, we weren't friends."

Parker rocks his jaw. "At the time, no."

Kylie braces herself through the awkwardness. "No reason we can't all hang out now."

"Yeah," I say, glancing at Wyatt. "Right?"

"Right." Wyatt unravels his arms. "But can we really go out if you left school early?"

"It's okay for me and Josie," Kylie says, stifling a laugh. "We're the good girls who get away with murder."

Amused by her comment, Wyatt's gaze moves over to Parker, getting a read on him.

Parker bats a hand. "There's only the boring classes left for the day."

Wyatt smirks. "Oh, okay then."

Kylie awes at Wyatt. "It's so incredibly good to see you."

"Thanks, you too."

"No, I mean, *really* good to see you," Kylie adds on. "We never thought this would happen."

The fun leaves Wyatt's expression. "No one ever thought I'd come back to town?"

"Why would you?" Parker says. "You have it made. There's no need to come back here."

"There's billionaires here," Wyatt offers.

"That's old money that built this town," Parker replies. "Not the same thing as reality TV new money."

Wyatt fidgets, not knowing how to respond. "Oh."

Parker draws a flatten palm towards Wyatt. "Can I get a loan?"

Wyatt recoils. "Huh?"

Kylie whacks Parker's arm, and Parker lifts his hands in surrender while laughing. "Kidding. Kidding."

The air in the room is stiff, almost to a choking point. I rub the cramp from my chest and say, "Shall we go out and get some fresh air?"

"Will you be okay around other people?" Kylie asks me. "You know, after..."

"It's cool," I blurt, so Wyatt doesn't get clued in. "Besides, everyone's still at school. Hardly anyone will be on Main Street."

Wyatt takes my hand. "Were you feeling claustrophobic?"

I hide the ick behind a smile. "I was around a lot more people compared to our time in Cherry Beach."

"Must've been a lot if you felt more overwhelmed at school than around the suits."

"The suits?" Kylie asks. "As in the people you work for?"

"Yeah," Wyatt replies. "I came back here with Josie to get away from their pressure."

"Must be intense," Parker says. "Especially after getting out of the hospital."

Wyatt smiles appreciatively. "Yeah, it's hard to get used to."

Parker motions toward the front door. "Then let's go do something fun."

Wyatt nods, looking my way. "Okay. Let's go."

We load into Parker's car, Wyatt taking the backseat with me, and we head into Main Street. After the short drive, Parker finds a parking space outside the café where Kylie works.

Kylie shifts in her seat, facing us in the back. "Maybe you don't want to go in."

Wyatt deadpans her. "Do you mean, me, sp-sp-specifically?"

Kylie bites her lip, glancing at me, then Parker, and then landing back on Wyatt. "This is a small town. People stare, and news travels fast."

Wyatt's Adam's apple bobs and his eyes shift in my direction.

"I'm just saying," Kylie continues on, "I could go inside and grab us something. Then we could lay low in one of the local parks."

Parker gives her a strange look. "How is that not as public?"

"We'll go to one that's not as popular," Kylie replies. "You know, like the one on Granger Street. No one's ever there. Plus, school isn't out yet."

Parker shrugs. "I guess it'll work."

Wyatt nudges me. "What do you think?"

The others turn in their front seats to face me, and I slouch, clutching my elbows. "I like the idea of not having people gawk at us."

"To be fair, it won't be at us." Parker throws a thumb at Wyatt. "It'll be at him."

Kylie and I groan at once. "Not helping."

"What, it's true," Parker argues.

"We don't have to do this," Wyatt says. "I don't want to make things awkward for you guys."

Kylie plants a hand on her chest. "It's not us we're worried about. We don't want this to be hard for you."

"I'm okay," Wyatt replies. "Really."

"But isn't it weird having people come up to you?" Parker asks. "You know, when you don't remember leaving and becoming famous?"

Wyatt puffs a laugh. "Actually, it's surprisingly easy."

"Really?" Kylie and Parker ask at once.

"It kinda came naturally," Wyatt tells them.

"Huh." Kylie thoughtfully looks off to the side. "So, the video in Cherry Beach was legit. You were cool with all those people around you?"

Wyatt nods. "I was." He then grabs my hand. "But I know Josie wasn't. So, maybe we shouldn't do this if me being there is gonna cause a scene."

I sigh, looking deep into his hazel eyes. "I don't want to be the buzzkill. I mean, maybe no one will notice?"

Parker smirks, muttering, "Wishful thinking."

Wyatt looks around the backseat. "Maybe I can go unnoticed. You got a baseball cap in here, Parker?"

Parker points behind us. "Back there on the parcel shelf."

Wyatt takes the cap and sits it on his head. "Am I just a regular kid now?"

Parker laughs. "I sure don't see anything special about you."

"Parker's giving you a hard time," Kylie says matter-of-factly. "Meaning you're just one of the boys."

Wyatt gives me a hopeful look. "Shall we test it?"

I smile and nod, because when I'm with Wyatt, I'm always safe.

Kylie walks us into the café, shows us to one of the rear booths, and then moves onto the counter to order for our group.

Wyatt and I take one side of the booth, with Parker taking the other side, awaiting Kylie's return.

I can't help noticing my best friend is a little sheepish when she walks back to the booth.

"My boss is a little skeptical," Kylie says in a low voice.

My stomach spasms. "What do you mean?"

"I told her you were away," Kylie says vaguely, avoiding eye contact. "And, umm, she asked who the guy was sitting next to you."

Wyatt slouches in seat, baseball cap shifted downwards. "Did she recognize me?"

"No," Kylie replies. "I just told her to act cool and not to make a fuss. She knows Josie doesn't like to be the center of attention."

"We can just tell her you're the new guy at school," Parker suggests.

Wyatt waves it off. "You don't have to say anything. Making things a bigger deal tends to make it worse."

I nudge Wyatt. "Don't hunch. Savanna will be unhappy."

"Right," Wyatt says, sitting taller. "Hunching is your thing."

I giggle at the kidding in his tone, and take in our surroundings. No one in the café has taken note of us.

Phew.

We might be in the clear.

"So, do I have to call your parents?" Kylie's boss asks, standing over our table.

Kylie glances around at our group, and then back at her boss. "What do you mean?"

Maddy, her boss, sets the tray of milkshakes and cakes down on the table. "*Hello.* You guys have cut class."

Parker mumbles a laugh. "Free period, Maddy."

"Uh-huh." Maddy deadpans him. "If I see any of your parents walk in here, I'll be telling them the truth."

Kylie beams at her boss. "We'll leave a big tip."

Maddy laughs to herself, moving back to the front counter.

Parker nods at Wyatt. "You can take care of that big tip, can't you?"

Wyatt grins. "Would be glad to." The corners of his mouth drop south and he palms his forehead. "Oh, man. I literally forgot. I have no way to pay for things."

"What does that mean?" Kylie asks as worry vibrates her tone.

Wyatt winces. "Everything got charged to the hotel before."

Parker lets out a belly laugh.

Kylie elbows him. "*Shoosh.*"

"Come on," Parker says, fumbling with laughter. "He's a mega star without the cash. That's funny."

Wyatt simmers with laughter, shaking his head at the tabletop. "I can't believe it never dawned on me that I'd have to figure out how to pay for things."

"I don't blame you," I say. "Life was pretty chill when we got to charge everything to the penthouse."

Kylie smirks. "Rub it in, why don't you."

Wyatt chuckles. "My bad, guys. I'll have to get the bill next time."

Parker bats a hand. "All good. I got it."

"No, I got it," Kylie and I say at once, and then end up laughing.

"Okay, let's split it," Parker says, dishing out the cakes left behind by Maddy.

We all agree and swiftly move on to trying the vegan strawberry shortcake, and dairy-free cookie dough milkshakes.

"My goodness, Kylie," Wyatt says, barely swallowing. "These are fr-freaking amazing. You make these?"

Kylie nods proudly. "If there's anything you especially want baked while you're in town, just let me know."

"I'm sure I'll love whatever you've got cooking," Wyatt replies.

Parker smiles at Kylie. "Give her a challenge, Wyatt. She loves it."

"Do you make donuts?" Wyatt asks.

Kylie sits taller, her gaze lifting as she thinks about it. "I've never made vegan ones. Challenge accepted."

After the cake and milkshakes have been consumed, and the check split three ways, we don't risk being made in the café. Instead, we head back onto Main Street.

There aren't a lot of people around, so we meander toward the closest park. It adjoins the skatepark, making it a popular hangout space. Although, it's still early enough not to have a crowd.

The afternoon sun gives the lush greenery a soft hue, and the gentle breeze has a calming warmth to it. I can't help smiling, marveling at the rolling hills surrounding us.

"Does it feel familiar, Wyatt?" Kylie asks.

"It's weird," he replies. "I remember it, but it also feels new. Not much has really changed, but I guess I feel like an outcast."

"Wyatt Hayes is no outcast," Parker quips.

"Hey, thanks for bringing us out here," Wyatt says to Parker. "It's really cool to hang out like a regular person."

"Glad you're into walking around Main Street," Parker replies. "It's literally a regular day for us."

Kylie gestures at the skatepark. "Over there is where Parker taught me how to ride a skateboard. Maybe when you're feeling up to it, you could give it a go?"

"My coordination isn't the best right now," Wyatt says with a laugh, "But, yeah, maybe."

"How long do you think you'll stick around for?" Parker asks.

Wyatt blows out a breath, slinging an arm around my shoulders. "I really don't know. Circle 8 might turn up tomorrow and demand I go back. I was excited to start recording, but my time in the studio wasn't exactly creative."

"What do you mean?" Kylie asks.

"Does soul-sucking mean anything to you?" Wyatt replies.

"Oh." Kylie frowns. "That doesn't sound fun at all."

"Definitely not," Parker agrees. "You really must've been miserable if walking around a park is fun for you."

I wrap an arm around Wyatt's back. "It's totally the company, right?"

Wyatt grins. "Totally."

We dawdle around the park, Wyatt and my pace lagging behind the others. I smile as Kylie and Parker hold hands and zigzag their way along the footpath. They're in their own little world and infatuated with each other's company.

"They're really cute together," Wyatt comments.

"I know. I'm happy for them."

Wyatt and I stroll along the sidewalk, coming close to a parking lot. My eyes wander across a group of students, who have gotten out of school early. I'm about to turn away when I hear a gasp and notice one girl hurriedly nudging another.

"Oh my gosh, Wyatt Hayes," one of the girls shrieks.

The girls bolt toward us, giving me no reaction time to get Wyatt away from them.

One girl's face is a mismatch of white and red splodges, like she's about to pass out.

Her friend holds her up, saying, "Holy crap! You've come back to town. This is so exciting!"

From a nearby pickup truck, a broad footballer-type plods over to the girls. "Sally, what are you screaming about?"

The girls point at Wyatt, bouncing up and down together. "Look! Look!"

The guy spots Wyatt and then stops dead. He then turns towards the pickup truck he came from. "Roy, Mckinley, get over here!"

Two other burly guys lift their heads with mild interest.

One of the girls points at me. "Oh my gosh! You're the girl in the video. The one who supposedly goes to our school."

"Oh, wow!" the other girl gasps. "It totally is. Why have we never seen you before?"

"Totally," the first girl says. "I was like, they're lying. I remember saying, I've never seen that girl in my life."

"Yo, Sally," the broad guy says, edging closer. "How are you talking to Wyatt Hayes right now?"

"*Hello*," she replies with an eye roll. "We went to school together, remember?"

Broad guy laughs. "Of course, I remember. I'm not a dumbass."

At that, something triggers Wyatt, and his expression quirks into a hardened frown. "You didn't want to know me when I went to your school."

"Sure, we did," they all reply.

Wyatt shakes his head slowly. "No. I was the dumb kid who got held back a grade. Besides one person, no one wanted to know me."

"That's not true," one girl blurts. "We, like, totally remember you from the school talent shows."

"Do you?" Wyatt's eyes turn to slits. "Or do you remember the footage of a talent show that was played on national TV?"

I jolt backwards.

How does he know that?

The girls glance at each other, uttering syllables.

Wyatt shakes his head. "I thought so."

"Dude, we were there," the broad guy says, folding his arms. "You just don't remember us being in the same class."

"I remember getting DMs after I won from people who, by all rights, used to hate my guts."

I double-take at Wyatt.

Wait...

Does he remember?

I clutch his arm. "Wyatt?"

He turns to me, and then grunts, grabbing his head in pain.

I grab hold of his other arm, looking him up and down as agony turns his frame rigid.

The surrounding people fuss and whine at the sight, but I refuse to take in any of their noise. Despite the fact it might hurt him, I shove Wyatt backwards, getting space from our onlookers. They continue to babble behind us, but they don't come any closer.

With a stable stance, Wyatt stands a little taller, wincing and rubbing his thumb in a circle between his eyebrows.

I clutch his arm and place my other hand on his back. "Are you okay?"

"I... I..." He strains to get the words out as he hunches forward. "It hurts, but... I... I think I remember."

My heartbeat speeds up, and my hands press firmer on him. "Remember? Remember what?"

Wyatt drops his hand and lets out a horrified gasp. He bumps my hands off his and takes three unsteady steps backward. His mouth hangs open, and his eyes widen with added shine.

"Wyatt?" I murmur, unnerved. "What is it? What's happening?"

His forehead scrunches, and he holds the sides of head as he leans forward. A guttural moan aches out of him, and I'm petrified with icy fear. My vision blurs with cloudy tears, and my muscles tense as questions leak from my brain.

I inch my way toward him, carefully taking hold of his arms. "What is it? Talk to me."

"My movie," he struggles to speak through gritted teeth. "I remember."

My jaw drops. "As in the film set? Do you remember being there? The accident?"

He frowns, which quickly morphs into a grimace as the pain scorches his face.

"Oh, Wyatt," I mourn. "I hate that you're suffering like this."

Wyatt moves out of my grip and blinks his eyes clear. I take half a step towards him, still giving him air.

"Oh, crap," it breathes out of him. "I have to go back."

I blink at him, hoping I misheard. "Huh?"

He holds his stomach and presses his lips together as a lump bulges in his throat.

"Hey, hey," I coo, rubbing the chill from his forearms. "Take it easy. Just breathe."

He shakes his head. "I've made a big mistake."

My heart drops. "About what?"

I can't bring myself to ask more, but my brain spirals.

About me? About us?

"Joze, I've let them all down."

Purpose strengthens my heartbeat. "Don't say that. You're doing your best to recover."

He shakes his head again, wincing from the pain. "No, you don't understand. If I quit, all these people will lose their jobs."

I swallow hard. "What people?"

"I have a contract," he rushes, looking off to the side as if someone's coming after him. "I have commitments. I've jeopardized too much by walking away."

"Wyatt, slow down."

His shallow breaths accelerate. "People depend on me." He pants hard. "They need me to show up for their own livelihoods."

I wrap my arms around him, hoping it'll ground him and help him calm down. "Wyatt, you haven't let anyone down. You're in recovery. You haven't quit."

His eyes grow glossy, and he has trouble steadying his eyes in one place. "But... But, I..."

"No," I say firmly, holding his chin so he has only me to focus on. "Those people were manipulating you into rushing back to work. You saw the journal entries in your own handwriting. You have nothing to feel guilty about."

Wyatt hugs me back, holding me tight like a security blanket. "Crap, Joze. They're stuck in my head. It's like a vice grip."

"I've got you," I whisper. "You don't have to go back. You're home."

He exhales slowly, trembling slightly. "I love you."

"Wyatt, you have my whole heart. I love you so much."

Kylie and Parker rush back toward us, and before they can ask us if we're okay, I ask Parker to drive us home.

Twenty-Nine

"Josie, what were you thinking?" Mom hounds me when we walk through the front door. "Skipping school?"

"Mom, we were..."

"I don't want excuses." Disappointment wrinkles Mom's face. "I couldn't believe it when the school called me. My daughter doesn't walk out on her classes. At least, she *didn't*."

I step in front of Wyatt. "Don't blame him. I did it all on my own."

Mom frowns. "Not according to the school."

I hold my middle as I droop with sadness. I didn't mean to get Kylie and Parker in trouble too.

"You're lucky they're not suspending you."

I gulp. "They're not?"

Mom steps forward and gently rubs my arms. "You have a good reputation, Josie. You don't want to wreck that."

My vision turns glossy, and I sniff hard. "I know, but people were talking about me in classes."

Wyatt steps beside me. "Who was talking?"

Mom shakes her head. "This is no reason to skip school."

I clasp my hands in front and let out a sigh. "I just couldn't handle it."

Mom steps aside. "We'll talk about this later. Go freshen up."

I move toward the staircase, but Wyatt grasps my arm. "Who was talking about you?"

I hunch, wincing. "Wyatt, I..."

"Tell me," he says softly. "What did they say?"

I lift my palms up. "Does it matter?"

He blinks at me. "Of course, it matters."

I shake my head. "Not now. You've got your memory back."

Mom gasps and clutches Wyatt's shoulder. "Is that true?"

Before Wyatt can respond, Casey and Callum race into the foyer.

"Did you ground her, Mom?" Casey asks with glee.

Mom waves them off. "Not now, you two."

Callum's lip upturns as he glances around at us. "What the heck is going on?"

Mom goes to shoo them again, but Wyatt stops her.

Wyatt nods at Casey and says, "I think I can answer some of your Circle 8 cult questions."

Casey lifts on the balls of her feet with interest. "You suddenly have intel?"

Wyatt rubs the side of his head. "My brain might be less broken now."

Callum gasps, hugging his arms around Wyatt's waist. "You got your memory back?"

Wyatt nods. "It's jumbled, but I'm getting there."

Mom ushers us into the living room. "What can we do to help you?" she asks, gesturing for Wyatt to take a seat on the couch.

Wyatt picks up his phone, which he left on the coffee table before we went to Main Street. "Maybe I should call my psy-psy..."

Mom gasps, motioning at the phone. "If you have a psychologist helping you through this stuff, you should definitely call them."

Wyatt mumbles a laugh. "Dang it. I thought I could say the word this time."

I lean into him for support. "No big deal. The fog inside your head is clearing. It's amazing."

Wyatt braces himself. "And scary."

Casey's eyes widen. "What if you remember stuff you don't want to know?"

Mom plants her hands on her hips in scolding-mode. "Casey, don't be heinous."

Wyatt blows out a breath. "She's got a point. I forgot this stuff for a reason."

I sit back. "What do you mean?"

"The doctors told me I'd suffer some kind of em-emotional shock." Wyatt takes a beat before continuing. "Something major happened, and I dealt with it by blocking it out."

"So it's more psychological than physical?" I ask. "I remember Dr. Fincher saying something about that. That your injury and your memory loss didn't exactly match up."

Wyatt rubs his forehead. "I remember a lot of shouting. Arguing. Just a lot of tension on set."

Mom gestures at Wyatt's phone. "Do you want to make the call? I can show you to Daniel's den."

Wyatt nods, thanking Mom and following her out of the living room.

As the twins speculate on Wyatt's recent memory comeback—Casey going wild on theories—I hear a distinct car noise out the front of the house.

I leave the couch and approach the foyer, nervous at the familiar sound.

Dad's keys jingle outside the front door, and I may as well be ten-years-old when I see the disappointment on his face.

"You're home early," I quip.

Dad sets his briefcase down and closes the door behind him. "I settled things with my last client after the school called me."

My insides spasms and loud warning sirens blare in my head to retreat.

I quickly B-line for the staircase, but only get a few steps before Dad's voice turns stern.

"Josie," Dad says firmly. "We need to discuss you cutting class."

"*Dad.*" I pout, turning toward him on the step. "Can we not?"

Dad crosses his arms. "The discussion isn't up for debate. I don't like this, Josie. You spent a week in opulence, and now what? You're acting like a brat?"

My jaw drops at the accusation. "I am not!"

Dad forces me to sit, and I take the third and fourth steps as my seat. Dad crouches before me and his eyes gleam with kindness. "Tell me what happened?"

I hug my knees and sigh. "I just can't imagine going back."

"Why?"

I shake my head, sinking deeper into the hunch. "The only future I see is homeschooling. Kylie will be fine without me. She has her boyfriend's friends to hang out with. I was fine being a loner. I was totally invisible." I sigh harder. "Now people will target me and hound me with questions."

"I know you have your mother's nervousness inside you," Dad says gently, "but you also have a strong resolve."

I shudder. "All I do is imagine all the eyes on me. It makes me sick."

A smile tugs the corners of his mouth. "It's the questions you're worried about?"

Something sour lines the back of my throat as I nod.

Dad's smile spreads. "Didn't you sign an NDA when you got to Cherry Beach?"

At that, the tormenting panic inside me pauses. I blink at Dad, my mind rewinding to my first moments in the presidential suite with Erika and Randall after I landed.

Dad chucks my chin. "Darling, you can't answer any questions."

With relief flooding through me, I launch forward and wrap my arms around Dad.

Dad chuckles as he rubs a circle on my back. "Feel better?"

I cringe. "I think the NDA was only about the clinic and Wyatt's medical stuff."

Dad hushes me. "It doesn't matter. Anyone starts hounding you, you just stop them. Say, you signed an NDA, and legally you can't say a word."

I pull out of the hug. "Won't that entice them more?"

"Initially," Dad agrees. "But when you keep giving the same answer, with the blankest expression you can muster, they'll get bored. Trust me."

I crack a smile, no longer feeling like eyes are burning into me.

"You promise to never cut class again?" Dad asks.

I give him my pinky. "I promise."

He links his pinky with mine. "Good girl. Where's Wyatt?"

"He's on a therapy call. He got his memory back."

Dad's mouth falls open. "Fully?"

"He said it's a bit scrambled, but the pieces are coming back."

"This is incredible."

"Hey, what's that?" Casey's voice sounds in the living room.

When I'm about to ask her what she means, I hear it.

The distinct sounds of cars parking.

The chatter between numerous people.

I move into the living room with Dad. "Is that coming from outside our house?"

The twins and I move to the front window. Instantly, I jump back with a gasp.

Outside our house, news vans are parking against the curb. Traipsing up our front lawn are reports with microphones, followed by people with camera equipment.

"What the heck?" the twins cry out at the sight.

"What is it?" Mom asks, making her way into the living room. "Daniel, you're home?"

Dad doesn't respond, stupefied by the sight beyond the window.

I point at the scene, horrified. "It's... It's..."

Mom moves past me, taking in the view. She gasps harder than I did and the knocking of her knees creates an echo. "How did... Why did..."

"*Duh*, Mom," Casey says flatly. "They're here for Wyatt."

Callum pulls a confused face. "How do they know he's here?"

The horror quakes through my body and I'm ready to keel over. "Because we were seen together." I retch. "Oh my gosh, it's my fault."

Callum's lip upturns. "Did you give them our address?"

"Ugh." Annoyance billows off Casey. "They know who she is after people saw them together in Cherry Beach."

"This is horrendous," Mom says, snatching the curtains closed. "They can't just camp in front of our house, waiting to catch a glimpse of Wyatt."

Three knocks thunder against our front door, making us all jump in alarm. The four of us huddle together, not daring to make a sound, as Dad creeps toward the front door.

"Don't answer it!" Mom shrieks.

"Is everything okay?" Wyatt asks, making his way back into the room. "I could hear the noise at the other end of the house."

I can't stomach the words. I don't want him to know what's beyond the curtain.

Casey breaks away from our group hug. "Reporters are here for you."

Wyatt recoils. "You're kidding."

Mom trembles, dropping her hands from around us. "Whoever saw you on Main Street must've leaked it to the press."

I think about those girls at the park. When I pushed Wyatt away from them, I can imagine them whipping out their phones and recording us. "Ugh. Or they put it online."

Wyatt moves toward the closed curtain, but Mom and I block his path.

"You don't have to look," Mom says softly.

"But it's my problem," Wyatt replies. "Not yours."

"I'm sorry," I utter, tears blurring my vision of him. "It's my fault they're all here."

Wyatt smiles gently. "No, it isn't. They're here for me."

"But I…"

"It's my fault," Wyatt whispers. "I should've known better than to leave the house."

Mom sighs. "We don't want you feeling like a prisoner."

Dad pounds on our side of the front door. "Get off my property!" Dad catches his breath, red-faced. "I was not expecting *this* when I got home."

"I'm sorry, Mr. Bartlett," Wyatt rushes. "I never meant…"

"Don't," I cut him off. "It's all me. If I didn't skip school, they wouldn't be here. Ugh. I feel sick."

Wyatt wraps an arm around me as Dad dashes past, checking out the scene from the front window.

"This isn't safe," Dad utters.

"Of course, it isn't," Mom murmurs, making her way to his side. "But what can we do?"

"*Duh.*" Casey's eyes roll hard. "Call the police."

Dad snaps his fingers. "Of course. They're trespassing."

"I'll let it slide, considering you're in shock," Casey mutters.

Dad pulls his phone from his pocket, but his fingers are shaking so much that he fumbles and drops the phone onto the carpet.

Mom bends down to scoop it up, and Dad's expression crumbles.

"Daniel?" Mom questions with trepidation, holding back the phone.

Dad gestures at the window. "This is after one day of you being here."

My core jitters when Dad's gaze lands on Wyatt.

"We can get rid of them today," Dad continues, "but what happens tomorrow?"

Wyatt nods, swallowing hard. "I know. I'm sorry."

I clasp Wyatt's hand hard. I don't want him to be sorry. It's not fair.

"We can't do this." Dad pulls his arm around Mom. "I know you didn't plan this, but I can't put my family's safety in jeopardy."

"Dad," I utter, stepping in front of Wyatt. "What are you saying?"

"I'm sorry," he murmurs, his aged skin paling. "Wyatt, we have to rethink you staying here."

"*Dad*," I balk.

"Josie," Mom says, tears welling in her eyes. "This is out of control. It's a mob out there."

With a tremble, Wyatt tugs on my hand. I turn and see the reluctant resolve in his eyes. "It's, it's okay," he stammers. "Th-they're right. I have to go."

My chest constricts and anger bubbles up from my gut. "No. You're not going anywhere."

"It's..." Wyatt gulps and stumbles, taking a step backward. "It's my fault."

"You didn't ask for this," I argue.

Mom's chin dimples. "The twins shouldn't have to witness this."

"No," Callum whines. "Wyatt can't go."

"Yeah," Casey says, hugging an arm around Callum. "He just got interesting."

My jaw aches and pain twists between my shoulder blades. "Where do you expect him to go, Mom? He doesn't have anyone but us." I glare at Dad. "Or maybe he only has me on his side."

"Joze," Wyatt whispers, tugging on my arm. "Don't do this. Don't fight with them."

"You're not leaving," I raise my voice. "There's no other place for you to go, but back to Ferndale."

Wyatt shrugs and his face droops. "Maybe th-that's where I belong."

My heart splinters. "You don't deserve to be miserable."

"I'm not kicking him out this minute," Dad says, surveying the crowd behind the curtain. "But we need a more realistic plan."

I stomp my foot to gain Dad's eye contact. "If the crowd wasn't here, you wouldn't be kicking him out."

Dad falters. "Well, I wasn't planning on it."

My heart races. "You need a plan to keep the reporters away for good?"

"It's not so simple..."

I backtrack toward the foyer. "I'll keep them away."

Mom and Dad have trouble computing my words, and I take the opportunity to reef the front door open. I hear the calls from my family to stop what I'm doing, but I slam the door behind me.

I'm not letting anyone take Wyatt away from me.

Even though there are eyes on me, and even worse, cameras pointed at me, the zing in my heart has me powering through. All the questions pointed my way, can't hurt me. I won't let them ruin what I have.

I trudge down the front path and my hands ball into fists as everyone circles around me. I stamp my feet, clench my eyes shut, and let out a high-pitched scream.

Once the ringing in my ears stops, I notice the surrounding voices have muted. Taking a few large breaths, I open my eyes, finding bewildered faces.

I stare back at them, my throat scratched and strained. "Get out."

Still, there's no movement or sound from anyone around me.

I stomp my foot again. "Get out!"

Two people on my left jump back from my outburst.

Before I can make my next move, sirens blare in our direction. As everyone faces the road, I contemplate their arrival being too soon, even if Dad's calling the police. Standing amongst the mass of stunned reporters, two patrol cars slow by the news vehicles, escorting a shiny black limousine.

My heart drops to the pit of my stomach.

A limo?

As in Circle 8?

Oh my gosh. Erika found us.

Okay, she already had my address and phone number from when she first called me to fly out to Cherry Beach. I just thought she'd give us more time.

My insides clench as the sheriff's department clears the press from our front lawn and ushers them to their news vans. I can't help keeping my eyes on the limo, sick at the thought of Erika dragging Wyatt back to Ferndale.

Is there anything I can do to stop her?

As the lawn clears of the violating press, the limousine driver exits the car. He's a tall and slim, older gentleman. Not exactly the burly type associated with Circle 8. The driver opens the passenger door, and a young man exits.

My heart stops for a millisecond.

It's Devon.

Thirty

Devon awkwardly waves at me. "Is Wyatt here?"

"You're... You're..."

He edges toward me, hand on his chest. "I'm Devon. I was Wyatt's assistant."

"I know. We were expecting you." I gesture at the limo. "How..."

"I've borrowed it from the Ashworths."

My chin drops at the statement.

Devon points at the house. "Can we go inside? I don't want a repeat of those vans showing up."

Hurriedly, I beckon him to follow. "Sure. Come on in."

My dad meets us at the door, sizing up Devon as he lets him follow me inside.

"Devon?" Wyatt utters as we enter the living room. "It's you."

Devon stumbles backwards. "You remember me?"

Wyatt rubs the side of his head. "A lot of stuff recently came back to me."

Devon moves in for a hug. "It's so good to see you, bro."

Wyatt yanks him into the hug, patting Devon's back. "Man, you too."

The boys pull apart and move further into the living room. Wyatt sits beside me on the couch, and Devon perches on the opposite armrest. Dad stands on the other side of the coffee table, surveying the room.

"I gave the twins ice-cream in the back room," Mom says, returning to the living room. "It was the only way they'd promise not to race in here."

"Mom, this is Devon," I introduce.

"My assistant," Wyatt is quick to add.

"So," Dad starts off. "Tell us how you got here, and the little show with the police out there."

"It's the Ashworths' limousine," Devon explains. "I still have some connections. Even if I need to go about things in the most roundabout way."

Dad folds his arms, getting a read on Devon. "Explain what that means."

"Right." Devon nods. "About a year ago, we got a call from someone who worked for Tom Ashworth. Apparently, his daughter Vanessa is a huge fan of Wyatt's and wanted him to perform at her birthday. It didn't work out, but I had some of the emails saved on my personal account. They had a phone number under the signature."

"Wait." Wyatt pauses, mulling something over. "I had a chance to come back to Victoria Falls, and I didn't take it?"

"It wasn't good timing," Devon says tentatively. "You weren't in a good headspace."

"Oh." Wyatt sighs. "Yeah, I wouldn't have wanted to see Josie when I was like that."

I recoil, hating the idea of Wyatt not wanting to see me.

He reaches for my hand. "Not that I wanted to avoid you. I just felt like a fraud. I wasn't good enough to be in your life."

I lace my fingers between his. "Has it gotten through your head yet? You should absolutely be in my life no matter what."

Wyatt relaxes into a smile. "Yes."

"So," Dad continues in drill mode, "you rang up someone who worked for Tom Ashworth? Now you're riding in one of his limos?"

"There was more discussion than that," Devon says, keeping his cool. "I managed to get in contact with someone in a higher position in the company. They heard me out. For one, they were concerned about Wyatt's security. Then, when I mentioned him being pushed back into work, they were concerned about what kind of contract he was under."

"How did you know he was being pushed back into work?" Dad asks. "Haven't you been out of the picture?"

"Portia's assistant, Jenna, filled me in." Devon then gestures at me. "She and Josie were talking at the hotel, which led Jenna to find me and ask for help."

"*Ohhh.*" Wyatt drags out the word, sitting back on the couch and staring up at the ceiling. "The contract. That's what the fight was about."

"What fight?" I ask.

Wyatt sits back, staring at Devon, stunned. "Richmond," he utters. "It was Richmond."

Devon nods. "Jenna told me they were told to lie. Telling people he was in Europe the entire time. But we know he came back to the set."

Wyatt's hands ball into fists, and a vein pops in his neck. "After what he did, he then came back with Portia. They forced me back into the recording studio." Wyatt stands with a grunt. "That jerk!"

"He's not getting away with it," Devon says, standing with Wyatt. "None of them are."

Dad stands between the boys. "Okay, everyone cool down. Talk this through."

"Richmond Salinger," Devon tells Dad. "He's a Circle 8 manager. He's the one who got into it with Wyatt and caused his injury."

My heart stops for a beat too long. I want to stand, but my legs have jellied. "That creep has been on Portia's case ever since. She never stops working. Then he has the gall to come back into your life like nothing ever happened? Ugh. I knew I hated that guy."

"If you're sure about this," Dad says to Wyatt, "you should press charges."

"Mr. Ashworth is prepared to help," Devon says. "We just need to get over to Ashworth Estate and meet with him."

Dad nods. "You should do that."

"Now?" Wyatt and I ask at once.

"They've got two suites in the manor waiting for us," Devon replies.

Wyatt sits next to me, rubbing his forehead. "Ugh. I can see Richmond's face, clear as day."

"I really thought it was Erika," I mutter.

Wyatt combs his hand through his hair, leaving sweat beads on his forehead. "Erika and I were butting heads. All I wanted to do was quit. I hate acting. Everyday on set, I f-felt like my soul was being cr-crushed. Any time I mentioned wanting to leave, they'd hang that fr-freaking contract over my head."

I rub his back. "I'm sorry."

"They'd guilt me about all the people who'd lose jobs if I walked out."

"They'll all be fine," Devon says. "If they have to, they'll replace you with another rising teen star. They've done it before. The only people who lose their jobs are those trying to speak out."

Wyatt sits forward. "How did you get blamed for my accident?"

"I heard you arguing with Erika, but by the time I got into the trailer, you'd left," Devon explains. "I thought maybe you'd gone to get something to eat and then found you in Richmond's grip. He shoved you hard into one of the heavy-duty lighting rigs that hadn't been properly assembled yet."

"If you saw what happened, why didn't you say anything?" Dad questions.

"I was pulled out of there so quickly," Devon replies. "I didn't know if Wyatt was conscious or not, walking or not, needing medical treatment or not. They kept me at arm's length for hours, until eventually my association with the company was wiped and I was forced off set."

Dad's skeptical expression doesn't budge.

Devon slouches in defeat. "It's a crummy excuse, I know. But, they kept Wyatt's condition a secret for so long. I didn't know if there was anything to say." Devon fidgets, meeting Wyatt's gaze. "I thought you wanted me out of the picture. It'd make it easier for you to toe the party line. You didn't need me, reminding you of your misery."

"I definitely wanted to forget the misery," Wyatt says quietly. "I remember walking out on Erika and thinking, if I'm stuck here, I want out of my head. Ugh. Man, I think I'd already blacked out before I got into it with Richmond. It's all such a blur."

"You remember to keep your psychologist on speed dial," Mom says anxiously. "This is a lot to process, and you already forced yourself to forget once."

Wyatt lifts his phone. "I will, Mrs. Bartlett. Thanks."

"Oh, good," Devon reacts. "You've still got the same phone."

Wyatt shrugs. "Not that I can do much with it. My eyes still hurt when I read the screen."

"At least you have access to your money."

Wyatt blinks at Devon. "I do?"

Devon gestures at the phone. "Yeah, didn't they tell you? You can pay with your credit card via an app."

Wyatt turns to me. "Tell Kylie and Parker I can shout next time we go out."

"You might not want to blow through your money," Dad warns. "You've got some financial things to work through. Might be a good idea to cap any spending."

Wyatt nods. "Yes, Mr. Bartlett."

Devon sits back down, looking at both my mom and dad in awe. "Wow, Wyatt, you've got some great adults on your side. This is what you've been missing." Devon smirks at Dad. "Especially you, Mr. Bartlett. I appreciate you giving me the third-degree for Wyatt's sake."

Dad nods. "He's been mistreated by Hollywood-types long enough."

"If only my parents cared as much," Wyatt mutters.

Devon folds his arms uncomfortably. "Things are still not good?"

Wyatt's jaw rocks. "I signed eh-emancipation papers."

Devon goes pale. "You didn't."

Wyatt recoils. "Huh?"

"I can't believe they talked you into it." Anger swells in Devon. "You didn't want to cut ties with your parents, but Circle 8 knows how to fan the flames between underaged talent and their parents."

Wyatt tilts his head. "I didn't want to sign the papers? Are you sure about that?"

"Does it feel right to you to cut off your parents?" Devon asks.

"Well, no, but they're not the same people I remember."

Devon gestures at Wyatt. "Do you remember becoming famous? Of course, they seemed different. They're used to having finer things. Dang it. They used your memory loss against you."

"No, my parents..."

"Your parents are scared of losing you," Devon says firmly. "They always have been. But they push you into work because they think it'll make you happy. Erika and the others drove the wedge, telling them that you'll cut them out if they don't encourage you to keep working." Devon sighs. "Ugh. It's such a mess."

Wyatt winces, rubbing his temples. "My head hurts. I don't know what to believe."

Dad moves beside Wyatt, patting his shoulder. "You should go to Ashworth Estate and hear Tom Ashworth out. At least, when it comes to contracts and the like, he has the expertise to clean up this mess. You've got your doctors and us to help clean up the emotional side of the mess."

Wyatt smiles and pats Dad's hand. "Thanks."

Mom moves closer and leans down to hug Wyatt. "You'll be okay. Somehow, things will work out."

Mom and Dad move aside, and Wyatt scoops me into a hug. He sighs against the nape of my neck, and I melt into him, rubbing a circle on his back.

"How do you feel, remembering the day of the accident?" I whisper.

Wyatt sighs again, and the forlorn tone tells me all I need to know.

When we pull out of the hug, Devon nudges toward the front door. "Are you ready to go?"

"Is it possible to say no and yes at the same time?" Wyatt asks, standing up.

Devon nods. "I've had that feeling since they forced me away from you."

I stand, gripping Wyatt's hand. "I can go with you."

"No, you can't," Dad cuts in.

I stamp my foot, turning in his direction.

"I'm sorry," Dad says matter-of-factly, "but I'm not risking your safety again. I need you home right now."

"I'm not disappearing from Wyatt's life," I argue.

"I'm not saying you have to," Dad says, linking arms with Mom. "But, right now, I don't want you being part of Wyatt figuring out his next step. I'm not letting this management company use you as a pawn, an excuse, or a scapegoat. You're staying here."

Wyatt squeezes my hand and kisses my cheek. "They're right, Joze. You gotta stay here."

"But..."

"I'll call you," Wyatt's quick to say. "I won't leave you out of the loop."

I pout. "Don't forget me."

Wyatt grins. "I definitely won't forget you."

Devon and Wyatt leave for the limousine. The driver came to our door, asking to collect Wyatt's things. It feels so final, seeing Wyatt's duffle, guitar, and walking cane being taken away.

"It'll be okay, Josie," Mom says, pulling me into a side-hug as the limo pulls away. "I mean that."

I lean into her. "For you to be saying that, you really must believe it."

Mom smiles. "I do. Now, don't fixate on Wyatt all night."

I slouch. "How can I not?"

"He's at Ashworth Estate," Dad replies, "the safest place in the mountains."

"He's back in opulence, and I'm kept away from him again."

"You know why he couldn't stay."

I nod. "I know. It wasn't safe."

"For any of us," Dad says. "I won't put my family in harm's way."

I lean into his hug. "I'm really annoyed, but I love you, Dad."

His belly jiggles in a laugh. "Love you too, Josie-posey."

Thirty-One

Dad's plan for me to answer every question with the fact I signed an NDA actually worked. During the first half of school, people were all over me with questions. I guess word traveled fast because, by lunchtime, the fascination with me had cooled down.

Thank *freaking* goodness!

It's amazing I got through an entire day of school. Maybe Wyatt not being at my house helped. I don't feel so rushed to get home. But all day, I've fantasized about being at Ashworth Estate. And when the final school bell rings out, I get to my locker with lightning speed. I need to survey the halls for one particular person.

Bingo.

Vanessa Ashworth strides along the hallway like she owns the place.

Okay, I think, technically, her family *does* own the school, but that's beside the point.

I surge toward her, my only link to Wyatt at this point. Ashworth Estate is gated with some of the best security in the area. No school bus will take me there.

I gain on her, but my words won't come out.

Yes, the Ashworth siblings go to our school, but I've never talked to one. I know, I've hung out with a celebrity all week. But billionaires are totally out of my league.

Vanessa notices me by her side. I maintain eye contact, but I choke on my opening sentence.

She arches an eyebrow. "Yes?"

I squeak the word out. "Wyatt?"

Vanessa halts, looking me up and down. "Are you Josie?"

I nod with desperation.

She beckons me to follow. "Come with me."

Too in awe to speak, I follow quickly behind the billionaire heiress.

Outside the school, a shiny black limousine idly waits. The driver holds the rear passenger door open, and Vanessa thanks him.

Vanessa turns to me with a smile. "Coming with?"

I nod again, sheepishly following Vanessa inside the limousine.

As I sit across from Vanessa Ashworth, she notes the apprehension mixed with wonder on my face. "First time in a limo?" she asks.

"Mm-hmm. Wyatt's crew used SUVs."

"My dad likes the spectacle of limousines and town cars."

"Where are we going?"

"Ashworth Estate. You wanted to meet up with Wyatt, right?"

"Yes, please."

"Then just chill. It's a twenty-minute drive to the estate, and I don't want you hyperventilating."

I lift my palms. "I'll relax. I promise."

Vanessa smiles and lifts her phone. Her thumbs tap wildly, probably replying to a text message.

For the entire drive, I hug my middle. I only look away from the window when Vanessa giggles at her phone. I don't know anything about her, but from the brightness of her cheeks and the light dancing in her eyes, I'm guessing she's texting a boy.

She notices me staring and puts her phone down.

I shift in my seat and clear my throat. "So, you're a big fan of Wyatt's?"

She smiles. "I'm a fan of anyone from this town making something of themselves."

I give a slight nod, unsure how to take her answer.

Vanessa taps on the window. "Here we are."

I am in awe of the sight outside the tinted window. Large iron gates open for our vehicle. The limousine drives up a winding path, framed with landscaped gardens, and ending at a massive, Tudor-style mansion.

"Incredible," I breathe.

The driver opens the door for us, and when I follow Vanessa to the front door, a man greets us wearing a uniform much like Hubert's at the Gran Palacio Hotel.

"Afternoon, Miss Ashworth," the man says.

"Hi Murphy," Vanessa says, handing the man her school bag. "This is Josie Bartlett. Can you take her to see Wyatt? I've got to get changed for my tennis lesson."

"Not a problem," Murphy says as Vanessa dashes further into the house. "This way, Miss Bartlett."

I squeak, "Thank you," and follow Murphy through the expansive hallway, decorated with large artworks, expensive vases, and ornate tables.

Murphy takes me to the rear of the mansion and opens the double doors to a large patio area. I walk across the tiled space, finding Wyatt and Devon kicked back on the outdoor furniture.

Wyatt leaps up at the sight of me. "Josie! I'm so glad you're here."

I rush into his arms. "I've missed you so much."

He kisses me hard. "Me too. It's been crazy without you."

I make him sit with me. "What's been happening? Are you okay?"

"Yes, I'm fine. We've had a lot of meetings," Wyatt says, curling an arm around my shoulders. "Circle 8 has more control over my choices than I do. Mr. Ashworth is getting his legal team to investigate how I get out of my contract."

My heart rate speeds up. "You really want to do that?"

He nods. "I don't want to go back to making movies. I know that's what they'll push to do. Plus, I want to make original music. They have no interest in letting me pursue it. That is, unless I'm collaborating with someone they see as better than me."

I hug my arm around him. "You have my full support. Being with Circle 8 won't lead to happiness."

He kisses the side of my head. "Thanks."

I wince. "Does this mean you're quitting show business?"

"It means he'll find new representation after his contract is dissolved," Devon explains. "Someone who'll work towards Wyatt's best interests and his goals. Not another machine looking for another cog."

"Mr. Ashworth also stopped the emancipation paperwork from being processed," Wyatt says. "Your dad was right. I shouldn't have signed it when I was dealing with memory loss. Mr. Ashworth and his associates were pretty horrified that I'd done that."

"That Circle 8 talked you into doing it," Devon cuts in.

Wyatt fidgets beside me. "I still did it."

"They manipulated your feelings so you'd push your parents away," Devon argues. "I've seen it first-hand dozens of times."

"Devon has talked me through some stuff with my parents," Wyatt tells me. "I even found entries in my journal that matched up. It's still really messy and confusing, but I reached out to them." Wyatt pauses, taking a slow breath in. "The Ashworths are going to fly my parents out here to the estate."

"And you're feeling good about that?"

"I'm feeling better than I was." He clutches my hand, frowning. "I still can't forgive them for making me cut you out of my life."

I suck in a hesitant breath. "I hope they can accept me being back in your life."

The corners of Wyatt's mouth tug upwards. "Joze, you're the reason for the head injury."

I sit back. "Excuse me?"

Nervous laughter simmers out of Wyatt. "I wanted you back." He squeezes my hand. "I wanted you back so badly, I forgot my life."

I shake my head. "I don't understand."

"The em-emotional shock Dr. Fincher was talking about," Wyatt replies. "I've spoken to Dr. Maxton about it."

"Your psychologist?" I ask.

"Right." Wyatt nods. "I was feeling like a fraud. So much time had passed. I didn't know how you'd accept me back into my life. The doc and I talked through it. He suggested that after I'd come to blows with Erika and Richmond, I had forced myself back to a safe place. The time when I wasn't famous, and I had you in my life."

I tremble as adulation buzzes through my veins. "I'm your safe place?"

Wyatt leans forward and brushes his nose against mine. "You're my perfect person. My whole heart."

I sigh with mixed emotions. "I wish you didn't have to go through this pain to bring me back into your life."

Wyatt smirks. "Don't worry. Richmond is gonna pay for that."

"Whether it's in criminal or civil court," Devon cuts in, "Richmond Salinger is going down."

I swallow hard but feel a heaviness lift off me. "He deserves everything coming his way."

Devon grins at me. "On a better note. Have you followed Wyatt's new social media pages?"

I stare at him blankly. "Umm, I didn't know there were any. To be honest, I've been avoiding looking at anything online."

Devon nudges Wyatt. "Show her."

Wyatt blushes, fumbling with his phone. "Ah, Joze, I have one post on there."

He drags out the last word, sending second-hand nervousness through me. Wyatt cracks a smile. "It's kinda blowing up."

"Kinda?" Devon splutters. "People are already using the sound to make their own content. This new song is gonna be huge."

A thrill springs inside me. "New song?"

Wyatt taps on a video and hands me the phone. I shiver in the best way, and my palms grow clammy. In the video, Wyatt sings and strums the guitar.

Oh.

My.

Gosh.

He's singing my poem.

He turned my poem into a song.

And...

People are listening to it.

"To love you then,

And love you now,

Another chance when,

You're here somehow.

In my heart near,

Body too far,

An ache it sear,

Longing for the star.

Grateful for a touch,

Soulful in words,

In memories and such,

Spirited like birds."

I look up at him, mouth ajar.

Wyatt braces himself. "Is it okay?"

"It's... It's..." My heart swells with a jittery bounce. "It's incredible."

"It's my love letter to you, Joze." Wyatt pulls me into his arms. "You're always on my mind. You've always been on my mind. I've never forgotten you, and I never will."

I melt into him, too overwhelmed to respond.

"Your words are magic," he whispers. "I wanted the world to hear them."

"I've never thought songwriting was on the cards for me. But maybe I should give it some actual thought."

We pull out of the hug, and Wyatt says, "I know you're more passionate about your short stories. But I want you to know I was serious. I want to collaborate with you when it comes to my lyrics."

"I'd do anything to spend more time with you," I gush.

"You know," Devon pipes up. "When Wyatt and Portia would do red carpets and other events, I'd chat with people on the other side of the velvet rope. I've made a few connections. If you ever want to publish a collection of your work, I could make some calls. It'd help you get a foot in the door."

I shiver at the thought and find myself grinning. "Wow, Devon. You'd do that?"

"It's all about who you know," Devon replies.

"Not that Josie needs the help," Wyatt says. "She's already an award-winning writer."

Devon claps. "Makes her an even easier pitch."

"Okay, stop," I say, fanning my face, "or I'm gonna black out from embarrassment."

Wyatt pecks my cheek. "Josie, I'm not going anywhere. We still have a chance to be together."

My heart is in my throat. "What are you saying?"

Wyatt beams. "Mr. Ashworth offered me a place to stay on the estate while all the legal stuff gets worked out. Joze, I'm staying in Victoria Falls."

I gasp and shoot my arms around his neck. "Are you serious?"

His hands press into my back, and I feel the thumping of his heart. "You've got me, Josie. And if you let me, I'll never let you go."

I sigh and rest against him. "Don't ever let me go."

Epilogue

Two Months Later...

Wyatt is still working on his mental health and personal growth. Right now, he's paused his tutoring. He decided to postpone his studies for one more year. I can't believe he's done this without talking badly about himself. The fact he was held back in sixth grade had cast such a dark shadow over him.

Now, he's made the choice to repeat a grade. With all the struggles he's had to overcome with his memory, eyesight, and mobility, I don't blame him. It's a sound decision I support one-hundred percent.

I have to admit, it's really hard going to school, knowing he's close by. He's found a comfortable place at the Ashworth Estate. They've even given him a dedicated recording space, and he still has Devon by his side.

Slowly, Wyatt's mending his relationship with his parents. They met on the Ashworth Estate, and Wyatt tried to keep an open mind. But when his parents looked around the mansion with dollar signs in their eyes, Wyatt asked them to leave. I told the crushing news to my parents, who then took matters into their own hands.

Mr. and Mrs. Hayes rented a room at a local motel, and my parents invited them to a diner meal. Dad said the couple needed "to get back to basics." With my parents' encouragement, Wyatt and his parents have met a few more times on neutral ground. I can actually say, without crossing my fingers, there's light at the end of the tunnel. A lot of damage was done over the years. However, with the help of therapy and support from my family, Wyatt can keep his parents in his life.

As for school, not everything about it is tough. Who knew, the quiet girl who kept to herself, would form an alliance with the Ashworth siblings? Those kids rule our school. They say something, and people listen. Now, the student body knows to back off and not hound me with questions about Wyatt. Yep, life at Ashworth Academy is a whole heck of a lot easier.

After school and on weekends, I see Wyatt as much as possible. We spend our time between the Ashworth Estate and my treehouse. Is there something wrong with my boyfriend that he prefers the treehouse? I guess nostalgia always wins.

Not only is our bond growing stronger every day, but our collaborations are like magic. Every night, after my homework, I work on lyrics for Wyatt. On our video chats, he always asks me to read them aloud. While listening to my voice, he strums and finds a beat that works.

I still can't believe there's a J inked into his skin. It's in a beautiful calligraphy-style on his arm, just above his wrist. It's not subtle either. Easily reaching three inches long. Wyatt is still not doing interviews, only posting teasers of his new tracks online. People have already been commenting on the tattoo, and I might keel over when he starts responding to the questions. I don't think I could handle someone famous announcing to the world that the permanent mark on his skin represents his love for me.

I think it'll be okay, though. Wyatt's so attuned to my disdain for the spotlight. It's something that gives him energy, and I love seeing him perform and interact with fans. Although, considering it sucks away my energy, we've already decided I won't join him at events. He'll get a fabulous publicist who'll work out all the details. Not being at crowded events won't make me jealous. I know that he'll be thinking about me and be excited for the next time we meet up.

Portia has tried a few times to coax Wyatt into the spotlight with her. She's flourishing without Richmond by her side. As soon as legal action was announced, Circle 8 immediately dropped association with Richmond Salinger. Wyatt asked Portia if she'll leave Circle 8, but she was clear about her happiness with her work. She'll age out of Circle 8's teen image one day. But she'll continue working and thriving in the industry.

Wyatt tells me we need a contract, so no one will rip me off, and I'll get paid for my words. I guess that'll come once he records a studio album. But for now, I'm having fun writing words I'm intending to share with the world. No longer am I hiding in my bedroom, creating love sonnets for the boy I feared I'd never see again.

Wyatt is mine.

I am his.

Nothing will ever break that.

Afterword

A few years ago, I was living with my grandmother. I went to the doctor's office with her for a check up. While we were there, the doctor conducted some memory tests. It was to check for dementia. She was first given three words that she would need to recall by the end of the session.

Apple, table, penny.

While she was doing the other activities, just like Josie, I began to forget the words. When it was time to recall the words, I'd completely forgotten them.

But my ninety-year-old grandmother had not.

"Apple, table, penny," she said proudly.

Throughout the rest of the day, I asked her what the three words were, and she continued to recall them. She'd also quip, "I don't know how the heck I remembered them!"

I found it remarkable that she continued to bring up the words. And five years on, they've stuck with me. Don't ever count anyone out. Even when they show signs of weakness, people are stronger than they realize.

About The Author

Milly Rose is an animal-loving romance enthusiast with a swoon-inducing book formula. Shy girl + hot guy + first kisses. Her YA sweet romance books will have you falling in love every instalment. Milly Rose is the quintessential shy girl, who you can contact via her mailing list and reply to her monthly email blasts! Milly spends her days vying for her cat's affection, dreaming up her next book boyfriend, and writing a fun meet-cute under candlelight with a lovely brewed cup of tea.

Join Milly Rose's Mailing List
millyrosebooks.com
Follow on Instagram @shy.author.milly.rose
Follow on Tiktok @shy.author.milly.rose

Also By

ALL BOOKS SET IN ASHWORTH ACADEMY

Shy Girls Can't Date Billionaires (Christie & Ash)
Shy Girls Can't Date Bullies (Ava & Beau)
Shy Girls Can't Date Frenemies (Jamie & Milo)
Shy Girls Can't Date Bad Boys (Vanessa & Dax)
Shy Girls Can't Fake Date (Kylie & Parker)
Shy Girls Can't Date Celebrities (Josie & Wyatt)
We Shouldn't Be Together (Tabitha & Kai)

www.ingramcontent.com/pod-product-compliance
Lightning Source LLC
Chambersburg PA
CBHW050612170726

48283CB00001B/218